Before I Wake

Something grabbed my arm, jerked me to a stop. I pulled against it, heart hammering.

"You shouldn't exist," a voice hissed near my ear.

I shoved hard. I don't know how I did it, but one moment I was afraid and struggling and the next I was free.

Reaching out, I found Noah and ran toward him.

The mist parted for me and began to swirl, taking shape.

I was on the threshold of Noah's dream now.

I stepped through the gauzy film, into Noah's world . . .

By Kathryn Smith

BEFORE I WAKE
LET THE NIGHT BEGIN
TAKEN BY THE NIGHT
NIGHT OF THE HUNTRESS
BE MINE TONIGHT

KATHRYN SMITH

Before I Wake

THE NIGHTMARE CHRONICLES

AVON

An Imprint of HarperCollinsPublishers

This is a work of fiction. Names, characters, places, and incidents are products of the author's imagination or are used fictitiously and are not to be construed as real. Any resemblance to actual events, locales, organizations, or persons, living or dead, is entirely coincidental.

AVON BOOKS
An Imprint of HarperCollins*Publishers*
10 East 53rd Street
New York, New York 10022-5299

Copyright © 2008 by Kathryn Smith
ISBN 978-0-06-134027-7
www.avonromance.com

First Avon Books paperback printing: August 2008

Avon Trademark Reg. U.S. Pat. Off. and in Other Countries, Marca Registrada, Hecho en U.S.A.
HarperCollins® is a registered trademark of HarperCollins Publishers.

Printed in the U.S.A.

10 9 8 7 6 5 4 3 2 1

This book is dedicated to Steve for all his support, love, and hand-holding. And for always saying, "No Sweetie, you don't suck" every time I ask.

Also to Nancy and Erika for all the encouragement and support and the "let's do this" enthusiasm that they both gave this project.

And finally, this book is for my mother—supporter of dreams, banisher of all things scary, and composer of dee-dee-dee songs. Thanks, Mom.

Chapter One

"You're a Nightmare."

Diet Dr Pepper halfway to my lips I paused, staring at the old man standing beside me at the Duane Reade checkout. My heart nudged hard against my ribs. "Excuse me?"

His face was the color and texture of a worn piece of leather, and his hair was a mass of tight, frizzy gray curls. But his eyes were as sharp as a child's. "You're a Nightmare, girl. What're you doin' here?"

I glanced around to see if anyone else in the drugstore had heard the old fella's surprising—and very *vocal*—accusations. If anyone had, they were pretending they hadn't.

He was just a crazy old man. No need to panic. No need to do anything. "Sir, I don't know what you're talking about."

"You are not of this *plane*," he insisted, doing this weird little stomp with his foot that made me wonder if he had to pee. "You shouldn't be here."

I took a step away just in case his bladder gave out. It was instinct, driven by pure self-preservation. One thing living in a city the size of New York teaches you is that some people just don't have the same boundaries as the rest of us.

Also, he creeped me out.

"Uh, okay. I shouldn't be here." I twisted the cap back on to my Dr Pepper as the cashier started scanning my items. Just a few more moments, and I'd be out of there. I should have gone straight home after work, but I needed tampons.

"You do know, don't you?"

I had hoped that agreeing with him would end the conversation. Apparently, I was wrong. "Know what?"

"What you are." He was staring at me now with a look of wonder. "Shee—oot. I bet you don't even know how you got here."

"I walked." I would not, however, be walking home. God, I hoped I'd be able to hail a cab pronto once I left the pharmacy. I never wanted to be somewhere else quite so badly in all my life.

He did that foot thing again, only this time his face twisted in annoyance. I took another step away. "I don't mean here. I mean *here*. On this earth."

I swallowed. My throat felt like I'd just swallowed a piece of carpet. "Sir, I was born here. Same as you." Maybe it was all the years of psychology classes, or maybe it was a little fear, but I needed to bring him back to the real world. *This* one.

He peered at me—a little too closely for my liking. "You may have been born here, girlie, but you don't belong. I wonder how you managed to slip through."

I wanted to get the heck out of there. What the hell was he talking about? "Just luck, I guess."

He stared at me with eyes that were slightly rheumy, but keen. "Luck, nothing. How old are you?"

"Sir, I'm not going to tell you that." Next he was going to ask my weight, and I'd have to kill him.

"Twenty-eight."

His voice rang in my head like a gong. He was right. If I was creeped out before, I was ten times that now. It could have been a lucky guess, but I doubted it.

"You're mature," he informed me. "At your full potential. No tellin' what havoc you might wreak."

That was *it*. I threw some money at the clerk. I hadn't heard the total, so I could only hope it was enough. I grabbed my bag and started for the door, grateful for once that most of my five feet ten inches was leg. The clerk didn't yell after me, so I assumed I had given her enough to cover my bill.

I miraculously hailed a cab right outside and jumped in. As we drove off, I looked out the window to see the old man standing on the sidewalk near the door, watching me. He was drinking a bottle of Brisk—bought with my change I bet. He waved as the cab pulled away, and he yelled something. I couldn't quite hear the words, but to my paranoid ears it sounded as though he yelled, "YOU. DON'T. BELONG."

I knew I didn't. The question was, how the hell did he?

I was six years old the first time my mother told me I was a Nightmare. I cried, because I thought she was mad at me. But then she took me up onto her lap and told me I was special because no other child on earth had the King of Dreams for a father. She told me I could dream whatever I wanted, that in my dreams I could *do* whatever I wanted, and I believed her.

I asked my father what it was like to be the Lord of Dreams. He didn't know what I was talking about. It was shortly after that I realized he wasn't my father. My real father was the man who played with me in my dreams, who put a sweet smile on my mother's face. The man I called Dad looked at me like he didn't recognize me, and at my mother as though he knew he was losing her to a man with whom he couldn't compete.

Was it any wonder that I soon found myself preferring the Dream Realm to the real world? Of course there were parts of the Dream Realm—The Dreaming—that my father told me to stay away from. Apparently my uncle Icelus had let some of his "creations" wander free. Since Icelus's domain was all things disturbing and frightening, I listened to my father and never ventured outside of his castle, terrified of these monsters and what they might do to me. I already knew to be careful of the eerie mist that surrounded the land.

My childhood seemed normal to me. I was in grade nine before I realized that something wasn't right. That *I* wasn't right. It never occurred to me that I was different, even though my mother told me in so many words. Other people didn't think of their dreams as being real. Didn't talk about them as though they were significant.

Jackey Jenkins picked on me mercilessly. She was petite and thin and blond, with a great tan and a perfect wardrobe. I was tall and curvy and so white I looked like Casper. She always raised her hand, and I only spoke when spoken to, and yet in the classes we shared, I made better grades. Looking back, I could say she was jealous. That she resented the fact that she worked so hard for what came easy to me. Despite being her polar opposite, I had good friends, and people tended to like me once they got to know me—especially teachers. Jackey reacted in the only way she could—she made my life hell.

One day I got my period at school. I wasn't prepared and spent the rest of the morning with a coat tied around my waist. As I was leaving school to go home to change, Jackey yanked up the jacket and showed everyone outside (and you know there had to be a crowd) the back of my jeans. People laughed. Not a lot of them, but some.

I was so mad, so humiliated, tears filled my eyes, which pleased Jackey to no end. I remember telling her that I was going to get her for what she had done.

And I did. It was the great *Carrie* moment of my life. That night I went into Jackey Jenkins's dreams, and I tortured her as only one teenage girl can another. It didn't make her nice to me. It just made her afraid, and I think that made her hate me even more. I didn't have quite the feeling of satisfaction I thought I should, not when every time I looked at her I could see in Jackey's expression just what a freak I was.

Shortly after that I heard she was seeing a shrink because she was afraid to go to sleep at night—and she became less and less pretty as the circles beneath her eyes darkened. Eventually I think she recovered, but I didn't.

Normal people didn't go into other people's dreams. Normal people *couldn't*. And if they could, they didn't go about trying to terrify young girls.

I had become one of the monsters my father warned me about.

After that I stopped playing with dreams. I built my own

little world that I could go into, and I didn't let my mother or my father, Morpheus, or anyone else inside. I was going to make myself normal if it killed me.

To say my mother was disappointed was an understatement.

After that, I managed to finish high school without anymore Freddy Kruger-esque behavior, and I went on to university in Toronto and got my PhD in neuropsychology. My grades were well above average, but it was my research on dreams that brought me to the attention of Dr. Phillip Canning—an associate of my mentor's. Dr. Canning was at the top of his field in sleep research. I had read all of his papers and his books on treating parasomnias and post-traumatic nightmares. You can take the girl out of the Dream Realm, but you can't take the Dream Realm out of the girl, and all that. I didn't need all my textbooks to realize that there was a part of me that *needed* to work in that field.

I needed to help people have a normal night's sleep—to help them protect themselves from the dangers of a world they thought harmless and "all in their heads." Weirdly enough, at the same time I needed to deny that world for all I was worth.

Now, here I am a genuine doctor of psychology and a full-time (albeit still plebeian) member of Dr. Canning's team at the MacCallum Sleep and Dream Research Center in New York City. My two years of proving myself and visa restrictions are almost up, and soon I'll be able to practice on my own. I do a little bit of everything as low man on the totem pole—clinical and research—but mostly I work in dream analysis and therapy, with heavy emphasis on nightmares.

So much for denial.

When I arrived at the clinic later that morning, Bonnie,

the receptionist, informed me in an all-too-smug and know-ing manner that, "He's heee-rre."

She sounded way too much like the kid out of the *Polter-geist* movies. I didn't have to ask who "he" was, not when Bonnie waggled her finely waxed eyebrows like that. Bon-nie was in her midforties and kept herself trim, dressed to the nines and was never seen without lipstick. Add a Brook-lyn accent, and it was no wonder I adored her.

I shot her what I hoped was a reproachful look as I hung my coat in the closet and retrieved my lab coat. "You shouldn't use that tone when talking about a patient."

"Oh, like you're not the least bit tingly over seeing him," she replied, not looking the least bit chastened. "He's still in the sleep room if you want to peek." Bonnie didn't treat me like the senior staff—either because she thought I was a kid, liked me, or because my lab coat was baby pink with rhine-stone buttons.

The coat had been a gift from a sweet grandmotherly pa-tient named Irene who thought women should be rosy and sparkly at all times. I'm not sure that I agree, but I have to admit, I felt perky and girly whenever I wore it.

"If you like him so much, Bonnie, maybe you should ask him out."

"Nah." She waved a perfectly manicured hand, her long nails blood red as the light bounced off them. "Poor thing, I'd break him."

I grinned. That was entirely possible. Bonnie wasn't a big woman, but she certainly had appetites, and apparently the stamina to support them. At thirty, Noah Clarke was obvi-ously too old, and too *fragile* for her to consider dating.

I pulled a hair clip out of my pocket and secured my hair

in a messy twist on top of my head. "Do you have Noah's file?"

"You bet." She lifted a thick folder from the pile on her desk and offered it to me.

I eyed her with suspicion—and a good dose of amusement. "How many times have you looked at the pictures?"

Not possessing an ounce of shame, Bonnie merely smiled. "A few."

I laughed at the blatant understatement. "You're twisted, you know that?"

Her smile broadened—her lipstick matched her nails. "And proud of it. Now, your patient is waiting, *Doctor*."

She got a kick out of calling me that. It wasn't like I was the only female on staff, but I had started working at the clinic before finishing my degree. Bonnie had been one of the first people to hug me the day I officially became a doctor—right after my brother, who had flown down from Toronto especially for the occasion. My sisters and father hadn't been able to make it, and my mother . . .

Well, my mother hadn't been able to come. She was the reason the rest of my family didn't come. None of them had been able to bring themselves to leave Mom's side "just in case." Just in case she woke up.

Of course she hadn't. Had I been able to have a discussion on the topic without being filled with an immeasurable rage, I would have told them not to worry about Mom. But then I would have to explain how I knew there wasn't going to be any miracle, and they would think I was crazy.

"By the way," Bonnie said, just before I walked away. "Canning and Revello are all buzzed about something. I don't know what, but I'd avoid them unless you want to hear about it."

Bonnie didn't think much of Dr. Canning. I wasn't sure why, but I knew firsthand how difficult he was actually to like. He was a great doctor, and he did fabulous work here, but I think somewhere along the line he started putting professional image ahead of patients. He had been on *Oprah* once, and had a framed photo of the two of them together hanging on his office wall behind his desk—right where you were forced to take notice.

I flashed Bonnie a grin. "I'll be careful."

I was still smiling when I left Bonnie, the thick file in hand. I flipped it open as I walked down the brightly lit, cream-carpeted hall with its sage-colored walls. I couldn't blame Bonnie for looking at the pictures taken of Noah for the sleep study he was part of. I wasn't part of that team, but had access to the file because of my own work with him. Tall, dark, and sexy when awake, he was just as appealing asleep. He wasn't one of those slack and openmouthed sleepers; he wasn't a drooler. In fact, he slept mostly on his back, arms at his side as perfect and poised as an actor on TV. A device which—I reminded myself—I watch entirely too much.

Noah was one of the few people I had ever met who faced the unpleasantness in his dreams. He was one of my special patients—a lucid dreamer. The most consistent I've ever witnessed. No matter the dream, Noah could fix it from inside his own head without waking up.

I hadn't been working with Noah long, but he was one patient who I truly got excited about seeing, and I don't mean in a personal way either—well, not totally. We met when he signed up for the sleep study. When I asked him to help me with a study of my own, he agreed without so much as a blink. I had other patients with varying degrees of lucidity in their dreams, but no one quite like Noah.

I loved discussing his dreams. He would tell me how he had changed things, how he had bent the dream to his own will, and I would write it all down as we dissected his dream and talked about what it might mean. His dreams were so vivid, I could almost imagine myself in them as he recounted them to me. I envied him. I worried for him.

Sometimes I worried for myself because Noah was the only patient who made me want to let down the walls in my head. I wanted to see his dreams for myself, watch him bend that world to his will, and cheer him on.

Through him I hoped to be able to help other people learn to free themselves from the nightmares that cripple them. To take control of their dreams within the Realm of The Dreaming, rather than allowing dreams to control them. That was my not-so-secret passion—to compile the most common abilities belonging to lucid dreamers and (hopefully) teach them to people suffering from chronic nightmares.

Because I knew that sometimes a bad dream was more than just a bad dream. And it was my way of sticking it to my father.

Dr. Canning and Dr. Revello were standing just outside the sleep rooms, talking in hushed voices. They looked excited—and guilty. There would be no avoiding them.

They looked up as I approached. "Something up?" I asked.

Dr. Canning cleaned his glasses with the end of his tie.

"Have you seen the paper this morning?"

"Uh, no." News was depressing. I avoided it at every cost.

"Another SUNDS case," Dr. Revello informed me. She was a fiftysomething woman who reminded me a lot of Katharine Hepburn, and was just as intimidating.

Ah, so that was the reason for the excitement—and the

guilt. Sudden Unexplained Nocturnal Death Syndrome was something our profession saw but rarely, and usually only in males of Southeast Asian descent, or sometimes in diabetes or epilepsy patients. Of course my colleagues were intrigued. And of course they felt bad for being excited about some-one's death.

Then it hit me. "*Another* one?" When I say *rare,* I mean rare, like one in hundreds of thousands. Healthy people usu-ally don't die in their sleep for no apparent reason. At least, not to my knowledge.

Dr. Revello nodded, little wisps of gingery hair escaping the loose bun on top of her head. "The fourth in two months."

"It can't be SUNDS," I insisted, "not at that rate. There has to be an explanation—like sinus arrest."

Both doctors looked annoyed, and I realized my mistake. I had doubted them out loud, and for that I got the "look."

"There were no signs of sinus arrest," Dr. Canning re-marked frostily. "I was contacted by investigators earlier this morning. They have no idea what might have killed these poor people, and they've asked me to consult."

Dr. Revello looked positively thrilled. "Can you imagine what this will mean if we actually manage to find a common trigger? The psychology world will sit up and take notice, not to mention most of the medical world as well."

"Well," I said, hefting my file. Noah was waiting after all. "Good luck with that." I said it with a genuine smile. I had my doubts that this rash of unexplained deaths was the result of a parasomnia—sleep disorder—but who was I to judge? *I* hadn't been asked to consult.

I continued on my way to the sleep room. These were individually decorated in different styles and colors to make

them seem more like bedrooms and less hospital-like.
Patients were able to choose which room seemed the most
soothing to them. Noah was in #6, which was decorated in
dark blue because, he said, we didn't have a black one.

I knocked on the door, trying to ignore the fact that my
heart rate had increased noticeably. This is what happens
when you have no social life outside of your work—you
start crushing on people you have no business crushing on.

"Go ahead," came the muffled reply from behind the door.

I turned the knob. This was ridiculous. Noah Clarke
wasn't even my type.

He sat on the side of the mussed bed, his bare forearms
resting on his cotton-clad thighs. Boots, faded jeans, and a
black T-shirt sat discarded near and on the chair by the wall
along with his motorcycle jacket and helmet.

He had obviously just woken up, and what composure I
had drained out through my toes.

He stood up as I entered the room and closed the door
behind me. The room suddenly seemed a whole lot smaller.
And warmer.

"Hey, Doc."

I smiled at the nickname and shivered just a little at the
low, rough timbre of his voice. "Hey, Noah."

My grandmother would have said that Noah Clarke had
presence—and she would have said that without the benefit
of seeing him in nothing but a pair of Batman pajama bottoms.

A little over six feet, he was just that much taller than me
that I had to look up to meet his gaze. He was lean and
broad-shouldered, like a swimmer. I knew from his file that
he was an artist and into martial arts. It had been a month

after our first session before he started talking about himself, and even then he didn't offer much. I don't think he was being standoffish; he just didn't talk a lot.

I liked Noah. Even if he weren't so powerful within the Dream Realm, I think I would still like him. He seemed to like me, too. Actually, I think he liked the fact that I could make sense of the things that happened in his head and that I didn't think he was a weirdo.

I wonder what Noah Clarke would think if he only knew what a weirdo I was. What would he think if he realized that some of the stuff he dismissed as being nothing more than his subconscious at work was real? He'd probably accept it. Creative people were a little more open to these kinds of things.

As an artist, I don't think "weird"—or personal grooming— was high on Noah's radar. Not that he was what I would call strange. Really, he wasn't. But sometimes his clothes looked like he had pulled them out of a thrift-store bag, and his thick black hair stood out from his head in a just-out-of-bed style that wasn't salon, but truly pillow-induced. He didn't care what opinion people formed when they looked at him. He just was what he was. I admired that.

Today, patches of beard covered his jaw and chin. He didn't have a lot of body hair, so the lean musculature of his body was perfectly accentuated by his golden skin. He had black eyes, too—or almost black. His complexion gave away that his background was mostly Caucasian, but the dark hair and eyes, and the faint curve of his nose hinted at something much more exotic.

Noah was exotic, even when smiling that goofy little smile that he always gave me. It was the smile that killed me, made me wonder if maybe there wasn't something between us other than a doctor-patient relationship. I had no business wondering, but how could I help it when the man stood before me in pj's with the Dark Knight on them, every inch of him an invitation?

Oh yeah, did I mention that he was totally hot?

"Sorry to barge in," I told him. "I wanted to ask if you were able to pop by my office for a chat?" This was part of our arrangement. Noah took part in a sleep study run by the clinic, and we always met afterward to discuss his dreams. Other nights, when he wasn't part of the study, I gave him exercises to try and we discussed those as well.

Was that hesitation? He seemed to freeze, just for a second, before nodding. "Sure."

But he didn't sound convinced. That was weird because Noah never balked at facing his dreams, no matter what they were. "Is something wrong?" What I really wanted to ask was *had something happened?* Color me paranoid, but I had never seen him look like that before.

Almost like he was afraid.

"We can skip a session if you want," I added. I didn't want to skip anything, but I was thinking of him. Or at least trying to.

A scoff and a shake of his head. He seemed annoyed at the suggestion. "No. Let's do it."

I gestured to the changing room, ignoring the light dusting of goose bumps his low, smooth voice always gave me. "I'll leave you to get changed then. Meet you in my office?"

He grinned as he scooped up his clothes. "Sure thing. Hey, Doc?"

"Yeah?"

He moved toward me, bundle of clothes in his arms, one

faded leg of his jeans pointing toward the floor. "You mind if I run out and grab a coffee?"

I smiled back, my confidence returning despite his nearness. "Sure." There was a Starbucks a couple of doors down.

A gaze as warm and personal as any set of hands ran over me. "How do you like it?"

Oh, how I wish I could misconstrue that question. There was no denying that his voice had dropped an octave, become even more deep and seductive. Lately, Noah had been getting in my space more and more, flirting. I knew better than to put any stock in it, but it was flattering all the same. He was my patient, and I respected that. "Cream and Splenda. Thanks."

He smiled. And all my respect couldn't keep me from wanting to lean up on my toes and taste that mouth of his.

"Doc?"

"Yeah?"

Dark eyes glittered. "I have to get dressed."

Right. Oh God. I chuckled in embarrassment. "I should probably let you do that then."

Amusement softened his features. "Probably." I was pretty sure there was an invitation to stay in there. That's why I turned on my heel and practically ran to the door.

"I'll meet you in my office," I tossed over my shoulder before walking out.

Fifteen minutes later, I had put myself in a professional frame of mind once more, but that didn't stop my heart from skipping when Noah entered my office. He looked just as good in clothes as he did half-naked. He had a backpack slung over one shoulder and a cardboard cup holder with two large coffee cups in his hand. His jeans and T-shirt were baggy and comfortable, concealing the lean musculature beneath. The T-shirt wasn't even tucked in, it just bunched along the top of his jeans, slung low on his hips. I found his lack of vanity very appealing.

I took the coffees from him as he tossed the backpack on the floor. Then, without me asking, he closed the door, shutting us into the tiny box that was my office, warming the air with the scent of flavored coffee and a hint of spicy vanilla that was entirely Noah.

I really should stop working with him, but I'd rather be uncomfortable than give him up.

He eased into the chair in front of my desk, and I took the one behind it. I took a sip of my coffee before speaking. "Mmm. Perfect. Thank you."

He slouched in the chair, watching me with blatant interest. "I think you must be a very sensual person, Doc."

I raised a brow. If I'd taken a drink then, I would have choked on it. "Excuse me?"

He took a drink from his own cup, making me wait for an answer, which came in the form of little more than a shrug, then, "You like things you can taste, feel, experience."

That would certainly explain my love affair with food. "I suppose so."

"Food with intense flavor," He remarked, tilting his head. "Music you can feel in your soul. Fabric that caresses your skin."

Whoa Nelly. I swallowed. His voice had dropped, and my pulse was pounding. He hadn't said anything inappropriate, and yet, I felt as though he'd seen me naked. He was right about all of it. And if I didn't take control of this situation, I was going to follow him wherever he led.

"Dreams that can be altered," I quipped, breaking through the tension.

Noah's gaze dropped to the cup in his hands. "You ever have a nightmare, Doc?"

"Sure. You?"

He nodded. "Most of my dreams are, until I change them."

"Nightmares aren't uncommon for creative people," I informed him, slipping into clinical mode. "I read once that 90 to 95 percent of all dreams by artists, writers, and the like are nightmares or disturbing at least."

"I used to think nightmares were bad, now I'm not so sure."

"No?" I was curious. "Why's that?"

His ebony gaze lifted, seized mine. "I think some Nightmares are there to help us."

I swallowed. The way he was looking at me made me feel like an animal in a cage—a strange and exotic one at that. And was it my imagination, or had he intimated that Nightmares were actual beings?

Christ, he couldn't know. Could he? But the old man had. Was there a freaking billboard somewhere that I didn't know about?

"Nightmares are often our subconscious way of working through fears and unpleasant memories."

He leaned forward, and so did I, not about to be intimidated or show fear. He wasn't trying to scare me, but there was a lot he wasn't saying, and that's what bothered me.

"I had a nightmare the other night," he said softly. "You were in it."

That was a surprise. "Me?" At his nod, I asked, "And what did I do?"

He smiled, a gentle tilting of lips that lit his eyes in a way that I couldn't be sure if it was meant to be warmth or suspicion. "You offered me your hand."

"It makes sense that you would see me in such a way in your dreams, given our work together."

His smile faded. "And then you pulled out a knife and slit my throat."

Chapter Two

I was thinking about Noah's dream when I opened the door to my apartment later that day. Obviously there was a reason for it—his own trust issues, I would imagine. Still, it made me uncomfortable, especially on the heels of the old man from the Duane Reade.

I could talk myself out of being too freaked-out over that as well. The old man had to have seen me leave the sleep clinic where I work, and that triggered his little . . . outburst. He didn't know anything about me. He couldn't. No human could.

I had to stop thinking about it. It didn't matter. I'd never see the old man again. I tossed my bag on the floor and resolved to forget the whole thing. Noah was a different matter, but I'd deal with that if his dreams continued.

My apartment wasn't much, but it was mine. Thanks to my father—the man who raised me—footing the bill for university, I was pretty much debt-free and could afford to live decently. That didn't mean I wanted to spend most of my salary on rent, though, so I had a roommate—my friend Lola. Yeah, that's her real name. We had a nice apartment in Murray Hill.

And by nice, I mean fairly simple. It was a walk-up in a prewar building, had two bedrooms and a kitchen separate from the rest of the living space—for which we were grateful. And the bathroom was huge, with a big tub, for which I was even more grateful.

My cat Fudge was sitting on the kitchen counter waiting for me when I set the plastic bag beside him. He shifted his furry black bulk long enough to sniff the bag, then turned back to me with a loud meow.

I checked messages while I fed him. One from my friend Julie wanting to know if I wanted to go out Saturday night, and one from my oldest sister, Ivy wanting to know if I was going to make it home this fall.

The thought pulled my attention to the family photo on top of the TV. It was too far away to see perfectly, but I didn't need the little details. I knew each face as well as I knew mine didn't quite fit.

I was the palest of the bunch—looking like a vampire alongside these robust mortals. I was the only one with blue eyes and full lips. At least my eyebrows were the same shape and my hair the right color.

I looked a bit like Mom—hence the eyebrows and hair—but nothing like my dad. Because I looked like her and was the baby, my brother and sisters accused me of being Mom's favorite, and maybe that was true, but it wasn't because of my looks.

My siblings wouldn't have teased me if they'd known the truth.

I made an egg-white omelet for supper—I was wearing my fat clothes this week and wanted to be back into the "thin" section of my closet by Monday. At my smallest I was still a size 12. Some of us just aren't meant to be skinny, and I'm one of them.

I followed the omelet with a small container of low-fat cherry yogurt, and wisely decided against coffee even though I desperately wanted one.

I e-mailed Julie while a cup of tea heated in the microwave and told her we were a go for Saturday, then ran a bath. I didn't return my sister's call. She always wanted to talk about Mom, and I never did. I'd call from work tomorrow so I'd have an excuse to make it short. I drank my tea in the tub and read a romance novel until the water turned cold.

With Fudge on my lap, I watched an episode of *Smallville* I had DVR'd, then I went to bed. See what a wild woman I am?

Dreams have always been an escape for me—mini vacations from life, if you will. Sometimes I like to crawl into bed and give in to the pull of my dreams and let them take me away. Today I hoped to dream as I had the night before—of being fireman-carried by David Boreanaz to a bed strewn with rose petals.

I wasn't so lucky.

I was in Central Park, sitting on a bench eating ice cream and listening to a young guy play saxophone nearby for change. He was playing the theme from an old TV show I couldn't remember the name of. I hate when that happens.

"Facts of life."

I looked up. It was the old guy from the Duane Reade. I wasn't afraid of him here. This was my *world. "Huh?"*

He sat down beside me, hitching his pants in the way that older men do before they sit. "The song he's playin'. It's the theme from The Facts of Life.*"*

"Oh." Of course now that he mentioned it, I recognized it. "I liked that show. I always wanted to be Jo."

"She the pretty one or the tough one?"

"Tough one." I spooned another mound of Cherry Garcia into my mouth.

"Huh. Figures."

I swallowed. "She was pretty, too."

"She was at that." He didn't look at me, but at a point some distance away. "Grew up to be a fine-lookin' woman."

We sat for a while listening to the music. Finally, I turned to him. "Why are you here?"

"I always come here."

"I mean here now—with me."

"Shucks, I don't know, girl. I's just walkin' through the park mindin' my own business, and there you were, sitting here like you was waitin' for me or something."

I shrugged. "I wasn't." Where the hell was David Boreanaz?

"I shoulda known you'd show up eventually. Didn't figure it would happen this soon, though."

"What are you talking about?"

He looked at me. Braced one bony hand on his bony leg and angled himself to take what my grandmother would have called, "a good long gander" at me. "You've been pretending so long, you've almost got yourself convinced, don't you?"

I shook my head, wishing I was anywhere but here. My ice cream was melting, and I didn't like this conversation. "I know you seem to think I'm a nightmare, but I have to be honest. I question your sanity."

He laughed. "I betchoo do. I bet you question your own sometimes, too."

He was right. I did, but only when I allowed myself to think about it.

Again, there was silence as we sat. The saxophonist was playing the theme from The Jeffersons, and my companion's foot was tapping like mad on the bald dirt below it. "I love it when he plays the stuff I can dance to."

My own foot started to tap as I tossed the empty ice-cream cup in the trash. He was right, it was a catchy tune.

Abruptly, the old man stood. "I'm gonna go now and leave you alone."

"Wait!" I stopped him with a hand on his arm. "What's your name?" It might come in handy if I needed, oh, say a restraining order.

"Antwoine. And you are?"

I hesitated, but figured, what the heck? "Dawn."

He laughed. "Whoever named you was not without a sense of humor." His mirth faded. "Bye-bye, little Dawn. You take care now."

"You too." I watched him walk away with a feeling bordering on sadness.

"Dawn?"

I looked up, and there, silhouetted by the sun was the man I'd been waiting for: David Boreanaz. Hello, Gorgeous.

"Fancy meeting you here." I batted my eyelashes at him.

"Yeah," He seemed really distracted as he sat down beside me, looking very much like he did as Angel—post-Buffy, of course. "Listen, there's something I gotta tell you. Something you need to know—"

And that's when a teenage girl with dark hair and big blue eyes jumped out of the bushes and drove a stake through his heart. Honest to God. One minute I was glorying in the feel of DB's thigh pressing against mine, and the next I was covered in vampire ash—and I had my mouth open.

The "slayer" had eyes that were so pale they were almost clear with an outer ring of black, but it was her grin that made my skin crawl—or maybe that was the gray soot covering me from head to toe. Gross, was that a clump of hair?

"Saved you, Dawnie."

I scowled as I brushed vampire leavin's off my sweater. "From what? It's daylight, for crying out loud!"

She leaned on the bench, all attitude and skimpy clothing. Her stomach was flat and decorated with a ruby belly-button stud. "From hearing things you know you don't want to hear."

I glared at her, my animosity stemming from more than just envy of her abs. What could possibly come out of DB's mouth that would bother me? "As if you would know what I would and would not want to hear."

She leaned down and actually kissed me—on the mouth! Her lips were soft and warm, but something about them gave me the wiggins—and it wasn't just the vampire gunk, or that she was a girl. It was how real they felt.

"I know you, Dawnie. I'd like to get to know you better." She was actually flirting with me!

"Or what?" I tried to sound all cool and composed, like

I had women hitting on me every day. "You'll drive a stake
through my heart?"

*She licked ash from her lips and gave me a once-over
that made my skin crawl.* "I could put it somewhere else."

*I jumped up. This was wrong. I shouldn't be here. She
shouldn't be here—not in my head, in* my *dreams. The
old man showing up I could probably explain, but not
this.* "I have to go now."

Creepy slayer-girl shook her head. "Nowhere you can go
where I can't find you."

*In the distance, I heard a familiar buzzing noise that both
annoyed and elated me. Was that my alarm?* "You're wrong,"
I told her. "I can wake up."

And then I did.

I hit snooze but didn't bother trying to go back to sleep for
the extra five minutes. I lay there, staring up at the white of
my ceiling and thinking about the dream that was already
starting to fade from my memory. I wasn't comforted by the
fuzzing details.

Bad dreams always find a way to come back.

At precisely 10:01 the next evening, as I sat on the couch
watching TV with Fudge purring loudly on my lap, the phone
rang. I knew who it was before I even checked the caller ID.
It would be Ivy. I had called her earlier from work and gotten
her voice mail. I knew I shouldn't have left a message.

I was tempted not to answer, but she was my sister, and
there was always the paranoia in my head that she might be
calling to tell me Mom's condition had changed—for better
or for worse.

So I picked up the receiver of my lip-shaped phone and
drew a deep breath.

"Hi, Ivy."

"Dawnie, thank God you're home."

She sounded distraught, and I was instantly guilty. "What's happened? Is Mom okay?"

"She would be better if all of her children were gathered around her."

Uh-huh. "She tell you that, did she?" It was a cheap shot, of course. Mom hadn't said a word to anyone in a very long time.

Ivy sighed in my ear—heavily. No doubt a million other martyrs around the world heard it and shook their heads in commiseration.

"You know perfectly well that she didn't."

"So how do you know what would make her happy? Maybe she's happy just as she is." In fact, I was pretty certain that was true.

"Oh, Dawn."

Okay, the sighing I could deal with—it was melodramatic and manipulative. The disappointment in her voice wasn't so easily shrugged off. This was my oldest sister, after all. I'd spent much of my life trying to live up to the example she set for me to follow.

Obviously I was *not* measuring up in her estimation.

"Look, Ivy, unless there's been some change in Mom's condition, I don't see how having me there would make one bit of difference." It wasn't like my mother would know I was there—at least not in the physical realm.

"She'd know her family was with her."

"You think Mom would be impressed with me leaving my job to sit beside her bed?" She wouldn't be. My mother had been—was—very big on personal accomplishment and pursuing dreams—no pun intended. She would not appreciate me brooding by her bed as though she were a corpse. Not when I knew the truth.

"Getting defensive isn't going to change anything, Dawnie."

"I know, and stop calling me that." I hated that she talked to me like a kid. I hated when she tried using her *Oprah*-learned psychoanalysis on me, too. I was the one with the degree, damn it.

I could help someone deal with bedwetting or nightmares. I could help someone find rest when they were having trouble falling asleep, but I couldn't get my own mother to wake up. It wasn't because I hadn't tried, but because Mom wouldn't come back to this world. The only way I could hope to wake her up outside of my field was to go into the Dream Realm after her, and I'd rather eat broken glass than do that. That would mean acknowledging what she had done. Acknowledging *her*.

"I can't come home," I told her. "I don't have enough vacation time yet." *And Mom can rot.*

"Can't you come for a weekend?"

And do what, watch Mom sleep? "That's an expensive weekend, Ivy."

"You're a doctor now, you can afford it."

The sound that came out of me was a cross between a laugh and a yelp. Fudge jumped off my lap. "I live in New York City."

A sigh—a gusty, long-suffering one—blew not so gently in my ear. "It wouldn't be an issue if you moved home."

Not this again. "I have to go now."

I was just about to hang up when I heard her, "Dawnie! Dawn, wait."

I pressed the top lip of the phone back to my ear. "What?"

"I'm sorry. I just . . . you're the only one of us who might be able to help her."

That melted my heart more than it probably should have. "I can't, Ivy." I didn't like admitting it, but it was true. Even if I did go into the Dream Realm and talk to Mom, there was no guarantee I could bring her back with me. If she wanted to wake up, then she would. Unfortunately, it was obvious to no one but me that she didn't want to.

"Sometimes I think she doesn't *want* to wake up." Ivy's voice was hoarse, as though she was saying something she thought she shouldn't.

Okay, so maybe I wasn't the only one it was obvious to. I didn't like the hurt in Ivy's voice. It was so much easier to justify not being there at home when I could be angry.

"She was so different before it happened," Ivy continued. "You know that. It was like she would rather be asleep than with any of us—except for you, of course."

I heard my sister's bitterness as surely as if she had been able to pour it through the phone lines and into my ear. Yes, Mom had seemed to have more tolerance for my company during the later stages of her "illness," and I spent as much of that summer as I could with her before heading back to class in September.

"Only because she knew I had to go back to school." Only because she wanted to talk me into visiting Morpheus and the rest of my "family" before leaving her own.

"Mm." Ivy didn't believe it.

"Look, don't go getting all pissy with me for something I have no control over, okay?" Defensive much? I shouldn't give in to the guilt. It wasn't my fault Mom was gone, and it wasn't like my sisters would believe me if I told them where she was.

"I'm just saying you're her favorite. I'm all right with that, especially if hearing your voice will wake her up."

"It didn't work the last two times I was home."

"This time might be different."

I sighed. "It won't. Look, Ivy, I love you, but I have to go."

"Do you think she'll ever come back to us?"

Once more I was ambushed from hanging up by another familiar phrase in my sister's anxious tone. We never used to be at odds like this. I have pictures of the two of us taken when I was a baby and Ivy treated me like her own big, amusing doll.

Ivy was just worried about Mom, and she was there, dealing with it every day. That wasn't to say that I didn't think of my mother every day—I just wasn't as charitable with my thoughts as Ivy probably was. And I didn't have to deal with the proximity of it.

And I didn't have to look at Dad. Which meant he didn't have to look at me. I think he liked that.

"I don't know," I replied honestly. "She'd better."

Ivy's laughter eased the tension from my shoulders. "That's what I love about you, Dawnie. You face life like it would be stupid to deny you anything."

"Maybe I can convince life it's true, what do you think?" This was my job in the family. I was the brat, the steamroller. I was also the one who tried to make everyone smile with a cocky attitude that was no more authentic than the Kate Spade bag I had bought on the street last spring.

"I think I miss you."

My throat tightened. "I miss you, too. Look, I'll be home for Christmas. If I can, I'll see if I can swing a few days before that." Part of me hoped I wouldn't be able to.

Awful, isn't it? To love your family and miss them, but at the same time dread seeing them? Actually, it wasn't them I dreaded; it was the expectations they had of me.

"Okay. Do what you can. I'll talk to you soon. Love you."

My throat got tighter. Pretty soon I'd be choking on air. "Love you, too."

I hung up. Two seconds later—and I mean two seconds. I didn't even have enough time to process any of the conversation I'd just had with my sister—the phone rang again.

"Hello?"

"Ivy call you?" It was my brother, Mark.

Laughter loosened my throat. "How'd you know?"

"I was talking to her earlier. I tried to call before she got to you, but as soon as I got your voice mail three times in a row, I knew she'd gotten you."

It had felt much longer. "Trying to run interference, were you?"

"I figured if I called first, she might get tired of trying and give up." There was a slight pause, and his voice changed—lost some of its usual humor. "She give you a hard time?"

I shrugged even though he couldn't see it. "A bit."

"You okay?"

"I will be."

"You wanna talk?"

I twisted the phone cord around my finger. "Not really."

I could almost hear his relief. My brother, as good-hearted as he was, was not good with feelings. "All right. I'll let you go then. Night, Tink."

I smiled. "Night, Idgit."

This time when I hung up I vowed to let voice mail answer if it rang again.

I ran a bath and sorted through my assortment of bath products as the tub filled. I needed something to relax me—ah, Cinnamon Buns bubble bath. That would do it. If I couldn't eat them, I could at least soak in water that smelled like 'em.

I pinned my hair up, grabbed the latest Bon Jovi CD and the newest romance by Lisa Kleypas, and tossed my robe over the towel rack. I settled into the hot, sweet-smelling water and read until Jon stopped singing. By that time I smelled delicious, had muscles as limp as Paris Hilton's eyelids, and had a head full of fantasies involving me and a darkly dangerous hero. If anyone tried staking David Boreanaz in my dreams tonight, I was going to be seriously ticked off.

I climbed into bed and was asleep shortly after my head touched the pillow. I drifted into my secret world and allowed the dreams to come:

I was on my way to the opera with Clive Owen, but before things could get interesting, I somehow ended up at my old high school, where I learned that I had forgotten to study for an exam. Clive was there, too, but he was attracted to the charms of Amy Dufresne—a skinny, skanky girl I sat behind in history class. I never did like her.

Then Amy and Clive were gone, and I was in a bedroom—an old one. It was like I was in a production of a Jane Austen novel. The bedroom was huge, the walls covered with paper that was hand-painted with hundreds of colorful birds. I touched it and felt the slightly uneven texture beneath my fingers.

My hair hung around the shoulders of my long cotton nightgown, which was pristine and unwrinkled. I was naked underneath it—not even underwear. Who was skanky now?

The door opened. In the lamplight—why had I not noticed how dim the lighting was before?—I saw a man enter the room. He came toward me, his boots falling heavily with every step. Out of the darkness he came, into the light.

He was beautiful. Tight black pants, leather boots, open white shirt, and tanned, muscular build. There was something familiar about his pale eyes, but I couldn't place it. He was like something right off the cover of a romance novel, only better. He was a complete personification of everything I thought physically attractive in a man, and he made my knees weak.

He didn't speak but simply took me into his arms—his very muscular, very strong arms—and kissed me. I swear to God, I actually swooned as he Frenched me. When I said this guy was perfect, I meant it.

He bent down and swept me up into his arms like I weighed nothing and strode toward the bed. I could hear the fall of his boots muffled by the carpet. I clung to his shoulders, terrified that he would drop me but knowing that he wouldn't.

"Beautiful, Dawn," he murmured as he placed me gently on the bed. "I cannot believe I have been so fortunate as to find you."

"I was just thinking the same thing." This close I could see the dark rim of his irises, smell the jasmine musk of his skin. Even the shadow of his beard was perfect—not too high on the cheek and not at all patchy. In his left ear was a ruby stud. Normally, I don't go for earrings, but on him it worked. It also made me frown. What was it about it that bothered me?

"Do you want me?" He was poised above me, one thigh

over mine, and I could feel every divine inch of him. He was hard. Very hard.

"Uh, yes," I replied, forgetting all about his earring. "I do."

He chuckled as his hand reached for me. Through the thin cotton gown I could feel the heat of his fingers as they stroked my breasts. He tweaked my nipples, pinching hard, but not enough to hurt.

And then he grabbed the neck of my gown and ripped. I heard the loud shredding noise and then the "pop" as the hem snapped. He laid both sides open and set that perfect mouth to work on my chest. Little silent darts of "oohs" and "God, yes!" rippled through me, heat pooling between my thighs. And he was only just getting started. His hands were everywhere at once. His skin was hot and smooth beneath my hands. I'd never felt anything so real in a dream before. I was hot for this guy, and from the tent in the front of his tight pants I knew he was just as primed for me.

He slid down, kissing my ribs, the soft flesh of my belly, then he was between my legs, and I swear he had at least two tongues—one of which was at least six inches long. He impaled me with it, moving it inside me like it was his cock while the other lapped at what I affectionately like to call my "magic button." Familiar tension built inside me and I moved with it, arching my hips. I grabbed at his hair, grinding myself on his mouth. Just a little bit more, and I was going to come.

Then he stopped. I actually moaned in disappointment, and he chuckled softly in response. Slowly, he slid back up my body. His pants were gone now, and I looked down to see the biggest, thickest, most impressive set of manly equipment I had ever seen. It scared me, and I looked up at his face. He smiled—so perfectly beautiful.

He slid between my thighs, and I looked down once more, nervous and unsure. But wait . . . it was just a normal penis now. I must have imagined that it was so terribly big. It was impressive, but not frightening—thick but not threatening. Tension eased from my muscles, and when he stroked the fat head of his cock against my wetness, I spread my legs and whimpered—just a little.

Oh, this was just too perfect, too good.

So why did it feel so wrong? He kissed me, and I wanted to pull away. Why did I suddenly want to cringe when he pinched my nipples again? Why did it feel as though his fingers were dirty and cold? The pressure of his lips increased. His teeth cut my lips—I could taste the blood. His breath was stale, like an old trunk that hadn't been opened in a long time.

I pushed at his shoulders, struggled against him. I didn't want this. Even if it was just a dream. I didn't want him.

"Stop."

He lowered his head, tongued and sucked at my breasts until I writhed with the sensations he elicited. God, it felt so good physically. I wanted him so badly, but I didn't want him at all.

I managed to push him off a bit, but not much. "Get off!" I yelled.

He grinned at me, his teeth bright in the dark. "I intend to."

I froze beneath him, all too aware of the hardness pressing against my inner thigh. He was still beautiful, but there was something twisted about his beauty. His eyes were clear and empty—like looking at nothing except for those thick, spidery black rims. He was cold and hard and more than a little scary.

I tried again, my jaw clenched to keep my teeth from chattering. "Get off me."

"You can't stop me, love," he murmured, kissing the side of my neck with lips that seemed to burn. "You don't know how."

My whole body was on fire—the kind of heat that comes with sexual arousal. As unpleasant as his touch was—as much as I wanted him to stop, I wanted him to continue as well. He bit me in places I didn't know it could feel good to be bitten—places that I wasn't sure if it actually felt good or was so painful that I was just grateful he stopped. He sucked and kissed and licked. I was going to have whisker burn on my thighs and my butt. He invaded me, slid fingers inside of me—God, in so many places—that were slick and set me literally spasming with lust. He did things I would never let anyone do—things that were borderline degrading, but he made them feel so damn good.

I cried out when he thrust inside me, unable to distinguish between pleasure and pain. And even still, I rose up to meet his thrusts. I welcomed every slam of his body into mine even though my mind recoiled in horror. I didn't want this, yet I had no control over him—and no control over the fact that regardless of what my mind wanted, my body wanted him.

He stared down at me as he moved inside me. "We're two of a kind, Dawnie," He said with a smile that was smug, even menacing. He took more pleasure from knowing what he was doing to me than he did from the actual act.

I tried to look away, but I couldn't. I hated him. I wanted to hurt him, but he held my hands pinned above my head. I wanted to throw him off even as my thighs tightened around his hips. I was throbbing—literally pulsing between the *legs. The harder he thrust inside me, the more I welcomed the pain, the more I wanted. I was battered. I was bruised, and I was so close to climax I couldn't stand it.*

"You can't stop me," he taunted, quickening his movements. I couldn't turn away from the dark brush of his breath. God, it was like death. "I'm coming, Dawnie. I'm coming and you can't stop me."

I looked him straight in those scary eyes. "Yes, I can."

I woke up shuddering—little shocks spasming between my legs. I might have stopped him from coming, but I hadn't been able to stop myself.

Chapter Three

I was going to puke.

Poor Fudge leaped off my bed with a perturbed mewl as I frantically tossed back the blankets and swung my shaking legs over the side of the bed.

I just made it to the bathroom. I retched until my stomach muscles felt like they were cramping. When my gut finally calmed down, I grabbed a wad of toilet paper and ripped. I wiped my mouth as the dispenser continued to spin. I flushed and used the vanity for support as I stood upright to look at my tear-streaked face in the mirror.

There was blood on my mouth. Sniffing, I wiped it—and the little piece of TP stuck to it—away with one hand while the other wiped at my watery eyes. I leaned into the sink to get a better look in the mirror.

My bottom lip was cut. I must have bit it during the dream. That would explain why my mouth felt so swollen and the musty taste on my tongue.

The thing in my dream couldn't have done it. It hadn't felt like an Oneroi—a creature of the Dream Realm—yet it hadn't felt quite human either. I must have conjured it myself—a manifestation of guilt and anger brought on by my conversation with Ivy. That was why I hadn't been able to stop it.

There was a knock on the bathroom door. A low, muffled voice penetrated the wood. "Dawn, you okay?"

It was Lola. Shit, I had woken her up. I opened the bathroom door. "Yeah. Sorry, Lo."

My roommate shrugged her round shoulders. "I'd rather make sure you're fine than sleep through it."

I tried to smile, but it hurt. "You just can't stand to miss anything—even if it's gross."

Lola grinned. "That too. Seriously, you okay? You look like shit."

At five feet, Lola MacIntyre made me feel like a giant. She had curly black hair, dusky skin, and boobs that defied gravity—pretty impressive given the size of them. She also watched *Forrest Gump* with me whenever I asked, which made her my best girlfriend ever.

Right now she was wearing boxer shorts and a tank top with a picture of *The Dukes of Hazzard* on it—the show, not that sacrilegious movie.

"I'm okay, really."

She frowned up at me, looking very young under the bright vanity lights. "What happened to your lip?"

"I think I bit it in my sleep."

"Oh. Did you eat something funky?"

I wish. "Bad dream."

Sharp eyebrows jerked upward. "That's weird for you."

"Yeah, well . . ." She was right, and two strange dreams so close together were even weirder.

"You wanna stay up for a while? I can put a movie in."

I was tempted to let *Forrest* run all this anxiety out of my head, but Lola had to work in the morning, and I wasn't going to have her fussing over me like a mother hen.

"Thanks, but I think I'm just going to brush my teeth and head back to bed. Rain check?"

She smiled. "You know it. If you change your mind, come get me, okay?"

I nodded. I wasn't going to change my mind, I knew that. As much as the dream had bothered me, I didn't want to share it, and I didn't want to let it keep me from trying to go back to sleep.

It was, after all, just a dream. They happened, even to me. Despite my heritage, sometimes the mind just had to work stuff out. During those times, my dreams were just dreams, and I let them happen, guiding myself through it and doing all that needed to be done to work it through. Maybe I had unknowingly done this. There was a reason why they called it the *sub*conscious.

But those weird, spidery eyes stuck with me. I had seen them somewhere before.

I gave Lola a hug, brushed my teeth—and my tongue—with cinnamon toothpaste, and went back to bed. My lower lip was sore, but at least I wasn't twitching with the aftershocks of orgasm anymore.

That had never happened to me before, and the fact that it had happened with such a disturbing dream was well, disturbing. Dreams had always been an escape for me—a world of promise and adventure. Now, I had been violated inside that world.

I thought back to when I was little. My mother used to hold me in her lap, wrapped in a fuzzy blanket, and rock me while she sang what I referred to as "dee-dee-dee" songs. The melodies were usually always different, but the lyrics remained the same—just "dee-dee-dee" over and over again. Sometimes, when I find it hard to fall asleep, I sing similar songs in my head.

My mother would also tuck me into bed every night—after singing to me—and tell me to have wonderful dreams. Even though I was usually on the brink of passing out by the time she put me in my bed, I remember her telling me she wanted to hear all about my dream-adventures in the morning. Of course, she was often there in my dreams, she and Morpheus.

Where was my so-called father when I was being raped in his Realm? So much for him being the Lord of Dreams. The walls I built shouldn't have stopped him, should they? Didn't he know everything that happened in his kingdom?

Screw Morpheus; I should have slapped that creep silly. If I had known more about myself and what I could do, I would have known how to react.

But I hadn't—and that bothered me more than the dream itself.

"I'm coming, Dawnie. I'm coming, and you can't stop me."

I rolled over onto my side as my stomach lurched. I had to stop thinking about it. I had to let it go. It was over now. I was safe. It was just a dream, and dreams couldn't hurt me.

Even though I knew that, it was a long time, and six "dee-dee-dee" songs before I fell asleep again.

* * *

When I first moved to New York I was certain I would be unaffected by the size of the city and the people in it. After all, I was from *Toronto*. I knew all about city living.

I was full of crap.

Part of New York's charm is that it is unlike any other city on the planet—not that I'm that well traveled, but I think it's a safe assumption. There are times when it is dirty and smells bad, and the people seem to be in too much of a hurry to care about anything but themselves. Then there are also times when the sun beats down between the buildings lining Fifth Avenue and makes the whole world seem bright and beautiful. There are mornings, when the streets have been sprayed down, that all you can smell is wet concrete and the freshness of a city waking up. There's a haze on the horizon, but the breeze is sweet—and there's no smell of taxi or subway urine.

A mariachi band got onto the subway on my way to work and played in the aisle as they passed a sombrero around. Only the tourists openly watched. I've been able to perfect an expression of boredom, but I still get a kick out of it. Although the break dancers that sometimes ride the subway scare me. I keep thinking one of them is going to kick me in the head or something. Somebody's going to lose an eye, I just know it.

New York, especially Manhattan, is so image-conscious, and yet I can pretty much guarantee you that the next Mid-East hot-dog vendor I meet will call me "pretty lady" or some variation thereof because he thinks my voluptuous form is the ideal. And while Torontonians can hold their own in terms of the brusqueness that comes with urban living, nowhere but in Manhattan have I ever been told that I need "more attitude."

I thought I was a city girl. I was wrong. I was becoming one now. I totally belonged as I strode purposefully down the sidewalk in the black suit I got for a steal at Daffy's and the huge diva sunglasses I bought from a street vender, along with my faux Kate Spade. The shoes were designer discount as well. I needed the window dressing to cover the fact that I felt like crap. Obviously, I hadn't slept well last night.

The clinic was on East Eighth Street, not far from NYU, and I spared a glance at the milling students as I climbed up the steps by the handicap ramp. The clinic was on the second floor. Normally, I took the stairs for a little exercise. Today, I took the elevator.

Noah was waiting for me in the reception area when I stepped off. For a moment I was ashamed to be seen with my Venti extra-whip latte, then I noticed the familiar white-and-green paper cup in his hand. I took a deep breath and smelled vanilla and sugar. I wondered how much whipped cream he had on his.

He stood when he saw me. I forgot about my sweet, decadent coffee when I saw the dark circles under his eyes. I wasn't the only one who hadn't slept well last night. Of course, he managed to make tired look hot, with his mussed hair and patchy stubble.

"Hey, Doc." He frowned—quickly, then it was gone. "You look like shit."

I might have been offended if I hadn't thought the same thing myself. And I was cranky enough to be honest right back. "So do you."

Bonnie watched this exchange with some interest. "Did the two of you get looking this way together?"

I shot her a look that definitely had a "shut up" vibe about it.

Noah glanced at her with what might have been genuine bewilderment, but I doubted it. He seemed amused by the question. "No."

Did he have to say it like it should be so totally impossible for us to have been together?

"What's up, Noah?" It came out a little abrupt, but standing around feeling like a joke was not my idea of fun.

Dark eyes turned to me, but his face remained impassive. "I need to talk to you." There was no inflection in his tone either.

I might have thought him totally vacant if I hadn't known how good Noah Clarke was at hiding his emotions. In my experience, the blanker Noah looked, the more there was wrong. This did not bode well.

"Come into my office." I glanced sideways at Bonnie. "If Mrs. Kinney arrives, give her a cup of coffee and the latest issue of *Cosmo*."

Bonnie saluted me, the diamonds on her fingers glittering under the bright lights. "You betcha."

Noah didn't follow me down the corridor like so many of my patients. He walked beside me. Being a doctor often made people treat me with a certain degree of deference. Noah never did.

"Pumpkin?"

I jerked, shocked at his attempt at conversation. "Excuse me?"

He nodded at my cup. "Your coffee."

"Oh." My cheeks warmed a little. Not a come-on then. "Yeah, it is."

"Mmm," he agreed as he took a drink. "My mother used to make pumpkin pie. Why do you look so bad?"

I was startled—and yeah, offended. "It's nothing, but thanks for the concern."

He must have heard the sarcasm in my voice—he'd have to be stupid to miss it. "Sorry. It's just . . . you usually look nice." His frank gaze met mine. "Real nice."

That warmed me. "I had a bad dream," I admitted, meeting his fathomless eyes for a second longer than I was comfortable with. "A nightmare."

He seemed surprised—sort of how I imagine you'd look at a mechanic who didn't have his driver's license, or an oncologist who had a tumor. Wonder and irony combined.

I opened the door to my office and gestured for him to step inside. He brushed past me with a whiff of warm vanilla and clove, and stood in the middle of the carpet, staring at his cup for a few seconds before meeting my gaze.

"Thanks for seeing me, Doc."

I sat down behind my desk, tucking my coat around me as I crossed my legs. "I get the feeling you want to talk about something important." And by important, I meant anything other than *my* dreams.

He looked at the cluster of photos on the wall by my desk. He didn't seem so eager now. "Is that your mother?"

He'd seen that picture before and never commented on it. It wasn't his fault, but his doing so now, on the heels of Ivy's phone call, brought a new rush of familial guilt.

"Yes." The photo had been taken when she was pregnant with me. She looked so happy—almost as happy as she did now, sound asleep. *"In the Arms of Morpheus"* the doctors called it. How appropriate. She wasn't a morphine addict, as the term sometimes implied. Rather, my mother had fallen into a deep sleep and couldn't be roused. There seemed to be nothing else wrong with her, and her brain patterns were normal.

The bitch was just asleep.

"She's pretty." He glanced at me. "You look like her a bit."

Was that a compliment or an insult? I was either almost as pretty as she or nowhere near it. "I don't think you came down here to talk about my mother."

He drew a breath, long fingers wrapping around his paper cup. "No."

Oh frig, what if he was going to tell me he didn't want to work with me anymore? Noah was one of the highlights of my job. It was pathetic but true. His ability to shape dream matter amazed me. I didn't want to lose that.

I didn't want to lose him.

But I couldn't just sit here in silence. "Noah, why are you here?"

He looked me dead in the eye. "I think my dreams are trying to kill me."

Chapter Four

"You *what*?" Not my most witty response, but I was thinking on my feet—and my balance wasn't that good at the best of times.

Noah shifted in his chair, leaning forward to rest his forearms on his thighs. The denim there looked thin enough to start shredding. "I know how it sounds . . ."

"I'm not here to judge." I winced. God, I hadn't just said that, had I? Most times I had trouble remembering I was a doctor, and now I was resorting to armchair-shrink lingo.

He blinked and rubbed his jaw with long, paint-stained fingers. "It sounds crazy, I know that." He also sounded perfectly sane, which scared me—and not for the reasons it should have as a doctor.

This was the point in the conversation where I was

supposed to tell him that he was wrong, or that I didn't like "that word." "But you believe it."

This time he didn't blink. He just held my gaze with the unflinching darkness of his own. "You think I'm crazy?"

"No." There was no hesitation on my part. There was something going on though. For a man who was normally so in control of his dreams to make such a claim, something had to have happened. I wasn't ready to assume it was something from The Dreaming and Noah's own mind. Not yet.

"Generally such dreams stem from a deeper issue—a fear or conflict that the subconscious is trying to sort out. In your case it might be something from your childhood." He never discussed his life before his parents' divorce—only the years after he and his mother went out on their own. And he never, ever mentioned his father.

He laughed—a sharp, harsh bark that startled me. "It's nothing from my childhood."

A little voice in my head spoke up. Something in his dreams might really be trying to kill him. Why did I have to know that was possible? It's rough trying to be clinical and analytical when you knew there were things out there that defied science—when you were one of them. But for now I had to approach this in a professional manner.

Noah believed what he was telling me, and what I believed didn't matter. For the moment, I wasn't going to entertain that there might be something in the night trying to harm him and treat this situation like a therapist should. Because that's what he expected me to do. I only thought otherwise because of my own recent experiences, and I should have known better than to bring anything personal into a session.

"What's happened that has you believing that your dreams are trying to harm you?"

"What's happened?" Disbelief and anger lit his features. He didn't like how I was handling this. Neither did I. "My dream tried to kill me."

I pressed on. There had to be a rational explanation. *Please God, let there be a rational explanation.* "Have you recently suffered an upheaval? Or a significant change in your life? It could be that your subconscious is reacting to this change in a way that leads your mind to believe you are in some kind of physical danger."

He eyed me for a moment. "Don't go all clinical on me, Doc. I came here because you're the only person I could think to turn to, not because I can't deal with reality."

His words humbled me. "I'm sorry, Noah. I've never encountered this kind of . . . problem before."

A slight smile curved lips the color of a juicy peach. "And you have a patient waiting." I'd fantasized a couple of times about kissing those lips, laughed more than a hundred times at the words that came from between them. Now the sight of them just made me feel sad—and more guilty than I was willing to admit.

I didn't question the stability of his mind. I didn't wonder if he needed more help than I could give. But even if something in his dreams was trying to kill him, I wasn't the person to help him.

"He wants you to be," that little voice whispered.

"I do have a patient waiting, yes, but—" He cut me off by standing.

"It's okay, Doc. I'll see Bonnie about an appointment." Stuffing his hands into the pockets of his battered leather coat, he started for the door.

After the mess I'd made of this, he was still going to come back?

"Noah." I couldn't stand the idea of him walking out that door thinking I didn't believe in him.

Still wearing that blank, but somehow disappointed, expression, he turned.

And said nothing.

I took a breath and pushed back my chair. "I'll be going to dinner at six. Want to come?" It was my duty to help him, and I wanted to help him.

Again with the slip of a smile—and just the tiniest frown. "Are you asking me out on a date?"

I smiled uncertainly—an expression that made me very attractive, I'm sure. I was crossing all kinds of lines I had no business crossing. "You're paying."

He nodded. "Of course. McDonald's okay?"

I must have looked horrified because his "slip" turned into a full-fledged smile. He had such great teeth. He must have had braces as a kid. Smiling made him downright beautiful. I basked in it, even after I realized he was teasing.

"Don't worry, Doc. Even I have more class than that. I'll pick you up at six."

He left, closing the door behind him—a fact I was thankful for as I sank into my chair like a boneless heap. What had I done? I'd just asked a patient out to dinner. Granted it sounded like he was screwed six ways from Sunday, but I had asked a guy out. I hadn't done that since . . . well, I never had.

I sat there for a second while the shock of what I'd done wore off. Slowly, a big-ass grin spread across my face. I was going to dinner with Noah Clarke.

Wait till I told Bonnie.

At 5:50 I said good-bye to a patient and pulled a brush and a small bag of makeup out of the top drawer of my desk.

I released my hair from its clip and let it fall. I ran the brush through quickly, then turned my attention to freshening my makeup.

I love makeup. I like to think of my face as a canvas that I can paint however I want. I've been blessed with fairly good skin—at least it looks good when I have a tinted moisturizer on it. My eyes are my best feature, and I play them up with colors that bring out the blue and green. I also have big lips, so I usually play them down unless I really want to make a statement. As a kid I was teased mercilessly for them; now, every lip gloss seems to promise "plumper" lips, and doctors offer to inject collagen into skinny mouths. You know I've actually been asked if my lips were real?

I brushed on a little extra shadow and used a fine brush—that great bent one that Benefit makes—to darken my eyeliner. A little powder took the shine from my T-zone and Clinique Black Honey gloss—a gift from the makeup gods—finished the transformation.

Not that it was much of a transformation, but I felt a little more prepared to be out in public with Noah.

I slung my lab coat over the back of my chair, grabbed my purse, and locked the door on my way out.

When I entered the waiting area, Noah was already there, being chatted up by Bonnie, who was watching him like a fat tomcat eyeing a lame pigeon.

Noah turned as I approached. I'd like to say that his jaw dropped at the sight of me, but it didn't. He just stopped and watched with an expression I couldn't read but warmed me right down to my toes.

He had shaved, and his hair was artfully mussed rather than accidentally so. He wore clean jeans—no rips—with a lightweight gray sweater underneath a leather coat in much better shape than his usual.

He cleaned up good. More importantly, he'd cleaned up for *me*.

He was staring at my head as I approached. "Something wrong?" I asked, feeling the top of my skull for foreign and potentially humiliating objects.

Noah's intense gaze shifted a little, traveling down to someplace around my shoulder. "I've never seen your hair down before."

"Oh." What else could I say?

He looked slightly bemused. "I was trying to think of the colors I'd use to paint it. Your hair, I mean."

I smiled. I wondered if he saw all of life as a potential subject for his art. "Did you think of any?"

He frowned in contemplation. "A couple. I'm not sure they're right, though."

"Well, maybe you'll figure it out over dinner." I turned to Bonnie. "I'll be back before the eight o'clock." I was doing some work for Dr. Canning tonight, and that meant I'd be hanging out in the sleep lab later.

She waggled her fingers in a wave. "You two have fun."

Noah said good-bye to her, and Bonnie waited till his back was turned to give me an openmouthed wink. I rolled my eyes.

It was a nice night, so we walked. I figured this would give me a chance to find out more about Noah, but I ended up doing most of the talking. It wasn't that Noah was curt, he just didn't waste words on himself. Maybe if I'd asked him about painting, he would have yakked my ear off, but I stupidly asked him about his family—about *him*. Obviously, he wasn't much of an egotist because he kept his responses as short and uninteresting as possible.

It made me wonder what he was hiding. Made me want to play doctor and not in a sexual way, because I was fairly certain he hid something that needed facing.

Luckily, we only had to walk a few blocks. The restaurant was a great little family-owned Indian place just off Sixth. I felt a little tingly as I remembered his assumption that I liked food with a lot of flavor. Sensuous he had called me.

We ordered drinks, appetizers, and main courses. I waited until the waiter had brought our drinks and appetizers before daring to open my mouth.

"Okay, so explain to me why you think your dreams are trying to harm you."

Noah took a bite of spicy potato and chickpeas. I can never remember the names of this stuff, only that it tastes pretty freaking good. He chewed and swallowed. "Not so much my dreams, but what's in them."

I loaded my fork as well. "And what do you think that is exactly?"

I looked up to see him staring at me—hard. "Are you mocking me?"

I stopped midchew and swallowed. If he only knew. "No." No, I was hoping he was imagining it all. Praying, actually.

He sighed. "Look, can you stop talking like you think I'm making this up?"

Yes, I could. I just didn't want to. "I don't think you're making it up."

"But you don't believe it really happened."

If I told him I did, would he think I was nuts?

"I don't even know what 'it' pertains to." I sighed. "Noah, my job is the human psyche—uncovering what inside you makes you feel this way and helping you make sense of it." I wasn't trying to aggravate the guy, but as someone trained in a scientific field, I wasn't supposed to believe that something in Noah's subconscious manifested itself and tried to kill him.

That scientific part of me didn't want to believe in dreams trying to kill people. But the nonhuman part of me believed and was afraid.

I tried again. "Why don't you tell me about it, so I can better understand what happened to you?"

He set down his fork. In the glow from the table lamp, the fatigue on his face was deepened. It didn't matter what I believed; it was obvious that something was keeping Noah from sleeping.

Regardless, this was my job. And Noah was more than a patient. I liked him, and I wanted good things for him. In a weird way I guess I looked at him as something of a friend.

Who was I trying to kid? This guy was on my top-five list of crushes, right after Johnny Depp and right before Jensen Ackles.

"It started a few weeks ago." He was looking at his plate, not me. "I tried to change a dream and couldn't."

It was unusual for him, but nothing surprising. Sometimes the subconscious was a little stronger. Or sometimes the dream dug its heels in. "That's happened before, hasn't it?"

He nodded and raised his gaze to mine. Leaning his forearms on the table, he closed much of the distance between us, closing in to what felt like our own little corner of the world. "That's why I shrugged it off. But it started getting worse."

"Worse, how?"

"There's this guy." His brow wrinkled, and I wanted to reach out and smooth it with my fingers. "I don't know who he is, but he started showing up in my dreams. At first he simply talked. I ignored him, then he started getting physical."

This was sounding a little too familiar. "Sexual things?"

He looked offended. "No. Jesus, Doc."

I shrugged, trying to hide that I was both relieved and bitter. He had gotten off easier than I had in my dream. "I need specifics."

"He became aggressive—pushing, trying to get me to fight him. Last night he tried to stab me, but I woke up."

It made me think of the "stabbing" the man in my dreams had given me. "Do you remember what he looked like?"

His frown deepened as he tried to conjure a mental picture. The fingers of his right hand touched the top of my left, stroking softly. It gave me goose bumps. I don't think Noah even noticed. "He had weird eyes. I didn't recognize him."

Weird eyes. Okay, that might mean anything. It didn't necessarily mean pale blue with spidery rims. "Dreams of a stranger often can mean fear of the unknown. As for the aggression . . . Do you feel pressure from some aspect of your life?"

He shook his head. "I have a show coming up in a few days, but nothing out of the ordinary."

I thought about it. The upcoming pressure of a show could certainly manifest in Noah's dreams, but it hardly seemed a likely catalyst for dream-violence of this caliber.

"Doc." Noah was pale as he regarded me across the table. "I tried changing the dream, and he took it away. It wasn't my dream anymore. It was his."

The words—and the look on Noah's face—sent a shiver

down my spine. Noah had been lucid in his dream—lucid and powerless. He must have been terrified. Dreamkin will shift a dream, but they won't take it away. They weren't allowed.

The thought that one had done this to Noah made me angry. *Very* angry.

"You said the man spoke to you." The therapist side of me was rapidly losing out to the Nightmare side. "What did he say?"

"He said he was coming, and neither me nor the nightmare would be able to stop him." His lips twitched, as though he tried to smile but couldn't quite manage it. "That's weird, right?"

Were it possible for a person's blood to turn to ice, I'd be able to sink the *Titanic* at that moment. It couldn't be. It was impossible.

"Yeah," I agreed hoarsely. "Weird. Any idea what he means?"

Noah shook his head, but when he looked at me, there was a strange glimmer in his dark eyes. "Not a clue. I thought you might be able to decipher it."

"Me? Why?"

"Because you know more about dreams than anyone I know."

Yep, I suppose I did. More than he could ever imagine. I smiled at the compliment regardless, then slipped into therapist mode. "How did this dream make you feel?"

He stared at me for a second, like he knew I was thinking more than I was saying. "Powerless." He said it so softly that I barely heard.

"Did that frighten you?"

His jaw tightened, the muscle there ticking. How did guys do that? "Yes."

He didn't like admitting to being frightened—who did? But it gave me something to think about. "Being made a victim is unpleasant for anyone." I watched his reaction; a subtle darkening of his eyes. "Perhaps you are afraid that you will be made a victim—or you have been in the past."

I've never seen Noah angry before, but I was willing to bet it looked a little something like he did now—only much worse. His nostrils flared with a sharp breath, his gaze brightened, and his cheeks flushed. "Maybe."

He wasn't going to give me any more, damn it. "Noah"—I tried to keep my voice gentle—"do you really believe something in your dreams was physically trying to harm you?"

He leaned closer, the fabric of his shirt pulling taut across his biceps and shoulders. A couple of inches on my part and we'd kiss. "Do you believe it's possible?"

I held his gaze and said the one thing I swore I wouldn't. "Yes."

Noah went very still, regarding me with something that looked like a mixture of relief and disbelief. "You do."

I was saved from answering by the arrival of our main course. I wasn't terribly hungry at the moment given the sudden lurch my stomach had taken earlier, but I wasn't about to waste good food.

Somehow I managed to speak as I dished out basmati rice for both of us. "Yes. Or, it could be anxiety over something or someone you would like to avoid but can't. Or, it could be a grudge you can't let go of. It might even be your unconscious telling you that you're working too hard."

He watched me carefully, as though seeing me for the first time. "But you don't think I'm crazy."

"No. I don't."

Something in my dream had raped me. Maybe something

in Noah's dream really tried to kill him. Logically, it went against everything school and society believed, but so did the fact that no one could wake my mother from what was basically a very long nap. I *knew* there was more to dreams than Jung, Freud, and every other therapist who ever lived. I was living proof of it, but I didn't know dick about anything thing further than just that.

Just enough to be dangerous. So before I panicked and went looking for answers in another world, I was going to do everything I could in *this* world.

"If you like, you can stay at the clinic tonight. If you dream of this man again, I can at least take a look at the effect the event has on your physiology." And I'd be there when he woke up, and the dream was still fresh. Details would be clearer then. If his description of the man matched the one from my dream—or any Dreamkin—then I'd know for sure what we were up against.

He looked surprised—or pleased, sometimes it was hard to tell the difference. "You'd do that?"

I nodded. "Buy me dessert and I'll even tuck you in." Flirting. I was flirting with a patient.

Noah smiled slowly, and I was very tempted to lean across all this food and kiss him like he deserved. "I'd like that."

I took a drink of water. I needed some serious cooling down. "Uh, you didn't have any plans for tonight, did you?"

"I did," he replied, "but I canceled. She'll forgive me."

"Oh." I felt a little bit like I did when I found out that Chris Cornell from Soundgarden was getting married back in the nineties. I knew there was no chance of ever having him for myself, but marriage made that realization so much more final.

I managed a smile. "Tell her sorry from me as well."

He was watching me with a mixture of amusement and hot intensity that surprised me. I'm not the brightest when it comes to men, but I knew at that moment that if I made an offer, Noah would have taken it. "I'm sure my mother will appreciate that."

I almost giggled—how prepubescent is that?

"I could be eating pot roast right now." He dipped naan in the masala sauce on his plate. "Don't tell my mom, but this is better."

"Your secret is safe with me." I picked up my fork. Suddenly, I was very hungry. "I'm technically done with work when the night shift comes on, but if you come back to the clinic later, I'll hook you up."

"Gee, Doc"—his voice felt like warm chocolate flowing over me—"from anyone else I'd take that as a proposition."

I know I blushed because my face was hotter than the chicken vindaloo on my plate. Somehow I managed a chuckle. "Don't tease me, Clarke. I can get you while you're asleep."

He dipped a chunk of naan into the buttered chicken on my plate as one of his dark brows arched almost coyly. Somehow the man made even food sexy. "I think I'd rather be awake for that."

I must have turned beet red because he actually laughed.

"I'm sorry," he said after. "I hope I didn't offend you."

Offend me? Was he nuts? "I'm made of hardier stock than that," I told him with a smile. "So, you'll be by the clinic later?" Maybe I was being overly paranoid, but best-case scenario Noah would feel safe with me around and get a good night's sleep. Hopefully worse case would be him having a nightmare, and I'd be there to talk about it when he woke. I just didn't feel right sending him off alone knowing what I knew.

He nodded. "It's a date."

A date, and he was going to sleep through it. Huh, wasn't that just my luck.

"Are you going to get into trouble for this?"

I shook my head as I led Noah into the green sleep room. It was shortly after midnight, and other than another patient—a patient who was someone else's responsibility, not mine—already asleep in a room down the hall, there was only me, Noah, and a small night staff in the clinic. The building provided security, and Joe, the night guard, would no doubt stop by later with coffee and donuts.

Donuts, which I would *not* eat. I had to make myself promise that now.

"It's not like I canceled another appointment to hook you up. If anyone asks, I'll tell them you're helping me with an experiment."

"An experiment?" Noah cocked a dark brow as he tossed his coat over the stiff, pinched little chair in the corner. "Sounds nefarious."

I smiled. I was beginning to sort out when he was joking. "You've discovered my dark side. I'll make something up. I wouldn't want you to get billed for something that was my idea."

He stiffened—just like in the movies when someone's been offended. "I can afford your rates, Doc." His voice actually dropped—in tone and temperature.

"I never said you couldn't." Actually I kinda had, I suppose. Deliver me from the fragile male ego. "You want me to bill you?"

He nodded—a quick, decisive jerk of his head. "Yes."

Since this was now a professional situation, it would have

been wrong of me to roll my eyes, no matter how badly I wanted to.

"Fine. I'll have Bonnie do the paperwork tomorrow. Now, can we get on with this?"

"Doc." His brows came together in a manner that was both mocking and endearing. "Do you treat all your dates this way?"

"Billing them? No. Besides, I don't date." Stupid, stupid mouth!

Anyone else would have looked uncomfortable, or maybe apologized, but not Noah. He looked curious—interested. The base of my spine tingled.

"Why not?" he asked, unzipping the bag he'd brought.

I might as well be honest, as painful as it was. It's not like I'd be able to tell from his expression if he pitied me or not. "The men I meet don't seem to find me attractive."

"Huh." He tossed a pair of Spider Man sleep pants over his shoulder, tilted his head and watched me with those fathomless eyes. "That's weird."

I arched a brow. "Weird?"

"That you actually believe that."

I opened my mouth at the same time he opened the door to the adjoining bathroom. He closed it behind him, leaving me alone to feel somewhat silly and bewildered.

Noah returned a few minutes later wearing only the sleep pants, and I tried not to think about the fact that I was alone in what was essentially a bedroom with one of the sexiest men I knew, and he was half-naked. Even the possibility of dream-killers couldn't dull that realization. It was no different than any other time Noah had done an all-nighter, but somehow, since we'd had dinner together and exchanged flirtatious remarks, it seemed strange and tense.

Once he was under the blankets, I focused on my job. It wasn't that difficult—I'm not a total flake. I got the equipment ready and in position and placed the electrodes on Noah's head and chest.

"I'm sorry if they're cold." It was what I said to him every time I hooked him up.

When he didn't respond, I looked down to see him staring at me. "Noah?"

"I thought of the colors," he replied, watching me closely. "For your hair."

Had he been thinking of that the entire evening? I wasn't sure how to feel about that, but you know I had to ask. "And they are?"

"Sable with burnt umber for the highlights and maybe a little titian."

I smiled. "You should work for Clairol. Good night, Noah."

"Night, Doc." He grabbed my hand and squeezed. "Thanks—for everything."

I nodded and beat a hasty retreat. If I stayed much longer with him talking about my hair and sounding all thankful, I was likely to climb in bed with him. Never mind that it might cost me my pride, it could cost me my career.

And not even a Jensen Ackles, Johnny Depp, and Josh Hartnett sandwich was worth that.

After leaving Noah, I went to the control room where I could watch him sleep and monitor the information detected by the equipment.

I sat down with a coffee. Danny, the night intern brought in a donut from Joe. It was homemade and had been warmed in the microwave in the lounge. My diet didn't stand a chance. I inhaled it, then licked the remnants from my fingers. Danny didn't ask about Noah and I didn't volunteer.

The sugar and caffeine gave me a nice little buzz, but an hour later my eyelids were drooping. The lack of sleep and low blood-sugar levels were catching up with me.

Noah hadn't shown any kind of unusual activity, so I leaned back in my chair and closed my eyes—just for a minute, of course. I am a professional, after all.

The sound of someone crying out in pain brought me to my feet with a startled grunt.

Startled doesn't begin to describe the rest of it. I looked around at my surroundings, shaking my head as I did so.

"What the . . . ?" My control room was gone. I was in a house—a house that was as alien as it was strangely familiar. The room was large, with a mishmash of furniture—most of which looked comfortable, but hardly used. The whole place was a riot of color with vaulted ceilings and huge, fantastic paintings covering the walls. I didn't know where I was, but I felt safe there. And I wanted to explore.

I had to be dreaming, but I'd never been so lost in a dream before—except maybe for the one I'd had last night. I didn't know this place at all, and I *always* knew my dreams.

I moved forward, around a rich, wine-colored sofa. I hadn't made it very far when I saw him.

"Noah?"

He was on the floor in the Spider-Man pants, struggling to lift his upper body. His arms visibly shook with the effort, the muscles straining beneath his golden skin. His chest and ribs—even his back—were bruised.

I dropped to my knees beside him, my hands instinctively positioned on his trunk to help him stand. His skin was clammy beneath my palms.

"Noah, are you okay?"

"Dawn?" He'd never called me by name before. "What are you doing here?"

"I don't know," I answered honestly, but I was willing to bet that neither of us was awake, at least not in the traditional sense. "Put your arm around me."

For once I was glad of my size. I could help Noah to his feet without hurting myself.

"Hello, Little Light."

I knew that voice. A man walked toward me. I watched, my hands still placed protectively around Noah, as he came forward. I knew he was who hurt Noah and had been stalking his dreams.

And then I saw his face. It was the same bastard who had raped me.

"Who are you?" I demanded, indignation and anger overshadowing everything else. "Where are we?"

The man looked around. "We are in a place of·his making." He pointed at Noah. "Ask him where you are."

"My dream," Noah replied, shooting me a frown. "How can you be in my dream?"

I ignored the question. "What did you do to him?"

The Dreamkin shrugged. "I might have broken him. I'm glad I didn't. I have use for him."

My heart raced, but I tried to ignore my rising panic. Noah was going to be okay. I didn't care what I had to do, or what happened, but Noah was going to be all right.

The dream thing kept talking, "Your name means 'awakening.' Did you know that? You were named for your aunt Eos, I suppose."

I frowned. His voice gave me the wiggins. "Who are—"

Suddenly, he was standing right in front of me. He

grinned. "Told you I was coming. Or did you think I meant that sexually?"

"You know him?" Noah demanded, his arm cradling his bruised ribs. "What the fuck is going on?"

I had to get out of here, had to escape. I had to do something. Had to . . .

"If you wake up, you'll leave poor little Noah alone with me," the Dreamkin said, reading my expression. "You don't want to leave him, do you? Not with me. If he's not broken now, he might be by the time I'm done."

His voice alone was enough to make my skin crawl, even as it pulled me in. How could I be repulsed and drawn at the same time? A cold, dry finger touched my cheek, slid down to my mouth. He shoved his finger between my lips, into my mouth. I bit down hard, and succeeded in doing nothing but smashing my teeth together.

The man laughed. He still looked like a romantic hero, but an even-more-twisted version than in my first dream.

Noah pushed me behind him. He wavered on his feet, but he stood alone as he faced the thing. "Stay away from her."

The Dreamkin laughed. "Little man, you should be hiding behind her."

Noah didn't look at me, but I saw the expression on his face—more anger than surprise. "Go to hell."

More laughter. "How cute."

The dream thing said if I woke up, I'd be leaving Noah behind. How was that possible if it was my dream?

Because it wasn't my dream. The realization came like a cold wind. I was in Noah's dream, and I had no power there. Did I?

How was this possible? And how had this thing managed to get inside my dreams? I had my own space. No one could get past the walls I'd built. Could they? Or had those walls started to crumble like all walls eventually did?

"You don't know how to control this place." The Dreamkin's smile was as cold as frozen tar, holding me in place. "You've so much power inside you and no idea how to use it."

"What do you mean?" As scared as I was—and I was scared—I wanted to keep him—it—talking. If he was talking, then I could think of a way out of this, for Noah as well as myself.

"Your mother should have told you."

"My mother?" What the hell did my mother have to do with any of this?

Long hands steepled in front of that disgustingly beautiful face. "I bet you were her favorite, weren't you? I imagine you were, being *his* daughter."

It knew who I was. It knew *what* I was.

It laughed. "You have so much of him in you, and you don't know anything."

I kept my hands still, even though I wanted to wring them, use them to push this thing away from me. "I'm nothing like him."

"Scares you, doesn't it?" The man shifted closer, edging past Noah, who was still as he watched, tense and ready to pounce. "How you survived I don't know. You must be stronger than you seem though I find that hard to believe."

My heart was pounding hard. Yes, I was afraid. I was afraid of this dream, afraid that what It said might be true.

This time when it—he—touched my face his fingers were hot—that same heat that I'd felt in my dream last night. My body was tingling from one touch—and my stomach was churning.

"You belong here, Little Light." The tingling increased deep inside me, low and sexual. "Why don't you stay?"

It was tempting. I wanted to stay with him.

For like a second.

And then Noah was there. "Dawn, don't trust it."

"It?" The Dreamkin said with a pout. "Noah, after all we've been through?"

I glanced at Noah. "If I go with you, what happens to him?"

"I have uses for him."

I didn't like the way that sounded. *This* was one of the monsters my father had warned me about. "What are your plans for me?"

White teeth, too straight and perfect to be real, flashed bright in the tan of his face. "I'm going to fuck you, kill you, then take your body back to your daddy for shits and giggles."

I swear to God my heart stopped at that moment. I was so terrified I was frozen like a stupid bimbo in a bad horror movie. I reached out and grabbed Noah's hand.

"Come on, Dawnie," the monster said, his face coming closer as his hands reached for me. "Let's get it on."

I screamed.

Chapter Five

I slammed back into the real world still screaming.

I was also in bed with Noah. I was pressed against him, his hand in mine. He was panting. I was panting. This might have been hot were I not so *freaked-out*.

He was solid and warm against me. His heart was a heavy pounding beneath my other hand, his chest a golden sheen of muscle.

My own heart kicked up a notch. Cardiac arrest seemed imminent.

I let go of him, but I didn't have the strength—or the inclination—to move from the bed. "What the hell just happened?"

"You were there." His voice was a hoarse whisper as he slumped against the pillows, the electrodes I attached to him in his hand. The sheets were tangled around his waist, his long legs still beneath the blankets. He hadn't left the bed. He hadn't moved, but I had.

"Sleepwalking." I nodded, numb inside. "I must have fallen asleep and heard you." Or maybe when I entered the Dream Realm, I really entered it—corporeal form and all. Was that possible?

I didn't know. I didn't know *anything*.

"You were inside my dream." He lay there staring at me, rumpled and surprised. "Inside my head."

I shook my own head with great determination. "That's not possible." It wasn't a total lie. I hadn't been inside his head, I had been inside his dream—there was a difference.

One look at his face, and I knew he wanted to believe me and also that he didn't. "No, but it happened."

I could have argued—I would have if the words and certainty had been there, but they weren't. This had never happened to me before. I was *always* in control of my dreams. No one got in, and I didn't get out. Morpheus's world did not encroach on mine.

My arm trembled as I braced myself on my elbow. Adrenaline pulsed in my veins—pumping through my heart as though I'd had ten espressos. I looked down at Noah, into his dark eyes, and saw so much there. He was looking at me as though I was the most amazing creature in the universe, and he didn't know whether to bow or run screaming. I could have kissed him right then, and he'd have let me. And then he'd wipe his mouth after.

"Are you okay?" I asked him.

He nodded, obviously still a little dazed. "You?"

I laughed. Not a good sign. "No, but I will be once I make sense of this."

Tossing back the blankets, he swung his legs over the side of the bed. He turned his head to look at me, his gaze dark and shrewd. "It knew you."

Shit. Once I admitted this, there was no coming back. No going back to pretending there was a sane explanation for what had happened. "I've dreamed it before." And I was beginning to wonder if It was what my dream version of David Boreanaz had tried to warn me about.

"You dreamed it before?" Now he looked disgusted. Pissed, even. "You've dreamed this thing, but when I told you about my dreams, you acted like I was crazy."

I sat up as well, holding my hands out in surrender. "Noah, I'm not sure *I'm* not crazy."

"That thing is real." He stood. "Don't tell me you need more proof."

Proof, no. I knew that thing was real, and I knew it was dangerous.

I looked up. The chiseled perfection of his chest was marred by flushed circles raised by the electrodes he had just ripped off. I couldn't even stop to appreciate the view because the bizarreness of my life had just caught up with me big-time.

He had bruises—bruises that hadn't been there when he first went to bed.

"What I need," I informed him in my best I've-got-a-handle-on-this voice, "is some time to think about this and figure out what is going on."

He offered me his hand, and I stared at it. Should I be a big girl and take it? Or should I be sullen and rude and get to my feet on my own? My natural tendency was to be dramatic and refuse his gesture, deepening the animosity between us that had no basis except fear.

I put my hand in his, allowing his warm fingers to wrap around mine and pull. I stood on legs that shook more than I wanted to admit.

"How did you do it?"

That was a question I wasn't ready to answer, so I just shook my head. He wasn't buying, but he didn't push.

"I'll take you home," was all he said, dark eyes unreadable. He seemed disappointed, and that was worse than anger.

I nodded, my mouth too dry to speak. He went into the bathroom and emerged once more dressed in his jeans and gray shirt. We didn't say much on the way out of the building. I guess we were both still a little shell-shocked from our shared experience.

He had a second helmet on his bike for me to wear, which I appreciated. I'm big on safety, especially when it concerns a person's brain. I gave him my address—not the least bit concerned about handing out such personal information—and climbed on the back of the bike. I was a little nervous, not having any leather or protective gear except the helmet, so I wrapped my arms around Noah and clung for dear life the entire drive home. I didn't let go until we were stopped in front of my building.

He lifted the visor of his helmet and watched me as I stood beside his bike—a sleek, black cherry and chrome machine that screamed speed and sex. I removed my helmet and combed my fingers through my smooshed hair.

"Thanks for the ride."

He nodded.

"Are you going home?" It was none of my business, but I felt somewhat responsible for him now. I think maybe he felt the same way about me.

"Yeah." His eyes were like black glass under the street-lights. "I'll probably paint for the rest of the night."

It was a brave man, I decided, who could admit that he was afraid to go back to sleep with such ease.

"Take a Vicodin. Have a drink, whatever. It will help you sleep." At his dubious expression I added, "Depressants suppress REM. I wouldn't recommend a steady diet of it, but it cuts back on the risk of dreaming."

He watched me, almost expressionless. But I knew he was picking apart everything I'd just said. And I knew that he took my advice as acknowledgment that there was truly something to fear inside his dreams. Funny, he looked almost relieved. "What are you going to do?"

"Knock myself out," I admitted. "In the morning I'm going to go looking for someone who might be able to give us some answers." My idea might be nuts, but it was the only one I had that was worth a shot. My other option was . . . well, *not* an option.

He didn't ask who I was going to talk to, or demand answers to any other questions I knew had to be swimming around his head right now. God knew I had a million.

What he did ask was, "Will you be okay here alone?"

"I have Lola. My roommate. You?"

"I'll be fine."

Notice that he didn't tell me if he had a roomie or not. If I invited him to stay, would he get the wrong impression? What was the *right* impression? As concerned as I was for him, offering him my sofa—or worse, the spot next to me—would definitely compromise the doctor-patient relationship.

As if we hadn't already compromised the hell out of it. And he'd only ask more questions I wasn't ready to answer.

"What did It mean with all that stuff about your mother?"

Questions like that. Nope, wasn't ready to answer it. "I'm not sure," I half lied. "Has It said what It wants with you?"

He looked away. "No." That was a half lie too. I'd bet my rent on it.

"Well," I said lamely, "good night."

He grabbed my hand as I turned to walk away. His fingers were cold, but his grip was strong. "What are you?"

I laughed, but it came out more like a sob. "I'm not real sure about that either."

He let me go. "Call me." It wasn't a demand or a plea, but he made it compelling all the same.

I nodded. "I will."

He waited until I was inside the security door before driving away. I know because I stood behind the glass and watched him go. And with him went any thought I might have had of my life ever being normal again.

I didn't work on Saturday, which was good because I ended up taking a Xanax before finally forcing myself to go to bed. I didn't wake up till noon.

Lola had already left for work when I emerged from my room. She worked full-time at a literary agency during the week and in a designer-discount store on the weekends. It was great. She scored me free books by the authors her agency represented and gave me a deal on clothes.

I didn't feel like putting on a full face today, so after coffee and a shower I sat down with a bowl of cereal at my vanity and rubbed on some tinted moisturizer followed by a coat of Xai Xai lip gloss by Cargo and a few coats of Benefit mascara that made my eyelashes superfat. I wasn't going to be signed to a major cosmetics deal anytime soon, but at least I felt reasonably human as I left my apartment half an hour later.

I took the train uptown, made a quick stop at Sephora on Fifth for a new heated eyelash curler, and walked the rest of the way to Central Park.

In the bright light of day it was a tourist trap; a horsecrap-littered haven in which people who live their lives on top of each other might find a little peace, but at night . . . well, we've all heard the horror stories about what happens to women who go into Central Park alone after dark. I've known women who have done it and haven't been raped or beaten, but I'm not the kind of person to tempt fate—it's just not safe. Of course, it wasn't safe in my own bed either. Not lately.

I knew exactly where to go, and I let my feet take me there at a comfortable pace. I knew there was no point in hurrying. The man I was going to see would wait for me. In fact, I thought he might be expecting me.

Something was changing in the Dream Realm, and I didn't know what it was. All I knew was that I had taken pains to keep that world out of my dreams, and it was no longer working. The old man—Antwoine—had told me I had reached my maturity. Did that have something to do with it?

It was a nice day—still warm enough for jeans and a light sweater—but there was a chill in my bones that had nothing to do with the weather. If I did this, there was no going back. This was admitting to someone other than myself the truth of what I was. I hadn't done that for a very long time.

The paved path was cracked and littered with leaves.

Autumn was my favorite season, but every year I mourned the falling of all those beautiful leaves. The sun shone down through the trees, igniting them in shades of gold, russet, and ruby. Life was slower here. People strolled—they didn't shoulder past each other. They sat on the rocky hills and on the benches, and they talked or read. Some just watched the rest of us.

I was on the mall, which had a black fence lining either side of it and benches facing the walkway. This is where I had once come with an old boyfriend and listened to a violinist play for money—and this is where David Boreanaz got staked in my dream. More importantly, it was where I hoped to find the strange old man.

I wasn't disappointed.

He sat alone on an expanse of wooden bench, slumped and sprawled, his head resting on the slightly curved back so his face was full up to the sun. He looked as brown and weathered as I remembered, but lacking the urgency he'd displayed in the Duane Reade. I stopped right in front of him.

One eye opened and peered at me for a second before closing again. "Sit down, girl. You're blockin' my sun."

I perched myself beside him on the bench and raised my own face to the warmth streaming through the trees. It was nice. It was calming, something I needed, although now that I had found the old man, I wasn't nearly as anxious as I had been.

"I was wonderin' when you'd show up," he said finally in that Southern molasses voice of his.

"Yeah?" Me so expressive.

"Been a long time since I had a pretty girl in my head. I figured you might have some questions."

He was right about that. "You know what I am, right?"

He peered at me out of the corner of his eye—all affronted-looking. "Anyone with any experience in the Dream Realm would know what you are, girl."

I sighed and watched a kid whiz by on a pair of those sneakers with the wheels built in the heel. "Great."

The old man turned his head toward me but not his body. "Is your name really Dawn?"

I nodded. "My mother liked it."

He chuckled, the corners of his dark eyes pleating like a skirt. His teeth were big and straight and white as snow. Forty or so years ago he had probably been a real Denzel kind of looker, but now he had more of a Southern Morgan Freeman vibe about him. "Morpheus your daddy?"

"So I'm told."

He took a sip from a bottle of water I hadn't noticed before. "You've got his eyes."

How the hell did this old fart know Morpheus? "You a buddy of his?"

Antwoine shook his head, a distant, sad expression on his weathered face. "We crossed paths almost thirty years ago."

And just like Forrest Gump, that was all he had to say about that.

Thirty years ago. Before I was born. Not much chance that he could help me then. "Oh. I thought maybe you could tell me about these dreams I've been having. About me."

He gave me a quick once-over. "You're a Nightmare." He said it with so much finality my heart sank.

"I know. A big bad dream, that's me." I mean really, who wants to be a nightmare? I've seen the painting; that poor woman with that ugly little gremlin on her chest.

"You don't know nuthin', do you?"

His sharp tone had me raising my eyebrows. "Excuse me?" I might not be a genius when it came to common sense, but I could kick ass on *Jeopardy* provided they didn't ask me anything political. I had my doctorate, for God's sake.

Now he turned his whole body toward me. He was small and wiry, and I had no doubt he could slap me silly. "Nightmares aren't as insignificant as minor dreams. You're a guardian of the Dream Realm. You're supposed to protect us."

Wait a second. My mother never said anything about my protecting anyone. Of course, I hadn't spoken to her in a long time. And even before that I wouldn't listen when she tried to talk to me about "what" I was. But I would think—hope—that she would have found a way to tell me something like this. "Us who? And protect you from what?"

"Dreamers—everywhere. From those dreams that would hurt us—like this thing that's been killing people in their sleep."

I forgot all about his "guardian" remark for a second. "Killing people?"

It was obvious from his expression how shocked he was that I didn't know what he was talking about. "All those people dying in their sleep, what else could it be? You don't really believe it's that Sudden Unexplained Death thing, do you?"

I didn't, now that I thought of it. And the thought of it made me cold—right down to the bone. Was that thing from my dream—and Noah's—responsible? I couldn't even protect myself. How could I protect anyone else from *that*?

The old man stared at me, obviously unimpressed with what he saw. "How can you be the daughter of Morpheus and not know this?"

"I haven't seen my . . . him in a very long time."

Another stare—a shrewd one this time that made me squirm. "So that's the way of it. Explains a lot. For a while there I was scared you was stupid or something."

I resisted the urge to correct his grammar and show him just how *not* stupid I was. "Can you help me?"

He shrugged narrow shoulders clad in a red leather coat two sizes too large for him. "Maybe, but not with what you're looking for right now. You want answers, and the only person who can give you those is your daddy."

As much as the idea of acknowledging my true father made me want to spit, it looked as though I was going to have to ask for his help in order to help Noah.

Not helping Noah really wasn't much of an option, was it? It was my job to help people, but even more important than that, Noah meant something to me. He trusted me. And maybe Noah saw that there was something different about me and it didn't bother him. Whatever reason—excuse—I wanted to use to justify helping him didn't matter so long as I did what I could.

He stood up, brushing the creases from his tan Dockers. "You want to keep any more people from dying, you have to stop this thing."

"*I* do? Wait one freaking minute—"

He pinned me to the bench with a stare that made me want to crawl under my seat and stay there. "It's your duty, girl. You're one of the few who can stop It."

"I don't even know what *It* is!"

"Most likely it's a Night Terror."

I blinked. "A Night Terror." Like the kind of thing that made little kids scream in their sleep?

He nodded. I might have laughed if he hadn't looked so bloody serious. "I've heard the name Karatos being tossed around in some circles."

"How could it get into my dreams?"

"Same as it does to anyone else, I s'pose."

Well crap.

He leaned forward, resting the elbows of his red leather coat on his thighs. "That said, it sounds like this Terror's been lookin' for you. It would have to have been to find you in your little fortress. You tell that to the King. He'll want to know that."

By "King" I assumed he meant Morpheus. "If you know so much, why can't you tell my *daddy*?" And why the hell couldn't he give me the answers I needed now? Why should I have to go to Morpheus at all? Couldn't he see that I was a big fat coward?

The old man smiled, but there wasn't a shred of humor in it. "I can't. He banned me from his Realm. I couldn't enter if I tried."

Banned? I'd never heard of such a thing. How could someone be banned from the Dream Realm? People had to dream.

"That's a conversation for another day, Miss Dawn. You run along now. Come find me once you've seen your daddy, and I'll help you if I can."

He turned to walk away. He managed to take a few steps before the ability to speak came back to me. "Wait!"

He peered over his shoulder. "Yeah?"

"What's your name?"

"Antwoine Jones."

"Will my . . . Will Morpheus remember you if I tell him we spoke?"

This time the smile had a little joy in it. "He should. I tried to kill him."

Chapter Six

I went to work Monday morning feeling like my eyes were on fire and my head filled with concrete. I'd spent my entire weekend (after my strange and somewhat cryptic meeting with Antwoine) trying to "find" my mother and Morpheus in the Dream Realm. I hadn't even made it out of my own little corner of it. Apparently stuff could get in easier than I could get out. Fabulous.

A lot of people think dreams take place in the subconscious mind, and to an extent that's true. The conscious mind of an ordinary human cannot enter The Dreaming, as the Realm had been called long before Kate Bush and Neil Gaiman used the phrase. There are some humans who have done it, but they're obviously *not* ordinary. However, the subconscious mind can easily span the dimensional portal between this world and the world of dreaming. In short, dreaming doesn't come to humans, humans go to dreaming. It's been that way ever since Ama, the creator of the Dream Realm, spun Her first web.

Which meant that even though I was part of the Dream Realm, I still had to move through it. And let me tell you, it's one hell of a big place when you don't know where you're going. I was worn-out from the preparation and the journey, and I still hadn't found my mother and her lover.

Eww. My mother and her *lover*. It sounded so very seventies of me, but saying my mother and my father—my parents—felt too much like a betrayal to the man who had actually raised me, who paid my tuition and sent me a birthday card every year.

My current patient didn't seem to notice that I was barely staying awake during our session. In fact, Mrs. Leiberman was well on her way to what seemed like an episode of manic-like giddiness. I might have given more thought to how strange her mood was, but, frankly, I was too tired to care. It was just nice to see her smiling for a change.

"You look well, Nancy."

She smiled; it was coy and struck me as out of place on her fortysomething, usually tired face. "I feel well. Work has been great, and I've met someone wonderful. I feel . . . good."

"I'm happy to hear it." And I was. "And your dreams? How are they?"

"They're good, too." There was such wonder in her voice I almost winced. Nancy had been my patient for almost four months, shoved onto me by another psychologist who would rather work her own kind of cognitive therapy in the Dominican Republic than help a woman who couldn't close her eyes without dreaming the most horrible things.

"Good?" "Good" was a four-letter word, and had already been bandied about more than it should have been. "Good" was too vague, too *easy,* especially in a case like this.

I suspected that Nancy had been abused as a child. She had already hinted at some things during our sessions that made the warning bells go off in my head. I was trained for this kind of thing, obviously. Dreams might be my passion, but when Nancy finally did find the source of her nightmares, I planned to be there for her. Whether or not she moved on to a counselor with more experience was up to her. The truth was buried deep inside her, but whatever had happened to her came back to haunt her in her dreams.

Her awful, bloody dreams. So, telling me now that, after almost two years of debilitating nightmares, two years of having an on-again, off-again relationship with sleeping pills, her dreams were suddenly "good" was not, well, *good enough.*

"Yes." She was obviously as confused as I was—either that, or she deserved a star on the Walk of Fame. I had no reason to believe she was trying to play me, so I at least had to try to believe that something had happened to make her demons go away.

Yes, I am by nature a suspicious person. So sue me.

"Can you tell me what you've been dreaming about?"

She smiled. "I love how you say that."

I stifled a sigh. Four years of living in the U.S., and people still made fun of the way I spoke. Though I could get through months without ever uttering an "eh," other words and phrases refused to die.

For the record I say "a-bout." Long *O*, like in oats. I do not say "a-boot."

"Nancy, I'm beginning to suspect that you don't want to tell me about your dreams. If you don't, that's okay, but I can't help you if you don't discuss them."

"That's just it." She leaned forward in her chair. "I don't think I need your help anymore. Dr. Riley, I think I'm cured."

I kept the surprise off my face—I think. "Excuse me?"

She didn't seem bothered by my reaction at all. "The nightmares. They're gone. I'm cured."

I stared at her. This had never happened to me before. What the hell did I say? "Of course I'm delighted to hear that you've gotten relief from your dreams, Nancy, but—"

"It's not relief. I'm cured." She was still smiling, but there was a determination in her expression that hadn't been there earlier. Had she had a break of some kind? Because excuse my technical phrasing, she looked totally cracked.

What had happened? The only new thing she had mentioned was seeing someone. Had this person talked her out of therapy? Or worse, had they convinced Nancy that they could "fix" her? "Nancy . . ."

She jumped to her feet so fast the chair she used staggered backward on its hind legs, swaying dangerously before slamming down onto all four again. "Thank you so much for all you've done for me, Dr. Riley." She offered me her hand. "I'll talk to the receptionist on my way out about canceling the rest of my sessions."

Dumbfounded, I stood and shook her hand. "Why don't you hold off on that, just in case?"

She was still grinning as she extricated her hand from mine. "No, that's okay. Thanks again. I mean it, you've been wonderful. Bye."

And then she was gone, leaving me standing there, staring at my open door like a Pez dispenser with its mouth stuck open.

I'd been dumped. By a client. I hadn't seen it coming, hadn't been able to stop it. It felt very much like it had in tenth grade when Mike Robbins decided he needed a skinnier, blonder girlfriend.

Of course, I was pretty sure that aside from being an asshole, Mike Robbins hadn't the same kind of emotional-health issues that Nancy Leiberman did.

What if something happened to her? What if she went home and killed herself? That was an extreme case, I know, but how much responsibility would be mine? Had I done everything within my power and reason to stop her from giving up on therapy?

I knew, beneath the shock and anxiety, that I had done everything I could for Nancy. Her will was her own, and in this case, I had to bow to it.

But that didn't stop me from going out to Bonnie's desk a few minutes later and telling her not to cancel Nancy's next appointment—just in case—an action that brought a smile to Bonnie's caramel-colored lips.

"You're a good kid," she told me, "No, you're a good doctor." I preened despite myself. Then one of her dark blond eyebrows rose ever so slightly as she glanced over my shoulder. Her green gaze took on an almost gleeful sheen as she cast me a sly glance, and I knew immediately who had just entered the reception area.

I turned. Standing there, beautifully rumpled in a black sweater and jeans, hands in his pockets, was Noah. Tension, hot and thick, bloomed in the room between us, pressing on my lungs as he stared at me with demanding black eyes. He wanted answers, and I knew he wasn't going to be satisfied until I'd given them.

"Noah. Hi."

He raised a brow at my breathless greeting. Never mind that I had seen him a couple of nights earlier, my heart kicked up as though I hadn't seen him in weeks. Plus, I was nervous. I had never told anyone details about my "other" life, and now this guy I hardly knew was going to know me better than my best friend.

"Hey, Doc. Got a minute?"

"Sure." And I did since my appointment had fired me. I gestured toward the hall that led to my poor excuse for an office. I didn't look at Bonnie because I knew her reaction would only get my hopes up. She would think Noah had come to see me because he liked me. It would never occur to her, thank God, that it was because I was a dream-invading freakazoid.

I closed the door behind me, making it less than a full step into the office when Noah turned, trapping me between himself and the door.

He really had lovely skin, golden and unblemished. And there was just enough light that I could see the hint of brown in the darkness of his eyes. He had a tiny scar above his lip on the left side and one at his temple. I wondered how he had gotten them.

He smelled nice, too—like spicy sugar cookies.

"You're staring," he accused, his voice all buttery and low.

"You're standing awfully close," I countered, as though that was an excuse.

He stepped closer, so that the heat of him seeped through my clothes, dotted my skin with goose bumps, and shivered down my spine. A long hand lifted and planted itself on the door beside my head. He had me boxed in on three sides, leaving me an escape route if I wanted it.

I didn't.

"Nervous, Doc?"

Ever try not to shiver? It's damned hard, but that's exactly what I was trying *not* to do when Noah spoke in that bedroom voice of his.

I met his gaze and lifted my chin with more bravado than I felt. "Should I be?"

A slow smile lifted one corner of his mouth. "Maybe a little."

Oh God. I swallowed. "How did you sleep this weekend?"

"Alone. You?"

He'd never been deliberately sexual with me before. I guess me walking into his dream had certainly grabbed his attention. But then, he'd been getting flirty before that, too.

"Like a baby," I replied, my voice annoyingly hoarse. "Did you take anything?"

"Yeah." Noah bent his arm more, bringing his body even closer to mine. Mere inches separated us now. I could feel his breath on my cheek. "You didn't answer my question."

"What question?"

His eyes sparkled. I could see my reflection in them. "Did you sleep alone?"

I was ashamed to admit it, even though he made it sound sexy. "That's none of your business." I needed to be away from him. Now. I moved to the left.

And his other arm came up, palm slapping the door,

cutting me off. I gasped, and my chest brushed his. I felt the tingle all the way down to my toes.

"I close my eyes and see you," he murmured, tension seeping into his voice. "And then you come into my dream. I need to know, Doc, when I'm alone in my bed thinking of you, are you thinking of me?"

My eyes widened. "You mean am I making you think of me?"

He chuckled. "No, but now that you mention it, are you?"

"No!" I glared at him. "Time to get over yourself."

He wasn't the least bit offended. In fact, he was grinning at me. "You do think of me."

My blush was all the answer he needed. He leaned in, chest to mine, stubble brushing my jaw as he put his lips close to my ear. "Who are you? What are you?"

It was the "what" that kept my knees from buckling, that gave me a surge of power I never knew I had. Some other part of me took over as I lifted my hand to cup the back of his head. His hair was like raw silk between my fingers as I pressed myself against him, feeling the lean, hardness beneath his clothes. I put my mouth against the downy curve of his ear.

"Nothing you've ever seen before," I whispered. And then I planted both hands on his chest and shoved. Hard.

Off guard, Noah stumbled backward, giving me enough room to flee to the safety of my desk. When I faced him again, he looked amused—and still very interested. How many times had I fantasized about him looking at me this way? And now that he was . . . wow. It scared me a little. Excited me, too.

And I wanted to jump him and damn the consequences.

"I want to know what's going on," he said softly.

That made two of us. "I'm still trying to figure that out."

He tilted his head. "You're not going to tell me anything, are you?"

"Not here," I replied. "I don't have time. I don't have all the answers."

"But you have some."

"Yes."

He moved toward the desk, and I braced myself, swallowing hard. If he came after me again—if he touched me—I was a goner. I think he knew that as well as I did, damn him.

He handed me a card. On it was the address of a gallery in Chelsea. "I'm having a show tomorrow night. Come."

Notice that he didn't ask if I would *like* to come, or that I would *want* to come. I wasn't sure of the significance of this, but there had to be one, right? If I were a Freudian, I could no doubt think of several.

"A show? You mean of your own work?" The idea of seeing Noah's creations was strangely exciting.

"No, Doc. Someone else's work." He softened the sarcasm with a smile. "Yes, mine."

It was amazing to me just how much a smile changed his face—how young it made him look.

It was also amazing just how freaking sexy laugh lines were. I'd take those tiny little grooves that curved up toward his brow and down toward his cheeks over rock-hard abs any day.

Fortunately, Noah had both.

"Okay," I agreed. "I'll be there."

His smile grew and changed into something slightly predatory. Now, if I weren't interested, it might have bothered me, but having Noah look at me like he was the wolf and

I was Little Red Riding Hood didn't scare me at all—at least not in a bad way.

I wondered what his reaction would be if I kissed him. I wasn't going to do it, of course, because he was my client, and we were in my office. But oh God, was I tempted!

I was saved from doing something totally unprofessional, not to mention potentially humiliating, by Bonnie of all people. She buzzed to tell me that Dr. Canning wanted to see me.

The tension between us eased. I actually found I could breathe easier, and Noah lost some of the intensity that surrounded him. "I'd better go," he said.

I could tell him to stay, that Dr. Canning only wanted the research I'd been working on for him. But I didn't. "I'll see you tomorrow."

At the door, he turned and regarded me for a moment. "Tomorrow night, I find out all your secrets."

I smiled coyly. "A girl never reveals all her secrets, Noah."

He returned the smile with one of his own. "Show me yours, I'll show you mine, Doc." And then he was gone, out the door leaving only the lingering scent of vanilla and cloves and the trembling in my thighs as proof that he had been there.

I sank into my chair and pressed my hands to my mouth to suppress nervous laughter. When he closed his eyes, Noah Clarke thought of me.

What was he going to think once I opened them?

That night I went to bed determined to contact Morpheus.

My bedroom was decorated like something out of the Mediterranean. The walls had been painted with a mottled effect in a muted, rich orange. Thick drapes in gold and blue hung in the window, matching the satiny bedspread that draped across my queen-size bed. I didn't have any art on the walls except for the headboard, which was an amazing, scrolling structure of towering wrought iron. I had a black dresser, armoire, and vanity, and a huge black candleholder that stood about four feet off the ground and held about nine candles. Multicolored rugs decorated the floor, and bright cushions covered the bed.

It might seem kind of obnoxious to some, but it worked for me. It was my sanctuary, my little oasis of calm in a city that didn't—well, rarely—sleep.

Dressed in a man's undershirt and boxers, I slipped between the purple jersey sheets and sighed. It felt good.

It's funny, but sometimes I have trouble going to sleep. Unless I specifically plan to go into the Dream Realm, sleep just doesn't come for me like it does some people. But, if I want to dream—boom—I'm asleep. Tonight was a "boom" night; I was in the land of dreams seconds after my eyes closed.

I was within the walls I had built, but it was easier for me to get out this time—I knew the way. I thought of the place as my own castle, and it appeared as such—a huge English manor house that looked as though it could be home to all manner of Darcys, Rochesters, and yes, even Heathcliffs. It was familiar and comforting and leaving it was harder than I wanted to admit, but I opened the door to my "house" and stepped outside.

Actually, it was ridiculously easy after all the struggling I had done before to find my way out.

It's difficult to explain what the Dream Realm really looks like. Any humans who enter it see it as their own design, which is true, but it's a design based on the rules and construct of The Dreaming.

Think of it as your own personal *Matrix* without Keanu Reeves. It may seem like it's all in your mind, but it's real. Very real.

It was nighttime here, as it usually is. Daylight only lasts a few hours unless a dreamer brings it with them. As a creature of this world I saw The Dreaming exactly as it was: a large kingdom shrouded in mist. The great city sat on the edge of a cliff, domes and spires bright and silver in the moonlight. And even more mist. I remembered what lurked in that mist and started walking. Fast.

Had I been better at this I might have been able to put myself on the front step of Morpheus's castle, or perhaps even inside, but it had been too long, and I was lucky to have found my way here at all on my own. As it was, I had managed to enter the world at the gates of the kingdom. I stood before the horn and ivory—much like those gates that guarded entry to the world itself—and waited for them to recognize me. The light of the full moon lit my face, made the horn and ivory glow, and filled me with a sense of strength.

A man bumped into me. I looked up to say something and found myself staring into familiar black-edged blue eyes. It was the Night Terror, but he didn't "feel" like he should. I couldn't quite put my finger on it, but he reeked of falseness.

"Little Light. How delightful to see you again."

My heart felt like it was in my throat, choking me with every frantic beat. "Karatos."

A smile of pure pleasure curved his lips. "You took the time to discover my name, how sweet."

Sweet, my ass. "Are you stalking me?"

He folded well-muscled arms across an equally impressive chest. He was so perfect and beautiful to look at, and yet there was an awful twistedness to him—a mockery of beauty. "'Stalking' sounds so dirty. I thought we had something better than that. I like to think of it as 'visiting.'"

I stared at him. My heart was back in my chest, but still pounding as though it might burst at any second. I wasn't concerned about him hurting me. Somehow, I knew he wasn't here to do that—he just wanted to scare me. "Why are you 'visiting'? What am I to you?"

He grinned, perfect white teeth gleaming in the moonlight. "Oh, it's not just me, Dawnie. It's what you are to all of us. Haven't you figured that out yet?"

Figured it out? All of us? I opened my mouth to ask another question just as the gates of horn and ivory creaked open beside us.

"That's my cue," Karatos said with a sigh of regret. Then he—It—grabbed me and kissed me before disappearing into the swirling mist.

The mist that was closing in around me. It was the guard dog of the Realm. I swear at that moment the damn stuff was whispering. I couldn't make out the words, but the tone was *not* friendly.

I whirled around and ran through the gates, into the heart of my father's Realm. I was safe from Karatos and the creepy mist here. The horn and ivory, symbolizing the real and the false, closed behind me, cutting off any thoughts I had of turning and running. I didn't want to do this, but it wasn't as though I had a choice. Karatos had killed people. It had hurt Noah. And It had, for all intents and purposes, raped me and made me like it. It was going to pay for that, even if I had to swallow my pride and grovel at Morpheus's feet to make it happen.

And now It was making comments about what I meant to "us." What the hell was that about?

I walked up the cobblestone path, breathing in the night-blooming jasmine and fresh air. My heart gave a funny twist. Jasmine was my mother's favorite.

Just ahead, looming high above all else, was the circular stone castle of Morpheus. It stood daunting and pale, its domes and pinnacles reaching for the starry sky. Looking at it, in all its shades of purple, blue, and silver, I wondered what colors Noah would choose to paint it.

Lights glowed from the many windows, giving this intimidating structure a welcoming cast. Music drifted on the breeze, along with the smell of something warm and delicious. I tilted my head back, lifting my nose to breathe in that heavenly scent. Was that funnel cake?

They knew I was coming. The funnel cake—one of my favorite things as a child—was proof of that. Some of my unease evaporated then. Neither my mother nor Morpheus would have conjured up funnel cake for my arrival were I not welcome.

The guards at the door to the castle—tall, onyx-skinned, manlike creatures with huge velvety bat-wings—bowed as I climbed the steps. The heavy wooden door, just like the gates below, opened for me without a word or a touch. I took a deep breath and walked inside.

If the outside of Morpheus's home was impressive, the inside was breathtaking. The floor of the main hall was golden marble, the walls alabaster, with delicate arches that rose to the ceiling—a good forty feet above my head. Classical sculptures lined the walls, and the glass in the windows shimmered like fine crystal.

In the middle of this grandeur stood a man and a woman.

She was average height, slim and brunette, with a smile that belonged in a toothpaste commercial. She was dressed in a crisp white blouse, jeans, and mules. He was tall and well built in boots, jeans, and a gray cashmere sweater. He was rugged-looking, with thick dark hair touched with auburn, and aqua blue eyes. My eyes.

"Uh . . ." I cleared my throat. "Hi."

"My baby!" My mother's dark eyes filled with tears, and she launched herself at me. I staggered back from the force of her exuberance. I didn't want to hug her, but she was clinging to me so tightly, and there was this burning in the back of my eyes . . .

Morpheus stayed where he was. Maybe he and I were more alike than I thought because he seemed to know that I wasn't ready for the big homecoming. My mother, on the other hand, probably knew this as well but just didn't care. She was just happy to see me.

I wish I wasn't so happy to see her. I mean, it was good, but all I could think about was how there were people back home in Toronto who had given up on living just to watch this woman *sleep*. Thinking of them, brought the anger back, and I dropped my arms, standing stiffly until she released me.

She eyed me sadly. I was unmoved. I was, damn it. "I suppose I deserve that," she said.

I met her gaze. "I suppose you do."

"You're a little bit old to come home just because you want something," Morpheus announced, his voice as low and cool as a shadow. "Aren't you, Dawn?"

He was obviously the one from whom I got my pride—and my bitter streak. I looked at him, saw myself in the strange blue of his eyes, the bit of red in his hair. "I wouldn't be here at all if you were doing your job."

My mother gasped and my . . . Morpheus's jaw tightened. I guess people didn't take my father to task very often.

"What would you know of my 'job'?"

"I know that one of your creatures is hurting people."

"How do you know that?"

"Because I was one of them."

And in that second, his expression went from mulish to anguish, then to something murderous that, I admit, had me shaking a little. "Explain."

I did—and fast. I told him about Karatos—what It had done to Noah, and some of what It had done to me. I just couldn't bring myself to admit to him that I had been so totally helpless. I told him that It was suspected of killing people, but I didn't tell him about Antwoine. If Morpheus really did hate the old guy, I didn't want that to stop him from stopping this thing from hurting any more people.

Morpheus seemed more concerned about what this thing had done to me and about the fact that It had been outside the gate when I arrived. "If It thinks to anger me through you, It is right." The lines of his face were harsh and unforgiving. I wouldn't want to be Karatos when the God of Dreams caught up to him. "I will find It and destroy It."

My shoulders sagged. "Thank you."

"On one condition."

My gaze jerked to his. WTF? "This *thing* of yours ra . . . beat me"—my mother winced at my raised voice—"and you have a condition?"

He stood tall and straight, and the gaze that met mine had no mercy in it. This was the King of Dreams. He was timeless, a god, and that side of him bowed to nothing, not even his own child.

"Karatos is not my *thing*," he informed me, as if that mattered. As though all the hurt it had inflicted, was negligible. "He belongs to your uncle Icelus." If I remembered my mythology—and my family history—correctly, Icelus was in charge of bad dreams and all things terrifying.

"He is still part of this world," I stupidly reminded him. "And this world is *yours*."

He moved closer. My mother inched between us, as though she might protect me with her tiny, delicate self. I didn't need her protection. My mother was an ordinary human.

I wasn't. I was as much a part of this world as Morpheus, even though I had chosen to leave it. I faced him with my shoulders back even though he scared the crap out of me. This mess was his to clean up, not mine.

"You are a Nightmare." Morpheus's voice had dropped at least an octave. "You are a guardian of this Realm, born to protect those who traverse it from things such as Karatos."

"Don't blame me for this. I haven't been part of this Realm for years."

"Whose fault is that?" I was shocked by the naked pain on his face. I had hurt him by turning my back on this world, and being a stupid kid I hadn't thought of how that would feel to a father. And later, when my mother went into her sleep and abandoned her family, I turned from him even more.

I opened my mouth to speak, and he cut me off. "You should have been able to protect yourself when he came for you, but you never learned how because you ran away."

"I . . ."

"And I let you." Darkness fell across his features. "I

should have made you come back. At least then you might have been able to defend yourself."

My mother left me to go to him, placing a comforting hand on his shoulder. She would always leave me for him. And not just me—everything. It still hurt.

I didn't want to be here any longer. I wanted to go home, to my bed. Go back to the world I knew, because in this one . . .

In this one I remembered good things, and I felt guilty for them. I felt too much a part of that very thing that had destroyed my family—was still destroying them.

"You said you had a condition," I reminded the quiet couple coldly. "What is it?"

Morpheus raised his head, pinning me with those glacial eyes. "That you learn what it is to be a Nightmare. That you accept what you are."

Accept it? Not freaking likely. But I could learn about what I was if it would keep me—and Noah—safe.

"It's what you are to all of us." Who was "us"?

"All right," I agreed.

He watched me, suspicion in his gaze. He knew me too well, and my capitulation had been far too quick. "That means spending time in this world. With us."

I looked from him to her, anger overwhelming me. "That's a better deal than your other kids get, huh?"

She turned white and looked as though I'd hit her. I wasn't the least bit satisfied, and the doctor in me was dying to shout out why. I told the doctor to shut up. I was going to be a child abandoned by her mother for just a little while longer.

Morpheus put his arm around her, held her close, but when he looked at me it was with sympathy. "Do we have an agreement, Dawn Marie?"

I nodded. Stiffly. "Yes." I would learn. I would do my time in their presence, but if he expected me to cave like some love-starved child and forgive them, he was in desperate need of some therapy himself.

He actually smiled. My mother did as well, though she couldn't meet my gaze. "When would you like to get started?"

I shrugged. "How about now?" The sooner I started learning, the sooner he'd bring Karatos down, and I could get back to my real world.

And who knows? Maybe I'd learn something useful.

Something that might force my mother to wake up and face the family she'd left behind.

Chapter Seven

He kicked my ass.

Not literally, of course, though I'm sure the temptation was there. It was a simple game—one we used to play when I was younger. Morpheus would create something from dream matter, and it was up to me to change it into something else. My father put the "morph" into "metamorphosis."

It was easy, and I got cocky—until he actually started throwing things at me. Nothing crazy, just snowballs. When I was little, he used foam balls. I guess he wanted to toughen me up a bit. I did okay, except for the times when I tried to be creative. I should have just morphed the damn things rather than wasting time thinking of what to turn them into. Did it really matter if I thought "bird" five times instead of something else each time? Hence the bruises.

Most of them were on my arms and shoulders. It wasn't very many, only three or four, but they were large. I wasn't ticked off that he'd given them to me, I could have prevented them easily enough. I felt foolish that he'd nailed me, because it just proved how out of shape I was. No, what bothered me was that the little black dress I had planned to wear to Noah's show was no longer an option.

I had no idea what to wear.

I've never been to a gallery before. I mean, I've been to museums, but never to a real art show where people express opinions and sip champagne like they do at these things on TV.

It was a cool night, so I finally went with black pants and a cowl-neck chocolate brown jersey top. For jewelry I added a necklace my aunt created that was lengths of gold chain, peridot, garnet, and aquamarine. I looped it around my neck so that one strand was like a choker while the rest fell below the neckline of my sweater. Then I added the matching dangly earrings. Brown leather boots, purse, and matching jacket completed my ensemble. I fluffed out my hair and applied an extra coat of Clinique Black Honey gloss before checking myself out in the full-length mirror.

"Not bad," I muttered. There was no concealing that I was a good-sized girl, but I was a put-together good-sized girl. I wouldn't be too underdressed in a more formal setting, and I wouldn't be too overdressed if the gallery proved more casual. Yayee me.

The gallery was in Chelsea. I took a cab. The ride gave me time to think about things I hadn't allowed myself to think about while getting ready.

What was I going to tell Noah? About his dreams, I mean. About this Karatos thing? He had believed that I had been in his dream readily enough, but how much truth could he handle before he started doubting my humanity? On top of that, how much was I allowed to tell him about the Dreamkin? We weren't supposed to be real.

I was definitely *not* going to mention the fact that I shouldn't even exist. One of a kind, that was me. A being straddling two worlds, able to live in both and belonging to neither.

Nope. Definitely not going to share that with Noah unless I had to.

But at least I could tell him that he didn't have to be afraid to go to sleep anymore. I'd just have to be careful about the details.

Morpheus would make good on his promise, and if Karatos hadn't been unmade by now, he would be soon. Creatures such as Karatos, who dealt in all things disturbing and scary—might belong to my uncle Icelus, but Morpheus was head honcho in The Dreaming. He'd take care of the Terror, not just because it was the right thing to do but because doing so meant I'd be spending more time at the castle with him and my mother.

The agreement left a sour taste in my mouth, but I had given my word. And maybe a tiny part of me—microscopic really—wanted to be a part of that world. The few minutes I had spent in it the other night had left me feeling a kind of peace I hadn't felt in a long time.

By the time I stepped out of the cab in front of the gallery on West Twenty-fifth, I had pretty much settled on what to tell Noah so that it sounded reasonable. I checked my hair and makeup in my compact and straightened my sweater, so that it didn't cling in an unflattering manner.

Inside the heavy black wood and glass door a European-looking man welcomed me, took my coat, and pointed me in the direction of the bar. Free booze. I was glad I wore cashmere—this was obviously a classier affair than I had first assumed.

The realization made me feel a little guilty. This gallery was far from the funky, urban setting I had expected. There was a good-sized crowd gathered. The air was thick with conversation, the clicking of heels on the stone-tiled floor, faint music overhead. I ordered a glass of white wine and moved toward the art rather than the people.

I'm not a big art aficionado. I'm that cliché who knows what she likes but couldn't tell you anything about it. I like color. I like beauty and maybe a little sadness. I'm not interested in anything aggressive.

Fortunately for my delicate sensibilities, Noah's work fell into my "like" category. He used bold, rich colors that were somehow subdued. Much of his work made me want to look inside myself. Looking at these gorgeous canvases on the stark white wall gave me more of an insight into Noah than a month of therapy.

Maybe it was all bullshit, but I admit, I was sucked in. There was vulnerability in his work, the subjects. There was a sense of melancholy, and yet strength and beauty as well.

I was glad I'd dressed as I had. Some of the men wore suits, the women cocktail dresses, but the general feel of the evening seemed to be dressy casual. Of course, casual for a lot of these people seemed to mean DKNY and Armani. I admit to being a little cowed, but having money meant that these people could afford to buy Noah's work, and Noah could use the money.

Or at least I thought he could. That thought expired the moment I saw him.

He stood in the center of the floor, partially surrounded by a group of men and women who seemed to be hanging on his every word. He was dressed in black trousers and jacket, a gleaming white shirt underneath, opened at the collar. His belt was as black and shiny as his shoes. He looked comfortable and relaxed; his shirt alone probably cost more than my entire outfit.

He had shaved for the event, his jaw smooth and golden. His black hair was brushed back from his face, but a bit fell over his forehead as he smiled at something one of the women had said to him. Skanky cow. Jealous? Yeah, I was.

I couldn't move. For the first time in our acquaintance, I was afraid to approach Noah. This was his world, not mine. Seeing him like this, I was now painfully aware that my assumption of his being a starving artist was waaaay off the mark. I had gone from being vaguely superior in my footing to inferior just by walking through the gallery door, and I felt really, really stupid and out of my league.

I could leave. I could tell him I had been there but didn't see him. Or better yet, I could tell him something had come up, and I hadn't been there at all.

All hopes for escape were dashed when he looked up—and caught me staring.

He smiled. A slow, eye-crinkling, lazy curving of his lips that had me tingling from the toes all the way up to my earlobes. I managed a smile in return—or at least I hoped I had managed one. Idiot that I am, I even raised my hand in a little wave.

Noah said something to the group, then walked away from them. A couple of the women watched him go, and I knew they'd look at me and wonder why he had left them to come see me. A part of me wondered, too, even though my heart was doing the lambada in my chest at his approach.

"Doc," he said in that mellow voice of his as he stopped but a foot away from me. He had a drink in one hand, the other was stuffed in his pants pocket. "You came."

He actually sounded surprised. Maybe he wasn't as sure of himself as I thought. I smiled. "How could I pass up the opportunity to see your work?"

He scanned me with a frank gaze. "You look great. See anything you like?"

Other than him? "I just got here."

I knew from the amusement on his face that he had been fishing for a compliment. He jerked his head toward the back of the gallery. "C'mon. I want to show you something."

The last time a boy had told me that, I'd seen more of Jason Lewis than I'd ever wanted to see, but I followed Noah regardless. But he didn't let me follow for more than a few steps before falling back to walk beside me, his hand on the small of my back as he steered me where he wanted me to go.

People watched as we walked past. Were they wondering who I was? What I was to the star of the evening?

As Noah guided me past several paintings, I stopped to look at one. He stopped as well, never taking his hand off of me.

The canvas was large—at least six feet across. The colors were all a mix of blue, green, and gray, blended into moody swirls. A woman in a nightgown lay on the floor, her arms covering her head as though protecting herself. Looking at it, I felt so anxious for her, so afraid and sad. I looked at the little plaque on the wall beside the painting. It was titled *Mother*.

Startled, I turned to Noah. The image was provoking enough, but to give it such a title was almost creepy. His face was totally blank as his gaze left the painting to meet mine. This was one of those times when he didn't want me to look beyond the painting. I knew it because that was the same expression he wore during so many of our therapy sessions. I was beginning to realize that it was all about self-protection.

"It makes me sad," I told him.

He nodded, and I noticed his shoulders slump a little, as though relieved that I didn't say more. "It's supposed to," he replied, then his hand gave a gentle push on my back. "This way."

We made it maybe three or four feet when we were stopped by a very tall man. He was fair-skinned with dark hair, dark eyes, a long nose, and a small mouth. Not classically handsome, but attractive nevertheless. Noah's fingers pressed into the small of my back.

"Noah," the man said, flashing a smile in my direction. "Sorry to interrupt, but I have to leave. I'll meet you after the show, all right?"

Noah nodded. "Warren, this is Dawn Riley. Dawn, this is my brother, Warren."

I had heard Noah mention Warren before. I knew that Noah's mother had married Warren's father after moving to New York when Noah was in his early teens. Dr. Edward Clarke had adopted Noah shortly after the marriage. And I knew that there was also a half sister named Mia. Other than a few other basics, Noah hadn't told me much about his family, but I had the distinct impression that he was very close to each member of it.

"Nice to meet you," I said, taking the hand he offered—it dwarfed mine.

"A pleasure to finally meet you," he replied in a smooth, deep voice that matched his stature. "I hear you're a psychologist?"

To *finally* meet me? "Yes. I work at the MacCallum Center."

He nodded, eyes sparkling, smile charming. "I went to school with Dr. MacCallum's son."

"Warren's a psychiatrist," Noah informed me, moving closer to me as he cast a small smile at his brother. Our legs touched. "He's been trying to shrink my head for years."

This was obviously not just an old joke between them, but a sore spot as well. Warren grinned at me. "I hope you have better luck than I have, Dawn."

I pretended to study Noah. It wasn't difficult given the subject. "I don't know. I think maybe his head is fine just as it is. Of course, it does look a little big . . ."

We all had a laugh, easing the tension between the two men. Was it just wishful thinking, or had Noah been not so subtle in marking me as his territory in front of his brother? Warren left after telling me again that it was nice to meet me. Noah steered me onward, and we finally reached our destination.

We were at the back of the gallery, standing at the middle of the wall. Here hung a huge canvas that was titled *The Nightmare*. Underneath in smaller script it read "artist's private collection."

I was almost afraid to look up, but look up I did. Noah stood beside me, silent and expectant, as I took in every detail I could before shock rushed over me.

It was me.

There was no denying it. The woman in this portrait might have been beautiful, but she had my face, which was weird because I didn't see myself that way. She was dressed in a flowing white gown, her dark hair—sable, burnt umber, and titian, I'd bet—hung full and loose around her shoulders. Her skin was creamy and luminescent, her lips full and rosy, and her eyes were large and such a strange shade of aqua that they seemed to glow within her face.

Was this how Noah saw me?

The me in the painting was bent over a bed. On it slept a man, his back to the viewer, but I knew from the musculature and from the spiky black hair that it was Noah. The woman in the painting smiled serenely as she gently stroked the man's hair. She was comforting him. Protecting him.

"What do you think?" There was genuine interest in his tone, and just a hint of challenge—as though he wanted me to deny it.

I turned to Noah, trembling. I was shaken more than I could possibly express. "It's beautiful," I managed to whisper. And it was, there was no denying that.

He was watching me carefully. "It's true, isn't it?"

I nodded. I felt a little hollow—numb. "How . . . How did you know?" No point in beating around the bush. No point in trying to pretend the truth wasn't there. And here I'd been worried about how much to tell him.

"That thing in my dreams. It told me. You're some kind of guardian for dreamers?"

I nodded. I tried to think of something to say that would make this all make sense. Noah seemed to be taking it all in stride. He was the one who should feel as though his world had just fell off its axis. Not me.

"Noah?" A soft female voice fell between us. "Who's your friend?"

There were two of them. One was a teenager with coloring similar to Noah's and enough of a resemblance that I figured out immediately that she was his half sister, Mia. The other was a petite, pretty blonde. She was almost as tall as I was in her high heels and several sizes smaller—of course. Her dress looked expensive, as did everything else about her.

Normally she would have cowed me, but I was still in shock from the painting and Noah knowing what I was.

Meanwhile, Noah looked at the pair of them as though he wished they would just disappear. I didn't miss the sharp glance he shot his sister, and I knew then and there that Mia didn't want her brother anywhere near any woman but this little blonde. "Mia, Amanda, this is Dawn. Dawn, this is my sister Mia, and Amanda."

Mia flashed me a falsely bright smile. "Amanda is Noah's wife."

"Ex," Noah growled. "Ex-wife." I'd never heard a man growl before. It might have been sexy if I hadn't been trying to keep from literally falling on my ass. Noah knew my secret, *and* he was married. Married!

No, wait. He wasn't married according to him. Not anymore. He had never mentioned Amanda to me. Ever.

I needed a drink.

Mia gave me a look that could only be seen as triumphant. She saw me as a threat. Should I be flattered or just smack her like I wanted? She smiled at me, even as Noah shrugged her off. "Semantics," she chirped.

Noah looked at her as though he could cheerfully strangle her. His movements were slow and controlled as he drew away from her. That hurt her, I could tell, but she hadn't come to us to win her brother's affection. She was there to chase me off because she obviously wanted him back together with Amanda.

I actually felt sorry for Amanda at that moment. There was no hiding her discomfort. And there was no hiding that Noah was uncomfortable as well. In fact, the only one of us who wasn't uncomfortable was Mia—the brat.

And this was just way too weird for me.

"It was nice to meet you," I lied. "Excuse me, but I have to go." I pivoted on my heel and began walking as fast as I could toward the man who had taken my coat. I didn't care if Mia thought she had scared me off. I didn't care if Noah thought she had scared me off either. If I was scared of anything, it was the realization that Noah knew what I was. What if he expected me to protect him in his dreams? Protect him from Karatos?

Too much responsibility, that was.

A hand clamped around my arm when I reached the center of the gallery. No doubt much of the crowd who noticed found it very interesting, Noah chasing some freaked-out woman across the gallery.

"Doc, stop."

I kept moving. I wonder how many others would notice if I dragged him all the way to the door?

"Dawn."

That was all it took—the sound of him saying my name. The plea in his husky voice stopped me as sure as a brick wall. I was a weak, weak woman.

I turned to face him. That was my second mistake. Coming to the gallery at all had been my first. He wore an earnest expression. At least he wasn't laughing at me. Not on the outside at any rate.

I met his dark gaze, wallowed in it a little and waited for him to say something.

"Amanda and I divorced two years ago." Oh great. So he knew I had a thing for him, too. What was this guy, a freaking mind reader?

"That's generally what 'ex' means." I sounded all cool and collected. Yayee me.

He didn't even blink. My remark just bounced off whatever armor it was that he wore. It took a lot of practice to get so removed, and of course, I wondered what had caused it.

"My sister has had trouble adjusting."

It was such a blatant understatement that I couldn't help but smile at the absurdity of it. "Really?"

Noah smiled too. "Stay." Somehow, he made it a request not a command. "Some of us are going out after the show. Come with us."

Another one of those commands that sounded more like an invitation. "We do have a lot to talk about," I remarked weakly. Who was I trying to kid? I wanted to spend more time with him even though I knew it was dangerous.

His hand moved up my arm. "Say you'll stay. That you'll come with me later."

My mind firmly in the gutter, I just about expired at his last remark. I nodded, despite protests from my brain. "I'll stay." Notice I purposefully avoided saying anything about coming.

Noah smiled. I was feeling pretty full of myself at that moment. So much so that when I caught Mia watching us with narrow-eyed interest, I grinned at her. I am *so* mature.

Noah kept me pretty close for the rest of the evening. I'm not sure if he was afraid I'd bolt if he didn't keep me by his side or if he genuinely wanted me there. What did it matter? I allowed myself to relax and enjoy the evening. I met new people, some of whom were actually interesting and unaffected.

You might be surprised at how many people found my job fascinating. I was. I lost count of how many times I was asked what I thought a particular dream meant. One older gentleman drew me into a debate over Freud vs. Jung. Noah, the ass, didn't even try to save me. He just smiled that little smile and offered me a glass of champagne. I grinned like an idiot as I took it from him. Someone came along and drew him away from me, and I turned away, not wanting to eavesdrop.

"I hear you're a psychologist."

I looked up. Or rather, I looked down—right into the chocolate brown eyes of Noah's sister.

I tried not to go rigid, to not show any reaction at all. "I am."

Relief washed over her face. "So you're Noah's doctor, not his girlfriend."

Maybe I should have been insulted, but I wasn't. There was nothing wrong about this kid's loyalty to her former sister-in-law. "Noah's helping me with a project."

"What project?"

I was pretty sure Noah wouldn't want me discussing him with his sister. "It's a personal study I'm doing."

She frowned slightly at that. "Does he ever talk about Amanda?"

"I can't answer that." Oh, but I wanted to tell her no. Nonononono. No!

Her eyes were angry as she looked up at me, as though I was somehow to blame for all her unhappiness. I couldn't— wouldn't—answer her questions even if I wanted to.

Everything Noah told me was confidential. "Did he mention the affair?"

Affair? No. No he hadn't. Whose affair? Amanda's or his? My surprise must have shown on my face because Mia smiled—gloatingly. "I guess not. He can't think that much of you if he hasn't told you about that."

I stared at her. Noah's sister or not, this girl was a brat. No, she was too old for that. She was well on her way to becoming a bitch. "I really can't discuss Noah with you. I'm sorry." I couldn't help adding, "But he and I are going out later, so maybe we'll get a chance to talk about it then."

She glared at me and flounced away in a huff. I'd never seen anyone ever flounce in real life. Aside from Miss Piggy on the Muppets, I'd never seen anyone flounce at all. Mia did it very well.

"Sorry 'bout that." Noah came up beside me as he spoke. From his expression, it was obvious that he had heard at least part of the exchange.

I shrugged. "She wants life to be the way it was, and every woman you talk to is a threat to that."

"Not every woman," he informed me with a gaze that had me hot right down to my toes. "Just you."

"Uh . . ." My eyelashes fluttered, and not in a flirtatious way either, but rather more spastic. "Okay."

He grinned. "You don't see it, do you?"

I blinked, eyelashes firmly under control once more. "See what?"

He moved behind me, hands on my shoulders. Oh God, he had lovely hands. The warmth from them seeped through my clothes and skin, right into my bones. He turned me to the right, so that I was facing the back of the gallery and the painting he had done of me.

"Her," he murmured in a warm chocolate voice near my ear. I shivered. Couldn't help it. The me in the painting just kept smiling. "When I look at you, I see her. You see some-one else. Someone less. You shouldn't."

His hand slid down my arms, rubbing the soft cashmere against my goose-bumped flesh. I was tingling in all the right places, and some I hadn't even known existed.

As Noah stood in front of me once more, his eyes were black and bright as his gaze met mine. His cheeks flushed, and his lips parted. "Christ, Doc. Don't look at me like that."

I knew then that Mia was right to see me as a threat, be-cause if we had been anywhere other than a crowded gal-lery, Noah would have kissed me right then. Kissed me and anything else I let him do. And I would be tempted to let him do anything he damn well wanted, even though his ex-wife had raised a niggling doubt in the back of my mind. See, I'm real big on trust, especially given my mother's infi-delity and what it had done to my family.

"Who had the affair?" I asked, a little breathlessly. "Amanda or you?"

The heat in Noah's eyes died a quick death, replaced with shock and yes, a little hurt. "Who told you about that?"

Did he really need to ask? "Mia."

"Fuck." Noah looked away, the muscle in his jaw clench-ing as he made sure there was no one close enough to hear us. Hands on his narrow hips, he was tense, a little scary and way too sexy. He swung his head back to face me. "What else did she tell you?"

"She just asked if I knew." Now that I thought about it, she had probably brought it up knowing this would be his reaction.

He stared at me, as though trying to get inside my head. I held his gaze, keeping my posture and expression relaxed and open. I didn't want him to feel judged, but I couldn't even entertain the idea of getting involved with him if I thought I couldn't trust him.

"She did." His voice was little more than a whisper. His gaze was flat. "Satisfied?"

Whoa. A lot of anger there—and entirely misdirected. I lifted my chin. "My mother screwed around on my father. I was the result."

There. We'd both shared something painful. We stood there, staring at each other. Anyone watching could probably see smoke rising off of us, so intense was our connection.

"I'm hungry," Noah said suddenly, breaking the tension. "You ready to go?"

I was. I told him so, and that was the end of our standoff. I don't know if this was the scheduled end time for his show or if he was simply cutting out early and I didn't really care. He spoke to a few people, shook some hands, and we left.

It was weird, but it felt as though something had changed between us—for the better. Sure, we were a little uncertain with each other, but it wasn't necessarily a bad thing.

It was a nice night, so we walked to the restaurant. As we walked we talked mostly about the show and that it had seemed successful. Noah would know in a day or two how much he had made in sales. We didn't discuss his income or mine, and that was fine. It wasn't important.

I thanked him for not offering *The Nightmare* for sale. "I'd feel creepy knowing I was hanging on a stranger's wall."

Hands stuffed in the pockets of his black peacoat, he shot me a sideways glance. "How do you feel knowing that it's hanging on my wall?"

I shrugged, hiding a smile. "I'm okay with that."

A crooked smile, a bit of cockiness in his eyes. "My bedroom wall."

Pleasure. Dismay. I felt them separately and at the same time. I stopped walking because my legs didn't want to work anymore. "Oh."

"That's it?"

I looked away. "Why are you flirting with me? Did the Terror tell you I was easy as well as a Nightmare?"

"Terror?"

I finally managed to look at him—and start walking again. "The thing from your dream. That's what It is—a Night Terror. Like a bogeyman."

"Why would It tell me you were easy?"

Because It had taken me so easily. I ground my teeth. "Did It?"

I felt him glance at me. "No." He was quite for a moment. "So it's real then—the Terror?"

I stuffed my hands in my pockets. "Yeah. It's real." I kept my gaze pinned straight ahead. "When did It tell you what I am?"

"A couple of weeks ago—before you came into my dream. I didn't believe what it said until then." He didn't sound like he totally believed it now.

I nodded. "It should stop bothering you soon."

Another glance. "Are you human?"

Damn, but he seemed to be taking this all much more calmly than I would be in his position. "Half."

That stopped him in his tracks. At this rate we'd never

make our reservation. His eyes were wide, as black as the night, reflecting the streetlights as he stared at me. People passed by, unconcerned. "What's the other half?"

This time it was me coming to stand before him. "Dreamkin," I replied. "My father is the God of Dreams."

"Morpheus."

I was impressed. "That's his most common name, yes. What else do you know about him?"

He knew the basics—that Morpheus was the son of Hypnos, God of Sleep. That he was the shaper of dreams. He even knew that he had brothers in charge of other aspects of The Dreaming. Everything that could be learned from doing a Google search. That was good—and it was all he needed to know at this point.

"My mother is human," I told him. "Right now she's asleep in Toronto—has been for a long time. My family thinks it's some kind of weird coma, but really she's in The Dreaming with my father. They want me to spend time there, too, in exchange for getting rid of the Terror."

Noah blinked. Looked away, then back at me. "You're not lying? Not saying this to humor the crazy guy?"

It was getting a little chilly just standing here. My nose was cold, but I made myself stand still. I met his gaze and smiled, hoping it looked as reassuring as I wanted it to. "You're not crazy. I wish you were."

"This Terror thing, why is it after me?"

"I don't know. I thought maybe because of me, but it sounds like It started bothering you before It came after me."

"And your father has promised to stop It?"

"Yes," I replied, hunching my shoulders as a sudden gust of evening air swept down my back with surprising chill.

Noah must have seen how pink my nose was—cold

weather did not promote attractiveness in my case—because he began walking again. "Tell me how this is possible."

And so I did. I told him how my mother had suffered a miscarriage before me, and how the depression that followed led to her sleeping for long periods of time. That eventually led to her meeting Morpheus and starting their affair. I told him how I was the outcome of that, and that I had spent a lot of time as a child in The Dreaming. I didn't tell him about Jackey Jenkins, but I did tell him that something had made me start putting up walls.

"I can't tell my family because they'll never believe me," I told him, for the first time revealing my deepest secret to another person. "They're so worried about Mom, and she's having the time of her life."

"You feel guilty because you can visit her, and they can't."

I managed a smile. "Maybe you should be the psychologist."

We were standing outside of our destination—a pub-type restaurant that was open late and served beer along with hearty food. My hips were going to hate me.

Hands in his coat pockets, he rocked back on his heels. "You went to Morpheus for me?"

He was sounding a little too strained, so I didn't want him to think it was all for him. "And myself."

He must have seen something in my gaze before I looked away because he asked in a low voice, "Did the Terror hurt you?"

My smile was tight. "Let's not talk about him anymore. Let's just go have a beer and a burger and forget all this stuff for a while."

He nodded. "All right. Sure." But I knew that wouldn't be

the end of it. When he held out his hand, I took it. His fingers were warm and strong—insistent enough that for a moment I felt as though I was suddenly in over my head.

We entered the pub and were embraced by its warm interior, where the air smelled like grease and french fries and all manner of other tasty things. The music was old rock, not too loud, and the conversation was at a tolerable level. There was rock 'n' roll memorabilia on the walls and an antique jukebox in the corner, and I swear the floor had a slight lean to it. All in all, it was perfect.

Of course, that was before I saw who was sitting at the dark, scarred table with Warren and Noah's friends.

Mia shot us a forced but sunny smile as we approached the table. "There you are!" she chirped, not seeming to care that Amanda was cringing beside her. "What took you so long?"

Chapter Eight

I should have simply stuck a fork in my eye and made an excuse to go home. That would have been less painful than suffering through dinner with Noah's ex-wife. She ordered a salad and a Coors light.

A salad.

I ordered nachos and a Corona with lime. Noah ordered a burger and fries and a Corona as well. His friends, Matt and Ellie, ordered real food, too. Warren was the only one who didn't eat, claiming to have had dinner earlier. He ordered a double scotch though.

I'd like to say that Mia wasn't the stereotype of the belligerent teenager, but she was. She watched every bite I took from her seat across from me. She didn't like my food. She didn't like me, and she didn't like that Noah sat beside me rather than Amanda. I had no sympathy for either of them, especially since it appeared that Amanda was the cause of their divorce.

Who in her right mind screwed around on a guy like Noah? He could be a little uptight and a little odd, but he was cute and he was blunt and I liked that. All my instincts told me he was a good man. He pointed at a jalapeno on my plate. "Dare you to eat that."

Puh-lease. I picked up the pepper with my fingers and popped it in my mouth. Chewed. Swallowed. Ta da.

"That wasn't much of a dare, Noah," Mia remarked. "Does she look like she wouldn't eat it?"

I smiled at her, much the way I supposed a shark smiles at divers in those cages. If I could just get through the bars . . . Everyone else looked confused or uncomfortable. I caught Amanda shaking her head at the girl in a disapproving manner.

Noah looked angry, and that warmed me a little. "It takes a lot of food for me to retain this figure," I informed the group, and got a few chuckles from the others at the table. Make a joke at your own expense, and people laugh with you, not at you.

Or at least that was how I hoped it went.

"Then please," Noah said, pushing his plate of leftover fries toward me. "Eat."

Everyone but Mia laughed. I managed an embarrassed chuckle as my face turned beet red. I hoped Noah saw the thanks in my eyes as our gazes met. He was looking at me like I was something he'd like to take a bite out of.

Sometime during our meal a guy had set up a karaoke system in the neighboring bar section. Matt and Ellie decided to go check it out and maybe sing a song or two. They asked Amanda if she wanted to go with them, and Mia followed after them with a sulk. I think the only reason she left the table was because Noah had gotten up to go to the bathroom, and she was hoping to snag him into hanging out with them on the way back. They invited me to join them, but I'd rather slit my own throat than willingly spend time with that little black widow, so I said thanks but no thanks and ordered my third beer.

That left me and Warren at the table. Warren, who was mellow after a couple of doubles and watching me with amused interest.

"I feel compelled to apologize for Mia."

I shrugged, but appreciated the sentiment. "It's not hard to figure out her motivation."

"She took the divorce hard."

I assumed he was stilling talking about his little sister. "Kids normally do."

"I haven't seen him smile so much in a long time." He gestured to Noah's empty chair, just in case I'd totally forgotten about Noah, I guess. "You seem to bring out the best in him."

I wasn't sure how to respond to that. "Thanks." And where the hell was Noah? He should have been back by now. I glanced over my shoulder and saw him talking to Mia near the entrance to the other section. Neither of them looked happy with the other, but Mia looked positively mutinous. Her big brother was obviously chewing her out for her behavior. Good.

I turned back, my companion noting the satisfaction on my face. Warren smiled, thin-lipped but genuine as he leaned his forearms on the marred tabletop. He didn't seem the least bit concerned about getting stains on his shirt, which looked pretty high-quality. "Has he talked to you about his past?" he asked, as the waitress set my beer in front of me.

This was the second time that evening I'd been questioned about Noah this way. I was beginning to wonder what the big deal about Noah's past was. And it was starting to tick me off. Amanda might have been an idiot, but this guy knew better than to ask. "You know I can't tell you that." I said it as nicely as I could.

A long arm lifted, bringing his glass to his mouth. "Yes. I do. He hasn't dated in a long time, and for him to bring you here . . ."

"He's my patient," I told him. I hated the word, especially where Noah was concerned. "Anything else would be ethically and morally unacceptable."

Warren arched a brow but wisely avoided the subject. "I hope he opens up to you, regardless. He needs to trust someone." Then he winked at me. "And he needs to get laid. Excuse me."

He got up and walked away, leaving me sitting there, red-faced and ready to climb under the nearest rock. Or perhaps just slither under the table. I took a deep chug of beer—like I needed to drink more.

I wasn't alone for long. In fact, Warren must have seen his brother coming and timed his exit because Noah slid into his chair mere seconds after Warren left his.

He tossed some bills on the table. "You want to leave?" he asked.

I reached for my bag. "Sure. How much is my half?"

I might have asked him to saw off my arm the way he looked at me. "This is my treat."

I cocked a brow, trying to look flirty and coy. "Does that mean this was a date?"

He shook his head. "No."

My heart plummeted. Talk about burn. But then he stood and held out his hand. "Dance with me, and we'll call it a date."

Dance? In the karaoke section, someone started singing a Bon Jovi song, a ballad, and I'm embarrassed to say that my legs were trembling a little as I rose to my feet. I love Bon Jovi.

"We can't leave now," Noah said, leading me toward the dance floor. "Not when they're playing your favorite band."

"How did you know?" How did he know? Bon Jovi was one of my guilty pleasures. I had every CD, knew the words to almost every song—especially the ballads.

Had Karatos told him that too?

He grinned. "Mouse pad."

My mouse pad at work was the *Have a Nice Day* CD cover. That Noah had noticed such a small detail was amazing to me. People I worked with probably couldn't tell you what color my eyes were, and Noah noticed my mouse pad of all things.

We walked into the other section, and I set my purse on the rail around the dance floor, where I could keep an eye on it. The second Noah's arms went around me, I stopped thinking about everything else. The products of our generation, we didn't waltz properly with two of our hands entwined. We didn't even waltz. We simply wrapped our arms around each other—his around my waist, mine around his neck—and began shuffling in a slow circle to the music. Still, at that moment I felt as graceful as any *Dancing with the Stars* professional.

We shared a gaze as we moved in silence. It was Matt rasping out the lyrics to "Bed of Roses." Had Noah put him up to it?

We were so close our bodies brushed together, our hips moving in unison. His hands were warm and strong against the small of my back and the curve of my hip, and his fingers moved lazily with the softest of caresses.

He pulled me closer, gently but without hesitation. I don't think I could have stopped him if I wanted to. Our bodies were now pressed together so tight that I had to hold his shoulder from the back with one hand, my arm against his, while my other hand tucked around his biceps. I could feel every hard inch of him pressed against me—his abs, his hips, his thighs.

My God, was he getting a hard-on?

He was still watching me, his gaze locked on mine. If it were possible for eyes to burn, then his were on fire. My hand tightened on his shoulder as I shivered—just a little.

Please don't let him feel my palm sweat.

It had been too long since I'd felt like this. It was a feeling I usually associated with being a teenager, a butterflies-in-my-stomach-heart-pounding feeling. I hadn't realized how badly I had missed it until now. It was both wonderful and terrible, being so drawn to a person, so physically affected. I had that tingle again, along with that sweet pressure between my legs that betrayed just how eager I was.

The song ended then, and Noah held me close until the last note faded and the band started a more lively number. Then he released me, leaving me damp, aroused, and more than a little shaky. Thank God I was wearing a T-shirt bra because my nipples were like chair legs. Damn him.

"I'll take you home now," he said, as we left the dance

floor. Was it my imagination, or was he walking faster than usual? Good thing he had my hand because I'm not sure I could have walked very well on my own.

I was tempted to tell him he could take me anywhere he wanted, but all I said was, "Okay."

We said good-bye to his friends, and I told Matt what a great job he'd done on the song. I purposefully ignored Mia, as looking at her would only ruin this slightly high, doughy feeling I was currently enjoying. I made the mistake of looking at Warren, however. He winked at me.

Outside, Noah hailed a cab, and we climbed in the back. I gave the driver my address, and we were off.

Despite the fact that New York is the "city that never sleeps," there is generally a surprising lack of traffic at night, and most of that is made up of taxis. We made the trip across town to my apartment fairly quickly and in silence. What we lacked in words we made up for in pent-up tension. Was Noah as anxious and twitchy as I was?

We pulled up outside my building, and I managed to pay the cabbie before he could. He shot me an annoyed glance but didn't argue as he stepped out onto the sidewalk. I slid out after him.

"Nice building," he commented, as we climbed the stone steps to my door. My building was an old brick structure with a stucco front that backed out onto a shared courtyard. It wasn't terribly luxurious or big, but both Lola and I had fallen in love with it the minute we saw it. We had been lucky to get it.

"Thanks," I said, unlocking the front door. "We like it." Behind me I could feel his presence as surely as if he had pressed his body against mine.

Inside, we climbed the stairs to the second floor, Noah

behind me. Was he watching me? And just how big did my
ass look from his angle?

The chain was across as I tried to open our door. I closed
it, took my keys from the lock and knocked. I heard the
chain slide open, and Lola opened the door. She was wearing Tweety Bird pajamas and had her hair in pigtails. "Hey,
chickie . . . whoa." In a second her expression went from
surprise to shit-eating grin. "Hello there, Mr. Hunky Pants.
Come on in."

That was Lola. She wasn't shy, but she wasn't a slut either.
She just said whatever the hell she felt like saying.

Noah gave her a lopsided grin. "Hunky Pants. I like that."

Closing the door behind us, Lola returned the grin. "Who
wouldn't?"

I made the introductions as she slid the bolts and chain
into the locked position once more. "Noah, my roommate,
Lola."

My friend winked at me as she shook Noah's hand. I
should introduce her to Warren. They could be obvious
winkers together.

"I'm off to bed," she announced. "Will I see you kids in
the morning?"

"Good night," I said, shooting her a halfhearted glare.

She merely grinned and skipped off to her bedroom.

See how pathetic my social life has been? I come home
with a guy, and my roommate is practically jumping out of
her skin.

With Lola gone, I was suddenly very aware of the fact that
I was alone with Noah. Totally alone. It made me nervous.

"Just put your coat anywhere," I told him as I tossed my
own on the back of the futon. "You want a drink?"

He shook his head as he shrugged out of his coat. "No, thanks. What does a Night Terror do?" He kept his voice low, and I appreciated that. I didn't want Lola to hear.

Back to that. I should have known he'd have more questions. I walked into the kitchen and grabbed a Diet Coke from the fridge, popping it open as I came back out. "Technically, Karatos is a kind of demon that brings terrifying dreams."

Noah was standing at the mantel, looking at the pictures there. Some of them were of my family, the rest of Lola's. He turned as I entered the room. "He seemed pretty intense."

Tell me about it. I could still remember how it felt to have Karatos inside me. Just the thought was enough to make me shudder. "He's a nasty piece of work, yes, but he is still answerable to Morpheus."

He was silent for a few seconds. I could see in his face that he was processing everything I had told him tonight. "And dreams are real?"

"Sort of." I smiled at his confused expression. "The Dreaming is a real place. Humans can't travel there in corporeal form, but your mind can. Think of it as another dimension."

He stared at me, obviously digesting this bit of info. "Were you born there?"

"No. I was born here, in this world."

"But you can actually go there." He frowned. "That's how you ended up in bed with me at the clinic. You didn't sleepwalk, you physically came out of the dream with me."

"I don't know." It wasn't a lie. I had an idea that I could move between the dimensions, but I had never actually done it that I was aware of, since I'd been asleep anytime I'd ever entered The Dreaming.

Noah shook his head in disbelief. "This is so fucked."

I had to laugh. "That's an understatement."

He took my Coke from my hand and took a drink before handing it back. It was a strangely familiar, intimate gesture that tickled me rather than grossed me out. "It's so surreal, but I know it's true because I've seen it."

I wished there was something I could do or say to make this easier for him, but I was having a hard enough time with it myself. But just like the rest of it, he seemed to be processing it all very well. "Most people would be pretty freaked after going through what you have."

Broad shoulders shrugged beneath his suit coat. "I'm not like most people."

"No," I agreed, raising my gaze to meet his. "You're not."

He took my Coke again, but this time he set the can on the mantel, and when he turned back to me he cupped my face in the warm cradle of his palms. "Neither are you," he informed me, and kissed me before I could even ask what he was doing.

And sweet God, the man could kiss! His mouth was firm, his lips warm as they came down on mine. He held me as though I was fragile. No man had ever held me like that, and it made my throat tight. I was so easy.

His chin brushed mine, slightly rough with just a hint of stubble. My fingers clenched the front of his shirt, fisting the material. A button bit into my palm; I ignored it. The kiss deepened, and I opened my mouth when he did, allowing his tongue to stroke mine.

Our breath mingled, shallow and desperate as our mouths

refused to unlock. Noah's tongue explored my mouth, brushed against my teeth, and I clung to him like I was afraid he might stop before I was ready. He tasted good—faintly of Corona and lime and my Coke. His mouth was warm and wet, and his lips and tongue were oh so talented. I'm not ashamed to say that my knees were weakening or that there were parts of me that very much wanted to rub against parts of him, but I couldn't move.

It wasn't until his hands slid down my shoulders, his gently kneading fingers finding the bruises left by my tussle with Morpheus that I pulled back.

Noah immediately held up his hands. "Too much?"

"No," I admitted, raising my own hand to one of the tender spots just above my left breast. "You hit a couple of bruises."

He frowned. "Did Karatos do that?"

"My father." As soon as the words left my mouth I saw the change that came over him. He stiffened, his expression darkening. I knew then that there would be no more kissing. The mood had been broken.

"On purpose?" His voice was low and soft, and strangely void of emotion, as though he was doing it intentionally.

"He hit me with snowballs," I explained. "He was trying to teach me to morph them into other things."

"Snowballs." If relief were a coat, Noah would have been wearing it right then. It might have been funny had it not been directed at me. "Good."

I thought about the painting called *Mother* and wondered if there was a connection between that and this weird reaction.

"I should go," he said, after a moment of silence.

I licked my lower lip. I was still too dazed from our kiss to be disappointed. "Okay."

Warm fingers came up and touched my cheek. "Tell me you are at least tempted to ask me to stay."

Oh. A huge pulse went off in my nether regions. "Yes," I whispered hoarsely. "I'm tempted." I was so frigging tempted.

This time it was he who licked my lip. "Good."

I released his shirt as he pulled away. I had totally crumpled it, but Noah didn't seem to mind. I concentrated on trying to steady myself as he walked to where he had tossed his coat. Maybe he moved a little stiffly, but he didn't seem nearly as discomposed as I was.

And then I saw the tent in the front of his pants. I felt a certain thrill, knowing I was responsible for it.

I walked him to the door, fingers trembling as I unfastened all the locks, aware that he was watching with those hot black eyes of his.

"Take something to suppress REM," I reminded him. "It should keep Karatos away."

He nodded. "I'll call you." He stepped into the hall.

"You realize," I informed him, "that this totally destroys our doctor-patient relationship?"

He grinned at me as he started to back away. "I hope so."

I watched him walk to the end of the hall and returned the little wave he threw me before closing the door and locking it once more. I leaned against the wood for maybe three seconds before I heard Lola's bedroom door open.

"Well?" she demanded, standing in the archway.

I grinned like an idiot at her. "Next time I say my life sucks, slap me. My life is fan-freaking-tastic."

I actually managed to believe that, for a while—that my life was fan-freaking-tastic. Even when I didn't hear from Noah the next day. Even though I had to suffer through Dr. Canning's treating me like his personal research assistant, getting me to dig up all I could on Sudden Unexplained Nocturnal Death Syndrome. He was very popular these days, it seemed, and now that another case had been reported here in the city, in Chinatown, he was taking advantage of the news coverage.

The death in Chinatown made a bit more sense than these others. At least this man had fit the genetic profile of most cases. The news of another death left me cold all the same. I was no longer looking at the situation as some kind of freaky medical mystery. I was beginning to wonder (and it was about time, I thought) if maybe these deaths weren't linked to my friend Karatos.

Was this what he had planned for Noah? The thought made me cold all over—panicked to the point of tears, so I pushed it away. No, if Karatos wanted simply to kill Noah, he probably would have done it by now. My instincts told me that Karatos wanted Noah for something. The fact that Noah was a powerful lucid dreamer was the most likely explanation. Dreamkin got their power from dreams. Even I wasn't immune. Jackey Jenkins had given me a high, and with Terrors, the more they scared someone, the more powerful they became. Karatos would see Noah like a generator, or maybe a big battery for his own personal supply of juice.

That was good. That meant Noah was more useful alive. Now, if he would just call me like he said he would, I would feel much better about that.

He didn't call that night either.

When people say they're going to call, they should give you a time frame. Having a time frame really alleviates the anxiety. I knew that with anyone else I wouldn't be the least bit concerned about them not calling me right away, but I wanted Noah to call because that would mean that he was safe.

At midnight, after watching *Forrest Gump* with Lola, I resigned myself to the fact that Noah would not be calling, resolved that he was okay, and went to bed. I had made a promise to Morpheus, and it was time to hold up my end. Fretting about Noah would have to wait.

I wasn't dreading entering The Dreaming as much as I'd thought I would. I wanted to learn more about what I was—anything that could help against Karatos. And I wanted to use whatever abilities I had to help my patients. If my father could help me with that, then I was more than willing to suffer through whatever he and my mother subjected me to.

It wasn't that I didn't love them—I did. Kinda. I was just so damn angry that it was hard to be reasonable. I blamed Morpheus and my mother for almost everything that was wrong with my life. How's that for honesty? My dad—the man who raised me—had hired someone to "sit" with my mother while he was at work. Someone to be in the house just in case she woke up, and meanwhile she was partying it up in The Dreaming. Pissed didn't begin to describe how I felt.

When I came into The Dreaming, I was on the shore. The Dreaming is an island surrounded by turbulent ocean and swirling mist. As a child, Morpheus used to make this beach a haven for me, but tonight I saw it as it was—a dark, creepy expanse of fog and sand that housed things much nastier than crabs or jellyfish.

The mist had a consciousness of its own. I should have

given more thought to where I wanted to enter. I should have opened a doorway right into the castle. I used to be able to do it, when I was a kid, but now . . . I was out of practice, and I just might get my ass kicked for it.

Okay, so I had two choices. I could panic and let my fear draw whatever badness was hiding in the mist, or I could try to concentrate on moving myself to the castle, where it was safe. It was The Dreaming after all, and I was only limited by my mind.

I closed my eyes and tried to ignore the damp tentacles of mist—or at least I hoped it was mist—wrapping around me. I opened my mind, pictured where I wanted to be and concentrated. And concentrated some more.

I felt the change as it happened—just as cold fingers curled around mine, trying to tug me into the fog, nails scraping my palm. I opened my eyes to find myself standing in the great hall of Morpheus's castle.

My hand was bleeding.

"Shit!" I cupped my other hand under the injured one to catch the drips.

The mist never had cared that I was Dreamkin. Or that I was human. It couldn't define me as one or the other, and therefore I was an anomaly. I was treated as such.

Suddenly, warm hands took mine and my bleeding palm was placed in a bowl of fragrant warm water that made the wound sting. It was Morpheus, looking more like a construction worker than the God of Dreams in a white T and jeans.

"You're lucky," my father told me in his low voice as he lifted my hand from the water and wrapped it in a soft towel. "An inch or two higher and it might have severed something."

"Yeah, I feel lucky." I would have rolled my eyes if they hadn't been watering from the ointment he was putting on the wound. "What is that stuff?"

He only smiled as he worked his own mojo. "It will help speed your body's own healing abilities. An infection is not something you want." He had me there. God only knew what kind of cooties the mist had.

When he was done, my hand was bandaged and hardly hurt at all, and I had a strange lump in my throat. How girly is that? My estranged father takes five minutes to fix my booboo, and I'm all watery over it.

"Thank you," I told him.

He smiled some, but there was tension around his extraordinarily blue eyes. "I could have healed it myself, but I want you to remember that you need to be careful, Dawn. Not only is the mist a danger, but there are those in The Dreaming who would do you harm if they could."

Oh great. After forcing me to return to this world, he tells me I could be in danger here. "Like who?" Karatos, for one. He had said something about "all of us" the last time I saw him. I had thought he meant the Dreamkin in general, but maybe he meant something else entirely.

Morpheus straightened his broad shoulders. He was incredibly well built, my father. Too bad I hadn't inherited those genes. "There are those who believe your ability to exist in both words is a portent of evil."

I stared at him. "I didn't ask to be born a freak."

He seemed offended by the word. "You're a miracle. I've never believed anything else. Dawn, you can do what even I can't."

Being a god, Morpheus could spend more time in the "real" world than all other Dreamkin, but he couldn't exist there, not like I could. And I was the only human who could manipulate the rules of The Dreaming. Lucid dreamers like Noah could bend the world to their advantage, but they still had to abide by the rules. I didn't.

Now that I thought about it, it occurred to me that having that ability was kind of cool.

"The Dreamkin who don't think I should exist, should I be afraid of them?" I needed to know what I was up against and be prepared. I was in no condition to fight any battles in this Realm. I knew what I had been able to do as a kid, but I should be more powerful now. Unfortunately, I was so rusty I wouldn't be able to protect myself much better than Noah or another strong dreamer could protect themselves.

I needed to be better than that the next time Karatos tried climbing into bed with me.

My father waved his hand, and the water and dressing he'd used on my hand disappeared, along with the table they had sat on. "There are very few who would risk my wrath by harming their princess. As uncertain of your abilities as they are, they would think twice before engaging you in battle."

Only twice? Maybe they could think a little longer. And Morpheus hadn't given me a straight answer. I was immortal in this world, but that only applied to a natural death. I could still be killed.

"But enough of that. You came here to learn." This time there was no wave, no shift in posture as my father dissolved and rebuilt the environment around us. The hall disappeared, replaced by a massive English-style library, complete with wingback chairs and a massive fireplace.

I noticed there were only two chairs. Two cups of coffee

on the table. "Mom isn't joining us?" I tried to sound like I didn't care, but I thought after all these years she'd be a bit more eager to see me. I should have known better.

Morpheus looked away. "She thought you might be more comfortable without her around at first."

The woman knew me better than I thought. "She was right." I walked over to a thickly padded chair and plopped myself into it. The leather was warm rather than cold, and it molded around my butt like a lecherous hand. Nice.

"Go easy on her, Dawn."

I stared at him—no, I *glared* at him—as he took the chair across the table from me. "She left her husband and her children. She abandoned her grandchildren just so she could be with you. She left me. So you'll excuse me for being as hard as I frigging well want."

He didn't even blink. "She didn't leave you. You've always known where to find her."

"Don't play me as the favorite." My temper was rising. "If I hadn't been your kid, she would have turned her back on me, too."

"Is it so wrong for her to want a little happiness?"

I clenched my jaw so hard I thought my teeth were going to splinter. "Yes."

Morpheus studied me for a moment, his face unreadable. Frankly, I didn't care what he saw there. I was totally justified in feeling the way I did, and he wasn't going to change that. Apparently, he knew better than to try.

"Let's make the most of your time here," he said, ever the diplomat. "I've spoken to Icelus, and he assures me he will see Karatos unmade immediately."

That took a lot of the anger out of me. "Thank you."

Those two little words put a pleased smile on his rugged

face. "I thought we might talk for a bit, discuss what you and I expect from each other."

I reached for the cup of coffee in front of me. Parental expectations. Fabulous. "I do have a few questions I'd like to ask."

"Such as?"

"Is it possible that Karatos is killing people in their sleep?"

"Unfortunately, yes."

"Would there be anything suspicious about the deaths?"

"No. They would appear to have died inexplicably in their sleep. In some cases Terror victims have suffered strokes or heart attacks."

So Karatos could be responsible for these SUNDS deaths. Bastard. "What would Karatos want with a lucid dreamer?"

Morpheus's tanned brow creased. "Energy, I suppose. A Terror could siphon a lot of power off a talented dreamer."

Just what I had suspected. Karatos was using Noah as his personal recharger. Killing had to take a lot of energy, and Noah topped the asshole back up.

"Why did Antwoine Jones try to kill you?"

He was so not expecting that question. All the color ran from his face, and for a second he looked as though I had smacked him. Then all the color rushed back into his cheeks—only more so. The mere mention of the old man obviously pushed some buttons with my father.

"How do you know him?"

I raised a brow. "You mean Antwoine?" At his nod I rolled my eyes. He wouldn't even say an old man's name! "I met him in a drugstore. He was the one who gave me Karatos's name. Why did you take away his ability to dream?"

Now he just looked morally offended. "I didn't! People

die without their dreams. No, I simply gave him his own little world so that he would stay the hell out of mine."

I'd never heard him swear before. "What did he do?"

"He broke the rules."

"Which ones?"

His jaw tightened as he gave me a frustrated look. "Mine."

"Oh, come on." I took a drink of my coffee. It was delicious. "Why won't you just tell me?"

The look on his face was a mix of murderous and pained. "He had a relationship with a succubus."

I made a face. "So? Isn't that what succubi do?" They were little more than oversexed pinups that drew power from sexing men up in their dreams.

"Not exclusively with one man."

Ahh. I got it. "And having 'exclusive' relationships with humans is taboo?"

He knew where I was going with this. I knew because his expression grew more pained. "Yes."

"Guess that rule doesn't apply to you, does it?" Gloat much? Why yes I will, thank you.

"That's different. You changed everything."

"Don't blame me. I was just the outcome."

He glared at me. I mean really glared. But I wasn't the least bit afraid. He was my father, and I knew that as mad as he could get, he would never do anything to hurt me. I might not like him, but I trusted him. Weird, huh?

"So Antwoine tried to kill you when you made him and his succubus break it off?"

He was clenching his teeth. Must be where I got it. "Yes. Can we move on to another topic now?"

I smiled at him, enjoying the brief pleasure of having discombobulated him. "Sure. What would you like to talk about? Your expectations of me?" Just as I finished speaking, there was a knock on the library door. I hadn't even noticed there was a door.

Morpheus smiled at me. It was a smooth, smug smile that instantly made me rethink trusting him. "Enter."

The door opened, and in walked one of the most impressive specimens of manly loveliness I had ever seen. He was tall with broad shoulders (I'm a sucker for shoulders), short, thick, dark hair, and eyes the color of ice. He had cheekbones to die for and a chiseled jaw. Best of all, he seemed totally unaware of his appeal. He definitely wasn't an incubus. From what I could remember, those guys were drag-queen vain.

"You summoned me, my lord?" his loveliness asked, addressing my father.

Morpheus gestured for him to come in. "Yes. I wanted you to meet my daughter, Dawn."

And then the lovely man turned on me with a look that I imagined a hungry lion might give a gazelle.

"Dawn." He said my name like it was synonymous with "eww."

I looked at my father. What the hell?

Morpheus's smile faded and I felt the fist of dread slam into my stomach. "Dawn, this is Verek, a sheriff of the Nightmare Guild."

"Oh?" One of the people who would do me harm? I wondered.

"He's going to be overseeing your training."

Chapter Nine

"No." I glanced at the gorgeous Nightmare who was watching me with a predatory gaze. "No offense, but I am not putting my ass in your hands."

"No offense taken," he replied in a silky voice.

My father seemed more amused by my refusal than anything else. "Verek is descended from your aunt Eos, Dawn. You were named after her, remember?"

I wasn't so lax in my family history that I didn't know who Eos, Goddess of the Dawn was. "I remember. Somehow I don't think the family connection is going to keep Leonidas here from slapping me silly." He did have sort of a *300* thing going on—without the leather Speedo.

"He's not going to hurt you," Morpheus claimed with more certainty than I felt. "But the Guild wants to know what you are capable of, and as a Nightmare, you are obligated to demonstrate your abilities."

There was something in his tone that made me suddenly very still. It sounded to me like he wanted me to impress Verek, but not overly so. Show him what he needed to see, not necessarily all I could do. Interesting. What kind of things did my father think I could do that would make the Nightmare nervous?

And what did it matter?

"What you mean to all of us," Karatos had said. Things were becoming a little bit clearer despite my lack of understanding.

"A Terror has become overzealous and attacked a dreamer," Verek said to me. "What do you do?"

It took me a second or two to realize that this was a test and not an actual issue. Given my current situation, I thought my confusion valid. I had no idea what the answer was, but I went with what my gut said, "Put myself between them. Get the Terror away from the dreamer and the dreamer to safety."

The Nightmare nodded. "How would you do that?"

People aren't supposed to remember Nightmares in their natural state. If you've ever had a bad dream in which you were in danger or hurt that suddenly faded into something else, that was the doing of a Nightmare. And anytime someone swooped to your rescue, that was most likely a Nightmare, too, whether or not they wore a familiar face.

"In a way that causes the least fear and confusion for the dreamer," I replied, as though I had always known.

Verek didn't look impressed. "Correct." Okay, so this guy was hoping I'd fail.

After a few more questions about nothing of consequence,

and a demonstration of my rusty morphing skills, Verek made his next move.

"Hand-to-hand combat," he said. "Can you fight?"

"Not real—hey!" I just managed to duck a large fist as it swung at my head. "What the hell are you doing?"

"Testing your agility, reflexes, and strength," he replied with a smile as he swung again. I dodged that one as well, but I had no illusions of my agility. He was going easy on me right now, but that wasn't going to last.

And my father wasn't going to intervene on my behalf, not unless he had to—which meant only if I was in danger of actually being killed. He had to let the Nightmare test me.

The next time he came at me, I sidestepped and brought my knee up into his groin. It was a dirty move, and I was very proud of myself for having made it—also a little surprised. Where had this speed come from? How did I know exactly when to dodge, duck, and strike?

My satisfaction was short-lived. Verek grunted and sagged to his knees, but the Nightmare had to have balls of steel because he shook off the pain and grabbed me by the waist of my jeans. He knocked my feet out from under me with a sweep of one long leg and had me on my back on the floor in a second. Before I could catch the breath that had been knocked from me, he was over me, hand on my throat, leg pinning mine.

He grinned at me—big teeth that were sharp white against the tan of his face. "What now, Princess?" This guy was almost feral—alpha to the extreme.

I didn't like it.

I shot a sideways glance at Morpheus. He was sitting on the edge of his chair, watching the fight with an anxious expression. But it wasn't for me, I realized. He was anxious for Verek.

Weird.

Something inside me was shifting, swelling. I could feel a pressure in my chest that had nothing to do with him and everything to do with me. How dare he threaten me! Heat rolled through me, sweet and strong. My eyes narrowed.

Verek blinked, icy gaze momentarily confused as he stared down at me. He noticed the change as well—and it surprised him. So much so that he loosened his hold on my throat just a fraction.

That's when I punched him in the throat. It was with my wounded hand, so I didn't hit quite as hard as I wanted, and it hurt like hell, but I connected with surprising force. His head snapped backward, and he let go of me. I was able to push him off me then and stagger to my feet, gasping for air, while he sat on the floor and did the same, his eyes watering.

My father stood and came to me. "Well done." Then he leaned in and whispered for my ears alone, "I'm glad you didn't seriously hurt him."

"Yeah," I replied, totally stupid. "Me too." How in the name of Freddy Flintstone could I hurt a man like that?

"She has potential," Verek announced as he rose. His voice was a little strained. "I would like to monitor her progress."

"Of course," Morpheus replied before I could, his smile tight. "Whatever the Guild requires."

Oh great. Now I was going to be like one of those show dogs who performed on cue. Someone give me a blue-freaking-ribbon.

The Nightmare raked me with a gaze that was a mixture of disdain and interest, which is a bizarre combination when you think about it. "You could just marry her off, my lord Morpheus. You'd have no trouble finding her a mate. That would make your life much easier I think."

"Marry me off?" I took a step forward. "Next time my knee's going to hit a lot harder, Spartacus."

My father made a sound that might have been a snort. "Thank you, Verek. I will keep that in mind."

The Nightmare bowed to my father as I seethed, then he exited through the same door he'd entered.

"I'm not performing for that creep or anyone else," I announced as I whirled to face Morpheus. "And I'm not getting married. You can't make me! And just what did he mean you'd have no trouble finding me a mate?" Overbearing, archaic ass.

"I'm not going to 'make' you do anything." He was openly grinning now. And then there was a mirror in his hand, and he was passing it to me. "See for yourself what he means."

I eyed both him and the mirror suspiciously for a moment. Did I think one of them might bite me? Not really, but I wasn't so sure they wouldn't either. Cautious, I wrapped my hand around the ivory handle of the mirror and lifted it to view my own reflection.

I literally gasped at what I saw. It was the woman from Noah's painting. Obviously, it was me, but I looked different. I looked . . . glowing. That was the only way to describe it. In this world something strange happened to me. I wasn't hulking, plus-sized, pale-faced Dawn Riley. I was still tall, but now I seemed statuesque even though I hadn't shrunk at all. My curves were soft and supple. My skin was pearlescent, shining from within like all those highlighters at Sephora promised to make you look. I was still me, only better.

Immortal. Dreamkin royalty.

It was almost enough to make me want to stay there. Forever.

Almost.

I shoved the mirror back at my father. He simply looked at it, and it disappeared from my hand.

"It won't work," I insisted. "I don't care what kind of tricks you play. I'm not staying, and I'm not marrying some Dream-jerk who thinks I'll be a good wifey."

"Tricks?" Someone's pride had been pricked. "You accuse me of trickery?"

"That's what you do."

"Not to you I don't. I can't."

Huh. That was news. "You can't?"

"You are of this world. It will not deceive you like it deceives others."

Interesting. "I'm still not staying."

He shrugged. "I never thought you would. Not this easily."

"I'm not. I have a life on earth. Sorta."

"Ah yes. You have friends and the family you try to avoid." Guilt leaped within me as I acknowledged the truth in his words. "Then there is that lucid dreamer you told me about." He looked thoughtful for a moment. "He dreamed of you the other night. He knows what you are." His gaze turned shrewd. "I wonder if he began to show interest in you before or after that realization."

The implication left me cold. So did the fact that my father was spying on Noah. Now was not the time for him to play the protective dad.

"Before," I gritted out from between clenched teeth, but I wasn't sure. I wanted to be sure.

"He's a very powerful dreamer, this Noah," Morpheus remarked, a little too casually, shifting in his chair. "With the help of a Nightmare, he could become even more powerful."

"And do what?" I demanded. "Nothing he could do in dreams would serve him in the real world."

"This world is every bit as real as the one you live in, Dawn. Don't ever forget that." His voice was low, calm even, but I felt the rebuke all the same. "If you knew what your friend dreams of, you might not be so flippant."

Another chill. "What do you mean?"

"I cannot say."

"Don't give me that." I snorted. "You can do whatever you want."

"And I don't want to tell you about Noah's dreams. Those are his own. I only want you to be careful."

Another snort. Pretty soon I'd be rooting for truffles. "Yeah, right."

He shrugged. I was getting really annoyed with this attitude of his. "Your choice," he said, rising to his feet. "Let's go for a walk. You'll have to leave soon and I think your time here is better spent remembering what you are and the things you are capable of."

I stood, too. And then the two of us walked. I spent the rest of the night refamiliarizing myself with this world within the confines of my father's castle. Another night he would take me out to meet others of our kind. Some of those would probably like me less than Verek had. I would do good to be prepared. I didn't want to be ambushed by another Nightmare or something even more fearsome.

But I was going to need help from more people than just my father if I was going to learn how to protect myself in this world. I was going to need Antwoine. And I was going to need Noah. I didn't want to admit it, but my father had planted the seed of doubt in my mind where Noah was concerned. And while I trusted Noah more than Morpheus at this point, it wouldn't hurt me to be a little cautious.

It was all starting to come together like the makings of a very bad dream. And unfortunately for me, there was no waking up.

Friday came, predictable and anticipated as always. I woke up feeling funky, the visit with Morpheus still all too fresh in my mind. I couldn't brush it away like a normal dream because of the simple fact that when I woke up I had a bandage on my hand, covering a wound that while almost completely healed and faded, hadn't been there when I had gone to bed.

Immortal I might be in the Dream Realm, but only to the degree that I would live forever if no one killed me. I could be hurt, and I could carry that hurt into this world. But that meant I had physically to enter The Dreaming. Had Noah been right when he supposed that was how I ended up in bed with him? Was my entire body being pulled into The Dreaming when I slept, or was I somehow moving myself between dimensions? God, it made my head spin. I knew portals were possible, but could I do that subconsciously?

Hopefully my uncle would have his little "pet" neutered soon and I—and Noah—wouldn't have to worry about it anymore. Of course, there was no bringing back the people it had already killed. God, if Karatos was responsible for those SUNDS deaths, there was no telling who else he had killed and made them look like natural deaths.

Was it any wonder I felt like curling up on the couch and losing my mind in front of the television instead of going to work? I was a Cancer. My first response to almost anything remotely threatening was to run and hide like the good little crab I was.

Hiding was not an option, though. I didn't get paid to hide. So, I tossed on a bright pink chenille turtleneck sweater, paired it with matching lip gloss, and set out to face the day, where everything is supposed to look brighter.

Only it wasn't brighter. It was raining. Cold and damp isn't a look that New York wears well. Everything looks dark and gray. The only bright spots were the bright yellow cabs chugging through traffic and the odd defiant umbrella that dared to be a color other than black.

On the train a lady with a cold sat next to me, blowing her nose so frequently I thought she must have blown most of her brain out as well. Her umbrella, dripping and slightly open, pressed against my leg, soaking the calf of my pants. Luckily, they were black, and the water wouldn't show. Not so luckily, the boots I wore beneath only came halfway to my knee, so I had a huge, uncomfortable wet spot rubbing against my skin by the time my stop came.

The clinic wasn't far, and I managed to trot up the street without getting much wetter than I already was under the flimsy protection of my umbrella. I pressed the buzzer for admittance since we didn't open for another twenty minutes and the door was locked. The elevator doors were open in silent invitation, so I stepped inside and pressed the button for the second floor.

The lighting in the waiting area was soft and meant to be soothing to our clients, but on dark days like today, when soft could be mistaken for depressing, the extra overheads

were switched on in an attempt to brighten the place up. I
don't know if it was an effective ward against depression,
but it did make it easier to see.

"Morning, Bonnie," I singsonged as I stepped inside.

The perfectly put-together receptionist stepped out of the
filing room. "Hey there." She slipped into her chair. "Nancy
Leiberman left a message on the machine last night. She
was wondering if you could squeeze her in today?"

That was fast. I figured the euphoria she'd exhibited during our last session would be short-lived, but not like this.
Her next scheduled appointment wasn't for at least a few
days. But if Nancy was having nightmares again . . .

Coffee in one hand, I hung up my damp coat with the
other. "Did she say what the problem was?"

Bonnie shrugged. "I wish. Then I could charge the rates
you guys do."

I arched a brow and tried not to smile. Bonnie grinned,
and I felt one twist my own lips as well. "Wench."

"She said something about a guy. That make sense to
you?"

Yeah. It did. A crush totally explained Nancy's manic
behavior. She had gotten a boyfriend and thought all her
problems would go away. I wondered if the boyfriend had
gone away as well, leaving Nancy with her terrifying dreams
once more.

"Would you call her back and tell her I can see her at
twelve thirty?" I'd shorten my lunch.

Bonnie raised her hand in mock salute, but the smile she
shot me was genuine. "You got it, kiddo."

Yeah, I know. It was totally unprofessional, my relationship with Bonnie, and I didn't give a flying frig. Did I realize
that Bonnie was a substitute for my own mother? Please. Ten

years of psychological study had made me nothing if not self-aware. But I was still human.

Or rather, half of me was.

I hadn't even made it to the closet I called my office when Bonnie called my name. She told me that Noah was outside, asking to see me. Should she let him in? The usual teasing note was in her voice, but I knew that if I said no, Bonnie would tell him to go away. I also knew that I shouldn't be so freaking happy to hear that Noah was here.

I had planned to call him later that day if I still hadn't heard from him. I still didn't want to seem overly eager, but obviously if he was at my work, he had something to share.

"Let him in." I didn't wait for her reaction before ducking into my office and checking my face in my compact. My mascara hadn't smudged, and my lip gloss was still obnoxiously pink. I was good.

Noah came in, looking more like the guy I was used to than he had at the gallery the other night. His hair was a little messy and damp, his jaw unshaven, and his clothes thrift-store casual. He looked tired though, tired and a little angry.

"Hi, Noah." It came out a little forced.

His dark gaze briefly met mine as he brushed by me to enter the room. "Hey."

If I had been expecting to be swept into his arms and kissed brainless, I wasn't going to get it. I guess I should have realized then that this wasn't a social call. As soon as I closed the door, he turned to face me.

"I thought you said that thing was taken care of."

Yeah, he was angry all right. At me. And I didn't appreciate it. "I was told it would be."

"It's not." He jammed his fingers through his hair, making it stand up even more. "It came after me last night."

My defenses immediately fell. I was right to have been worried. "Are you all right?"

He moved away when I tried to touch him. Ouch. "Yeah. It wanted me to deliver a message. To you."

Oh-oh. That's why he was so mad. Can't say that I blame him. I wouldn't like being used as a Night Terror's messenger either.

"What did It say?" My voice trembled just a little. The only thing worse than being the messenger was being the messenged.

"That It would be sending you a present."

I frowned. "That's it?"

His jaw ticked. "Sorry, but I didn't press for details."

I frowned at him. "How did he find you? Didn't you take something to keep It away?"

His gaze turned defiant as well as a little sheepish. "I forgot."

Arms folded over my chest, I bit the inside of my lip to keep from saying something smart-ass. It didn't help much. "So you didn't take my advice and Karatos found you, and that's my fault, how?"

Black eyes bored into mine, so full of frustration and anger that I took a step backward. Noah hated not having control. Hated being used as a puppet. And right now the only place that frustration had to go was at me.

He lifted his hand, pointed at me. "Is this thing using me to get to you?"

"I don't know," I retorted, snappier than I should. "I don't know what It wants from me, other than to piss off my father. If either of us should feel like we're being used, it's me. At least you're a source of energy for It."

He blinked. "Excuse me?"

Well shit. I stepped into that one. I sighed and rubbed the back of my neck. I had a killer headache starting. "The Dreamkin, especially Terrors, draw their power from dreamers. A lucid dreamer like you is a big power bar to them."

"Great, so I attract these things."

"And you have the power to protect yourself as well." For the most part, but I didn't mention that.

He was silent, mulling everything over in his head. No doubt he was trying to figure out whether he should still be mad at me.

"Look," I said finally when it became obvious he wasn't going to speak. "I don't like this any more than you do. We'll stop this thing, I promise."

He moved toward me, stopping when there was barely breathing room between us. "We?"

I swallowed. I couldn't read his expression and didn't know whether it would be better to cover my ass or be totally honest. I squared my shoulders and looked him straight in the eye. "Unless you'd rather go it alone."

A hint of a smile lifted his lips as he took a tissue from the box on my desk. "No, not alone." Then he started wiping at my lips with the tissue. It stuck to my gloss, and I turned my head, trying to stop him.

"What the hell? Stop that!" But it was too late. I wiped at my mouth with the back of my hand and licked my lips, ridding them of fibers. I glared at Noah. "Why did you do that?"

"I hate the taste of that stuff," was his reply. And then he kissed me, and suddenly I didn't mind so much that he'd wiped all my gloss off. I didn't mind that he'd been angry at me. I'd been angry at him, too. All that mattered was that Noah was kissing me. Again.

He had me against the bookcase, all snug and flush against him. All I could smell was damp leather and the spicy scent of his soap on clean skin. Oh yeah.

Noah lifted his head too soon. I would have stood there forever I think. He gazed down at me with those incredibly black eyes, and there was no anger there anymore. There was heat and something that looked a little bit like wonder.

"You're out of my league," he murmured.

I swear to God the man had a voice that could melt ice. My left knee practically buckled at the sound of it.

"Really?"

Noah pulled away, but he was smiling. "How can I help you stop this thing?"

Good question, but luckily one that didn't take much thought on my part. Pulling myself together, I straightened away from the wall. "You can help me in the Dream Realm. Maybe if we work together, we can track It."

A black brow shot up. "Or It will find us."

I shrugged. "Either way I can deliver Karatos to my father."

The idea seemed to appeal to him. "All right. We can try that. Tonight?"

"Let me talk to Morpheus first, and we'll take it from there." I felt guilty for leaving him vulnerable for another night, but I had to make sure my father would come when I called him. I had to make sure that I could call him.

Noah nodded. "I'll talk to you later then." He kissed me again—quick and hard—jacking up my heart rate again. God, if Dr. Canning caught us, I'd be in so much crap.

I walked him out of the office to the reception area. We

shared what I thought was a smoldering glance before he left, and my world went back to normal.

"Might want to powder your chin before your first appointment," Bonnie informed me, not looking up from her desk. "Whisker burn."

My cheeks burned at the laughter in her voice. Shit. I whirled around and started back to my office, only to be cut off by Dr. Canning, who raked me with a gaze that was anything but approving.

"I'm still waiting on that research, Dawn," he said coolly. "Perhaps when you're done having *private* visits at work you can get that to me, ASAP?"

Oh yeah. Today, despite a blistering kiss from Noah, was not shaping up to be a good day. At least Dr. Canning hadn't seen who I had been kissing. Things would be way worse if he knew it was a patient. I would be in so much crap if that was the case. "Of course, Dr. Canning. Right away."

I spent the rest of my morning—when not counseling my own patients or doing clinic-related work—doing Dr. Canning's legwork so he could publish his papers, be quoted in the newspapers, and look like an expert on TV. These SUNDS deaths had people worried, and there was a growing fear that they were actually caused by some kind of contagion. Obviously, the authorities did not want people freaking out, so Dr. Canning was in high demand on the local news and talk shows. All he had to do was smile a charming smile and calmly explain that SUNDS was in no way contagious and that he was personally doing all he could to discover the cause of these unfortunate deaths.

At noon I scarfed down a tuna sandwich and vegetable soup at my desk. I had just disposed of my trash and was reapplying lip gloss when Bonnie buzzed.

"Is Ms. Leiberman here?" I asked.

"Dr. Riley"—I knew right then something wasn't right. Bonnie never called me that—"there are a couple of police officers out here who would like to speak to you."

I dare anyone to hear that phrase and not have their blood turn to ice. Of course the first thing I thought was, *what have I done?* And then I thought of Lola, because we were each other's emergency contacts.

"I'll be right out." Maybe I should have had the cops come to me, but I wanted Bonnie with me regardless of the reason for their visit.

I straightened my clothes, smoothed my hair, and walked toward the waiting area as quickly as my shaking legs would allow. Sure enough, two uniformed members of the NYPD were standing in front of Bonnie's desk, watching me.

"Dawn Riley?" one of them asked when I reached them.

I nodded. "Is there something I can help you with, Officers?" Ohh, how professional and calm I sounded!

"Do you know a Nancy Leiberman?" The other one asked. They were both big guys with heavy New Yawk accents, but they weren't trying to be intimidating, so I relaxed a little.

"Yes." I nodded as I spoke. "In fact, she's due here any moment."

"Yeah, we heard Ms. Nadalini here leave a message on Ms. Leiberman's machine. Is there someplace a little more private that we can go to discuss Ms. Leiberman's therapy with you?"

They had been at Nancy's house when Bonnie called? They wanted to discuss Nancy's therapy? I couldn't do that unless . . . A cold chill settled in my chest. "My office," I croaked. "What's happened?"

Their expressions were sympathetic. "Ms. Leiberman's

daughter found her mother dead this morning. We have reason to believe it might have been a suicide."

A suicide. Behind me I heard Bonnie gasp. Dr. Canning and Dr. Revello had come out to see what was going on, and they, too, looked shocked—which gave me hope that they were human after all.

"Come to my office," I told them hollowly. "I'll tell you whatever I can."

As the police followed me down the hall, I thought of Nancy and how happy she had been the last time I saw her. I thought of her nightmares and how they had simply vanished—and her call asking to see me. And then it all came together in one blindingly clear flash.

Nancy Leiberman hadn't committed suicide. Nancy Leiberman had been murdered.

Karatos had sent me a present all right—big bow and all.

Chapter Ten

Nancy Leiberman had pills and alcohol in her system, but not enough to kill her. It seemed as though her heart had simply stopped—no explanation for it. Her death was considered from natural causes then. Dr. Canning thought it was SUNDS. And if he brought it up one more time, I was going to make him eat his clipboard.

This had to stop, and as I went into The Dreaming that night to continue my training, I made myself a promise that I would stop it myself if I had to. If I was going to have any kind of "normal" relationship with Noah, if I didn't want cops coming to the clinic to tell me my patient was dead, Karatos had to be stopped. And by "stopped" I meant killed. Destroyed. Unmade. Whatever it was my father did to Dreamkin who had broken the rules.

That was, of course, if my father could find Karatos. According to him, neither my uncle Icelus nor the great King himself had been able to find the Terror.

"Jesus Christ," I swore as I concentrated on turning a pencil into a stiletto. "How hard can it be to find a freaking Night Terror when you're god of this world?"

My father didn't like that. Of course, he had to admit I was right. "I will find him," he assured me, creating something else for me to alter.

I knew he would try. I also knew now that it was up to Noah and me to find Karatos. At least if I found the Terror, or rather more realistically, he found me, then I could call out to Morpheus, use the psychic bond that existed between us in The Dreaming, and bring some Dreamkin smack-down onto Karatos.

"Why haven't you found him already?" I pressed. "How can anything escape *you*?"

The bafflement on his face didn't help. "I don't know. It's as though the Terror isn't in this world."

That would terrify me if I thought for a moment it might be true. "That's impossible."

My father shot me a look of pure indignation as I turned a swan into a pig. "You think I don't know that? One of my own creatures escaping my detection."

Yeah, that had to be humiliating. "It killed a patient of mine." I knew I wasn't helping, but I felt like he needed to know how desperate the situation was becoming. "It's threatening me and Noah. It has to be stopped."

"I *know*." His voice was a deep, rumbling shadow that sent shivers down my spine. If—no, *when*—my father finally caught up with Karatos, he was going to destroy the Terror. I hoped I was still alive to watch.

"I'll see if I can draw It out." I couldn't believe I was actually offering myself up as bait. It was almost heroic of me. But seeing as how I didn't see any other solution, I wasn't ready for the Wonder Woman suit just yet.

"You're not strong enough yet," Morpheus told me, easily turning my pig back into a swan to make his point. So much for a father's faith in his daughter.

"Then I'm going to have to get strong." Where the bravado came from I couldn't say, but I knew it was truth. And I had the pig to prove it once more. If Morpheus couldn't help me, I was on my own, and putting my shields back up wouldn't help. Karatos had found a way around them before, and he knew he could get to me through Noah or any one of my patients.

The pig disappeared entirely as my father turned to me. "Are you saying that you are willing to embrace your destiny?"

I made a face. "You sound like something out of a bad sci-fi movie."

To my surprise he chuckled. "Where do you think all those movies come from? From dreams."

I rolled my eyes. "Great. My father is responsible for *Bill and Ted's Excellent Adventure*."

He grinned. "If I remember correctly, you liked that one."

He was right. "Look, I'd really like to play Ebert and Roper with you, but I have to go. I have to see if I can find Noah."

"Are you going to see your mother before you go?"

"No." I had managed to avoid her this long, and I was going to keep going for as long as I could.

"Dawn."

"Stay out of it." I gave him a look that told him I wasn't going to bend. "I can't deal with her. Not yet."

He nodded sharply. "Fine. You'll be back tomorrow night? We'll work on reshaping dream matter."

It was about time. I had to remember how to reshape what was already there before I could summon the dream matter to my own will. If I practiced, someday I might be as adept as Morpheus himself. I couldn't fathom it, personally. Me, a shaper of dreams. I was his heir. Verek hadn't just been sarcastic. I was a princess here.

I really had no idea what I was capable of. I needed to sit down.

He was smiling as he approached me, looking all too human in jeans and a sweater. He placed his hands on my shoulders and kissed me on the forehead. In a moment of weakness I leaned into his embrace. He was so solid and strong, and I knew nothing could ever hurt me with him there to protect me. If I could just let go of the bitterness inside me, I could take my place there beside him and my mother. I could be what they expected.

But I would be running away from the world I knew, and I'd be turning my back on all the people I cared about. I couldn't do that.

I pulled away. Morpheus didn't try to stop me, but I could see the regret in his eyes. "See you tomorrow."

He nodded. "Focus on where you want to go, on who you want to find. Your friend is very powerful, but he protects himself. You'll have to look hard for him."

Okay. I closed my eyes and pictured Noah in my head. I imagined reaching out for him, parting the mist and moving toward his signal. I can't explain how it's done, but it's like I'm a tracker following the scent, or a magnet following a pull. I moved through the mist of The Dreaming quickly, so nothing could grab me. I knew where Noah was; I just had to get there.

Someday maybe I could just think it and be where I wanted, but for now I actually had to travel through the Realm.

I could feel Noah's presence growing stronger. I was almost there.

Something grabbed my arm, jerked me to a stop. I pulled against it, heart hammering.

"You shouldn't exist," a voice hissed near my ear. It was like blood running down the side of my head, the sound of that voice. Blood coming from my ear.

I shoved hard. I don't know how I did it, but one moment I was afraid and struggling, then next I was free, with nothing but the cries of the thing I had expelled echoing around me. I really had to get a grip on this fast.

Reaching out, I found Noah again and ran toward him. The mist parted for me and began to swirl, taking shape. I was on the threshold of Noah's dream now. I stepped through the gauzy film, into Noah's world.

I was in a kitchen. It was nice and neat with a tile floor and lots of light. Someone was crying. A woman. I turned my head, and there was Noah, dressed in jeans and a white T-shirt. He was barefoot, standing over a woman who was on the floor at his feet, her back pressed against a cupboard. She was crying, wiping at her eyes with the back of her hands. A large bruise was forming high on her cheekbone, and her lip was cut.

And Noah just stood there, frustration etched on his face.

"Noah?"

He whirled around at the sound of my voice. I saw then that his mouth was cut, too, and there was blood on his T-shirt. Had the two of them fought?

"What are you doing here?" he demanded, coming toward me.

I didn't know what to do, but the look on his face scared me. "I had to talk to you," I told him.

"You shouldn't be here." Two splotches of color stood out on his cheeks. "You have to get out."

"I'm sorry. It's not like I could knock."

The woman staggered to her feet. "Noah? Who is it?"

We both turned to look at her, and as soon as I saw her face, I recognized her. She was the woman in the painting called *Mother* that I had seen at Noah's show. Now that I took a good look, the resemblance was unmistakable. This was Noah's mother.

Had he hit his own mother? No. He always spoke highly of her. He hadn't done this. Someone else had.

"What's going on?" I asked. I was answered by the sound of loud, booming footsteps. It was as though someone was coming downstairs, but amplified to the point where it sounded like a giant stomping on every step. Noah's head jerked up at the sound.

"You have to get out," he told me, grabbing my arm. "Get out of here." He was afraid of what was coming, and I had a pretty good idea of who that someone was.

I tried to hold on to him, but he wouldn't let me. "Let me help you."

"I don't need you to protect me!" The anger in him startled me, but I had a feeling only a sliver of it was directed toward me.

"I just want to help you," I told him.

His eyes were wild as his gaze met mine. "I never gave you permission to come into my dreams."

Okay, this was nuts. "I didn't mean—"

The pounding grew louder, and if anything, Noah looked more agitated. He didn't want me to see what was coming. "Get out!"

And then it was like a door slammed in my face. I couldn't believe it. I was standing there, staring at him, then nothing. I was on the other side of a huge black wall that stretched on for as far as I could see. Noah had shut me out—literally.

I would have slid down that wall and bawled were I not terrified of the things lurking in the mist. I woke myself up instead—or at least that's what it felt like. What really happened is that I opened a dimensional portal between the realms and stepped back into the human world. Only when I opened my eyes, I was in my bed, with Fudge curled up beside me.

I wished I could cry, but nothing came. I couldn't even cry for poor Nancy Leiberman. I was too scared and helpless to cry. Crying meant you still had hope.

I was running out.

The next day was Saturday. I spent some of it Googling Nightmares. There wasn't much that applied to the actual beings, but on the 232nd hit I found a small site on obscure mythology that had a couple of pages on Nightmares as guardians of The Dreaming. They were said to be so powerful even the Terrors feared them. Obviously times had changed because I didn't seem too terribly powerful.

I took a break from studying for food and an attempt at relaxation. I ordered flowers to be sent to the funeral home where Nancy Leiberman's body was, and I sent a bouquet to her family as well.

I tried not to think about how much my life had changed in just a couple of weeks. In fact, I was trying really hard not to think about anything except what I had to. Otherwise, I started to feel like my throat was closing up, and my head was becoming a balloon. I knew anxiety when I felt it. I was also determined to run from it.

When Noah called at two o'clock, I let voice mail answer even though part of me wanted to hear his voice. I was still a little freaked out, but mostly I was hurt that he had shut me out like that. I hadn't meant to intrude, but dreams didn't have doorbells. I would have announced myself if I had known how.

And I had to be honest. As much as I liked Noah, reasons to stay away from him were starting to pile up. He was closed off and a little weird. I could handle weird if I knew the reasons for it.

He knew I was a Nightmare, for God's sake. And I *had* been his psychologist. I should know way more about him than I did. Why was it such a hassle getting him to reveal anything about himself? I assumed his father had been physically abusive toward his mother and possibly toward Noah himself. That wasn't such a dirty secret anymore, so why would he hide it?

So let him leave a message. It might do him good to know I wasn't sitting around waiting for him to call. Well, actually I had been doing just that, but he didn't have to know it.

I made myself wait a full two minutes before dialing the mailbox to hear what he'd said.

"Doc? It's Noah. I . . ." There was a lengthy pause. *"Call me."* And that was it. He hung up.

Had I been expecting something more substantial? Something a little more . . . oh, I don't know . . . groveling? Yes. Granted, he sounded embarrassed and uncertain in his message, but just how sure of that can I be when all I had to base that opinion on was six words? I could be bitter and say screw him. I could count my losses and move on, write him off as a problem I didn't want.

Thing was, I didn't want to move on. I wanted Noah, and I couldn't turn my back on him. I was going to call him back, but just not right away. No matter how much I both dreaded and wanted to hear what he had to say, I needed a little more time before I finally let him say it.

I went to bed and practiced putting myself to sleep and waking up again. If I sang one of my mother's "dee-dee-dee" songs in my head, I could put myself under with startling ease. Maybe it was because she was rooted in The Dreaming through sleep that I found it easy to follow the same path. Or maybe it was because the God of Sleep was my paternal grandfather. Regardless, I was asleep within minutes and standing at the gates of my father's castle. Waking myself up took less effort. All I had to do was concentrate on returning to this world, and my eyes opened.

Someday I'd be able to cross over awake. That was, if I continued on with this Nightmare stuff. Maybe once I was sure Noah and I were safe, I'd say screw it and go back to my normal life.

No, I didn't see it happening that way either.

I played with the sleep thing a few more times before it exhausted me, and I had to stop for a real nap. When I woke up it was after five and the phone was ringing. It was Julie, wanting to know what time I was going to come over that evening. We were going to have a couple of drinks at her place before heading out to our favorite club.

"Were you asleep?" she demanded with a hint of laughter in her voice.

I slumped against my pillows. It was almost full dark outside now, the fading daylight little more than a smudge of orange peeking through my window. "Yeah."

"Loser."

If she only knew. "I'll be over around nine."

"Bring pineapple juice. I've got coconut rum."

I grinned into the receiver. "Now you're just talking dirty." I love coconut rum. And by love I mean drink it like a thirsty fish.

"Now, if only I could get you to put out," she joked. "See you at nine, Hoser."

The etymology of the word escaped me. How the hell had Canadians managed to come up with such a pathetic insult anyway? I hadn't heard anyone but Bob and Doug MacKenzie—brought into the American mainstream by the movie *Strange Brew*—use the term "hoser" in my entire life.

I shrugged it off and crawled out of bed, trying to shake off the sleep that wanted to reclaim me. For a second I saw Karatos standing in the mists on the shore of The Dreaming, a mocking smile on his lips. He looked dark and dangerous and repulsively sexy. I felt a pressure inside, as though there was a string attached to my soul, tugging.

I was still just enough in The Dreaming that he was trying to pull me all the way in. The son of a bitch. He had been waiting—maybe even watching for his chance to grab me unaware. Unprepared.

Vulnerable.

Rage seized me, and I pushed back. I could feel power

ripple down the invisible tether between us. In my mind's eye—that part of me still in the Dream Realm—I watched as Karatos staggered backward, then was gone.

That would teach him to fuck with me, I thought with a smug smile. But wait. He was in The Dreaming. How the hell could he be in The Dreaming without Morpheus knowing? Had the Terror thought to suck me into The Dreaming and use me as a bargaining chip? Or was Karatos acting with my father's permission?

I couldn't believe that—not totally. Unless it was all a ploy to get me back into the paternal bosom. I wasn't so sure I wanted to believe that either. Regardless, the doubt was there.

Frig. Seems like I was doubting a lot of people lately. Naturally suspicious, that was me. My sister Anne used to accuse me of having a persecution complex, but then she was always picking on me.

I made French bread tuna melts with lots of cheese for supper and ate them in front of the TV while watching a *Dark Angel* rerun on the SciFi Channel. Jessica Alba kicked serious butt on that show. Was that what I was in The Dreaming? A Nightmare. Guardian. Asskicker?

I'd be lying if I said the idea didn't have its appeal. I'd love to bash Karatos's beautiful face in until he looked as ugly as he should.

The fact that he was in The Dreaming still bothered me. I should have put myself under again and gone to my father, found out just what was going on, but I was afraid. What if Karatos was still there, and he got me? What if I wasn't strong enough to save myself? In fact, I was pretty sure I wasn't—not yet.

There was always the chance that my father had caught

Karatos during his little abduction attempt. Maybe right now, as I sat here, a lump of tuna and bread in my throat, Karatos was being slowly and painfully unmade by his maker. I liked that thought more than all the others. I might check in on that one later.

I finished my melts and put a pot of coffee on. If I was going out with Julie, I was going to need all the energy I could summon. While the coffee brewed I ran a bath. I poured some scented oil into the tub, along with a bubble bath that smelled like chai, then popped my iPod into the stereo base I'd bought for it and pressed play. My clothes dropped to the floor as "Temptation Waits" by Garbage began playing.

I slipped into the tub with a mug of sweet, creamy coffee and thought about conjuring weapons and morphing objects in The Dreaming. Morpheus had made certain that was one of the first things he and I worked on together.

I closed my eyes and leaned back against my tub cushion. *Please, please, please. Don't let him be a bad guy.* I couldn't tell you who I was praying to. Maybe God, or perhaps Ama, the great spider, weaver of dreams and spiritual mother of all Dreamkin. It didn't matter. I was praying to anyone who would listen. I might not respect my father much given what he'd done to my human family, but I wanted to believe in him. I wanted to be able to trust him.

Many of the weapons my father had shown me looked like something used in martial arts. I knew nothing about martial arts except that the people who were good at it were beautiful to watch. How was I supposed to use these weapons once I conjured them? Would I instinctively know? That wasn't a chance I wanted to take.

Noah knew some kind of martial art. We had talked about it before. Maybe, if we managed to work out this crap between us, he'd teach me. If not, I'd have to sign up for classes.

I shaved my legs and under my arms, pumiced my heels, and used a fruit-enzyme scrub on my face that always left me looking glowy. I took my sweet time, enjoying every second of this pampering session. I took a full two hours to do my hair and makeup, toying with primers, contouring, highlighting, and blending as my hair sat in a huge pile of hot rollers on top of my head. These were the moments that I loved being a girl.

By the time I was done and dressed, it was time to leave. I stopped by a grocery for the pineapple juice on my way to the train.

Julie lived on the Lower East side, in a trendy building that boasted at least one punky artist and goth drag queen. I really wished Julie would become better friends with the queen. Goth wasn't a good look for me, but she was almost seven feet of incredible makeup, hair, and clothes, and I wanted to know her secrets.

I buzzed, and Julie's boyfriend Joe let me in. Julie and Joe—too cute for words, right? Joe wasn't going with us tonight as he hated the club we always went to, but he gave me a hug when I walked in and had a drink in my hand in under three minutes.

Julie was a petite brunette with thick curly hair and a big grin. I could tell just from the expanse of teeth she flashed me that she was already a drink or two ahead of me. I had to catch up.

Three Malibu rum and pineapples later, Julie and I left for Scritti's—an eighties-themed bar within walking distance of Julie's apartment. They had posters and banners of eighties pop and metal bands all over the walls, lots of neon and

Day-Glo and a dance floor that looked like it was made out of Rubik's cubes. My favorite table—which we managed to snag—was right below the huge poster of Bon Jovi circa 1986, with big frosted hair, animal-print jackets, and leather pants. I loved it.

I ordered a rum and Sprite as did Julie, and after the drinks arrived, we hit the dance floor—which was also very close to our table, so we could watch our stuff.

We danced to Madonna's "Holiday," laughing at our own silliness. It was the most fun I'd had in a long time, and I needed it.

Of course that all came to a screeching halt shortly after eleven, when Noah walked in.

My heart leaped at the sight of him, standing by the bar in a black Henley and jeans, a bottle of Corona in his hand. His hair was its usual sexy mess, and he hadn't shaved this morning. His black gaze moved around the club. He was looking for someone.

He was looking for *me*. My heart leaped a little higher.

"Noah's here," I told Julie. Of course I had told her all about him—well maybe not all. She didn't know anything about Karatos or the fact that I, her best friend, wasn't quite human.

"Where?" She was up on her toes, peering through the crowd, weaving like a sunflower in the breeze.

"Tall guy all in black by the bar. He's drinking a Corona."

She made a face. "*That's* Noah?"

What the hell was *that*? "Yeah. What?"

She came down off her toes but didn't look at me. She was still looking at him. "He's not what I expected."

"And that was?" Seriously, I was getting a little ticked.

She didn't have to agree that Noah was possibly one of the sexiest men on the planet, but she didn't have to talk like he was something stuck to the bottom of her shoe either.

Julie frowned as we made our way back to our table. "Dude's a little intense-looking."

Yes, she actually called him a "dude." That wasn't surprising—she called me "dude" all the time. What was surprising was her thinking Noah was intense. I glanced across the bar again. I suppose he could be.

"It's just his eyes," I told her. He could control everything, close down everything but his eyes. It was all about retaining control with Noah. No wonder he had freaked out when I walked into the dream that he *had* to control on his own.

If he had come here looking for me, it was a big step for him, and the least I could do was meet him halfway.

"I'll be right back," I told my friend, as she sat down; and then I turned to make my way through the crowd.

I kept my gaze fastened on Noah as I weaved through the wall of bodies separating us. He looked to the right, then slowly brought his head back . . . *bang*. Our gazes met. Surprise flickered briefly in his eyes as he straightened, then he moved forward, also braving the throng to meet me.

The crowd seemed to disappear. I know how hokey that sounds, but at that moment, when Noah was walking toward me, there was no one else in the world but he and I.

Neither of us spoke until we were standing inches apart— there was no point when the music was so loud.

"Hi," I shouted.

A small smile twitched at the corner of his mouth. "Your roommate told me where to find you."

Ahh, Lola. She was either a genius or a busybody, I hadn't quite decided. I leaned toward him, feeling the heat of him through his clothes and mine. God he smelled good. "Well, you found me."

A warm hand on my back stopped me from pulling back. We were so close we might as well be slow dancing. "I need to talk to you," he said loudly near my ear.

I met his gaze for a second, feeling suddenly more confident than I ever had before with him. "I need to talk to you, too."

"Can we go somewhere?"

Yeah, we could. We could go to my place, or we could go to a restaurant, but all of those were safe for Noah because they didn't require letting me into his world. They didn't require trust. I trusted Noah with the secret of who I was. It was time for Noah to trust me.

I locked my gaze with his. "Let's go to your place."

Chapter Eleven

"My place?" Noah's mouth was so close to my ear when he spoke that I felt the moist heat of his breath on my skin, shivered under the low timbre of his voice.

Shaking off the goose bumps he'd just given me, I smiled in what I hoped was a confident manner. "Yes. Your place."

"You sure?" I knew what he was asking. He wanted to make certain I'd be okay with whatever happened once we were at his place. I couldn't say, but we needed to talk, and he'd feel more in control on his own turf.

And okay, maybe part of me was hoping he'd make a move. I wasn't sure I was ready for sex, but I was ready for something.

I nodded. "I'm sure."

"Okay. Let's go."

My heart was pounding at this point. What the hell was I doing, going off to Noah's place? I didn't know where he lived—should have memorized it from his file. What if he turned out to be the psycho? Couldn't imagine it, but I suspect that's what a number of assaulted or dead women would say about their attacker.

I got my stuff from our table and told Julie where I was going. She immediately turned to Noah. "What's your address?"

To my surprise, he rhymed it off. He lived in the Village. No real big surprise there. Julie asked his last name as well and wrote the info down on a napkin that she stuffed in her purse. She smiled at Noah. "No offense, but I don't know you."

His head bobbed in another of those sharp nods of his. "None taken. I'm glad Doc has someone looking after her."

I almost rolled my eyes at the sentiment, as sweet as it was. Julie, however, shot me an amused glance. No doubt she'd tease me about "Doc" next time I spoke to her.

"Call me tomorrow," she ordered, as I slipped my purse over my arm.

"I will," I promised, and gave her a quick hug. "You going to be okay here?"

She waved away my concern. "I'll call Joe. He'll come meet me."

I felt better knowing she wouldn't be walking home alone, and turned to Noah. "Let's go."

We got our coats from the check counter. I was still buttoning mine when we walked out into the surprisingly balmy night air. Noah hailed a cab—smart boy knew better than to drink and drive—and we were in the back and in motion before Noah even gave the address.

We didn't speak during the drive. I sat on my side and stared at the city passing by. Noah sat on his side and did the same. But on the seat between us, his fingers found mine and entwined.

Finally, the cab stopped, and I slid out behind Noah after he paid the driver, my hand still in his. As the taxi pulled away, I straightened my coat and took a moment to look around.

The street was narrow, punctuated with large, dense trees that had lost most of their leaves, leaving the sidewalk and small lawns covered in a blanket of orange. Most of the buildings looked residential, but one had a restaurant in the basement.

Noah's building was a big redbrick block with huge windows on the second floor and smaller, barred ones on the bottom. The bars had been painted black and had the look of old wrought iron.

"Rent or own?" I asked, as he slid the key to the lock on a very heavy wooden door.

"Own," he replied. "Warren and I bought it. He teaches aikido downstairs."

"Aikido." I arched a brow. "Neat." Not to mention, it could be useful.

Noah didn't reply, he just looked at me as though he was trying to figure me out. I wished him luck. Then he pushed open the door, stepped inside, pushed a few buttons on a keypad, and gestured for me to come in. "After you."

I walked into the closet-sized foyer. There was just enough room for Noah and me to stand there at the foot of a wide staircase. The lighting was soft, casting Noah in a glow that made him more golden. I fought the urge to stare and started up the stairs. I heard the door close and lock behind me, then Noah's footsteps followed.

At the top of the stairs was a set of French doors with thick glass panes. They were locked, so I waited for Noah to come up behind me with the key. His chest brushed my shoulder as he leaned forward. I wanted to turn around and wrap myself around him.

But I didn't.

The doors opened, and I walked in, my mouth dropping at the sight that met me. I knew Noah had money, and I was willing to bet he had done most of the work himself, but the floor was gleaming hardwood slabs. That same slick wood formed huge door arches and wide window frames. The windows had to be eight feet tall and four wide. The ceilings were easily twenty feet. There were thin strips of that same wood where the ceiling met the cream-colored walls, thicker strips at the floor where a hip-high length of the wall was painted a reddish chocolate color. This carried through the wide, massive space that was the main area of the apartment. From where I stood I could see living room—decorated in chocolate and beige—dining area, and kitchen. Farther down the length of the building there was a door to the right—the bathroom probably—then another set of doors passed that—to what looked like a studio. A set of stairs off the living area led to a loft area, which I assumed was Noah's bedroom.

What did his bed look like, I wondered? And would I ever find out?

"I'll never think my apartment is nice again." I was only half-joking.

He shrugged out of his jacket. "I like your apartment. It's warm."

I didn't pursue it. When he held out his hand for my coat, I took it off and handed it to him. He stared at me.

"What?" Had I spilled something? Was my zipper open? Oh God, not the zipper.

He gave his head a shake. "Sorry. I've never seen you in jeans before."

I glanced down. Just boot-cut jeans, nothing special. I liked them because they had spandex in them, so I could wear them a little snug without developing muffin meat above the waist.

"Nice blouse," he commented, and pivoted on his heel to hang our coats on the iron stand by the door.

I smiled. I understood now, thick as I was. The blouse I was wearing was a dark wine cotton peasant blouse, gathered at the waist so it accented my figure. It also was a little low cut. I'm not lacking in the boob department, and the girls were standing high and firm in the bra I'd chosen. I have nice cleavage, if I do say so myself, and apparently Noah thought so, too.

"There's something I have to do before I can talk to you," he said as he walked back to me. I opened my mouth to ask what, but never had the chance to say a word. The something he had to do was kiss me—and very well I might add. His lips were soft and warm, not demanding or insistent. Still, my heart sped up at the taste of him. He took his time tasting me. It was a hot, lazy kiss that said, "We have all night to do whatever we want."

When he finally pulled away, he planted a small kiss on the tip of my nose. "Had to do that." He grinned. I grinned back.

He offered me a Corona, and I took it, then we went into his living room. I took my boots off despite his assurance that I didn't have to. I had been raised to believe that it was rude to traipse through someone's home with my shoes on.

We sat on his sofa—a chocolate brown, overstuffed, micro-fiber monstrosity that snuggled against every nook and cranny of my body. Bliss. He was on one end, and I was on the other, turned toward each other. Our knees touched, both of us having hiked our legs onto the cushions.

"You have a great place," I told him.

"Thanks." He looked down at the beer in his hand, before setting it aside. "Listen, about the other night . . ."

"Me too," I blurted, interrupting what I was sure was going to be an apology.

He looked at me for a moment before nodding. "You came into my dream for a reason. What was it?"

It was like a black cloud settling over my head, the memory of the police at the clinic, telling me that Nancy Leiberman was gone. "I wanted to tell you that I got the present Karatos sent. He killed one of my patients."

Noah looked astounded. Or horrified—maybe both. "Shit."

"That pretty much sums it up, yeah."

He reached for his beer, sitting on a stone coaster on the coffee table. After a deep swallow from the bottle, Noah held the Corona in his lap and turned to me. "Why is this thing after us?"

"I don't know. Maybe because you're a lucid dreamer. He would draw energy from you. I'm not sure what he wants from me—revenge against my father maybe."

"How do we stop it?"

"I'm not sure." But I would find out. I would.

"Great." Slapping his thigh, he rose to his feet. He strode to one of the huge windows and looked out at the night and all its twinkling lights.

"Hey," I began lamely. "At least you're still alive." That was more than Nancy Leiberman could say.

He shot me a scowl. "Oh thanks, Doc. I feel so much better." His head shook. "I'm tired of being this thing's cat toy."

"I'm tired, too." And I was. I was supposed to be able to destroy this thing, or at least give it a good ass-kicking, and I had no idea what to do. I just wanted my life back.

"What's he done to you?" He was on the offensive now.

"It raped me." I couldn't stop the truth from pouring out, and I couldn't call Karatos "he" like Noah could. I just couldn't.

Noah went as still and quiet as an animal in headlights. "What?"

I had come this far, I might as well keep going. "In a dream. I couldn't stop it." I wasn't going to admit how the thing had made my body like it. That was too personal and something I would rather forget.

There was anguish on Noah's face as he came back to the couch. He set his beer on the table and sat closer to me this time. I didn't try to stop him when he reached for me, instead I allowed him to pull me against his chest and wrap those deliciously strong arms around me.

"Oh God, Dawn." I closed my eyes at the sound of my name on his lips. I hadn't cried over what Karatos had done to me. In fact, other than anger, I was pretty numb about it, but Noah's concern tightened my throat. And the little kisses he planted on my forehead made my eyes sting.

"You okay?" he murmured against my hair.

I nodded, my cheek rubbing against his shirt. This felt good. So very good. "Yeah."

"I'd kill the bastard if I knew how."

He was serious, and I was strangely touched. But I didn't want to be treated like a victim, so I pulled free of his embrace. I sat up, but I didn't move away. "Thanks."

Noah didn't seem bothered by my actions. He simply reached over and put his hand on my thigh. It was a comforting gesture rather than a sexual one. "How can he . . . It be doing this without your father knowing?"

"I don't know."

He eyed me for a moment. "Is there anybody other than your father who might know how to kill this thing?"

Antwoine. Why hadn't I thought of him before this? "There's an old man I can talk to. I'll look for him tomorrow."

He looked dubious—which for Noah was little more than a lift of a brow. "An old man can do what the God of Dreams can't?"

I managed a half-assed smile. "I don't imagine, but he seems to know a lot about The Dreaming, and he's tricked my father himself. He might know how Karatos is managing to hide himself."

"Good."

Silence stretched between us for but a few seconds, until I asked the question I should have asked a long time ago—had I thought of it. "Noah, you pulled me into your dream at the center. How?"

"I don't know. The Terror-thing was kicking my ass, and I remember thinking I didn't want to die in front of you. The next thing I knew you were there."

"So all you had to do was think of me?"

He shrugged and took another drink of beer. "I guess so, yeah."

"If Karatos comes back I want you to try it again. He can't take both of us."

He made a scoffing sound. "You don't think?"

"I'm a Nightmare." I said it with more confidence than I felt. "I'm supposed to be able to kick this thing's ass."

"Supposed?"

"I can do a lot of the same tricks he can mentally, but I'm not much of a fighter."

His gaze brightened. It was hope I saw there—and a little bit of vengeance. "I can help with that."

I was hoping he'd say that. "You'd teach me?"

"I have keys to Warren's dojo. We can start tomorrow if you want."

"I want." We could start training in this world, then move it into the Dream Realm. We'd be just like Morpheus and Neo in *The Matrix*.

The glow in his eyes shifted, warmed as he looked at me. I knew what was coming, and I wanted it, too. As Noah's lips met mine, I gave myself up to his sweet, warm taste. I melted into his arms and let my mind empty of any thoughts that weren't of him. I let myself believe that I was a normal woman and he was just a normal man.

And I did believe it. For a little while.

Antwoine was waiting for me on the same bench as last time.

"For someone banned from The Dreaming, you sure are easy to find," I commented as I sat down beside him. The worn wood was cold through my jeans, and I wished that I had worn a hat. Antwoine was wearing one—it was red, yellow, and purple, and had a pom-pom on top.

I had searched him out last night—from my own bed—and sent him a message that I would be in the park today. That I needed to talk to him.

I stayed at Noah's for an hour or so before getting a cab home. We made out for a bit on the couch, but after my big revelation, I don't think he wanted to try to take things further. Since I wasn't sure I was ready to have sex, I didn't mind his restraint. There were no similarities between him and Karatos, and I wanted Noah like ice cream wants cake, but I wasn't in a hurry to have him.

Antwoine's chocolate brown eyes turned to meet mine. "He just sent me to the Outlands. Couldn't ban me altogether, not without getting blood on his hands."

"He" was Morpheus, and it was nice to know he wasn't a complete asshole. "So, that's how you can still dream?"

He nodded. "And how you call me up like one of them folks tryin' to sell me something whenever you want."

I wondered what Antwoine dreamed about. I didn't ask. "I thought you might appreciate a 'call' more than me simply popping by your dream unannounced."

The old man's eyes narrowed a little as he looked at me. "Got yourself into some hot water, did ya?"

I looked down at my boots, dug their toes into the grass. "You could say that."

Antwoine chuckled then—it was raspy and broken, and sounded more sympathetic than humorous. "What happened, child, your man dreamin' of another woman when you walked in on him?"

"No!" I scowled at him. But what if Noah had been? God, that would have been so awful. I hated to say it, but that would have bothered me more than the violence he had been dreaming of. I glanced at my boots again. "He didn't like that I could just walk in."

"Ain't nobody who would like that. Imagine if someone just showed up inside your private world."

Like Karatos. Shit. I had gone into Noah's dream like Karatos had done to both of us. No wonder he had been upset. I was such an idiot.

"Now don't go getting' all down in the lip on me," Antwoine chided. "It isn't your fault, you were just doin' what comes natural to your kind."

My kind. He didn't make it sound like an insult, but I felt segregated—freakish—all the same. "I'll never do it again."

He laughed, and this time there was humor in it. "Sure you will. Maybe he'll be okay with it, maybe he won't. Loving a succubus was hard enough. I can't imagine trying to have a relationship with a Marae."

"Marae" was the old name for what I am. The name later became confused with "Mara," which are somewhat nasty daimons, and that's what led to Nightmares being thought of as bad things rather than the guardians they are.

"You know a lot about Dreamkin," I remarked.

He nodded slowly. "I spent a lot of time in that world before your daddy tossed me out."

My daddy. He hadn't liked Antwoine and his succubus being together. He didn't seem to like me and Noah either, even though we were hardly "together." Would Morpheus take drastic action if Noah and I did take our relationship further? We hadn't even had a real date yet, and we might be over before we even started.

I would not allow my father to screw with my life that way. But first, I needed to deal with Karatos, so Noah would stay alive long enough for us to burn that bridge when we got to it.

"Do you know how to kill a Terror?"

"No, child, I don't." He fixed me with that dark gaze. "Doesn't your instinct tell you anything?"

Instinct? Oh yeah, because I was so good at that. I guess

maybe I should be. "I know I should be able to do it. I know I should know how, but I don't."

"You have to learn. You have to become more familiar with what you are and what you can do."

No shit. "But even if I can't find this thing, Morpheus should be able to, right?" I didn't like suspecting my father of actually allowing Karatos to sexually assault me, but I had seen the Terror in The Dreaming. Morpehus was all-powerful in the Dream Realm. How could anything escape him?

"It's possible that the Terror has figured out how to cloak himself so your father can't find him."

"Is that possible?"

"It ain't easy," he replied with a shake of his head. "Only ones I ever saw do it were the succubi. They could take life force and wrap themselves in it—that's how she'd hide from Morpheus when she was with me. If he went lookin', all he'd sense was me. 'Course the night he just simply showed up was another story."

And one that could wait for another time, regardless of my curiosity. "She'd take your life force?" That was pretty scary-sounding.

"She was a succubus, child. That was part of her job."

I didn't ask to what purpose. I didn't want to know.

"I need your help. You know things about the Dream Realm—things Morpheus won't tell me."

"Serves his purpose not to tell you."

I tried to ignore that remark. Antwoine hated my father, and it only made sense that he trusted Morpheus about as much—or less—than he'd trust a sewer rat. Still, I didn't trust my father much myself, so the words rang in my head.

"Will you help me?" I asked. "Teach me what he won't?"

I could tell it was a tempting proposition. Helping me would be a middle finger to Morpheus.

Of course, it occurred to me as well that Antwoine might like to use me to hurt Morpheus. Get a little revenge through the baby girl. I wasn't sure if I could trust either of them, but I needed them all the same.

Antwoine thought for a moment. Then a light came on in his eyes. "I'll help you on one condition."

Uh-oh. "What?"

"You find my Madrene. Find her and let her know I . . . You let her know that I'm okay."

His succubus. I could do that. I could *so* do that. "All right. And you'll tell me everything you know?"

He nodded. "Everything."

"Great. When can we start?"

He smiled—big and toothy—as he pulled a wicked-looking dagger out of his coat. "How about now?"

Chapter Twelve

I froze. The blade in Antwoine's slightly gnarled hand glinted in the watery sunlight. "Put the knife down, Antwoine."

He chuckled at the caution in my voice. "I'm not gonna stab you, idiot. This dagger is a gift for you." As if to prove that point—and make me feel even more like an idiot—he handed me the blade, hilt first.

I took it after a quick glance around. There was a fair bit of traffic in the park, but no one was the least bit interested in the big white girl and the little black man sitting together on a bench with a dagger between them.

The blade was thin and razor-sharp. The hilt was un-adorned except for a large oval moonstone embedded in it. The stone sat just above my hand when my fingers closed around the smooth bone. It fit my hand perfectly. In fact, it grew warm in my grasp, and I knew that it recognized me as its owner.

"It's a Marae blade," Antwoine said, answering my unspoken question. "Made especially for Nightmares."

That was why it felt so right. I couldn't take my eyes off it. My father hadn't told me about these. I turned it this way and that, admiring how the light hit that amazing stone. "How did you get it?"

He passed me the sheath for it. "Stole it from one of the Nightmares your daddy sent to *escort* me out of The Dreaming."

That made me look up. That was why I hadn't seen one before this. They were just for those in the Nightmare Guild, and I wasn't one of them. "But Nightmares are supposed to protect dreamers." This dagger wasn't of The Dreaming, I could feel it. Items from the Dream Realm were supposed to eventually deteriorate in this world. Whatever had made this, hadn't been human, and they hadn't been Dreamkin.

He gave me an odd look. "Nightmares are supposed to do what their maker tells 'em."

And that was something else that made me different. Morpheus could tell me to do whatever he wanted, but he couldn't make me do it.

Antwoine seemed to know the direction of my thoughts. "He's your daddy, and I'm sure he loves you and wants what's good for you, but like any daddy, he's going to think he knows what's best. You keep a close eye on him."

I slipped the dagger into the sheath and dropped it into my backpack. Antwoine watched with an amused grin. "You even know how to use a dagger?"

Now it was my turn to smile at him. "I don't have to. That blade will do whatever I want it to." I knew it as surely as I knew my own shoe size.

His grin widened. "Now you're startin' to sound like a Nightmare. Good girl."

I preened under his praise. The opinion of an old man whose sanity I had yet to confirm meant a lot to me. Just like I knew that the Marae blade would obey me, I knew that Antwoine Jones was going to play an important role in my life.

I checked my watch. "I have to get going." I had half an hour before I had to meet Noah, and I wanted to grab lunch on the way.

Antwoine rose when I did. "You take care of yourself, Little Dawn. Call me anytime you want, y'hear?"

I was by nature an impulsive person—compulsive even at times. It was something I tried to tamp down and keep under control, but today I threw it out the window and gave in to the impulse to hug this little man who smelled of tea and aftershave.

"Thank you," I murmured as I let him go. "I just may need to call you again sometime."

He patted my shoulder with a smile. "I'll be here. Now go. You'll be late for that boy of yours."

I don't know how he knew I was meeting Noah, and I didn't ask. I gave Antwoine a little wave as I walked away, then hurried down to Eighth to catch the subway. I grabbed a hot dog on the way. It tasted every bit as good as something that bad for me should.

I arrived at Noah's right on time. I even remembered to dig out my compact and make sure I didn't have mustard on my face before pressing the dojo buzzer. My cheeks and nose were pink from the chill in the air, but there was nothing I could do about that. I wasn't wearing much makeup today because it would only smear, but I had mascara and a little tinted lip balm. I really didn't think Noah would care.

He answered the door in his bare feet, wearing a gray T-shirt and a pair of black pajama/lounge pants with Batman on them. I supposed they were easy to move in.

He smiled, brightening his gaze. "Hey."

I smiled back, feeling like a kid when he looked at me like that. "Hey. Nice pants. I'm sensing a superhero complex."

Grin widening, Noah stepped back so I could enter. "My little sister gives them to me. I think she's the one with the complex."

I didn't let the mention of that little monster spoil my good mood.

"Come on," he said, "I'll show you where to change."

I followed him through the large, open space. The floors were polished hardwood, scuffed and faded in places. One wall was nothing but mirror. The walls were painted sage rather than white, which I assumed marked too easily. Rows of lights ran along the high ceiling—as bright as sunlight.

A door in the back led to a hallway. Noah led me past a door marked OFFICE to one that said WOMEN. I thanked him and went inside to change.

It was obvious that Warren didn't have many female students. Only four of the lockers had locks on them, and the tile floor had a fresh look to it. I was hardly the right one to comment, however. When I was a kid, the last thing I would have wanted to do was learn martial arts. Of course, if I had known then what a fabulous way it was to meet boys, I would have signed up in a flash.

Since I was alone I didn't bother using one of the curtained cubicles to change. I did move into the corner, though, just in case Noah happened to come back. I had no objection to him seeing me half-naked, but if it did happen I'd like for it to happen under softer lighting and maybe after he'd had a beer or two.

I changed into sweats and a T-shirt and put my hair up in a ponytail. Barefoot, I went out to meet my own personal Mr. Miyagi. Wax on. Wax off. Yeah, I know that was *The Karate Kid,* but I'd take Pat Morita over Steven Seagal any day.

Noah was sitting on a large tumbling mat in the middle of the dojo, stretching his arms over his extended legs. I joined him and began stretching, too. Exercise might be a dirty word in my dictionary, but even I understood the importance of loosening my muscles before any kind of activity.

"Aikido is about defense," he explained as he leaned forward, pressing his chest to his thigh. "It's nonviolent. Meant to neutralize attacks rather than retaliate."

"But don't I want to retaliate?" I mean, I didn't want to get my ass kicked!

His lips twitched. "What you want is to keep your opponent from hurting you and exhaust him at the same time. Fighting back disrupts your harmony."

"Have you ever fought back?" I asked. I immediately regretted the question when I saw the life leach from his expression. The perfectly serene mask I knew so well slid into place.

"Sure," he replied, expressionless. "But first, you work on defense. Then later, we can work on other stuff if you're still interested."

I figured I would be. Interested, that is, and not only in ass-kicking. Noah had a lot of baggage—maybe more than

anyone should want in a boyfriend, but I was willing to risk
it. The question I had to ask myself was—did I want him in
my life because I liked him as he was, or because I thought
I could fix him?

Maybe "fix" was too strong a word, but I can't deny that
the need to help him was there inside me, right beside the
urge to bonk his brains out.

"The point of aikido is to use the attacker's energy and
momentum against them," Noah said as we stood. "The
movements are circular, using the hips rather than the upper
body."

"Finally," I quipped. "My hips are good for something."

He grinned, and oh, it was sexy! "A few things."

I actually blushed. "Okay, so no upper body."

"Right. If someone tries to hit you, you block and push
their arm or foot beyond, so that the extension throws them
off-balance. Pretend that you're going to slap me."

I did, swinging my arm slowly just in case. Noah's own
arm came up as he sidestepped, blocked mine without hurting me—he was going slowly as well—and then pushed my
arm farther into the arc so that I was forced to lean forward.
My center of balance was gone, I couldn't retaliate, and neither of us had gotten hurt.

"That's obviously pretty simplified," he remarked, helping me straighten up. His hand was warm around my arm.
"But you get the idea."

"If aikido's so kind and gentle, why the mat?"

His dark eyes shone brightly as his gaze met mine. "Aikido's kind and gentle. I'm not."

I was pretty sure that was meant as a mock threat. I was
also pretty sure it turned me on.

We started out slowly—not much faster than his example

exercise. Since we were working at less than warp speed, my movements felt heavy and clunky. It was like reliving all those dance classes my mother made me go to as a kid in the hopes that I'd stop tripping over my own size eleven feet. Once we got a few basics down, however, Noah picked up the pace, and my confidence increased.

Thirty minutes later, I was sweating and breathing through my mouth. My back was damp and icky and so was the flesh between and underneath my boobs. Noah had sent me sprawling only once so far, and I was feeling pretty confident as we circled each other, him instructing and me doing what I was told.

That was, of course, before he sent me sprawling on the mat for the second time. And the third. Somewhere between two and three we stopped to discuss how to take a fall so I wouldn't hurt myself. It helped—a little.

The fourth time I knew what was coming, and I managed to get my leg in around his. If I was going down, this time he was coming with me. I wasn't going to be the only one with bruises on my butt tomorrow.

We landed in a tangled heap—and not in a graceful, sexy way either. He landed on top of me—hard—and knocked the breath from my lungs. He swore. I swore. Thank God for the mat, or I probably would have knocked myself out.

I was almost afraid to look at him, convinced he was going to be pissed.

"Nice move," he remarked drily, with just a hint of amusement. "You hurt yourself more than you hurt me."

I tried to grin, but it felt more like a wince. "I'm good that way."

He pushed up on his elbows, but his chest was still on mine. I could feel his heart pounding, feel every breath. One of his legs was between mine, and I tried very hard to ignore the lovely pressure of his thigh.

From this close I could actually make out the pupils of his eyes—a bare shade or two darker than the irises. I'd never met anyone with eyes so dark before. I could see my face reflected in their shining blackness. God, I was a mess. Noah didn't seem to mind. As his gaze flickered over my features, I saw nothing but appreciation in the bright depths. I liked it, even though it worried me. It seemed so sudden, his attraction to me, and I wasn't so sure I could trust it.

And then, he was obviously overcome by the ruddy flush in my cheeks that happens every time I exert myself. Or maybe it was the sweat beading in that little valley above my lip that did him in. The next thing I knew, Noah's lips were on mine, and our tongues were doing the tango. Mentally, I sighed in delight, and let him have his way with my mouth.

He tasted faintly of toothpaste—sweet and minty. His lips were soft against mine, firmly coaxing a response. I met every nip and nuzzle, opened myself to the hot wetness of his tongue, and stroked it with my own.

Warmth tingled in my veins. Want blossomed in my stomach. I could smell the salty heat of our damp skin, feel the insistent hardness of his body pressed into mine. I adjusted my hips to better cradle his, torn between wanting to gyrate against his erection and pull away from the bruising arousal of it.

It was obvious that he liked kissing me, that wasn't the problem. The problem was I didn't know if his interest stemmed from a genuine attraction to me or if it had been "influenced" by Karatos and The Dreaming. For all I knew, the Terror could have done something to Noah to make him act this way. He could be using Noah to get to me.

Scary.

Once Karatos was gone, what would we have? As far as I knew, we had very little in common except for some power in the Dream Realm. I was willing to take a chance on a relationship with Noah—risk having it all fall through—but I wasn't going to be the only person to take that risk. How could I give all I had when the man I was with only gave half back?

I might not have my pick of men, but I knew what I wanted and settling was not an option. If Noah didn't want me the same way I wanted him—if he wasn't ready for a relationship of some sort—then what was the point?

One of his hands—those beautiful, strong fingers of his—was easing up my ribs toward my chest. Tight and tingling, my body was anxious for him to reach that very destination, but I knew it wasn't a good idea. If he touched me like that—if he started something more serious than just kissing—I'd let him, and I wasn't ready to go there yet.

I pushed against his shoulders, even though my fingers itched to dig in and hold on. He lifted his head and gazed down at me, all heavy-lidded and delicious-looking, but my resolve was firm.

And oh boy, so was he.

He didn't speak, but his gaze was questioning. I heard his voice in my head as clearly as he had spoken out loud. *What's wrong?*

"I can't do this," I told him. "Not here. Not now."

The golden skin between his brows puckered. "Do what?"

He could play coy all he wanted, but I wasn't totally stupid. "Have sex with you on a dojo floor."

"You think I want to have sex?"

I arched a brow. "Unless you're carrying a zucchini in your pants, yeah."

He rolled off me completely, and a chill rushed up the front of me where his warmth had been. "*That* has a mind of its own."

Yeah, and I was pretty sure what that part of him had in mind. I sat up to face him on an equal level. "Are you saying that you wouldn't have taken it further if I had let you?"

He shrugged. "I was just enjoying myself. I thought you were, too."

That was quite possibly the most words I had ever heard him speak at one time. "I was. I just don't want us to rush into anything."

He was scowling now. He knew there was more to my lame protests than I was saying. "You think I'd just fuck you, then I'd disappear?"

"No." I was getting agitated—we both were, obviously. "I think you'd wait until Karatos disappeared first." Oh, that so hadn't come out the way I meant it.

Noah paled, and I felt cruel. "Nice to know you have such a high opinion of me."

He rose to his feet, so I stood as well. "Noah, that's not it."

Defiantly, he faced me, muscled forearms folded over his chest. "Then how is it?"

"I have to focus on stopping Karatos. I can't have any distractions." Was that toes I tasted in the back of my throat? Had to be, for I certainly had my foot in my mouth.

"I'm a distraction." His voice was so quiet and low that I shivered at the sound of it. Noah was dangerous at that moment. He was either going to shut down or lash out, and I had no idea which one I'd prefer.

"Of course not."

"Then what?"

I couldn't answer. What words could I possibly use? Did I tell him I'd been infatuated with him for months and risk that vulnerability? How could I explain that I was very much afraid that he was my strength without making myself weak?

He raked a hand through his hair, pulling the silky black strands back off his forehead.

My silence obviously spoke to him. The high planes of his cheeks darkened as his eyes narrowed. "I don't need you to save me." His voice was still that low, controlled pitch. "I don't want to be some pathetic victim you feel the need to rescue and protect."

At least he hadn't accused me of wanting to "fix" him.

"Noah . . ."

He stopped me with a look of undisguised bitterness. "Find someone else to show you how to fight Karatos. A victim like me can't be much help. I'll be fine on my own."

Anyone else, and I might have rolled my eyes at the martyred tone, but as Noah walked away, I felt like crap for letting something that had started out so wonderful go down the toilet in such a spectacular way. I knew that he wouldn't be all right on his own. Karatos would come for him.

And it would be all my fault when the Terror took him.

"Stupid is as stupid does."

From now on this sage phrase from Forrest's mama was going to be my personal motto. Stupid was as stupid did, and I felt really stupid about the fight I'd had with Noah. I just needed to know that he liked me, and that maybe he planned to stick around once our Night Terror problem was solved.

Because I wasn't investing my heart or my energy for less.

"Kleenex?" Lola asked from where she lounged beside me on the couch. On the TV screen, Forrest was still at Jenny's bedside, but we both knew what was coming next. I pulled two tissues from the box.

Even though I had watched this movie more times than I could count, I still teared up when Tom Hanks says, "You died on a Saturday." In fact, the entire Jenny's grave speech never fails to make me cry like a baby. Lola is the same way, hence the box of tissues on the cushion between us.

It's these moments that make me miss my family. I refuse to watch *Little House on the Prairie* reruns for the same reason. Sentimentality gets me every time, and I end up longing for home, my dad's fried bread, and, yes, even my mother.

So it was perfect timing when my sister Joy called at exactly the right moment to catch me vulnerable. Instead of letting the call go to voice mail, I picked up, suddenly needing to hear my sister's voice, regardless of the topic.

"Is this a bad time?" my sister asked after I said hello. Joy was the closest to me in age, being six years older. I thought of her—and the others—as my full siblings regardless of who my biological father was.

I sniffed and wiped my nose with a Kleenex. "No. Lola and I just finished watching Forrest Gump."

A soft chuckle rang in my ear. "So that's why you sound like you've been bawling."

Another sniff, but I was smiling. "Yeah. What's up?" It

wasn't that I thought she had to have a reason for calling, but Joy normally didn't call just to say hi.

"Ivy was going to call you, but I thought it might be better if I did."

My soft and sappy feeling evaporated, replaced by a frisson of fear. "What's wrong?"

"Nothing's *wrong*." I knew there was a "but" coming. "We've arranged for a specialist to see Mom."

I frowned. "What kind of specialist?" That I knew of there were none.

"Ivy found a neurologist from Boston who has agreed to take a look at mom's case."

Of course it would be Ivy. I shouldn't be this annoyed. Ivy was only worried about Mom. She didn't know what I knew—that she would be wasting her money—Dad's money—on trying to bring back a woman who didn't want to be with us.

"We've had three different neurologists look at Mom already," I reminded her. "It hasn't done any good. No one can figure out what is wrong with her." No one except for me, and no one would believe me.

"This one has a theory."

"I bet he does. What's his rate?"

"It's going to cost five thousand for the consult and treatment."

"Jesus. And Dad's going to pay it?"

"He wants her back as much as the rest of us, Dawnie."

I didn't want her back. "Right."

"He thinks the coma might be psychosomatic. Of course, you know what that means better than I do."

Well, shit. Maybe this doctor wasn't trying to make a

quick buck after all. But that didn't mean he could bring my mother back to this world. "So, what does this guy think he can do for Mom that the others couldn't?"

My sister hesitated, as though trying to think of the best way to phrase her words. "He says he can wake her up."

Chapter Thirteen

What the hell was I supposed to do with this?

After hanging up with Joy, I sat on the couch trying to figure out if I should tell my mother and Morpheus what the family had planned. I couldn't confide in Lola since she seemed to think I was sane, and I didn't want to do anything that might change that. I told her that they were calling in another specialist, and that was it. She thought maybe I was afraid to get my hopes up. She was partially right.

Was it wrong of me to hope that this neurologist might actually succeed in breaking the "Arms of Morpheus" spell? My mother was happy where she was, but I wanted her to face the family she'd abandoned. I wanted her to face the pain she'd put them—us—through.

But I also didn't want anything to jeopardize my standing

within The Dreaming—not that I had any plans to spend a lot of time there, but if Mom woke up, Morpheus might decide she was more of a priority than apprehending Karatos. Or worse, he might decide to go all vengeful on my family. I wish I could say I trusted him not to be so petty, but I didn't. He was a god, and gods were known to behave like over-grown children.

I was going to have to tell them. I didn't want to, but it would save a lot of trouble in the long run. Chances were that the specialist wouldn't be able to wake Mom up after all. My father was all-powerful when it came to dreams, and I had my doubts that any mere mortal could stand against him.

Of course I could be wrong. If a dirtbag like Karatos could fool him, maybe Morpheus wasn't as bright as I thought. Either way, it sucked. And I was on my own.

Lola decided to take a bath, so I called Julie to make a date for the weekend. She and Joe were headed out of town on Friday, so we made plans to do lunch after they got back instead.

I wondered what Noah was doing Saturday night. Not me, that was for certain.

Had I been out of line with him? Didn't I have a right to know if a guy liked me or was under supernatural influence? Normal people didn't have these worries.

I went to bed shortly after saying good night to Julie. As I walked down the hall to my room, I could hear Lola snoring gently in hers.

I changed into my boxers and tank top and climbed into bed. The sheets were a little cold, as was the temperature in my room, but I pulled the comforter up under my chin and snuggled down. I would warm up soon enough, and there was nothing better for sleeping than a warm bed in a cool room.

Instead of waiting for the veil of sleep to transport me to The Dreaming, I decided to try meditation. I should be able to cross over when awake. Having to be asleep was just one more thing holding me back from my true potential, plus it put me at a decided disadvantage.

I emptied my mind—not an easy task for me. Then I imagined a lovely warmth entering through my toes and working its way up to my head. Usually, I started thinking of other things when I did this, but I managed to keep my thoughts clear. Maybe there was hope for me yet. By the time I was warm all over, I was also totally relaxed.

My eyes opened, heavy and unfocused. Hovering in the air before me was a shimmering opalescent sliver of light. It flickered and pulsed, like the glow from a TV through a partially closed door. This was the entrance to The Dreaming. Eventually I would be able to conjure it with a simple thought, but for now I was pretty puffed up at myself for summoning it this quickly. Now to see if I really could physically enter the world.

I sat up and reached out both hands. Warmth spilled over me as my fingers slipped into the bright crevice. I pulled at the fissure, peeling it back to widen the void. I was like a butterfly, breaking through the fragile membrane of its cocoon to emerge transformed. The comparison was not lost on me. Entering into The Dreaming was a transformation as I left mortal Dawn Riley behind and became grace and power—more than mortal. I wasn't willing to think beyond that because thinking of myself as a goddess was too weird even for me.

The "door" was wide enough for my shoulders now, so

I eased through, crawling out on the other side. As I entered The Dreaming, I clothed myself in jeans and a T-shirt and ballerina flats. It was more for my own sense of coverage than anything else.

I was in the great hall of the castle. I could have put myself into my father's personal rooms, or even in the rooms set aside for me, but the hall felt more impersonal. I didn't want to let myself to be too familiar with the castle, but I didn't want to put myself outside, where the mist and the things living in it might get me.

I looked up and saw my father coming through a vaulted door at the far end of the hall. He was very lord of the manor in a crisp white shirt and pressed black pants.

"You look like an Abercrombie & Fitch ad," I told him with a reluctant smile when he was close enough to hear.

He grinned. "That's exactly what your mother said."

That killed whatever good mood I might have been nurturing. "Yeah. Is she around? I need to talk to the two of you."

The pleasure on his face was hard to ignore, but I tried. He didn't seem to notice that I wasn't exactly excited about this meeting. If I wanted a touching reunion with my mother, wouldn't I be more enthusiastic?

Morpheus didn't move. Didn't even say a word, but within a minute of my saying I wanted to talk to Mom as well, she was coming through the same door he had, looking as impressive as he had in ivory cashmere slacks and sleeveless turtleneck. I looked away from her hopeful expression. It made my eyes burn.

"You wanted to speak to us, Dawn?"

I glanced at her; it was all I could manage. "Yeah. Joy called me earlier tonight."

Morpheus turned to her. "Your daughter?"

"You don't know her." My mouth was my greatest downfall. "She doesn't know about you either."

My parents turned to face me as a unit, and I felt the combined weight of their disappointment. I sighed.

My mother lifted her chin. "How is she?"

"She's fine. Your grandchildren are good too." Burn.

"I know. Morpheus shows me their dreams."

I glanced at my father. "Aren't you just adorable." How could either of them think that a little dream-spying was good enough?

His face darkened, and he opened his mouth, but I cut him off before he could say a word. "She called to tell me that the family is bringing in a new specialist. A neurologist."

My mother didn't look worried. "They've done that before."

I didn't like her certainty. "This one isn't treating your condition like a coma. He's treating it like something you've done yourself. He says he can wake you up."

Morpheus answered that one. "They won't."

I disliked his certainty even more. "Does this even bother the two of you?"

My mother stepped forward. "Dawn . . ."

I held up my hand. "Your family misses you. They've spent thousands of dollars on doctors because they want you back, and you don't even have enough feeling to give them the consideration they deserve." My throat was tight. "They think you were taken from them. They have no idea you left on your own."

She took another step toward me, and my vision started to blur despite my anger. "Dawn, I had to think of my own happiness."

I backed away as she touched me. I didn't want her hands

on me. "What about Dad—your husband? His life is on hold while you fuck around with your lover boy here."

Morpheus straightened, shooting me a look that no doubt made most mortals tremble. "Do not talk to your mother that way."

"Back off." I glared at him. "You don't get to play daddy, not when you're the cause of all of this."

"I never meant to hurt anyone," my mother insisted, her expression strained. "There was no other way."

When I thought about how much my brother and sisters missed her, how much her grandchildren missed her . . . "You could have killed yourself." Cold, but true.

Both were staring at me as though they couldn't believe I had just said what I did. I didn't stop there. "The dead can come here, even I know that. You're just selfish."

My mother literally snapped backward. My father's face was pale, and mine had tears streaming down it. "I was an idiot to come here," I ground out. "An idiot to think I could do this. I can't stand what you've done to your children. I can't stand knowing the truth. And I can't stand the sight of you."

Morpheus found his voice. "That's enough."

I wiped my eyes with the back of my hand. "You're right, it is. I'll keep my end of the bargain and come here until Karatos is caught, but after that I'm done. I won't betray my family like she did."

And then, just like a heroine in a novel, or a movie, I turned on my heel and walked away, back to the portal to my bedroom. I never looked back.

Even though I wanted to.

I might not have looked back, but I eventually *went* back. That night, in fact. It was unavoidable. As soon as sleep took me—and I was as susceptible to it as any human, although physically traveling to The Dreaming could refresh me as sweetly as any nap—I allowed myself to drift consciously into the Realm, rather than invite my own dreams.

I needed to go someplace soothing to think. Someplace that made me feel comforted, secure, and calm. It wasn't a surprise, then, when the world around me faded, then came back, bright and vivid as the beach near my grandmother's house in rural Nova Scotia, where I had spent many summers growing up.

I sat high up on a sandstone outcropping about twenty feet up the steep bank. Trees kept a tenuous hold at the top, digging their roots deep into the rich red-brown soil to keep from toppling to the sand below. Another few years and the maples and evergreens would lose the battle and be ripped loose by erosion.

The breeze that combed through my hair was warm and salty, clean and fresh. The tide was almost fully in. It wouldn't reach the bottom of the bank as it sometimes did, leaving not even an inch of beach. I wouldn't let it come in that far.

I had great respect for this water, its moods and unpredictable nature. I'd heard the stories of people being caught out on the flats when the tide turned, of boats being stranded, children drowned. I had swum in its chilled waves, learning that an afternoon tide was the best on a hot day because the water would be warmed from rolling over the sun-warmed flats. Maybe I would stay long enough for the tide to reverse its path and go out once more. I could dig some clams and steam them on the beach over a driftwood fire.

But for now, I was content to sit on my rough perch in shorts and a halter, my feet bare as the sun warmed my skin and made the water sparkle like a bowl of crystals. Life was sweet here. Peaceful. I was small and insignificant on a mile-long stretch of empty beach. I'd never seen more than a dozen or so people on it at one time, and as a kid it had seemed my own private haven. That feeling returned now.

The sound of approaching footsteps made me look up with a sense of doom. I expected to see Morpheus or worse, my mother. Instead, I was surprised to see Verek nimbly climb up to sit beside me.

Fabulous.

He was dressed in red surfer shorts, a white tank top, and black sandals. He was tanned and gorgeous in Ray-Bans and a shark-tooth necklace.

The shark teeth were a bit much. He grinned—or maybe it was a grimace—when I told him as much, his own teeth big and blindingly white. "But I pulled them from the shark myself."

I bet he had. Poor shark.

He glanced around us, face tilted slightly toward the sun. "Nice place."

I didn't say anything. I suppose my silence was answer enough. I really didn't want to reveal myself or my feelings to a guy I was pretty sure was just a spy for my father. Plus, I didn't know if he was here to talk or to kick my ass again.

Verek wasn't daunted by my lack of conversation. "You know, Morpheus is doing all he can to find Karatos."

"Yeah?" I turned my head. "How do you know that?"

"He asked me to head the search personally."

I studied him for a minute, so gorgeous and still. He had lifted the sunglasses, so I could see his eyes, and he let me search his face for any trace of untruth for as long as I wanted.

I saw none. "So why aren't you looking?" I asked, looking away once more. I was shut up like a hermit crab in its shell.

"I found you instead."

Sighing, I wrapped my arms around my knees and rested my chin in the "V." "Are you my friend or my father's lackey?"

He didn't jump at the bait. "Neither."

"Why are you being so nice then."

His eyes narrowed as he turned his incredibly muscular body toward mine. His expression was—surprise surprise—grim. "Get something straight, Princess—this world is not nice. You're not going to meet many 'nice' people, what you're going to get are people who are either loyal to you or not. I'm loyal to the Nightmare Guild, but I'm also loyal to your father, and because of that, to you."

I swallowed. "Is that why you tried to kill me?"

"I was testing you. The Guild has to know your potential."

That sounded ominous, and I purposefully avoided asking any more questions.

After a few seconds silence, Verek spoke again, "Morpheus has taken a lot of criticism for his relationship with your mother."

"Good."

"And for you."

That softly spoken remark got my attention. I turned my head to gaze into clear eyes. I wasn't that surprised, since Karatos had insinuated as much already. "Me?"

Verek's face was impassive. "You're not stupid. I think you know why you would cause some . . . anxiety in this world."

I nodded. The whole one-of-a-kind thing was clearly the issue. "I shouldn't exist."

"But you do."

And there it was. What more could I say?

"Why do you think Morpheus has been so hesitant in presenting you at court?"

I didn't even know The Dreaming had a court. It wouldn't have been something I'd know about as a child, and I had already cut myself off when it would have become important information.

"He wants you to be comfortable as a Nightmare, in your position as his daughter, before he introduces you to the kingdom."

"And your job is to make sure I don't embarrass him or the Nightmare Guild?"

He pinned me with those scary eyes. "My job is to determine whether or not you're a danger to The Dreaming."

"And if I am?" Hadn't I just decided not to ask questions I didn't want answered?

He smiled/grimaced again, and I knew the answer without him saying a word.

Fuck.

"His enemies will use you against him," Verek informed me with absolutely no inflection. "I cannot let that happen."

Could someone overthrow Morpheus? This was his kingdom. It always had been. But if there was discontent amongst the Dreamkin, that wouldn't be good. I didn't like thinking I was a part of it. I didn't like thinking of what that might mean for me.

"What can I do?" The petulant child in me rebelled against doing anything that might help my father, but thankfully the mature side of me—the side that wasn't about to put myself in any more danger if I could help it—won out.

"Learn to be a Nightmare," Verek replied smoothly.

I arched a brow. "Why didn't I think of that?"

He smiled at my sarcasm. "You don't like my shark teeth? Then get rid of them."

I moved closer, lifting my hands to search for the clasp on his necklace. He eased out of my reach. "No. Don't remove it. Get rid of it."

I understood now. I think. "How? Just by thinking about it?"

"You can bend everything in this Realm to your will."

"Because I'm a Nightmare?"

"Because you're the daughter of Morpheus, *and* because you're a Nightmare."

Obviously I still had a lot to learn, because I wasn't sure what the difference was—unless my parentage made me even freakier.

And damn, wasn't that something I *should* know? I was so tired of being an idiot when it came to this stuff. And yet, it was as though I couldn't quite bring myself to embrace it totally, to let that freakiness inside.

I didn't want to be a freak.

I pushed that thought away as I focused my attention on Verek's necklace. "*Get rid of it,*" he had said. As I stared at the teeth, I imagined what his neck would look like without them—I pushed the thought outward, demanding that the necklace be gone.

And then it was, and there was nothing but tanned flesh where it had been.

Verek grinned. "Excellent." Then he held up his wrist where several shark-tooth bracelets had appeared. "Now, try it again. Only this time I'm going to try to fight you. Take it slow, one at a time."

I focused on the first bracelet and tried to will it away as I had the necklace. As I made the demand, I felt the answering wall of Verek's will opposing mine, pushing me back. I pushed harder. So did he.

Sweat popped along my hairline as tension crept into the muscles and tendons up the back of my neck and shoulders. I could feel the pressure in my head. My only satisfaction was seeing the strain on Verek's face as he fought me. It wasn't easy for him, and that made me want to push harder—even though I was afraid my brain might explode.

But my will wasn't in my head. My will—my personal power—was inside me. Some people called it the soul, that intangible, essential part of ourselves. Others might think of it as the id—that primitive part of each of us that is all about survival. However you wanted to think about it, it was that place deep inside my core that gave me power. Calling upon it was like locating my diaphragm or isolating my abs. First I had to find it, then I had to figure out how to work it, but when I did, I could feel the energy flooding me from the bottom of my feet on up.

And then I unleashed it at Verek.

The blow struck him hard. There was a blast of light, and I ducked, shielding myself even though the light was all my own. When I looked up, Verek was on his back on the sandstone, looking dazed.

He was also naked.

I was horrified, but that didn't stop laughter from building in my chest. Hand over my mouth, I went to him as he eased himself into a sitting position. "Are you all right?" I asked.

Unabashed by his nudity and seemingly unharmed, he blinked at me. "If you wanted me naked, all you had to do was ask."

His humor was so unexpected that I laughed, then I offered him my hand. He took it and stood. "I guess I didn't focus on the bracelet intensely enough."

"You're concentration was fine," he informed me as his clothes suddenly materialized once more. "I think what we have to do is teach you to control your power. You have a lot of it."

Despite his grim expression—which I was beginning to accept as his normal look—that simple statement gave me a grin. Better yet, it gave me hope. "Really? You think I'm powerful?"

Suddenly, he was very serious. "I think you're very powerful, Dawn. And I think that should be our little secret for the time being."

A faint hum of dread settled over my heart. "All right."

But then he smiled—and I saw what the shark had—as a new necklace and bracelets appeared on his skin. "Oh, and don't tell anyone you saw me naked."

I would have rather gouged out my own eyes than go to work the next morning. In fact, I looked as though I had tried to do just that. Stress had me bleary and red-rimmed as I slogged through paperwork and research for Dr. Canning.

I tried not to think about last night with my parents. There was nothing I could do about it. Nothing that I wanted to do about it. I wished I could talk to Noah, but he probably wouldn't want to offer a sympathetic ear. I had to admit there was part of me that wanted him to know that I had spent most of the night with another man—a gorgeous, if scary, one at that. But how sad was it that the one man I had managed to get naked was not the one I wanted to get naked with?

But regardless of that, Verek had helped me learn how to change elements of the Dream Realm, and he had helped me focus and control that power. I felt like I had accomplished something—like I just might be able to stand on my own against Karatos eventually, and I was grateful for that.

I had told him that as well, as we parted ways just before dawn. I also told him that I thought it was possible for him to be both my father's lackey and my friend. He had grinned then and given me a hug. A friendly hug. For now, friends were all we would ever be, and I'd be lying if I didn't say I resented Noah at that moment. I resented him for being the one I wanted to be more than friends with because it would be so much easier with Verek.

So I threw myself into work and tried not to give my mother, father, Verek, or Noah another thought. I was paging through an article on SUNDS and wondering just how many of these deaths had been natural and how many had been the work of a Terror like Karatos, when Dr. Canning knocked on my door. I knew it was him because he walked in before I could say a word. Guess you can afford to be rude when you run the place, but I could have been with a patient or adjusting my bra or something.

"Dawn," he said in his low, cultured tone. "A moment?"

I closed the periodical and straightened in my chair. "Of course, Dr. Canning."

He didn't sit but remained standing. I'm pretty sure he did it to intimidate me. He was good at things like that.

"Noah Clarke called me this morning. He's withdrawing from the sleep study."

My heart pinched. Crap. "Oh?"

"I thought you might know something about his reasoning."

"Why would I know that?" But I did know. He had left the study because of me, and it made me want to puke.

"I've heard talk that the two of you are . . . friendly."

Bonnie. She wouldn't have done it with the intention of causing trouble, but she had opened her mouth and speculated to the wrong person. And that person had been more than eager to blab to Dr. Canning.

"That wouldn't be very ethical of me," I reminded him uselessly. It was easier than admitting the truth. "Not to mention it could have ramifications on my own research."

"But it could explain why he withdrew." Dr. Canning watched me closely. "So he hasn't said anything to you?"

I sat back, fingers gripping the arms of my chair. "I haven't seen Noah Clarke for days." It wasn't really a lie. I hadn't seen Noah for a while, and I didn't imagine I'd ever see him again. That realization hurt.

Dr. Canning nodded slowly, as if my words had given him something to think about. "I'm concerned about you, Dawn."

"Sir?"

"Your work has shown a noticeable decline these past two weeks." He folded his arms over his chest. "Is there something you'd like to discuss?"

His mouth was saying one thing, but his body language was saying another. He didn't want to know my problems. He didn't care. All he cared about was this clinic and how he looked in the media. The police had been looking into him since Nancy Leiberman's death—nothing big, but I bet it embarrassed Canning no end. Of course they were going to investigate him. He'd gotten a lot of exposure from the SUNDS cases, and a lot of business as well. I understood why he would want to take that frustration out on someone. I just wished it was someone other than me.

"No." Even if he did care about my personal life, I wouldn't share it with him. "I've been distracted by some family issues. I won't let it interfere with work anymore."

"Your mother?" Dr. Canning asked with a frown.

So much for body language. "Yes. My family has found a specialist who thinks he can wake her up."

Canning made a scoffing sound. "Wake her up? Does he think she's merely asleep?"

"Something like that." We were not going to have this conversation. Dr. Canning was not going to mock my family, even if through association.

"Fool."

I remained silent. After a moment, Dr. Canning realized that I hadn't agreed with him and turned his attention to me. I kept my face blank.

A dull flush crept up his fair cheeks as the silence deepened. He cleared his throat. "Well, I wish your family the best, of course, and I hope that this will no longer affect your work."

I nodded. "I will do my best, Dr. Canning."

I could tell from the look on his face that he thought my best sadly lacking. I was getting so tired of this. I would give the clinic as much energy as I could. Next week the restrictions on my visa would be lifted, and I could work for whomever I wanted. The day after that became official, I was going to start looking for a new job. Maybe even before.

But first I had a Night Terror to slap around. And somehow, I had to protect Noah from that Terror, even though I was pretty sure Noah would prefer Karatos's company over mine.

"I'm such a shit." Bonnie took a sip of her Cosmo. "A big-mouthed shit."

"Bah," I voiced, plucking the cherry out of my Tom Collins. Bonnie had been done with work at the same time as I, so I'd invited her out for a drink—more to vent then to give her a hard time. She was doing a good job of that all by herself. "You're not a shit. I'm not going to argue the big-mouthed thing though."

She smiled gratefully as I grinned at her. "I really am sorry, sweetie. If I had thought that Nadine would squeal to Canning, I never would have said anything. I was just so happy for you."

Nadine was an intern working at the clinic, who I was pretty sure saw me as some kind of threat. Maybe she had a thing for Canning, or maybe she wanted my job. It didn't matter.

I took a deep drink, the tart cocktail flooding my mouth with sweet ginny goodness. "Stop apologizing. I forgave you an hour ago."

"I just can't believe that little shit tossed you aside." She drained her glass. "He seemed so yummy."

"It's not his fault. Not entirely." I was big enough to admit that after two drinks. "My mouth opened, and garbage came out."

Bonnie flagged a waitress for more drinks. "He should have jumped at the chance to have you."

"Yeah. Well, he didn't." I really wanted to be okay with

that. Noah and I didn't have a relationship. We never got that far, so why did I feel like my heart was broken?

Beneath a layer of champagne eye shadow, Bonnie's blue gaze turned sympathetic. "You like him, don't you?"

It was like being in high school again, being asked if I "liked" a guy. "Yeah," I admitted, knowing that she wouldn't repeat the shameful admission despite her earlier transgression. "I really do."

I liked Noah—a guy who didn't want me to know much of anything about him or his life. A guy who dropped out of a sleep study just to avoid me. Me=loser.

She patted my hand. "It will fade, kiddo. It always does."

Practical advice. And not the least bit romantic. I wanted to believe it even as the sappy side of my nature insisted it was impossible.

We stayed at the bar until eleven, then parted company. The buzz I'd built had started to fade, and I just wanted to go home and crash. I was starting to think about Noah again after a few hours of forgetful numbness, and I really didn't want to go down that road again.

I walked into my apartment to hear Lola screaming.

Scared sober, I quietly slipped through the apartment—almost forgetting to close the door. Instinct had my hand inside my coat, grabbing the Marae blade. If someone was attacking my roommate, they were going to be awfully surprised.

My heart was pounding as I slunk toward the door to Lola's room. It was partially open, and I peaked around the edge before slipping inside.

Lola was on the bed, thrashing. She was alone. Her limbs flailed against an invisible assailant as she cried out in her sleep. She was caught deep in the throes of a nightmare.

If I had been a fully powered Nightmare I could have

slipped inside the Dream Realm and eased her terror from there, but since I was such a newbie, waking her up in this world would be much easier.

I set the blade on the nightstand and crawled onto the bed. My alcohol-shot equilibrium was thrown even further out of whack by Lola's tacky purple satin sheets.

"Lola!" I tried to grab her shoulders, but my knees kept sliding on the slippery bedding, and Lola kept twitching. It was almost impossible to get a grip on her, but finally I did. I shook her. "Lola!"

Her eyelashes fluttered, then ripped open to reveal terror-wide eyes. It took a second for her to focus on me. "Dawn?"

I smiled. "It's me."

She threw herself on me with a grateful cry, hauling me against the generous pillow of her chest. "Oh, thank God! I had the worst dream."

She was singing my song. I sat back on the bed, breaking her hold on me. I took her hands in mine so she wouldn't feel abandoned. "Want to talk about it?"

There was no hesitation. "We were downtown at a club, you and me. And there was this gorgeous guy who wanted to dance with us."

Were she a patient, there were plenty of questions I could ask right now to ascertain the meaning of her dream, but it was more important right now for Lola to simply talk it out. "Then what?"

She pulled her hands free of mine, gathering up a pillow to hug it tightly against her. "We were dancing to Leo Sayer— 'You Make Me Feel Like Dancin'—and it was great. Then he grabbed you." Her forehead creased as she played the scene in her head. "He had you by the throat, and he was strangling you. You fought him, but it didn't seem to matter. He wouldn't let go."

I was creeped out. "Go on."

Lola's gaze met mine, and there were tears in her eyes. "He killed you. He killed you, and all I could do was stand there and watch."

I hugged her, which was awkward because she still had a death grip on the pillow. "It's all right, Lo. It was just a dream." Oh, the irony.

"He was going to kill me, too. He said you wouldn't be able to save me. He was coming for me, and you wouldn't be able to stop him."

I stiffened. Those words were a little too familiar. Dry-mouthed, I eased back so that I could look Lola in the eye. "What did he look like?"

"He was gorgeous, but he had these freaky eyes—clear blue with a black ring."

Karatos. I looked away before Lola could see the fear in my eyes.

Her voice was low, thready. "It was so real."

I just bet it was, but I couldn't tell her that. "You want to sleep with me?" I honestly couldn't think of any other way to keep her safe. If that sonovabitch hurt my friend, I'd have his balls for breakfast.

Like a kid, she nodded. "Yeah." Then she laughed. "I must seem like such a baby to you."

I kissed her forehead. "You're my roomie, and I think you're great. I gotta brush my teeth. I'll see you in my room."

Lola bounded out of bed, and I went to the bathroom and brushed my teeth and washed my face. Then I made sure all the locks were secure on our door and padded into my room. My roommate was in my bed, blankets around her ears, already sound asleep.

And she was sleeping on my side of the bed. I probably would have chuckled if I hadn't been so angry and afraid.

After changing into my boxers and tank, I crawled into bed and turned off the lamp. I lay in the darkness willing myself to sleep. I went into The Dreaming that way rather than by opening a portal. I couldn't risk Lola's waking up and seeing it. Worse, I couldn't risk her following through it, not when I knew what was on the other side.

I set myself on the beach, on a rocky shelf high above the mist that swirled and whispered my name. There, I called out to Karatos, daring him to come and face me.

And then I waited.

Chapter Fourteen

"You called, Little Light?" Karatos drifted up from the depths of the mist as though the thin tendrils knitted themselves together to give It form. It didn't look like a trick. Everything in this world was formed from the essence of the world itself, their molds created by my father.

But Karatos didn't "feel" like something of this world. It was weird, but in this world, everything had a smell . . . no, a *sense* about it. And to my senses, Karatos was more like Lola than Itself. So much so that I almost had trouble hanging on to my hate. Almost. Knowing that this bastard was hiding behind the essence It had stolen from my friend was enough to keep my rage stewing.

"I'm surprised you came," I answered, my anger and fear mixing into a shaky cocktail in my stomach.

A sardonic smile curved Its lips. Karatos was so beautiful to look at, yet so disgusting. "I come just at the thought of you, but that Lola—mm mm." It smacked Its lips. "I'm going to have to get me a piece of that."

My stomach lurched, rippling upward until I thought I might throw up. I held it together and hid my reaction from Karatos. It would get off on knowing It could generate such a response.

"Lovely," I replied as sarcastically as I could. "You have all the class and charm of a drunken frat boy."

It pressed a hand to Its chest. "You wound me." It was meant to be mocking, but I caught a thread of truth in the tone. The Terror glanced around us, at the rocky, barren ledge. "The least you could have done is conjure me up a place to sit."

"You won't be staying that long."

It shook Itself in a mock shudder. "Planning on calling your daddy?"

In retrospect, I probably should have called Morpheus the moment Karatos arrived. I planned to remedy that immediately.

But the Terror knew what my silence meant, and before I could even think my father's name, It backhanded me with enough force that my feet left the ground, and I landed several feet away. Pain shot through my face as I struggled into a sitting position, my arms trembling with adrenaline. Karatos stalked toward me like a wolf.

"Pathetic," It sneered. "You don't even know how to shake off the pain. You should be so much more of a challenge."

It was right. I should be; the little training I'd had hardly gave me the ability to fight Karatos on an equal level. Only confidence and experience could do that, and I had too little of both. Too much time in the "real" world had dulled my ability to see my own potential in this one. What the hell had I been thinking calling It to me?

So when Karatos grabbed me by the hair and pulled me to my feet, I screamed and clawed at Its fingers rather than kicking It in the balls as I should have. Rather than tearing It limb from limb as I might have, had I known myself.

"So much power," It snarled. I stumbled, hunched and crying. "You can walk in both worlds, and yet you're useless in both as well. You're no threat to any of us." It shoved me, releasing the grip on my hair as It did so, and I stumbled backward.

I pulled myself together, shook off the tears, and whirled around just in time to block another blow. Pain raced up my arm from where it had met the Terror's arm, but it was better than allowing It to knock my teeth out. Surprise made Karatos hesitate, and I used that against It. I slammed my knee into Its crotch, something I had never done to any man. It crumpled just like I'd hoped It would, and I took that opportunity to punch It as hard as I could in the face.

"Leave my friends alone." I was panting, high on adrenaline, but the words came out clear enough. "You understand me, you sonovabitch?"

Its reply was a punch in the stomach that sent me to my knees seeing stars and gasping for breath. It was followed by a kick to the head that in the real world would have broken my neck.

I was lying on my back, feeling as though I was going to vomit, when Karatos came over and lowered Itself over me, one hand braced beside my head.

"I could kill you," It murmured, running the fingers of Its free hand down my cheek. "I'm supposed to, but I like your spirit."

Supposed to? "Gee," I rasped. "Thanks."

Karatos leaned closer and ran Its tongue over my dry lips. I tried to jerk my head away, but pain exploded behind my eyelids at the movement. "It doesn't have to be this way," It told me in Its silky voice. "I don't want to hurt you."

I stared up into that beautifully creepy gaze. "I suppose you don't want to hurt Noah either?"

It smiled. It really was gorgeous, but even the smile was full of menace. "I have no intention of hurting, Noah—yet. He's very important to me."

Dread washed over me. I ignored the implied threat to Noah's safety. "Important how?"

The smile faded. "Uh-ah. You know I'm not going to tell you that."

No. That would be too easy, wouldn't it? "If he's so important, why do you keep kicking the crap out of him?"

"Sometimes you hurt the people you care most about. Your mother could tell you all about that."

Lucky I was in so much agony, otherwise the barb might have actually stung. "You don't know anything about caring. You don't know anything about me."

Karatos traced the fingers of Its free hand along my cheek. "I know I could teach you how to reach your full potential, Dawnie."

I stared at It. "Thanks, but I already have help. I'd rather you kill me."

It shrugged. "As you wish."

As he drew back, I reached into my sleeve and pulled the Marae blade free from its sheath. I didn't know how the dagger made it into The Dreaming with me. I hadn't been aware of it at all until I'd thought of how nice it would be to have it with me and noticed the straps of leather binding it to my arm. I lurched upward, ignoring the pain but blinded by it all the same, and drove the blade into Karatos's chest.

I hoped I'd hit something vital.

The Terror's screams echoed in my aching skull as I fell back upon the rock, and I smiled. I'd hit something all right.

My vision began to clear, and I saw Karatos struggling to Its feet, the dagger sticking out just below the breastbone. Damn. Its face was white as he reached for the hilt of the blade. The dagger came out with a sickening, slurping sound. Karatos lifted Its head and looked at me.

Shit. Now It was pissed off and armed.

The hand was smoking where it touched my knife. It wasn't meant to be used by anything other than a Nightmare, but that didn't mean another couldn't wield it—the dagger simply made it damn difficult for that to happen.

It was going to kill me, and suddenly I was struck by how much I did not want that to happen. I acted without thinking—something that normally doesn't work well for me—and opened my mouth. "Morpheus!" I screamed. "Morpheus!"

Karatos stopped dead, Its gaze darting around for any sign of my father. I took that moment to will the dagger back to my hand. The Terror glanced down at Its empty fingers, then to me—astonishment plain on Its features—before running into the mist. It swallowed the Terror whole as It leaped from the edge of the rock, disappearing from my sight.

Morpheus was suddenly beside me, his hands gentle as they touched me. "Dawn? Lord Zeus, are you all right?"

"No," I croaked. "No, I'm not."

He lifted me into his arms, and within the time it took me

to blink, we were in my old room at his palace. He placed me on the bed, which felt like heaven. My mother was there, too, wringing her hands.

"What happened?" Her voice shook.

"Karatos," I answered, looking at my father. "My fault. I thought I could take It. It was going to kill me."

Morpheus's expression was murderous. Thunder rolled outside and shook the very walls of the palace. Hades hath no fury like a pissed-off god.

He touched my mother's arm. "Look after her. I'll be back as soon as possible."

And then he was gone, leaving me alone with my mother, and I was too sore and tired to protest. Besides, she was crying, and I really wanted her to make everything better, even if it was only temporary.

She held my hand, and I didn't pull away. I didn't have to be a therapist to know that much of my anger fueled itself on the love I still held for her. She was my mommy, and she had left me, but I knew in that moment that she loved me. Maybe not enough, but she loved me nevertheless.

She talked me through the healing process. It wasn't something she could do herself, but she spoke to me in a soft voice, telling me to reach within myself for the ability to repair the damage Karatos had done.

Two hours later I was almost totally healed, and I had done it myself. I was feeling pretty proud of my accomplishment. Maybe I'd make a go of this Nightmare thing after all.

But then my father returned.

"The Terror is gone," he announced in a flat, black voice. "It's hiding, either by Its own means or with assistance."

Assistance. So it was true then. Morpheus had enemies

who would see him removed from his position. Enemies wouldn't mind at all if their king's freaky half-breed daughter died in the process.

"It said I was no threat to 'us,'" I heard myself admit. "It said It was supposed to kill me."

My mother's face went white as she uttered a little gasp. Morpheus, however, didn't look as surprised as I had hoped.

"Do they want to get to you?" I asked. "Or do they want me dead because I'm a half-breed?"

"Both," he replied quietly. He sat on the side of my bed and took my hand in his. His fingers were strong and warm, and I clung to them as any frightened child would, a little stunned and silent that he had confirmed my fears.

"I'm so sorry," he whispered. I saw him as a father then—a true father—and it broke my heart to see the vulnerability and fear in his pale gaze. "I've failed at protecting you."

"Teach me how to protect myself." I wanted to tell him that I was sorry, too. Sorry for turning my back on him and who I was all those years ago. If I hadn't done that, I would know how to fight Karatos. I wanted to tell him that, but pride kept me from doing it.

"I'll alert the Nightmare Guild. The violence Karatos has leveled against dreamers will be enough to move them to action."

I think seeing that uncertainty in his eyes almost drove me over the edge of what emotional control I had left. "So long as they don't know that I'm involved."

He nodded. "There are those who don't . . . approve of you being a Nightmare."

Approve was an understatement. It was a hell of a lot more than disapproval if he couldn't trust them to help me. To help him. What was all that crap Verek gave me about loyalty? I guess just because Verek was loyal to my father, I shouldn't assume that all Nightmares are.

Other than his Royal Guard, my father and I were on our own. I knew then that it didn't matter if I could heal myself in a couple of hours. Karatos had more friends in this world than I did. And if I didn't get my act together, the next time we met, the Terror was going to make good on Its promise to kill me.

The bruises I had left had faded considerably by the time I left The Dreaming. I couldn't heal nearly as quickly in the mortal world, and so I had a pale purple, green, and yellow shadow on the side of my face, high up around my cheek-bone. I wasn't sure if it was from the slap or when Karatos kicked me.

It was Saturday, so I didn't have to worry about going to work and trying to explain why I was sporting healed bruises when I hadn't had fresh ones the day before. I could spend the day on the couch, watching the *Monk* marathon on TV, but that wasn't really an option. Karatos had eluded my father and threatened to kill me. And I knew that there were other Dreamkin who wouldn't mind seeing me gone either. But more importantly, Karatos had revealed to me that all this bullshit was linked to Noah. It was Noah who was the prize, not me. That, at least, made me feel a little better. At least I knew that this whole mess wasn't about getting rid of me.

So even though I'd rather get my nipples pierced than face Noah again, I got dressed and made my way across town to his flat.

It was unseasonably warm, and I was sweating beneath my light sweater and suede coat as I rang the buzzer. The dampness between my shoulder blades itched in a spot that was impossible for me to reach, and I was grinding my back into the doorjamb when I heard a familiar voice.

"Let me guess, you're auditioning for *The Jungle Book* on Broadway."

I stopped squirming and straightened, itch barely satisfied. Warren was walking toward me with a friendly smile on his little lips. He was carrying a gym bag over one broad shoulder, his lanky frame dressed in jeans and a sweatshirt. He had an aikido class today, I remembered.

I smiled back, but the soreness in my face made it tight and uncomfortable. "Think I'd make a good Baloo? You sure know how to flatter a girl, Dr. Clarke."

His grin grew, squinting his dark eyes. "And I have the social calendar to prove it. You here to see Noah?"

"Yeah." I gestured to the door. "I guess he's not home."

Warren was close enough now to get a good look at me, and the smile melted off his face when he saw the bruising. His eyes widened in horror—and not because I looked so awful but for another reason entirely.

"Noah . . ." He swallowed and locked his gaze with mine. "Has he seen that?"

"No." I touched the darkened patch of skin with my fingertips. It wasn't even that sore anymore. "I haven't spoken to Noah since before it happened."

Warren was obviously relieved, but the doctor in him wasn't satisfied. "Do you need help, Dawn?"

I smiled. Hell, I almost laughed at the irony. Help? Shit, I needed more help than Gretzky had hockey sticks. "Not the kind you think, Warren." He didn't look convinced, so I added, "You should see the other guy." I might be bruised, but I had put a hole in Karatos, and my dagger had the blood on it to prove it.

He chuckled a little at my bad joke. "You'll have to get Noah to ramp up your lessons." Then he sobered and gestured to my face. "That won't be a regular thing, will it?"

God, I hoped not. "No, but I think I'll have to get my lessons elsewhere." He stared at me, seeing more than I wanted. Then he gave a little nod. "I have a class coming. Why don't you sit in? You can help me demonstrate some new moves to the kids."

"Thanks, but I'm hardly dressed for it."

"I have some clean sweats in the office you can borrow. They'll be big, but you'll be able to move in them."

Because he was being so generous and because I really did need all the help I could get, I said okay and followed him inside.

It was warm inside the dojo and had the slightly musty smell of a place that had been closed for a few days. I guess Noah hadn't been back after our . . . spat? fight? disagreement . . . either. I didn't want to think about that right now. Didn't want to think about Noah or his lips, his eyes, or anything else related to him. I really didn't want to think about what Karatos was going to do to him. I was going to have to warn him, however. If I couldn't do that face-to-face today, then I would have to call and leave him a message.

Hopefully he wouldn't allow his anger at me to cloud his judgment.

Once inside, Warren dug out the sweats he promised me and went to get changed himself. I changed once again in the ladies' locker room, and this time came out wearing a sweatshirt that hung past my hips and sweatpants that I had to cuff twice. Warren was six inches taller than I and a fair bit broader—a fact that made me like him all the more.

Obviously I was attracted to the wrong brother. Warren was a much better match for me—not as volatile (or at least I thought he wasn't), in the same field, and tall enough to make me feel dainty. Unfortunately, he didn't inspire the same tingly feeling that Noah did. And my heart didn't give a hard thump at the mere thought of Warren like it did whenever I thought of Noah, the big jerk.

I sat on a mat by the front wall of the studio while Warren's students trickled in, some alone and some in small groups. There were boys and girls of all shapes, sizes, and colors in the twelve to fourteen age bracket. They had acne or braces, or both, and their hormones were so fired up I felt bad for them. I remembered what it was like to be that age and feel so awkward in my own skin, to want to be seen as something different than how I saw myself.

One plump little girl stood back from the others, who were more athletic and clearly more confident. I wanted to go up to her and tell her that she was prettier than those other girls, that she'd grow up and show them all, but I couldn't promise that, and so I stayed where I was.

Warren introduced me as his friend, who was going to help him demonstrate some stances and moves. It was obvious from the response that the kids, especially the boys, thought I was his girlfriend. Not surprising then, were the glares I got from a few of the girls, who obviously had a crush on their teacher.

For the most part I just watched the kids, unless Warren needed me. I think he could have used one of the students for the demonstrations more easily than using someone as inexperienced as me, but I appreciated him wanting to make me part of the group.

Afterward, when the kids had left, Warren taught me a few new moves and worked on some that Noah had already shown me. I was sweaty, tired, and laughing at something Warren said, when the door to the dojo opened.

Noah crossed the wood floor, his boots leaving new scuff marks on the faded surface. He kept his gaze fastened on me, and I couldn't seem to tear mine off him. It was like something right out of a movie, or a book.

"I have some stuff to take care of in the office," Warren remarked suddenly, almost cautiously. "Dawn, it was good to see you again. Noah, lock up if you leave after I do."

And that was it, my champion left me to fend for myself with the wolf.

"What are you doing here?" Noah demanded as soon as we were alone. He stood directly in front of me, hands shoved in his jeans pockets, leather jacket bunched and open to reveal a faded gray Henley.

"Making a play for your brother," I replied sharply, not liking his tone. "What does it look like? Warren was teaching me more aikido."

He studied my face for a moment. I stood perfectly still while he did it. If he was looking for a lie, he wasn't going to find it.

"Warren didn't give you that bruise."

"It was a gift from Karatos. It says hi, by the way, oh, and you're the one It's coming for—after It kills me." I should have said it differently. I should have been more gentle, a little kinder, but it all poured out of me like a bucket of water kicked over onto its side.

He paled but didn't say anything, so I kept going, "That's

why I came here, just in case you're interested. Since you won't be coming back to the clinic, I had to come here."

"Dawn, I . . ."

I held up my hand. "Save it. I'm so not in the mood. You don't want my help, I get it. But you'd better get used to it. It's my job to stop this thing, and if that means walking into your dreams or showing up where you don't want me to be, then I'm going to do it—screw your personal space."

He stared at me, looking a little startled. I didn't blame him. I was starting to freak myself out, too, but I couldn't stop. "I am not going to let It use you or hurt you, so you're going to be seeing a lot of me, Noah, whether you like it or not. Until Karatos is destroyed, I'm going to be in every fucking dream you have, got it?"

I couldn't tell if he wanted to kiss me or kill me. Maybe it was a little of both, but he nodded all the same—stiff and awkward. "Got it."

"Good. Now I'm going to get back to my lesson unless you have something else you'd like to say to me."

His jaw clenched as he stared at me. "Yeah, I have something to say."

I swallowed, some of the bravado leaking out of me as his shoulders straightened. "What?"

He moved toward me, closing the distance between us with a few quick steps. And when there was nothing more than a few inches between us, his hands came down on my shoulders, warm through the damp fabric against my skin.

"I left the sleep study so I wouldn't be a 'distraction' for you anymore."

I really hate having my words thrown back at me, especially when I had been such an ass to say them.

"Noah . . ."

He pulled me closer. "I only joined the study because it was a way to see more of you."

"Oh." All the breath left my lungs.

He tilted his head, an inky black lock of hair fell over his forehead. "You scare the shit out of me. There aren't any boundaries with you, no defenses. I haven't told you half my secrets, and I feel like you know them already."

It wasn't meant to be a compliment, but it warmed my insides like one. "I'm not going to apologize—" He cut me off with a kiss so hard and fierce I couldn't breathe, couldn't think. I just grabbed the lapels of his jacket and hung on as my knees began to tremble, and my heart raced. I could feel my blood pounding through my veins, feel my nerves tingling in awareness even though only Noah's hands and lips were touching me. I could feel him everywhere.

I wanted to feel him everywhere. Who was I trying to kid? I wasn't afraid of giving him my body or my heart. I was afraid that neither would be good enough, and that was just stupid.

I kissed him back, letting him know that I wasn't about to back down from trying to get to know him better. I wasn't going to be any less scary if he continued seeing me. I liked being scary.

Noah broke the kiss. Breathing heavy, he touched his forehead to mine. "If I'm stuck with you in my dreams, then you're going to be stuck with me, Doc. You might be afraid of what's between us, but I'm not. I know you think you can do this alone, but you can't. You need me. And I need you."

It was quite possibly the most words he'd ever said to me in one go. And probably the sweetest. "Okay."

He arched a brow. "Okay?" A small smile curved his lips on one side. "That means I'm going to kiss you more. I'm going to touch you—and if I can get you into my bed, I'm going to do that as well."

Maybe I was stupid. Maybe I was desperate. But at that moment I felt a happiness that I didn't want to analyze. "I think I'd like that."

If we both survived, that was.

Chapter Fifteen

"Move the blade upward, like you're gutting a fish." As he spoke, Morpheus gestured with the blade, slicing upward in a smooth fluid motion.

"I've never gutted a fish," I replied, trying to replicate the movement. My dagger may do what I want, and always find its way back to me, but it would be that much more efficient if I knew *how* to wield it.

"Never gutted a fish?" My father's rich voice vibrated with amusement. "We will have to remedy that."

I sneaked a sideways glance. "No, I don't think so."

Chuckling, he turned toward me. "No fish then. Why don't we spar instead. I'll attack you."

Now, I had no doubt as to which of us was the superior

fighter, but that didn't stop me from asking, "With real blades? What if I hurt you?"

He looked as doubtful as I felt, the jerk. "I'll heal."

I was skeptical, but I knew I wouldn't come close to hurting him, which sucked because I would really like to have kicked his butt.

It occurred to me then, as it had occurred to me several times since deciding to embrace what I was and use it to defeat Karatos, that maybe I was being a little hard on myself. I was trying to make up for thirteen years of avoidance in a few weeks, but since the alternative was letting Karatos get away with murder—and one of his victims might be me—I didn't see that I had much choice.

"Um, what if you hurt me?" I asked. That was really the question I should be asking.

He gave me a challenging look. "I guess you're just going to have to make certain that doesn't happen. That's the point of using real blades."

Fabulous. He must have seen the look on my face because he chuckled. "You'll be fine, Dawn. I promise."

How he could keep that promise I wasn't certain, but I believed him all the same.

Grinning, Morpheus crouched a little, the posture making his midsection a more difficult target. He began to circle me. "Come on, Brat. Take your best shot."

I grinned back. "I don't respond to goading, Old Man."

"Sure you do." His grin widened. "Wimpy."

I did attack then. Not because he called me a wimp, but because it was a waste of precious time if I didn't. He dodged the lunge, but just barely, and I had to stifle the urge to congratulate myself. Almost didn't count. I was also pretty sure that the fact that I didn't want to hurt him was going to make me pull back, which wasn't doing me any favors either.

"Good," Morpheus said encouragingly. "Next time don't hesitate."

I didn't. I didn't think, didn't pause. I went for it, and was rewarded with the sickening feeling of my dagger sliding through muscle as my torso rushed up to meet his.

His eyes widened briefly, then closed tight as he shuddered against me. I drew back in horror. I had stabbed him. I had one flickering moment of victory before the awfulness of what I had done crashed down around me. His blood was on my hands—sticky and hot.

I was going to puke.

Morpheus's lashes fluttered, then a clear golden gaze met mine. "Rule number one," he rasped as his fingers closed around the hilt of the knife sticking out of his gut. "*Never* leave your weapon with the enemy."

I watched, both fascinated and repulsed—and a tad chagrined—as he pulled the blade from his body just as Karatos had done. I should have learned this lesson already.

But unlike Karatos, my father simply wiped the blade on his shirt and handed it to me hilt first. I took it with numb fingers and watched as he lifted his shirt to reveal the bloody wound beneath. It was awful-looking. So much blood.

He placed his palm over the gash in his gut. I blinked. A soft glow emanated from around his hand. Soon, the sweat disappeared from his brow, as did the furrows of pain. The lines of his face relaxed, and the blood on his skin drifted back toward where it had originated. His body was drawing it back in, repairing itself. When he finally lifted his hand, after maybe fifteen or twenty seconds, all evidence of my violence—except for the rip and blood on his shirt—was gone. He had healed a much more vicious injury in a fraction of the time it had taken me to recover from Karatos.

"That's quite the talent," I joked hoarsely. I really was going to puke.

He smiled. "Thanks. It's come in handy over the years." He gave me a strange look. "That was good. I never saw you attack."

I just stood there, dumb and heart pounding. "What?"

"You moved so fast, I never saw you coming."

It hadn't seemed that fast to me. "Huh. How about that?"

He was still watching me. "Not many in this world can move like that."

I tried to smile. "Well, at least I'm not alone." I had company in my freakiness. I was about to say as much when I caught the scent of something familiar. It wasn't so much a smell, but yet it was. It was like . . . a feeling—a deep knowledge of a presence. *Lola.* I could feel her close by, and yet it wasn't her. It wasn't vivid enough to be my roommate. Lola pulsated with light and life and joy. But this was almost as if Lola had been watered down and mixed in with a bunch of other people. This was Lola-lite, and it set off warning bells in my head, reminding me of another time I had been struck by such a feeling. I remembered what Antwoine had said about his succubus being able to hide the two of them from my father.

My head snapped up. "Karatos."

Morpheus's face tightened and paled. "Where?"

I looked around, but there was nothing. I knew he was close . . .

In the time it took to blink, my father was gone. Or rather, I was gone. Another Nightmare power that I hadn't known about and couldn't control. I had teleported myself to the source of the "Lola" feeling, and guess what? I had company.

I was standing in the middle of the dirt floor in a Roman amphitheater, complete with cheering crowd. I could smell the sweat and animals. I could feel the barely restrained aggression of the crowd, their desire for blood. And just a few feet away from me, dressed like an emperor of old, complete with gold coronet, was Karatos. He was beautiful enough that the look worked on him. He was smiling smugly at Noah, who was slapping dust off his jeans and bleeding from the mouth.

"Nice outfit," I called out, grabbing Karatos's attention.

The Terror looked up in surprise, and Noah seized the moment, delivering a vicious kick to Karatos's windpipe that send the Terror sprawling. Pivoting on his heel, Noah ran to me.

"You need to get out of here," he told me with a scowl. His hands pushed at me, trying to get me to run away.

"Don't be an idiot," I replied with a scowl of my own, pulling free of his grasp. "You aren't in control here, Noah. As much as I hate to be the one to tell you that, I'm the only one who can save your ass."

"Since Karatos is on his right now, I think I'm doing okay." Nope, he didn't like my interference much at all. I thought we were "stuck" with each other?

I pointed past him, feeling much more confident than I should. In fact, I was pretty freaking close to jubilation. I had tracked Karatos all on my own. "He's not on his ass anymore."

Noah turned his head, and we watched together as Karatos straightened his coronet and adjusted his leather breastplate. It might have been amusing if Noah's blood hadn't been dripping on my shoes.

"Dawn!" Karatos greeted me with a huge grin. "How lovely of you to join us. Did you bring that little pigsticker of yours?"

"You know it," I answered cheekily. "Did you lie to me, Karatos? You said you had no plans to hurt Noah."

An expression of sheer indignation crossed his rugged face. "Hurt him! Of course not. But you know how kids can be, Dawnie. Sometimes you've got to show 'em who's boss before they'll fall into line." He flashed a grin at Noah. "You know all about being brought into line, don't you, Noah?"

I saw something on Noah's face then that I had never seen before. It was more than embarrassment at having me witness Karatos's remark. It was shame. I wouldn't have been half so alarmed to see anger or even fear. What had happened to him?

"I'm not going to fall 'into line' for you, asshole," Noah bravely replied, his jaw tightly clenched.

Karatos gazed at him with mock sadness. "I didn't want to take you by force, boy, but you leave me little choice."

Something in his words made me shiver. Take Noah? Where was he going to take him? And for what purpose? Karatos claimed that he didn't want to hurt him, and certainly the Terror could have killed him several times over by now, so what did he want with Noah? Why did he insist on beating him down, physically and emotionally? He seemed to want Noah weakened, but not broken.

"And *you*."

My head jerked up at the force of Karatos's tone. He stalked toward me like a lion with a gladiator lunch in mind. "You are beginning to seriously piss me off, Little Light."

All my cockiness was gone in the face of his anger. Karatos might not want to kill Noah, but he'd cheerfully murder me, and do God only knew what to my corpse before sending me back to Morpheus.

"I can't let you have him, Karatos." I kept my tone calm. "You know that."

He sneered, twisting that handsome visage into something grotesque. "I might be more impressed if you truly were a full-blood Nightmare, but you're nothing more than a little girl without a mommy desperately trying to win the attention of a boy who can never love her."

"Maybe you're right," I replied, pulling my dagger from its sheath. "But I'm also the daughter of Morpheus, heir to the throne of this Realm, and you will yield to me or die."

Oh, such brave words! Karatos looked every bit as shocked by them as I was. Stranger yet was that I felt the power and truth of them rushing through my blood. I took a step toward Karatos. "In fact, why don't we call my father right now and get his opinion?"

Karatos whirled around, and I reached out to grab him, thinking he was going to escape. Instead, he lunged toward Noah—who wasn't prepared and hadn't had enough time to launch any kind of defense. I'd never seen anything move as fast as Karatos did. I was standing there, still dazed, so all I could do was watch in horror as the Terror literally shoved his hand into Noah's chest.

Light burst from around Karatos's arm, where it was buried past the wrist in Noah. Noah screamed as the Terror groped around inside him. It was the scream that finally broke through my shock and propelled me forward. I lunged at Karatos, and this time I knew how fast I moved. I was like a streak of lightning.

And I still wasn't fast enough.

I flung myself into Karatos, knocking him backward to

the dirt. With both hands wrapped around the hilt, I thrust the Morae dagger through the Terror's throat with all my strength. I felt it pierce flesh and bone, felt the blade embed itself into the ground below. I stared the Terror in the eye for a split second, taking a perverse, bloodthirsty thrill in the pain and surprise I saw there. I could hear the blood gurgling in his windpipe as I jumped to my feet.

Then I remembered my father's number one rule, and I yanked the dagger from the Terror's neck.

I ran to Noah's side, screaming for my father like a banshee on acid. Noah was shaking when I reached him. Pale and pasty, his skin was covered with a thin sheen of sweat, and there was a huge burn mark in his shirt. Beneath the smoking fabric, a four-inch circle of skin on his chest was blistered and raw.

"Don't you dare die," I told him, shaking now myself. I couldn't wait for my father to come. I could only trust that he would and that he would find Karatos bleeding to death when he did.

As carefully as I could—as I dared—I gathered Noah's upper body into my arms and closed my eyes. I pictured the one person who I knew could help him. I pictured the one place where he would be safe.

And when I opened my eyes we were in my bedroom at Morpheus's castle, and my father was waiting.

Chapter Sixteen

Morpheus fixed Noah's physical wound within minutes, but it was going to take more than a touch to fix what was going on inside Noah, I was afraid.

"I've done my part," Morpheus said softly, as we stood on the other side of the room from where Noah lay on the big canopy bed. "The rest is more your specialty, I think."

He meant my mortal-world specialty, obviously. Right now I wasn't sure I could manage even that much. I had managed to tell my father that Karatos was somehow cloaking himself, hiding behind other dreamers—like Lola—as a way of camouflage.

"Thank you for your help." It seemed trite, but it was all I could think of to say.

"I would have followed you if you hadn't hidden yourself

from me," he said softly—with just a hint of hurt and accusation. "Why did you?"

I stared at him. "I didn't." Hidden myself? Frig, I would have welcomed his help. And here I'd thought maybe he had left me on my own. I mean, there had been that brief second I had thought that it would be nice if I could handle Karatos on my own, but that didn't mean I *wanted* to.

He watched me for several seconds, his expression purposefully unreadable, and I knew that he believed me. I also knew that bothered him.

"I'm going to join the Guard in the search for Karatos." The father gave way to the Lord of Dreams as he lightly touched my arm. "You and your friend are safe here."

I thanked him again and watched as he left the room. I wasn't sure if he had to leave that way or if he chose not to teleport. There was so much I didn't know that I should, and I was angry at myself for not knowing it. If I had, Noah wouldn't have gotten hurt.

"Who was that?" Speak of the devil.

"Morpheus," I replied, walking toward the bed on knees that were still shaky. "He healed you."

Noah was a study in gold and ebony against the snowy sheets. Aside from a faint discoloration on his smooth chest, where the skin had been charred not even half an hour earlier, he looked perfectly normal. My father had even healed the cut in his lip. Only there was a strange brightness in Noah's eyes, a brightness that made me careful not to get too close.

"The God of Dreams," he muttered almost bitterly. "He wouldn't need you to save him."

"No, because that's what being the God of Dreams is all about."

He fell silent, jaw clenched so that the muscle there pulsed beneath the skin.

"Look," I said after it became clear that he was just going to lie there and seethe. "Karatos knocked the crap out of me, too, and I'm supposed to be able to beat him. The fact that you stood up to him at all is amazing."

He turned his head to look at me. He still didn't look quite right to me although I couldn't put my finger on it. "He makes me feel weak. You make me feel weak."

My temper spiked. Fuck that he had come close to dying, or that he had made my abilities sound like a good thing not too long ago—before kissing me senseless. "Yeah, well you know what you make me feel, Noah?"

He threw back the covers and jumped out of bed. Thank God Morpheus had removed his shirt, not his jeans. Still, Noah half-naked was a pretty impressive, pretty angry sight. "What?" he demanded. "What do I make you feel?"

I held my ground regardless of his approach. "You make me freaking crazy. All I've ever wanted is to help you."

"I should be able to help myself."

"And I should be able to destroy Karatos." We both knew how well that was going.

We stood there, just staring at each other for what seemed like the longest time. Instead of calming him, this standoff seemed to make Noah even more agitated.

"I don't feel like I'm in control when I'm with you," he blurted. "I want to be with you, keep you safe. No matter what I do, my trouble always seems to find you."

I couldn't have been more surprised if he'd dropped his pants and revealed a pink lace thong. "I'm sorry," was all I could think of to say.

"No you're not." And then he was kissing me, and I was kissing him back. He was right, I wasn't sorry.

Noah's mouth was the softest, firmest mouth I'd ever kissed. He tasted warm and salty, and when his tongue nudged my lips, I opened them and let him inside. His fingers bit into my arms, and I could feel a slight tremor in his body as it pressed against mine.

If this was what happened when he lost control, I was all for it.

My arms went around his neck, and he spun me around, dancing me backward until my legs hit the edge of the bed. One of his legs came up the side of mine, then he was lowering me onto the bed, his weight balanced on the knee he had pressed into the mattress. He followed me down, and it never crossed my mind to stop him. I didn't want to stop him.

For a second I thought of Karatos and what he had done to me, then it was gone. This was not the same, and I wasn't going to give the Terror any more power over me.

Noah broke the kiss to undress me, but he kept his gaze locked on mine the entire time. The look in his eyes made my skin hot and made me tingle in the most delicious places. My leather boots were the first to go. They landed on the floor behind him with a thud. Next came my socks, then my jeans, then my shirt.

Normally being naked in front of a guy scares the crap out of me, being as self-*aware* as I am. I was still in my bra and panties—new and a matched set, yayee me—and had yet to feel that niggle of embarrassment in the back of my brain. It wasn't just that I looked good in this world, it was that sudden awareness that I looked good to Noah, no matter what I thought of myself.

He slid between my legs, levering himself on his arms so that his body hovered above mine. His jeans were rough against my thigh, and as his hips pressed into mine, the ridge of his erection was so hard I thought I'd bruise from it. He moved against me, and I raised my hips to match him. I literally ached—throbbed even—he felt so good.

He kissed me again, his lips and tongue hot and demanding. When one of his hands came up to cup my breast, my hand went between us, fumbling with the button of his jeans. Why did they make these things so damn hard to undo? Finally, the button slid free, and I eased the zipper down, gasping and wriggling against him as his thumb flicked my nipple.

It had been too long since I'd had sex. And it had been longer still since I'd wanted a guy this badly. I was damp and ready and eager enough that as soon as I had him naked, he was mine, mine, mine.

Noah's mouth left mine to plant hot kisses on my jaw and my neck and finally close around my breast. Every muscle in my body tightened, and I pushed at his jeans and underwear.

"Naked," I panted. "Now."

Lifting his head, he stared down at me, eyes as black as night, cheeks flushed, lips deliciously damp. "Okay." His voice was hoarse, little more than a whisper, and if I hadn't been certain of his desire for me before this, I was now.

His body lifted from mine, and I felt the loss like a chill. I watched as he slid the remainder of his clothes down his legs. Socks and boots went as well. And then he straightened, standing before me beautiful and naked and not the least bit self-conscious.

Noah had a beautiful body. His legs were long and muscular,

like someone who biked a lot, and he had the pert little butt that only lean men seem to have. Every inch of him was golden and warm and firm—some inches firmer than others.

I licked my lips.

Smiling like a cat after a mouse, he hooked his fingers in the sides of my lacy pink panties and pulled. I lifted my hips, and the flimsy garment slid down my thighs, past my knees to the floor. I spread my legs, inviting him between.

He knelt on the carpet and held me open with his fingers and then . . . oh! His tongue made me shiver and moan, and I think I might have actually started begging. I'm not sure. But I was still gasping when he slid his body up over mine and replaced his tongue with something infinitely harder and bigger.

One thrust, and he was inside me. I barely had time to adjust, to enjoy the feeling of being so filled, before he withdrew and thrust again. I cried out and clutched at him with my legs and arms, rocking my body against his.

He braced himself on one elbow, shoving his free hand into my hair, twisting it around his fingers, tugging on my scalp. I let him pull, opening up my neck to his mouth. He ran his tongue along the sensitive skin, nipped with his teeth. I shuddered and wrapped my legs even tighter around him.

His mouth moved to my ear, sucking on the lobe as he continued to fill me with short, aggressive strokes.

"Dawn," he whispered, breath hot and moist on my skin. "*My* Dawn."

That did it. I, a woman who usually didn't orgasm without a little mechanical help, came with such force I stopped thinking—hell, I stopped breathing. My body tensed, arched, and spasmed all at the same time.

It was fantastic. And as I rode out the amazing sensations, Noah gave a little groan, and I felt his back stiffen. His fingers tightened in my hair as he buried his face in my neck. His hips stopped pumping, and I felt the warm flood of him deep inside as he eased his torso onto mine.

We stayed like that for a bit, fitted together like pieces of Lego, simply touching one another in silence. It was a strangely intimate experience, this quiet comfort between us. I smiled. He smiled and played with strands of my hair, draping them over the bed and over my shoulder. I didn't even bother to fix my bra, which was pulled down on one side, leaving me bare, the underwire digging in under my arm.

"Thank you," he murmured, his voice husky and rough.

"For what?" I was almost afraid of what he was going to say—that it might ruin the moment.

His brows knitted slightly, his expression as restrained as always. "For being you."

I had to blink back tears, and I kissed him rather than trust my voice.

That was the sweetest thing anyone had ever said to me.

I wasn't surprised to find Noah gone when I woke up. I wasn't hurt either. He would have woken up in his own bed, back inside his body. I could only hope that what had happened between us didn't seem like a dream to him. It was still wonderfully real to me.

The Dream Realm was a lot like the *Matrix*. In fact, I often wondered if the Wachowski brothers had been inspired by The Dreaming. Of course, they probably wouldn't know it even if they had been. The techno aspect was obviously different, but the similarity remained—what happened inside the Matrix was real, even if your physical body wasn't there to experience it. The Dreaming operated on the same principle. In either world, all you had was the abilities and strength your mind gave you—unless, of course, you were me and able to take your body with you.

So while Noah would wake up and only have the memory of what had happened, I woke up with the smell of him on my skin and all the physical evidence of what we had done to remind me.

I got up and showered and pulled some clothes out of the closet. When I was a kid, the dresser and closet had been filled with clothes in my size and favorite colors, and that hadn't changed. I didn't know where they came from or who was responsible for them, and I didn't ask. I didn't need more guilt where my mother and Morpheus were concerned.

Dressed in jeans, a sweater, and my own boots, I went looking for the two of them. It was 6:00 A.M. in New York, but the sun had yet to rise in The Dreaming. I wasn't sure how that worked either or why. It wasn't as though Morpheus ever slept, so the change between light and dark didn't serve as any kind of clock—not for him at any rate.

I found my parents in the study, sitting in the big leather chairs in front of the fireplace, sipping coffee and eating croissants. It was a very Continental scene.

"Did you get him?" I didn't bother with good morning. I didn't care if that seemed petulant or not. I cared about Noah and whether or not he'd be able to go to sleep at night without worrying about something trying to kill him.

Morpheus put down his coffee and rose to his feet. He was dressed very similar to me while my mother wore cream-colored slacks and a gray silk blouse. There were tension lines bracketing her mouth and around her eyes. It didn't make me happy to see the worry in her face, but I liked it all the same.

"No." He didn't mince words. "My Guard is scouring The Dreaming for him even now."

I stared at him. No, I glared. "Why can't you find him? I told you how to find him. Why can I find him, and you can't?"

If my little outburst bothered him, he hid it well. "I searched everywhere. I found your friend Lola, but she was alone. Her essence was nowhere else to be found."

This wasn't possible. "Noah!" I grasped at his name with new conviction. "Did you look for him?"

"Safe in his bed," my father replied. Then, more drily, "After leaving yours."

Now was not the time for blushing, so I swallowed the bitter mortification that threatened to turn my face beet red.

Morpheus pressed a mug of coffee into my free hand. "Drink this. It will make you feel better." I knew without trying it that it would taste exactly how I liked it. I also knew that he was right. It would make me feel better.

"I don't understand," I whispered, more to myself than the two people in the room with me.

"Obviously he was hiding behind someone else."

I peered up at my father. "No kidding."

His smile was one of sympathy. "If you think you feel foolish and helpless, imagine how I feel. I can't even protect my daughter from one of my own creatures. It's embarrassing."

"No doubt that's part of Karatos's motivation. He hates you."

Morpheus nodded. "Comes with the job."

"But you're supposed to be all-knowing here."

"Again, embarrassing. I think the Terror might have siphoned energy from some of the people he murdered and used that to cloak himself."

I was beginning to understand. It was what Antwoine had suggested. I had found him when he used energy from Lola, but if he was using the essence of his victims . . . "And you can't track dead people, only dreamers."

"That's right. You know that the dead sometimes travel through The Dreaming?"

"Yeah. I read that in the book you gave me." It made perfect sense. The Dreaming was like a rest stop for those moving on to the Shadow Lands—or Heaven and Hell, whichever you prefer. Sometimes the spirit didn't want to let go right away, and it came here, where it could still have contact with the living. A spirit could exist in this world, but couldn't affect it, and was just as much of a ghost here as in the human world.

If Karatos had indeed learned to do that . . .

"It's going to be very difficult to find him," Morpheus stated, finishing my thought. "That's why I want you and Noah to stay out of The Dreaming."

"And just how do you suggest we do that?"

He looked at me like I was a child, which I suppose to him I was. "Take pills or imbibe alcohol, whatever you humans do to escape darkening my door."

"But I want to help find him." When had I started thinking of Karatos as "he" and not "It"?

"No."

"I'm a Nightmare, it's my job."

"I said no." His voice had a weird kind of echo to it—it was his "god" voice. "And my word is final." With those words still ringing between us, a portal opened beside me, a bright sliver of light that I knew instinctively led to my apartment. I could hear Fudge meowing on the other side. My poor neglected cat.

"Go."

So I went. After all his coercing me to stay, now he was booting me out, and funnily enough, I didn't want to go. Since I didn't have a choice, I went. The portal zipped shut behind me as I stepped into the early-morning brightness of my bedroom. Fudge was on the bed, watching with big green eyes.

I scooped all eighteen-plus pounds of him into my arms and hugged him close, listening to his wheezy purr. "I'm not turning my back on what I am this time, buddy," I told him, not caring how TV-drama it sounded. "I'm a Nightmare, and it's about time my father and Karatos figured that out."

Chapter Seventeen

I was late for work. Not by a lot, but late—and you can be sure that if Dr. Canning didn't already know, it wouldn't be long before he did.

Bonnie gave me a motherly once-over when I walked in. "Sweetie, are you okay?"

I nodded. Bonnie was on my side, so I knew she wouldn't go squealing on me. "I'm fine, thanks." What else could I say? The bruise Karatos had given me had almost faded, but my makeup today was half-assed, and I looked pale and drawn. Those things, coupled with the smugness a night of great sex brings, served to make me look how I thought a crack addict must look as she chases a new high.

She didn't push it, and I was grateful. She wouldn't believe it even if I told her, and the thought of Bonnie looking at me differently made my chest tight. Bonnie wasn't the kind of person to believe in dream demons and half-goddess co-workers. At least I didn't think she was.

"The police are here again, talking to Canning," she informed me in a low voice. "If you can avoid him today, do it. If he asks, you were here on time."

I smiled my thanks and left her. Dr. Canning blamed me for all the attention the NYPD was laying on him because Nancy Leiberman had been my patient. I might be responsible for her death, since Karatos had killed her to send me a message, but Dr. Canning was the one who had smeared his face all over the news and declared himself an "expert" on SUNDS.

In my tiny office, I hung up my coat and flopped into my chair, careful not to spill my coffee. I rotated half a circle, then back again, spinning the chair back and forth as I looked at my schedule for the day. I had a couple of patients that morning—one who was part of my lucid dreamers study and another who was suffering from nightmares related to post-traumatic stress disorder. The rest of my day would be spent helping out in the sleep clinic. Great. An afternoon under Canning's watchful eye was not what I needed at that point.

I was still sipping my coffee when my first appointment arrived. Megan Murphy was a university student who had been able to control elements of her dreams since puberty. She wasn't as strong as Noah, but her abilities had been increasing as of late. I wasn't sure what that meant. Maybe nothing. She was stressing over school, and that could explain the increased dream activity.

Still, I made a note in her file to keep watch and possibly "visit" her some night when this mess with Karatos was over.

I was getting paranoid—understandably I thought—about creatures in The Dreaming messing with my dreamers.

I had fifteen minutes after Megan left, so I ran to the bathroom, then called Noah. He answered on the fifth ring, just when I was mentally composing a message for his voice mail.

"Hello?" He sounded like crap.

"It's Dawn." I twirled the phone cord around my finger. "I wanted to check in and see how you're doing. Did I wake you?"

"Yeah." His voice was dry and rough, but he sounded happy to hear my voice. "But I forgive you."

I smiled. "How are you feeling?"

"Tired. Sore." His voice dropped to a seductive timbre, "I had the best dream."

The shiver that ran down my spine was warm, spreading heat down my arms and legs—and other places. "Are you sure it was a dream?"

"Had to be. It was too good to be real."

I flushed, grinning into the phone. "You'll have to tell me all about it."

"I'd like that."

Whoa, was it getting hot in here, or was it just me? I was pretty sure it was me.

Then he yawned. "Sorry. I took some Vicodin earlier."

I wasn't offended. In fact, I was impressed that he remembered what I had told him about depressants suppressing REM. Not something you want to take on a regular basis, but for now, little white pills were the only defense—other than me—Noah had against Karatos.

"I'll let you go back to sleep." His body needed rest more than it needed to flirt with me. "I'll call you later."

" 'K. See ya, Doc."

I said good-bye and hung up. Seconds later, Bonnie buzzed and told me my next appointment was there, and so I put thoughts of Noah on hold for the next forty-five minutes. I was saving those thoughts for later, when I'd be working with Dr. Canning and in dire need of them.

My next patient was a young man, plagued by terrible nightmares about a particularly horrible incident he'd been involved in that killed several of his friends. They'd been in the wrong place at the wrong time and got caught in the middle of a gang assassination attempt. I could handle my Dream-Realm weirdness and horror pretty well, but the stuff that humans do to each other really scared me.

John, my patient, and I had met several times already. In our earlier sessions I had him describe the incident that haunted his dreams to me in several different ways. This process helped me to isolate certain parts of the incident that had affected John the most. By doing this, we could concentrate on those elements in therapy and hopefully get John back to sleeping—and functioning—in a healthy manner as soon as possible.

John's main issues were feelings of helplessness as he was unable to save many of his friends. He also had what many refer to as "survival guilt." John had escaped the shooting with a bullet in the leg—the least serious of all the injuries. He had come out of it fine, while some of his friends were dead, one was paralyzed, and another had been in the hospital for weeks, finally coming out of the coma with significant brain damage, some of which was permanent.

It was no wonder the poor guy was messed up. But I was seeing improvement. The dreams were fading in intensity, and the more we talked—the more I listened and provided nonjudgmental support—the easier it was starting to become for John to integrate the experience into his life and move on.

By the time John left, I was feeling a little drawn from the emotional work, but all in all it had been a fabulous morning. I found comfort in dealing with him and Megan. Their issues weren't related to Terrors—not the kind with physical form, not really. While there were beings in The Dreaming responsible for the images John kept seeing, they were trying to help—trying to force him—to face the bigger issue. They weren't trying to kill him.

In other words, they were the kinds of dreams I was more than prepared to help my patients face.

At lunch I had a craving for soup and a sandwich, so Bonnie and I went to this little deli just around the corner from the clinic. I ordered tomato soup and tuna salad on whole wheat—comfort food or what? Bonnie ordered a Reuben with extra slaw.

We sat at a corner table near a window, so we could watch people walk by. Unfortunately, they could watch us too.

"So," Bonnie began just after I'd taken a big bite of sandwich. "Was Noah as good as I always thought he'd be?"

I choked, of course. I think that might have been her plan. Then I took a drink of water and swallowed.

"What the hell?" I croaked. "Jeez, Bonnie! Are you trying to kill me?"

She patted me on the back, like burping a baby. "Sorry, sweetie. But that is what has you all doughy-looking today, isn't it?"

I could tell her it was bloat, but what was the point? If there was one person who would stand up and cheer for my sleeping with Noah, it was Bonnie.

"He's not my patient anymore." Bonnie might not care, but I wanted that out in the open first.

Bonnie arched a tinted, perfectly waxed brow. "You can still play doctor."

"That is so wrong!" But I laughed anyway. We both did.

"Are you happy?" she asked after taking a drink of her iced tea. "Does he make you smile?"

I shifted in my seat, a little uncomfortable with the question. I looked down at my sandwich and picked at the bread. "Yeah. I think so. It's . . . complicated." Oh God, now I sounded like something off a TV teen drama.

She smiled—sympathetically, I thought. "I'm here if you need me, kiddo."

I nodded, my throat strangely tight. "Thanks."

We finished eating and headed back to the clinic with five minutes to spare. After being late this morning I couldn't afford to take a long lunch as well, especially when I was expected to be in the lab with Dr. Canning for the rest of the afternoon.

He was civil to me when I got there, but I could tell from the look he gave me that the police visit this morning had him in a pissy mood. I hadn't needed to be any higher up his shit list, but I knew I was. He blamed me for Noah's leaving the study, and he didn't like the fact that this place wasn't my life. I suppose I couldn't blame him for either because he was right. Noah had left because of me, and ever since Karatos came to town, I had started spending more and more time embracing the part of me that wasn't human—the part that didn't pay the bills.

I was going to do whatever he told me to do, suck it up and take it—even his crappy attitude. Not for the first time,

I entertained the notion of looking for another job. It was time for me to move on. I'd gotten good experience in the clinic, but I wanted to do more counseling, more research, and less watching people sleep.

Less listening to a man who used to be my mentor and was now little more than an arrogant windbag.

Of course, my plans to behave and be the model employee were shot down by a simple phone call. I was in the middle of listening to Dr. Canning and Dr. Revello discuss a patient with severe sleep apnea when Bonnie's voice crackled over the interoffice telecom, informing me that there was a call for me on line two.

Neither of the senior doctors looked impressed when I asked them to excuse me, but they didn't say anything. I went over to the phone on the wall and punched the blinking button as I picked up the receiver.

"Dawn Riley. Someone had better be dead."

"I know you don't mean that." It was Warren, and the concern in his voice immediately turned my stomach into a churning pot of anxiety. I could think of only one reason why he would call me at work.

"Warren. Is Noah all right?" I had to keep my voice low and turn toward the wall because Dr. Canning was watching me, and I had already lied (sorta) to him about my relationship to Noah.

"I don't know," he replied honestly. "Have you been talking to him today?"

"This morning. He sounded tired, but fine."

"I'm worried about him. I think he's coming down with some kind of flu bug, but he won't go to the hospital. He's just lying on the couch doing nothing."

How was I supposed to tell him his brother was fine without him asking how I knew that? "It probably is just a bug. He was fine when I . . . spoke to him last night."

"Would you do me a favor? I'm on my way out of town. Would you check in on him for me later? I'll leave a key under the mat."

"I'm at work until five, but I can check in before I go home, sure." What did it say that I was tickled just to have an excuse to go see Noah without seeming the clinging type?

A soft sigh blew through the line into my ear. "Thank you. Give me your cell number, and I'll text you the alarm code as well."

Ah, good. I liked that he wasn't foolish enough to put a key where someone else might find it without a little added security.

I gave Warren my cell number and listened as he repeated it back to me. He thanked me again, and we hung up. Dr. Canning was still watching me.

"Is something wrong, Dawn?"

"No, sir."

"I thought perhaps there was since that sounded like a personal call."

It was none of his business. This wasn't a prison last time I checked. "You misheard, sir." I said this as coolly but professionally as I could, holding my boss's gaze.

Dr. Canning caught the slight barb and flushed. Proper thing. Maybe he wouldn't be so quick to eavesdrop next time, jerk. He cleared his throat. "Very well then."

I walked up between them, a little cocky now that I had the faint taste of victory on my tongue. "How's work on the SUNDS case coming?"

"There haven't been any more cases," Dr. Canning replied, but he didn't look at me. "The police think it may be a bacterium, or maybe a biological agent. I'm inclined to think it wasn't SUNDS at all."

That was a convenient way of putting the blame on the police and not themselves for not finding the "link" they wanted. I had told them it wasn't SUNDS, but I wasn't about to bring that up. They would only mock me or ask for my theory, and I could hardly tell them that a Terror from the Dream Realm was killing people in their sleep in order to siphon their essence to cloak himself from Morpheus. It sounded crazy even to me, and *I* knew it was true.

"That's too bad." I didn't sound all that sympathetic, and I didn't care. "The clinic could have used the publicity." I picked up my clipboard and walked away. I could feel the two of them watching me. They'd be talking about me as soon as they were sure I was out of earshot, and I just couldn't bring myself to care. People were dead. Karatos had killed them, and nothing could change that.

Not even me.

Noah's apartment was silent as I stepped inside. I punched in the alarm code and relocked the door before calling out his name. No answer.

At the top of the stairs, I slipped out of my boots and looked around. "Noah?" Still nothing. I checked the kitchen, which was empty, but there was a bowl with a spoon in the sink and half a pot of cold canned chicken soup on the stove.

The living room was also silent but had signs of life. A rumpled quilt was bunched up on the sofa, an open book spread like a butterfly facedown on the coffee table. Noah had been here, so where was he now?

I went up the stairs to the "second" floor of the apartment, which was really more of a loft. Because the space was open and airy, the rapidly sinking sun managed to peek through the many windows and cast an orange-and-golden glow over the smoothly polished floor. Two heavy square columns rose from floor to ceiling, flanking the foot of the king-size bed. The headboard sat between two partial columns built into the eastern wall. The bed was unmade, the snow-white sheets and marshmallow-plump pillows a crisp contrast to the gold-and-bronze duvet that lay half-buried beneath them and spilled onto the floor.

"Let me guess—"

I yelped at the sound of his voice, body jerking around as my heart leaped into my throat.

Noah grinned. "Warren sent you."

He stood in a doorway on the far side of the room in nothing but a pair of low-slung jeans with a towel slung around his neck. His tanned skin was flushed from the shower, and his inky hair was damp, sticking up in thick spikes around his head.

I pressed my palm against my chest. My heart was trying to squeeze through my ribs. "He was worried. Did you tell him you were sick?" And damn he looked good. I could have started at his toes and licked my way up.

Noah held the ends of the towel around his neck as he approached me, a faint smile curving his lips. He looked a little drawn, but I'd seen him look worse after an all-night painting session.

"It was either that or tell him that I was attacked by one

dream thing, healed by another, then spent the remainder of the night having a really good Nightmare."

I grinned—and even blushed a little—at the double entendre. "How good?" Ego, it was a horrible thing.

He chuckled and tossed the towel on a chair just a few feet away before stopping right in front of me. He smelled warm and clean, and I wanted to bury my face in the hollow where his neck met his shoulder and just take one deep breath.

His eyes did that glow thing that made me all warm and mushy inside. "Very good," he murmured, slipping a hand behind my head. Then he pulled me close and kissed me, and my stomach flip-flopped in response.

I wrapped my arms around his waist and pulled him close, so that we were pressed together from knee to chest. Both of his hands held my head now, in that gentle but firm way that kept me from pulling away—as if I would.

He tasted like vanilla-mint toothpaste, his mouth hot, wet, and sweet as our tongues moved together. I slid my hand down the small of his back to cup one firm, round butt cheek. He had such a great ass.

My stomach growled. Probably I should have been mortified, but I wasn't. I started laughing instead. Noah did, too. We laughed with our mouths still touching. Leave it to me to ruin the moment with a need to feed.

Noah grinned as he lifted his head from mine. "I was just about to order in. You like Vietnamese?"

I do, and I told him that. He made the call, pulled on a T-shirt, and we went to the kitchen, where he took down some wineglasses and poured us each a glass while we waited for the food.

"Wine on an empty stomach," I mused, swirling the dark

red liquor around the bowl of my glass. Usually I didn't like red, but this was good. "You're not going to get me drunk and take advantage of me, are you?"

A lopsided grin crossed his face as he hooked a finger in the waist of my pants and pulled me closer. "Do you need to be drunk first?"

I couldn't even fake chagrin. I just laughed and kissed him.

We took our wine to the living room and sat on the couch. I'd only taken two more swallows before we were kissing again, and Noah had me pinned beneath him on the over-stuffed cushions. We ground against each other, necking and panting and groping like teenagers.

I was so glad Warren had asked me to go over and check on Noah!

I was two humps short of an orgasm when the buzzer went off. I hadn't been so horny since high school. Noah lifted himself off me with a rueful grin.

"Don't look so disappointed," he told me with a kiss on the nose. "You're not the one who has to answer the door with a hard-on."

A hard-on that was all because of me, thank you. The silly thought occurred to me as he padded down the stairs, hunched like an old man. I smiled at the sight of him. I was feeling pretty giddy—pretty high on womanly sexual power. I wonder how many men realized that we got off on arousing them just as much as they seemed to like turning us on? I know there are a lot of men out there only concerned about their own pleasure, just as there women like that, too, but Noah and I obviously weren't amongst them.

Oh, I was in such danger where he was concerned. I had

to slow down, or I'd be in love before I knew what hit me. If I wasn't in love already.

That was a sobering thought. I polished off the rest of my wine in an attempt to forget it. When he came back upstairs, Noah took one look at my empty glass and shook his head in amusement. He brought the bottle in, and we sat on the couch, each with our own carton of noodles, chicken, and vegetables. We split the order of crispy spring rolls, and I was tickled to learn that Noah didn't like fish sauce either. We used a mix of hoisin and hot sauce as dip. We listened to music and talked as we ate.

We finished dinner and the wine while snuggled on the couch watching TV. You would think I would be satisfied with that, but I wasn't. I didn't like not being satisfied either. Everything was great—better than I even dreamed it could be. I was comfortable enough with Noah to be confident, but just on edge enough to enjoy the sexual tension. The problem, though, wasn't with us. It was with Noah.

I couldn't put my finger on it, but something wasn't right with him. It was like something was missing. Maybe it was my paranoia, or maybe some kind of residual hangover from the injury he'd received from Karatos, but there was something. Both Verek and my father said they couldn't find anything wrong with Noah, but had they looked past the physical? What if Karatos had done something to him?

I knew I should just be glad that Noah was safe, but I wasn't. Karatos wanted him for something and until I found out what it was, I wasn't going to be content. Since I'd been banned from The Dreaming, I wasn't certain I would even be allowed entry if I tried to get in that night. No doubt Morpheus had created my own personal detention room. But there was one person I could contact. Antwoine. If anyone on this plane could figure out what Karatos was up to, it was he.

Around ten o'clock I decided that as great as the evening had been, it had to come to an end.

"I'm going to head home," I told Noah as I rose from the couch. On the TV, the end credits rolled for the show we had been watching in between bouts of making out.

He stood too, hands in his pockets in a posture that struck me as vulnerable. "Stay."

He hadn't said please, but it was in his tone. I didn't have to ask why he wanted me to stay either. It would be easy to assume that he didn't want to be alone, but that wasn't his personality. In fact, if I didn't stay, he'd probably go to bed and walk boldly into The Dreaming, daring Karatos to come get him. His determination not to let fear rule him, not to be a victim, was going to make him just that one of these days—if it hadn't already.

No, Noah wanted me to stay because he wanted me in his bed. And I wanted to stay for that same reason.

"I don't have any clothes." It wasn't meant to be a protest, just a simple fact.

His mouth took a sexy curve. "You don't need them."

Ohh, spoken just like one of those romance heroes I love so much. If I didn't make light of the situation, I'd be quivering all over the place. "You don't mind if I wash my underwear in your sink?"

He closed the distance between us, hands still in his pockets, his black gaze locked on mine. "As long as they're off, I don't care what you do with them."

"Oh my God." Yup, couldn't help it. I said the words out loud.

Smiling, he pulled one hand out of his pocket and wrapped it around one of mine. He paused long enough to press the OFF button on the TV remote, then led me through the living room, now lit by nothing more than the lights of the city outside. I followed him up the stairs to his bedroom, my knees trembling ever so slightly.

Why was I so nervous? We'd had sex last night, sure, but this was the first time with Noah in this world.

"Condoms?" I asked when we were standing beside the bed. This world had consequences that didn't exist in The Dreaming.

His fingers busied themselves with the buttons on my shirt. "Taken care of."

I raised a brow. "Were you hoping for this, or are you just a whore?"

Laughter brightened his face as he peeled my shirt down my shoulders. "Hopeful." His hands settled on my rib cage, and I fought the urge to suck my gut in. "Doc, you're the first woman I've been with in a long time."

"Oh. Wow." I guess I didn't need to wonder what he thought of me, did I? I was just going to enjoy that new revelation. Enjoy it for a while.

But if Noah was out of practice, he hid it well. I orgasmed twice before he even slipped inside me, his mouth and fingers having already turned me into Jell-O. I was on my stomach with him on top of me, moving with slow, deep thrusts, one of his hands beneath us as he stroked between my thighs. Number three had me practically drooling into the pillow. By four I was boneless and mindless, which I guess was his intent, because after that he quickened his pace until his fingers bit into my hip, and he stiffened, groaning as he slumped on top of me.

Neither of us moved for a while. We lay together like spoons in a drawer, still joined as the sweat dried and our heart rates slowed. Eventually, Noah got up, but he was back in a few minutes, tucked against me as sleep tugged at the edges of my mind.

I wasn't going to try to have a conversation with Antwoine tonight. I'd "call" him and arrange to meet him tomorrow. Probably he'd tell me I was just paranoid. There wasn't anything wrong with Noah. Nothing at all.

He kissed my shoulder. "I'm glad you stayed." The whisper was warm against my bare skin.

Tears teased the back of my eyes with a rush of unexpected heat. I turned in his arms so I could kiss him, wrap myself around him, and hold him tight. At that moment, I never wanted to let him go. "So am I."

And then he kissed my forehead and hugged me close. For someone who knew just what a freak I was, Noah had a way of making me feel completely wonderful. That was something worth fighting for. And I was going to fight as hard as I could.

Chapter Eighteen

Were I a normal person, I might have thought I was dreaming, waking up next to Noah the next morning. But I wasn't normal, and my dreams of late had been far too real.

He was propped up on his elbow, watching me. His hair was a mess and his eyelashes were at half-mast, heavy with sleep that refused to let him go just yet. He looked warm and sexy and far too yummy for first thing in the morning.

"Stare much?" I asked groggily, as he popped two white tablets in his mouth.

"I like watching you." He smiled and held out a little plastic container. "Tic Tac?"

I laughed. "Slayer of Morning Breath. Yes, please." I took two and gave the mints back. "What time is it?"

He twisted, glancing over his shoulder at the clock on the

bedside table. "Eight twenty-five," he replied as he came back to face me. His fingers found my shoulder and stroked my bare skin. "Do you have to work?"

I shook my head. "I'm calling in sick. I have some things I need to do today." I wasn't going to play hooky with Noah, no matter how lovely it was to wake up next to him. Canning wouldn't like it, and I was playing a prickly game with my job, but if I didn't do this, more people might die—and that was way more important than Dr. Canning and his disapproval.

All good humor drained from his face. "Nightmare things?"

"Yeah. I'm going to Central Park to meet a man who might be able to help us figure out what Karatos wants with you."

"Someone from this world?" He was surprised and rightfully so. "Who?"

"Antwoine," I replied, not bothering with his last name. "He's been asking questions for me."

His head tilted, dark eyes narrow. His expression was shrewd, almost angry—and it didn't look right on his face. "Asking questions of who?"

"I don't know." Probably I should ask, but I had enough on my plate right now without opening another can of worms.

Now he looked vaguely amused. What the hell was going through his head? "And you trust him?"

I didn't have to think about it. "Yeah. I do." Antwoine might have good reason to hate my father, but he didn't hate me.

Noah stared at me, a smile tugging at his lips. He looked more like himself, and I relaxed a little. "And I thought I gave abrupt and cryptic answers."

I chuckled and took his free hand in mind. "You trust me?"

His smile grew. "Yep."

"I'll fill you in on everything I find out later, okay?"

He nodded. I knew this was hard for him, given his control issues, but he was doing really well. Hopefully, we'd be rid of Karatos soon. His shadow was too big, looming over my relationship with Noah. I wanted us to have something normal—or as normal as possible.

For a second, I almost wished Karatos would stick around a little longer, so Noah and I could have the time together. Would the attraction between us be enough after the Terror was gone?

Noah was still watching me with soft, dark eyes, that tiny smile flitting around his lips. "I love you," he said.

My heart lurched—and not because I thought he meant it. My hand twitched, but before I could do anything, it was pinned to the bed, and Noah hovered over me, his fingers wrapped around both my arms with strength far beyond human.

"Don't you go trying to summon that pigsticker of yours, Little Light," he murmured, voice dark with amusement as his eyes faded to pale blue. Only dark rims remained. Dark, spidery rims. Those eyes were horrible in Noah's face.

I should have known it was a dream. I should have known it was Karatos trying to get information out of me, fucking with my head.

But I hadn't, not right away, because he had felt like Noah, smelled like Noah. Was he that good at fooling me, or had he siphoned some of Noah's energy as well?

"Get off me," I said.

"Oh, come on." The lopsided smile grew into something oily and coy. "It was so good last time. Think of what it could be like—my finesse in Noah's package."

"I said, get off me."

"What are you going to do, call your daddy?"

I could, but Karatos would be gone before I could blink, and cloaked as he was, there was no way my father could find him. I should have taken a pill last night. Then I realized that Noah hadn't either.

Oh God, what if Karatos had gotten to Noah again?

It was almost as if he read my thoughts. "Don't fret, Dawnie. Noah's safe. For now."

For now. "I said, get off me." I didn't struggle. That would be like writhing beneath him, and Karatos would like that far too much. "Now."

Lips widened, the grin growing until it took up more than half of Noah's face. Disturbing didn't begin to describe it, but I didn't flinch, didn't look away. "Or what?"

I met his gaze and held it, feeling a little smug despite being naked and vulnerable. "This."

I did what I had done to Verek when I wanted his necklace gone—only this time I wanted Karatos off me. I reached down inside myself, found that will, and pulled it up—hard. It wouldn't have worked had the Terror been expecting me to put up such a defense. But Karatos wasn't expecting it.

The look on his face as his fingers loosened on my arms was magical—the expression that followed as he was yanked off me, downright priceless. The power inside me grew, spreading warmth from the top of my head to the tips of my toes. I had to let it out, or I would explode.

I let it go. I took a moment—and just one—to enjoy the Terror's shock as he flew up into the air, across the room, and hit the wall with a loud thud. He slid to the floor in a crumpled heap.

I didn't wait for him to recover. Once he recovered, he'd

be angry and attack—and I wasn't prepared for that. I needed to check on Noah. I needed to meet with Antwoine. I needed to get prepared.

I woke up.

Noah—the real Noah—sat on the side of the bed. He was dressed in nothing but a towel, his skin humid, hair damp from the shower. He was freshly shaved, scrubbed and smelling of cloves and vanilla. If I wasn't still shaky from Karatos, I'd be on him like butter on warm bread.

"You all right?" he asked, watching me carefully—tenderly.

I nodded. My throat was tight, my stomach rolled, and I wanted to cry, but I nodded. "Bad dream."

His expression didn't change, but there was a flicker of something dark in the depths of his eyes. I wasn't fooling him—not much. "Want to talk about it?"

"No." I almost laughed—hysterically—at the suggestion. "Not now." No way in hell was I going to tell him that Karatos had stolen part of him, or that the Terror had entered my dream pretending to be him.

Shit. I had told Karatos about Antwoine. Even more reason to go looking for the old man.

Some of the gentleness in Noah's eyes was replaced with wariness. He knew I was keeping stuff from him. "I'm not fragile, Dawn. You don't have to shut me out."

"I'm not." Could I feel any guiltier? "What about you, did you sleep okay?"

He stared at me for a moment, letting the silence stretch between us to the point where it was almost uncomfortable. "Yeah. Was it Karatos?"

I was going to have to tell him something just to get rid of this tension between us, but there was no way I could explain what the Terror had done without freaking him out.

I wasn't prepared to answer what questions he might have, so as far as I was concerned, I wasn't saying anything I didn't have to. I nodded. "He was just talking crap. He didn't visit you?"

"Must've thought he'd give me a break this time." He managed to sound amused and bitter at the same time.

"No doubt," I replied. But Karatos had merely wanted to freak me out—and show off what he could do. It had nothing to do with Noah and everything to do with gaining power over me. Again, I wasn't going to share that.

His hand settled over my thigh, his fingers warm through the sheet that covered me. For a second all I could think of was Karatos's touch, and I had to force myself not to flinch. I was not going to let that sonuvabitch ruin what I might have with Noah. I put my hand over his and squeezed. Take that, Karatos.

I saw the worry in his face—and the fear. "He didn't hurt me." Not much anyway. Not compared to what I had done to him—that made me smile.

Noah smiled as well. It was half-assed, but at least it was warm and genuine. "I'm glad. Get up. I'll make breakfast."

Noah had put my clothes from yesterday in the washer earlier, so while they dried, I took a shower. Then he started breakfast while I called Bonnie and told her I wouldn't be in today. I said I had a headache and a fever and that I was worried I had that bug that was going around. I hadn't been scheduled to see any patients as it was a clinic day, so nothing had to be rearranged because of my absence. I didn't like lying to Bonnie, but I liked knowing I wouldn't have to deal with Dr. Canning for the rest of the day.

Bonnie told me she hoped I felt better tomorrow, and I assured her I would. Then she told me to say hi to Noah for her. I muttered something in shamefaced response and hung up. I joined Noah in the kitchen. We worked side by side making bacon and eggs, toast and hash browns in his huge kitchen. He even made fresh orange juice and ground the beans for coffee.

"Tell me you don't eat like this all the time," I remarked, as we sat down at the island in the center of the kitchen, our plates loaded with food.

"Only after sex," he replied, shaking the ketchup bottle. "So a coupla times a week, yeah."

I stared at him, fork frozen halfway to my mouth. His face was blank, but there was the tiniest sparkle in his eye. "You're lying."

He snorted. "Yeah."

But I couldn't just let a sleeping bear lie. I speared some hash browns with my fork. "How long has it been since you had sex?"

He checked his watch. "Eight hours."

"Before me," I amended, letting my exasperation show.

"Why?" He poured ketchup on his hash browns.

"Because I'd like to know."

Flipping the top closed on the bottle, he set it in front of me. He looked amused—annoyingly so. "No, you don't."

"That's a little presumptuous."

"Women never want to know." He licked a drop of ketchup from his thumb. "You say you do, but you don't. Men never want to know either."

"You're either very enlightened, or you had sex with someone two hours before I got here and don't want to tell me."

He laughed then. Not a chuckle, but a full-on bark of laughter. "You're so suspicious."

I shrugged. "Well?"

He folded his forearms on the edge of the table and leaned toward me. "There's a difference between sleeping with someone and getting laid. You're the first woman I've slept with since my divorce."

Oh. The sharp, sweet heat of pleasure blossomed in my chest. His explanation should have been good enough. "What's the difference?"

Sighing, he plucked a piece of bacon off my plate and held it out to me. I took it. "The difference is that we're having breakfast."

I smiled as I reached for the ketchup. In fact, I was probably grinning like an idiot, but I didn't care. "I like breakfast."

Noah glanced down at his plate for a moment before lifting his gaze to mine. I liked what I saw there in the tar black depths of his eyes. He seemed a little less composed than he had a few minutes ago, and it warmed me. "Me too."

I left after my clothes were dry, showered and belly disgustingly full. Noah walked me to the door and kissed me good-bye. He was going to paint for a bit before meeting his mother for coffee that afternoon. I walked down the street feeling lighter than I had in weeks, and I only looked back once.

Noah was still standing at the door. He waved and I waved back, grinning like the idiot I am.

By the time I reached my own apartment, a lot of the glow had worn off, and I was back to thinking about Karatos and what the hell to do about him. Noah and I would never have a normal relationship until the Terror was gone, and so that had to become my top goal in life. Not just for my own sake but because lives depended on it.

I checked my voice mail—nothing. I wondered if my family had set a date with the specialist yet. Would anyone tell me when they did? Maybe I was better off not knowing. Then I wouldn't have to decide how to act or feel like a traitor to one side or the other.

I called the number Antwoine had given me. He answered on the third ring, and from the sound of it was in line at the grocery store. He told me he could meet me in a couple of hours, and I hung up to get ready.

I changed my clothes and put on a bit of a face. Oddly enough, I hadn't minded that Noah had seen me without makeup. I was more upset about having gone to bed without washing my face first. I never did that—it was bad for the skin. I called and made an appointment for a facial to make up for it.

Antwoine and I were going to meet at a Starbucks on Fifth, so I had an hour before I needed to go. I thought about Karatos, of course, and Verek and my father and Noah. All of them seemed to think I had this great potential, but I had yet to truly tap it. Surely what I had done to Karatos that morning was an improvement? But there were so many things I should be able to do and nothing to tell me how to learn those powers. Supposedly I'd been born with them, but I didn't know how to call them forth.

I needed a mentor. I needed to find an older, more experienced Nightmare who would help me unlock my potential. Did they have a Big Brothers, Big Sisters for Nightmares? My father had helped me a fair bit, but he was king and not exactly impartial. My best bet was probably Verek, who would teach me out of loyalty to my father, and therefore to me.

Finally, it was time to leave. I pulled on black leather boots and a matching coat. The black went well with the cranberry chenille turtleneck sweater and jeans I was wearing. I slung a black leather messenger bag over my shoulder to complete the look and off I went. It wasn't very PETA-friendly of me to be wearing so much animal hide, I know, but I liked the feel and durability of leather, and since I ate cow, I saw no problem in wearing it as well.

It was cool, but not too crisp, so I walked the few blocks to Fifth and up another couple to the Starbucks where Antwoine and I had agreed to meet. It was warmer than Central Park, and I could make sure Antwoine had something to eat while we were there. I wasn't sure if he worked, or if he even had a place to live, and I cared enough to want to help him if I could.

Antwoine was waiting for me, wearing that same old reddish leather jacket with a dark brown sweater and old cords. He looked like he'd had a haircut and he smiled when he saw me. I smiled back, genuinely happy to see this strange little man who knew what I was and was okay with it.

I needn't have worried about Antwoine's financial situation. When it came time to pay for our coffee and treats, he whipped out a wallet fat with cash and plastic and paid for mine as well. I managed to mumble a thanks. You would think someone with my amount of education in the study of people wouldn't fall victim to assumptions, but I had and I felt stupid for it.

"What is it you do, Antwoine?" I asked when we sat down.

"I'm retired," he informed me. "Won the New York State Lotto a few years back." The look on my face must have been something, because he started laughing when he looked at me. Then he shook his head and took a drink of his coffee.

"You didn't call me here to discuss my financials, did you, girl?"

Somehow, I found what sense I had left, and my voice. "No. I wanted to ask you a question, but I have to tell you something first."

He broke a piece off the top of a bran muffin and popped it in his mouth. "I got a question for you, too. Did you find Madrene?"

His succubus. God, I had totally dropped the ball on that. Still, I had a good excuse for letting it slip my mind. "No. I'm sorry Antwoine. With all that's been going on—"

He held up a hand. "Don't apologize. I just had to ask."

"I'll find her, I promise."

He nodded, taking me at my word, and I planned to keep it. "Now, what did you want to tell me?"

This was hard. I felt like an idiot, like I had let him down. "I think you might be in danger."

He didn't even blink. "Nothing new there, girl."

Just who did this guy associate with? "From the Terror. He visited me last night disguised as Noah and asked me questions. I told him your name before I realized it was Karatos."

Antwoine frowned. "He came to you in a dream as your young man?"

"Yeah, the bastard. I almost believed it."

"The Terror must've taken some of Noah's energy."

"That's what I figured. He did the same thing to my roommate, but he didn't pretend to be her."

"Unless she knows what you are, there'd be no point for

the Terror to do that." Antwoine was still frowning as he
took a drink of his coffee. "Don't you worry about me. That
thing can't touch me where I am. Nothing can."

That was a huge relief. "Oh, thank God."

He flashed me a grandfatherly smile. "You take too much
responsibility upon yourself, child. Now, you had a question
for me?"

"Karatos's fascination with Noah. Why would a Terror
routinely stalk a lucid dreamer?" I swallowed. "Why not just
kill him like he did the others." Except for Lola, of course.

Maybe he's coming back for her, a voice in my head whispered. I tried to ignore it.

Antwoine took another nibble of muffin. "A Terror could
feed off one of them for a long time."

"Karatos says he doesn't want to hurt this dreamer. Says
he has *plans* for him."

Antwoine's leathery brow wrinkled. "Plans?"

"Yeah. Any idea what those plans might be?"

Shifting in his chair, Antwoine sat up ramrod straight.
"You say this Terror's been killing other dreamers?"

I nodded. "Not all of them have been lucid dreamers, but
many seem to have been strong dreamers or plagued by terrible dreams."

"Of course he would be drawn to those with a predisposi-
tion toward horror. But he hasn't killed everyone he has
come in contact with?"

I thought of Lola again. "No, thank God."

He thought for a moment. "And he keeps coming back to
this one dreamer."

It wasn't a question, but I responded anyway. "Yes."

"A strong lucid dreamer."

"Very strong."

"Who he has had plenty of opportunity to kill but doesn't."

"It's like Karatos is trying to see how far he can push Noah before he breaks him." The implication of the words sank in seconds after they left my mouth, leaving me with an awful shaky feeling in my gut.

Antwoine rubbed a hand over his face. The second knuckles on his fingers were large and a little crooked with arthritis. "I think the Terror is trying your friend on for size."

I didn't get it. "Trying him on?"

He leaned forward on his elbows, moving in close so he could whisper to me. "He's trying to cross over into this world."

I shook my head. "That's impossible. Dreamkin, especially Epiales, can't survive in this world."

"They can if they find a dreamer powerful enough to bring them in. A good host, and they're all set."

"Like demonic possession?"

He snapped his fingers. "Exactly. This thing has been stealing the essence of his victims. Probably he's been doing it for a long, long time, building up that human feel. Once he's built up enough power, worn a human disguise long enough, he's going to climb inside your friend and cross over into this world."

I couldn't believe what I was hearing, but the horror of it cut through me, leaving behind nothing but numbness. I couldn't let Karatos take Noah.

Oh my God. What if he had taken him already? What if that was the difference I saw in him?

I was going to be sick.

My chai tea was thrust into my hand. "Take a drink. Now."

I did as I was told, and it helped a bit. "How would I know if this had already happened?"

Antwoine picked at his bran muffin again. "A newly hatched Terror would be just twitchin' to get out and cause some damage. If your friend seems manic, aggressive—like everything is new and fascinating, then I'd worry."

Relief washed over me like a bucket of warm water over my head. Noah was none of those things. Not yet.

"Don't going sighing on me just yet, missy." He took a drink of coffee. "If this thing crosses over, he's gonna make Jack the Ripper look like Prince Charming. You need to keep your friend out of The Dreaming. He can't cross over without a body. He can't survive here without a body."

I nodded. "I'll make sure Noah stays safe."

"Your friend's not the only person you need to worry about." At my puzzled gaze, he continued, his expression both grim and worried. "If that Terror crosses over, who do you think his first victim is going to be?"

Chapter Nineteen

At the end of the day, what it came down to was that I was a big fat chicken shit.

I left Antwoine outside of Starbucks. He must have seen how messed-up I was because the poor guy hugged me before I stumbled off like the zombie I was. I needed to walk for a bit. I needed to work off this trembling, impotent anger before I exploded.

I kept my head down, my hands shoved in the pockets of my coat. My gaze was fixed on the sidewalk ahead of me, and I shifted and veered according to the crowd around me, but I kept walking.

Karatos. He had forced me back into The Dreaming. He had toyed with my dreams and me. He might not have hurt me, but he had raped me all the same. Hurting me came later—physical hurt, I mean. He had killed Nancy Leiberman. He'd taunted Lola. He had treated Noah like a cat toy, and wanted to use him as a puppet. The Terror had fucked my life and the people I cared about for the *last* time.

Heat ran through my veins, burning just beneath my skin until I felt like a kettle about to boil. When I was a kid I used to pretend I was one of the X-Men—Storm or Phoenix. I'd point my fingers at something and pretend I was zapping it with lightning or lifting it with telekinesis. I felt like doing that now, but I had the weirdest feeling that if I did, something really would happen.

Someone bumped into me, knocking me backward as he slammed into my shoulder. "Watch it," he barked.

At that moment, I wanted to take this stranger's head off. Slowly, I looked up, meeting the guy's snarly gaze. His features slackened, the belligerent light in his eyes fading to something disconcerted, uncertain. Afraid? "Sorry," he muttered, and shouldered his way through oncoming pedestrians like the cops were after him.

Frowning, I glanced at myself in the window of the building right beside me. What the hell?

My heart was pounding as I ducked around the corner onto a side street with less traffic. I put my back against the cold stone and swung my backpack off my shoulders. Inside I had a compact and I grabbed it, opening it so I could look at myself in the mirror.

Holy Shit. Some of the color was coming back, but there was no mistaking what had freaked the guy out.

My eyes were so pale they were almost colorless. As I watched, the blue started filling in once more, but those awful spidery black rims were slower to fade. As the anger in me gave way to awe and yes, fear, my eyes slowly morphed back into their normal appearance.

It wasn't so odd for my eyes to change. Many Dreamkin had pale eyes with dark rims. Karatos did, and sometimes my father as well. They were more light-sensitive, making it easier to peer into the darkness of dreams. No, it wasn't strange to have that kind of eyes in The Dreaming.

What was weird is that I shouldn't have them here. Human eyes didn't just switch color like that, not so completely.

The change in my eyes had corresponded with a feeling of great power and I was glad I hadn't given in to the urge to release what I had felt. I didn't know what it meant, but I knew I was going to keep my mouth shut about it for the time being.

Whatever it was that had just happened to me, it wasn't good.

I was at home, on the sofa with Fudge, trying to distract myself with television, when Noah called.

"Come for dinner." It was a command, he expected no refusal on my part.

I stared at the phone. Was this the beginning of aggressive behavior? Had Karatos already taken him over like I feared? No. If Karatos had taken Noah, I'd know.

I'd be dead by now. Karatos would have played with me for a bit, but he wouldn't have been able to contain himself for long.

"What are you having?" I asked, smiling in relief.

"Indian."

"My favorite. Where are you ordering from?"

There was a chuckle on the other end. "I'm making it."

My heart flip-flopped as my mouth began to water. A man who could cook. And not only cook, but cook Indian?

"What time do you want me?" I asked, flirting shamelessly.

"Hmm, trick question." His voice had dropped considerably, to a low, sexy growl. "What time would you like to come?"

Shivers. Big, delicious shivers running down my spine. Tightening in places already tight and oh, there was throbbing. "I have to get a bath and change . . ."

"You could take a bath here." More of that sexy voice.

He had to know I would think of him in the tub with me. He had to. Noah, wet and slippery. I closed my eyes. "Don't tempt me." I couldn't take a bath at his place. I needed to soak a little of the day out of me before I went to see him.

"Come over whenever you're ready." I could hear the smile in his voice. "I'll be here."

"Okay. I'll see you in a bit."

I was just about to hang up when he stopped me. "Dawn?"

"Yeah?"

"Bring an overnight bag." Then he hung up.

I stood there, phone in hand, slightly dazed and shaky. This was going so fast. Too fast maybe. But I had no intention of slowing it down. I don't think Noah did either.

I ran a bath and soaked for as long as my hormones would let me. I'm not ashamed to admit that I wanted to get to Noah's in the worst way. I wanted to see him, touch him, taste him. As long as I was with him, I knew he was safe. I felt safe.

So I rubbed myself down with a sugar scrub that smelled like coconuts, made sure I hadn't missed any spots shaving my legs or armpits, and took a brand-new pumice to my feet.

Then I dried off and lathered my still-damp skin with a moisturizer that matched the scrub. I fixed my makeup and got dressed in stretch jeans and a teal blue sweater that really brought out my eyes—which had fully returned to their normal color, thank God. I left my hair pinned up and put a pair of big gold hoops through my ears. Satisfied with my appearance, smell, and overall touchability, I dug out a leather overnight bag I had gotten through a Lancôme Christmas offer and packed clothes for work tomorrow. I tossed my robe in as well, and my makeup bag. There. I was good to go.

I left a note for Lola because sometimes she worried. I worried about her, too, especially with Karatos knowing who she was. But Morpheus had someone watching over her, and I knew she was as safe as she could be.

By the time I got to Noah's almost two hours had passed since he'd called. He answered the door barefoot, in frayed jeans and an old gray T-shirt. He took my bag as I stepped inside. As he pushed the door closed, he moved farther and farther into my space, until my back was against the wall, and he was just as hard against my front. He kissed me—not tenderly or hesitantly, but like a man who wanted to eat me alive. My heart immediately began slamming against my ribs—I think it was trying to throw itself at Noah's feet. And my breath—well I think I forgot to breathe, because when he stepped back, breaking the kiss, I was gasping like a floundering tuna.

He held my hand as he tugged me up the stairs behind him. The apartment smelled of tikka paste, garlic, and coriander. My stomach growled. The fragrant warmth wrapped around me, so inviting and homey. I felt like I belonged here, like I was welcome and wanted.

"Dinner's ready," Noah told me as he set my bag at the foot of the stairs leading to the bedroom. "Wine?"

"Sure. Can I help with anything?"

"Nope," he called over his shoulder as he disappeared into the kitchen. "It's under control."

A few minutes later we were at the table, which was filled with delicious-smelling food, and lit with warm, vanilla-scented candles. A bottle of wine sat in the middle of it all, adding its own lush bouquet to the potpourri that was dinner. Everything smelled and looked amazing, and I told him so.

We sat, and he poured me a glass of wine. I wasn't ready to tell him about what Antwoine had said, so I stuck to safer topics. "Did you get any painting done today?"

He shook his head. "Didn't feel like it. I had lunch with my mother instead. You?"

I shook my head. "No, I didn't paint either."

He grinned. "Smart-ass."

I wanted to tell him what had happened with my eyes. Other than Antwoine, he was the only human I could tell, but I couldn't bring myself to do it. It was freaky even for me, and Noah already had a lot to get used to where I was concerned. I didn't want to add something I couldn't explain to the list.

Dinner was one long mouth orgasm. The chicken tikka masala was to die for, as were the sag paneer, chana masala, and lamb vindaloo. There was basmati rice, too, just the way I like it. And the naan was delicious. He had cooked far too much, but we made the biggest dent we could in it.

"You're amazing," I told him, unable to stuff another bite in. "That was fabulous."

"Take some for lunch tomorrow," he said, as we cleaned up later. "I won't eat it all."

How very domestic of him. He even put some in a divided plastic container for me.

We were on the sofa, Damien Rice drifting softly from the stereo speakers, when Noah gave me a half smile over the rim of his wineglass. "Spill it."

"Excuse me?" I had a hunch he wasn't talking about my own wine.

"You've been fidgety ever since you got here. What happened today?"

No more dodging. I sighed. "I spoke to my friend today—the guy I thought might know what Karatos is up to."

When I didn't say anything else, Noah arched a brow. "What did he say?"

"He could be wrong." I just wanted to get that straight. "Just because he has experience with this kind of thing doesn't make him an expert. He's not Dreamkin, he's human."

"Okay. Now tell me the rest." He really was showing a lot of patience. I would have taken my head off by now.

"You need to stay out of The Dreaming, though, okay? It's too dangerous. Morpheus will have people watching out for you, but I don't want to risk your safety, not when Karatos wants you so badly."

Noah was watching me carefully, with his face perfectly blank. "Why does he want me so badly, Doc?"

I looked down. Then away. Anywhere but in Noah's eyes. "Antwoine thinks he wants to use you to cross over into this world." After the words left my mouth I dared glance at him. He was still watching me, expression unchanged.

"How?"

I forced myself to hold his gaze this time. "I suspect he's going to try to possess you."

"Possess me?" His brow lowered dubiously, scoffing even. "That's not possible, is it?"

"I think it is."

"Shit!" He jumped to his feet. Holding his wineglass by the rim, down by his thigh, he paced in front of the windows. "Fuck."

I knew how he felt. "We'll stop him, Noah."

His gaze flew to mine, and I saw the anger there. "*We'll* stop him? You mean *you'll* stop him, right? I'm not even supposed to dream, for Christ's sake."

The only time I ever saw Noah angry was when he felt like his control was being taken away—when he felt helpless. I wasn't afraid of him, but I felt for him.

"Yeah. I'll stop him."

He shook his head, mouth set grimly. "I don't like this. I don't want you fighting my *fucking* battles."

"Noah . . ."

"And I'm just supposed to sit around and let you. Too fucking weak to do anything else."

Okay, he was really getting overheated.

"Noah," I said in my firmest tone as I rose to my feet. "Karatos didn't choose you because you're weak. You know that, don't you?" I tried to put my hand on his face, but he pulled away. "He chose you because you're *strong*. Strong enough to host a creature that can't survive on its own in this world."

He stared at me, still stiff and full of anger. "He'll hurt you. I don't want to—I don't want you to get hurt."

I don't know if it's possible for the human heart actually to swell with emotion, but mine felt as if it was doing just that. "I'm not going to be alone. I'll have Morpheus with me. But I can't beat him if you let him in, Noah. None of us can."

I could see the change in his body as some of his agitation eased. "What will happen if he crosses over?"

I crossed my arms over my chest. "He'll be free to do whatever he likes. He lives on fear, so I'm assuming he'll hurt people. Probably rape, torture—your basic serial-killer stuff." How calm I sounded—so in denial and disconnected.

"And he'll use me to do it."

I nodded. "I figure he'll start with people familiar to him."

It didn't take long for the implications of that to sink in. "You." He sounded as sick as I felt.

And Noah's family, but I didn't say that.

The muscle in Noah's jaw ticked. "You really think we can stop him?"

I smiled at "we." "I do." Oddly enough, it was true. "Without you, he's nothing."

A harsh bark of laughter escaped him. "Great."

This time he didn't draw back from my touch, and I put my hands on the solid wall of his chest, felt the heat and hardness of him beneath my palms. His free arm went around me, pulling me tight against him.

"Be careful," he warned.

I nodded. "I will be."

"If he hurts you . . ." The rest of the sentence hung unfinished between us as our gazes locked. I couldn't fathom what he was thinking, but I was warmed by it regardless. Men didn't talk like this unless they cared. Unless they cared a lot.

I don't know which of us leaned in first, which one of us gave in first, but the next thing I knew we were kissing like our lives depended on it. Maybe they did.

Noah set his wine on the coffee table, then he bent down and swept me up into his arms. The beautiful man actually picked me up!

"Noah, no. I'm too heavy . . ."

"Quiet," he growled. "You're perfect."

Oh yeah, I was in so much danger of falling for him.

He carried me up to the bedroom, and I stayed quiet like I was told. He undressed me slowly, caressed, kissed and teased every inch of me with excruciating slowness. It seemed like he had something to prove—that by driving me to the point of sexual madness he was somehow regaining the power Karatos took from him. I didn't mind.

When he finally slid inside me, our bodies were slick with sweat and mine hummed with tension. I wrapped my arms around him, gripped his ribs with my thighs.

"Look at me," he commanded, voice low and raw.

I did. We moved together, our gazes locked. It was so strange to gaze into a man's eyes as he made me quiver and gasp. To see the need and desire reflected back at me in the darkness of his gaze as his body pumped into mine.

What I saw in Noah scared me as much as it thrilled me. Forget Karatos's plans to possess Noah. Noah wanted to possess me.

And I wasn't certain I wanted to stop him.

At exactly 2:15 A.M., I slipped out from beneath the warm, heavy weight of Noah's arm, drew on my robe, and tiptoed downstairs. I didn't have to worry about finding my way as ambient light from the neighborhood did that for me. Noah obviously wasn't a big fan of curtains because there weren't any in the entire apartment. There were windows every-where, but in his bedroom the windows were on the west wall only. No morning sun to wake him up, but plenty of twinkling lights to lull him to sleep.

He was snoring softly as I padded across the living room to the kitchen. It was either there or the studio to use for portal casting, and since I was thirsty, the kitchen seemed the best bet. I took a bottle of water from the fridge, drank half of it, and set my mind to opening a gate to The Dreaming.

Slowly, I breached the walkway between my two worlds. The familiar sliver of light formed and hovered before me, and I peeled it open until it was large enough to step through. I walked into my father's study. It was his power that brought me there, not mine. Mine wasn't focused enough to pinpoint a particular spot just yet. However, I had no doubt that I could close this portal and open another and still end up in the same spot because that's where Morpheus had decided I would go.

I suppose it was safer that way, but it also gave him entirely too much control over my movements.

"Hello, Dawn."

The sound of my mother's voice damn near broke my heart. How long was it going to be like this? How long was I going to alternate between loving her and hating her like I did?

"Hi," I replied. "Morpheus around?"

Her youthful face held an expression of hopefulness, an eagerness that I hated being the cause of. "He's out with the Guard, but I expect he'll be here shortly now that you've arrived. Tea?"

I shrugged. Why did she keep trying to win me over? "Sure." I closed my portal before joining her at the little table near the fireplace. A china teapot and matching cups and saucers sat on a tray in the center, along with a plate of little sandwiches. I couldn't help but smile at the sight of it, especially when I saw the pile of fat, spiced sugar cookies on the side.

"It looks just like Nan's," I remarked. My grandmother had insisted upon tea every day at exactly the same time, and she always had little sandwiches with the crusts cut off. Sometimes they were cucumber or egg. Sometimes salmon or chicken. I liked being there for tea on any day except for salmon. I still didn't like the canned stuff.

But my mouth watered at the thought of those cookies. I hadn't had them in years.

My mother smiled, too, as she sat down. "I even have sugar cubes."

Nan always used cubes at tea. She had the little tongs for them and she would let me plop the cubes into her cup for her, just because I liked playing with those little silver tongs.

I sat down and let my mother pour the tea, then she let me add the sugar to both our cups. She smiled at me across the table, and I smiled back, until I remembered not to.

I watched as the pleasure drained from her face. She looked older. Sadder. "Dawn, are you ever going to forgive me?"

I thought of my sisters and my brother and my father. I thought of the grandchildren my mother would never know. And I thought of how happy she was here—happier than I had ever seen. "No," I told her. Her doelike eyes filled with tears. "But I'll try to understand you."

The tears didn't dry up, but they didn't fall either, so I suppose we had reached some kind of agreement. "Thank you."

Silence stretched for a moment. "Was it easy?" I heard myself ask the question I'd wondered for so long.

She tapped the spoon on the side of her cup before setting it on the saucer. "What?"

"Leaving us."

Her hands folded around her cup, but not before I saw the tremor in her fingers. "No. Of course not. But I haven't left any of you."

Now that was just a lie. "What do you call walking out of our lives without a good-bye?"

"You walked out of your father's, remember?"

"It's not the same." I was pretty sure it wasn't. I snatched a sandwich off the plate and shoved it into my mouth. I wasn't hungry, but it was the most defiant thing I could think of to do.

"You turned your back on him and this world. You wouldn't even let him into your dreams. I visit your brother and sisters regularly in their dreams. I see my grandchildren, too."

She had mentioned that before. Once in a while someone would tell me they dreamed about Mom, but I usually tuned it out, not wanting to hear. Or worse, I treated it like I would a patient's dream and told myself that my siblings were using dreams to compensate for what their real world lacked.

"I watched over you, too, after you left."

My heart jumped, making my body lurch with it. "How?" I had put up walls. Built my own world.

She gave me a patient smile. "Your father is master of this world. Do you really think you could keep him out? The only thing that kept him from forcing you to come back to us was that he knew we'd lose you forever."

I swallowed. I thought I had been so clever, so rebellious. I didn't owe her an explanation, but I gave one anyway. "I wanted to be normal. I didn't want to be what I am."

She sighed. "Honey, you can't run away from what you are. Those walls didn't stop you from being you, they just postponed it."

"Don't remind me." Because I had tried so hard to deny my heritage, I was paying for it now. Was that how Karatos had found me? Because my walls hadn't been as strong as I'd thought? Or had he simply taken his time looking, wiggling his way in by chipping away at my shoddy defenses?

Or, maybe, someone more powerful had helped him. Were my father's enemies conspiring against him? Was that the "us" Karatos mentioned? Was I just a pawn to get to Morpheus?

And how much did my mother know about all of this? Not much, I'd bet. I wasn't about to offer her up for sainthood just yet, but she'd be a lot more freaky if she thought someone was trying to hurt me just to get to her lover, and Morpheus struck me as the "must protect my little woman by keeping her in the dark" sort.

A slim hand reached across to pat one of my larger ones. She was so dainty, my mother. How she'd ever managed to birth a lumberjack like me I'd never know. It had to be those immortal genes.

"I love you," she informed me matter-of-factly. "And no matter what, you'll always be my baby girl."

Oh God. I couldn't swallow, my throat had closed up so tight. I couldn't see because my eyes burned with tears. Not now. Not freaking *now*.

Like the answer to my unspoken prayer, my father chose that moment to enter the room. It wasn't like he opened a portal as I had, or that he came through the door like a person would. He seemed to walk out of the air, not interacting with the world but rather part of it.

"I thought I felt you here," he said in way of greeting as he grabbed two sandwiches off the plate and practically swallowed them whole.

"Did you find Karatos?" I knew it was a pointless question. If he had found the Terror, I'd know about it.

"No. We've come close a couple of times, but then he slips into a new guise. Don't worry, he'll reveal himself eventually."

I managed a wry smile. "And when he does, you'll be waiting?"

Morpheus smiled. It was like the snarl of a hungry wolf—no humor but plenty of anticipation. "How's your friend?"

He seemed to have an aversion to calling Noah by name. "As well as can be expected."

He lifted his face, like someone catching the scent of fresh baked pie. "His presence is muted. You've made him take something to stay out of this world."

Drugs were tricky. A little bit was good for suppressing REM, but sometimes drugs induced strange or wonderful dreams in the sleeper, which was why morphine had been named for my father.

"I had to," I told him. "It's not safe for him here with Karatos planning to possess him."

My parents both looked at me with almost identical frowns. "What do you mean?" My mother asked, pouring a cup of tea for Morpheus. There had only been two cups before. Now there were three.

I looked at my father. "You know what I mean, don't you?"

Face stony, Morpheus glared at me. "You've been talking to Jones again, haven't you?"

"You mean Antwoine? Yeah. He's been very helpful to me—much more forthcoming with information than you've been."

My mother glanced back and forth between the two of us, but Morpheus and I never took our attention off each other.

"I can just imagine how helpful." My father sneered. "What does he want in return?"

"He wanted me to ask after Madrene."

The darkness in Morpheus's face grew. He looked like a thundercloud about to burst. "You can tell him that she is well."

"And that's it?"

"That's it."

I suppose it was something. Given my father's feelings on the subject, the fact that he had volunteered any information at all spoke volumes. Antwoine would probably be glad for it. I'd keep my word and look for her once this was all over. "Thank you."

Morpheus merely nodded. Then he turned that piercing blue gaze to me. His eyes weren't as creepy as mine had been. Did he change them for my mother's benefit? And since he'd been such a shit about Antwoine . . .

"Why would anyone want me dead?" I asked. "If I die in the human world, I'm going to come here anyway, so it's not like they can get rid of me."

Morpheus's face tightened, and the answer came to me. "But then I'd belong to one world and only one. That's what this is about, isn't it? The fact that I'm the only half-breed ever to be born."

"The first ever to survive," he corrected.

"And they hate me for it." Prejudice was alive and well in

The Dreaming. W00t! Bring out your pitchforks! But they had known about me for years. Why now?

Because I was twenty-eight. What had Antwoine said the first time we met—I was mature. I was coming into my power, and now I could be a potential threat. But to what?

"You must have really pissed someone off if they're targeting me, especially when I haven't been here in years. Why do they want to hurt you?"

Morpheus didn't say anything. He just stood there, with his jaw tight, looking somewhere over my shoulder. My mother's pretty face broke into a frown—a scared one—as she lifted her gaze to his. "Answer her." Her voice might have been soft, but the emotion behind it wasn't.

He glanced at her, his face softening. Then he looked at me, and the softness disappeared. "I have enemies, as all kings do. I've always been accused of having too much love for humans, that's part of the job. Because your mother is human there are some in the kingdom who do not approve of her living here with me."

"And they don't approve of your half-human child," I added.

His gaze practically bore a hole through me. "My half-human heir."

Well shit. That certainly shone a brand-new light on the situation. Suddenly, everything was a lot more clear in my mind. "Great. No wonder they want me dead."

"Who wants you dead?" my mother demanded. The look she shot Morpheus could have ignited tinder. "You said it was just the Terror. It's more than that, isn't it?"

Morpheus sighed the sigh of a man who knew he was in deep trouble and that there was no way out.

"I don't know exactly," he told her. "But I suspect that

part of the reason Karatos has slipped through my grasp so easily is because he has help."

"From your enemies," she supplied. Her mouth tightened at his nod. "Enemies who want to kill our daughter just to make a point."

"Maggie . . ."

"Fix this, Morpheus," she demanded. "Fix this now. Make her human—do something to keep her safe!"

"He can't do that," I told her, knowing it to be true and feeling bad for her because of it. "He can't make me something I'm not." I turned to my father. "What do we have to do?"

He rubbed a hand over his jaw before stuffing both in the pockets of his jeans. "This could be a small group testing the waters to see how far I can be pushed." Or there could be a large mutiny brewing in The Dreaming. Either way, it had to be stopped, or the human world could suffer as well. I didn't want to think what might happen if someone who had less love for humanity took over my father's rule.

And I'll admit it—I didn't want to think of the fact that I'd have to be dead for that to happen.

I gave a sharp nod. "We need to stop Karatos quickly—and brutally."

My father looked surprised and strangely proud. "Yes. I have no doubt that the promise of humanity is his reward for targeting you. He'll be on earth, where he can do lasting damage."

Christ. And he was going to use Noah to do it. "So, what do we do?"

"It's not safe for your friend to go too long without dreaming. If Karatos doesn't reveal himself soon, we may have to lure him in."

"Lure him in?" Suddenly I understood. "I suppose Noah would be the bait?"

"Yes."

"No."

"It's either that, or he dies."

And if he did, some of the responsibility for that would fall on me. "Not if we use me as bait instead." God, when did I become a hero? Since I'd started falling for Noah. A human being couldn't survive without dreams, and Noah could only deny them so long. Dreaming recycled the soul. It was the psyche's version of an oil change. Dreaming was for getting rid of the garbage and holding on to the good.

My mother looked horrified. My father did, too—he also looked proud, and that pleased me, I admit.

"Fair enough." I also admit I expected him to put up at least a bit of a fuss.

My mother grabbed him by the wrist. "No. I won't allow Dawn to be put in any more danger."

Anger and bitterness aside, I realized at that moment that my mother, regardless of her great and huge faults, loved me. Too bad I had to be facing total annihilation for that realization to happen.

"We're not putting her in more danger," he countered. "We're trying to get her out of it." Morpheus drained his cup and set it down on the table. "I have to get back to the search."

"Wait." My voice stopped him as he began to walk away. "What can I do?"

He turned and came to me, smiling a father's smile. "Stay safe, and let your instincts guide you."

With that said, he bent and kissed my cheek and, after

kissing my mother—who was not impressed with him—he disappeared, much the way he had appeared to begin with.

"That went well," I said, slightly dazed. I had to accept all of this and fast, or this constant fog of disbelief was going to get me killed.

I picked up another sandwich. I couldn't wrap my head around having the kind of power my father had—or that my mind seemed to think I might possess, but three weeks ago I wouldn't have been able to wrap my head around opening portals or having my eyes change color.

My mother's eyes looked too big in her pale face. "Promise me you'll be careful." She actually choked when she said it—like on a sob.

I could do that, even if it might prove to be a lie. I could give her a little hope because I wasn't a total bitch, and I couldn't bring myself purposefully to hurt her at the moment. "I promise."

It was time to leave—before she hugged me or something. I had to remind myself not to get too close. Regardless of what she said, or how caring and frightened she appeared, she had abandoned me and the rest of her family, and a woman who would do that once would do it again in a second.

I said good-bye and opened a portal. I hopped right through. Either I was getting better at this, or I'd been given a lucky break.

I took another drink of water from the bottle I'd opened and left the rest on the counter. Then I quickly tiptoed back upstairs and slipped into the soft, inviting warmth of Noah's bed. He stopped snoring and shifted, his body easing toward mine. He reached for me, and I went willingly into his arms. I needed to be there.

"Where were you?" he asked, pulling me close so that he was spooned around my back.

"I had to get a drink." It wasn't really a lie if I left stuff out, was it? I had been thirsty after all.

"I thought I'd lost you." His voice was a warm mumble against my skin.

"No," I said, snuggling deep into his embrace. "You're not going to lose me." *And I'm not going to lose you.*

Chapter Twenty

I hated keeping secrets.

Normally I was the kind of person who couldn't hang on to a secret no matter how hard she tried. Oh sure, I did an okay job of keeping the fact that I was a Nightmare hidden, but that was self-preservation. Who'd go to a psychologist who claimed to be half-immortal?

Secrets slipped through my fingers, tumbled from my lips. I just wasn't good at holding things close. Sometimes I would tell one person who I was sure would never say anything—but then I'd feel guilty for telling.

Patients' secrets were different. That was my job. Yes, I'll admit that sometimes I talked about patients, but I never revealed names. Never told their stories just for the sake of telling. That was just too much like betrayal.

But mostly, I was bad when the secret was my own. I wanted to share. So was it any wonder that I was having a hard time keeping a lid on several secrets in my life? I hadn't told my father about the weird thing that happened with my eyes. And I certainly hadn't told Noah that my father wanted to use him as bait for Karatos. Was it any wonder, then, that I was practically vibrating with the need to unload some of this stuff?

"You okay, hon?" Bonnie asked me at work on Thursday. "You seem a little jittery."

I waved away her concern. "I'm fine. Just tired. It's probably too much caffeine." In fact, I had just returned from another coffee run, carrying offerings for Bonnie, Jose, and one of the kids in the lab. Of course that's when Dr. Canning showed up.

"Dawn," he said, expression stern, "can I talk to you?"

Oh God. "Sure."

We went into my office, me leading the way like a kid bound for the principal's office. I didn't waste time once the door was closed, however. I turned and popped the lid on my latte. "Is there a problem, Dr. Canning?"

He studied my face, his own set in disapproving lines. "You were sick on Tuesday?"

Now lying, on the other hand, was a different story from keeping secrets. I was fabulous at lying. "Yes, sir. I was. Spent most of the day in bed."

"So you wouldn't have been out on Fifth Avenue that afternoon? One of the girls in the lab could have sworn she saw you."

I just bet. This place was terrible for backstabbing. Every little intern who came through those doors wanted my position. In less than a week they could have it. Maybe it was that sense of finality that drove me onward.

"You ever get tired of having your ass kissed?" I asked.

Dr. Canning blinked, his pale eyes wide. "I beg your pardon?"

"Don't you ever get annoyed at the number of people who try to win your favor by talking trash about others? I was sick, Dr. Canning. And if I was seen on Fifth Avenue, it was because I went to the doctor and had to get a prescription filled."

He stiffened. No doubt he was not used to people talking to him with such obvious disdain, especially not an underling.

"Do you have the prescription with you?"

"It's at home." The lie fell easily off my lips. I was too angry to feel bad about it either. "It's a twice-a-day antibiotic. I can go home and get it for you if you like. You can have your little friend in the lab follow me."

That might have been going too far, and if Canning had decided to call my bluff, I'd be screwed, but luck was on my side. Or maybe I had succeeded in making him feel silly enough as it was.

"I don't like your tone, Dawn."

"I'm sorry, sir. But I don't like being told on and scolded like this was elementary school rather than a work environment."

He flushed a deep red. "Your behavior . . ."

I cut him off. "Are you dissatisfied with my work?"

"There have been some incidents—" He meant Mrs. Leiberman and the police questioning him. He meant Noah's leaving the program.

"My *work*, sir. Has there been anything I've done for you or this clinic that has not met your standards?"

His face flushed even darker, making his hair and eyes

all the paler. For a moment, I thought his head might explode. "No."

"Then your problem with me is personal?" I had him then. A personal issue could be pursued in all kinds of ways—most of which would have him in the papers, looking less than professional. I was a younger woman with a good work and academic record, and the press would jump all over the story if I decided to make trouble. Plus, there was the fact that Dr. Canning had been particularly close to a couple of the lab rats, as I liked to call his little female militia.

At that moment I knew that Dr. Canning would gladly fire me on the spot if he only could. "You're on probation, Dr. Riley. From now on I'm documenting everything you do. I'm going to evaluate all your cases. You'd better hope I don't find anything."

I met his gaze, bold as brass and proud of it. "That sounds like harassment, sir."

Dr. Canning pivoted on his heel and stormed out of my office, leaving me giddy, shaking, and a little high on my own power. Where had all that ballsiness come from? But I knew where. It came from knowing that I was stronger than he was. It came from knowing that I had strength, and from knowing that the bottom would not fall out of my world.

And let's face it. After facing down Karatos on several occasions, confronting Dr. Canning was like taking on a toad after going a few rounds with a *T. rex*.

At lunch, Bonnie asked me what happened. "Canning came out of your office looking like he was going to have a heart attack. What did you say to him?"

So I told her. I gave her every little detail. Not because I couldn't keep a secret, but because I didn't want to keep it.

Just in case anything ever happened, it would be good to have someone who knew my side of the story and witnessed some of it.

Bonnie laughed when I was done. "I would have loved to have been there for that."

I dipped a chunk of bread in my soup. "You don't like Canning much do you?"

She eyed me for a second with something that looked like speculation. She was trying to decide whether or not she could tell me something. Whether or not I could keep a secret. When she started to speak, I knew she had decided in my favor. "After Tony died, I was real lonely, you know?"

I nodded. I had no idea what it was like to lose the love of your life, but I could imagine how horrible it would be.

"Dr. Canning was very good to me. I guess you could say I became needy where he was concerned."

My jaw dropped. "He seduced you?"

She shrugged, picking at her meatball sandwich. "I suppose so although I think I made the first move. I'm fairly certain he'd been setting it up. Anyway, he was the one who ended it by moving on to someone younger and needier."

I had to force myself to swallow I was so disgusted. "How can you work for him?"

Another shrug as she tore off a big chunk of bread-covered meat. "I make good money as a receptionist. I've got benefits, and I've got kids to think about. They were young enough then that I had to put them first. And now . . ."

And now she was in her mid- to late forties and figured no one else would hire her.

"That sucks." I reached for my Diet Coke. "Really. How can you stand to look at him?"

She swallowed the food in her mouth. "It's not that bad anymore. Sometimes I forget. But every once in a while he'll say something that's meant to be like a private joke or something between us."

I gestured at her with my pop can. "When I have my own practice, I want you to come work for me."

She grinned. "I'll hold you to that."

I bought her a tea before we left, and we walked back to the clinic, Styrofoam cups in hand. We didn't talk about Dr. Canning anymore, but I thought about him. I was thinking that he needed to be taught a lesson in contrition.

And then I thought of Jackey Jenkins. Yes, Dr. Canning needed to be taught a lesson, but I wasn't the Nightmare to do it.

When I arrived at Noah's that evening—yes, it was becoming a habit—I found him and Warren beating the crap out of each other in the dojo. Or at least that's how it looked.

They were both sweaty, dressed in those white pajama things you see martial artists wearing all the time. Their hair clung to their heads, and I could hear both of them gasping for breath—and grunting—as they circled each other, striking out with hands and feet, sometimes getting blocked and sometimes landing a blow.

I winced as Warren landed a fist to Noah's midsection, then winced harder when Noah seemed to lift Warren right off his feet and slam him to his back on the mat. This was different from the aikido they'd both taught me. How could they do this and not seriously hurt one another? Years of practice, I supposed.

As soon as they noticed me, they stopped.

"Am I interrupting a brotherly feud, or are you two always so hard on each other?"

They both smiled, breathing hard and sweating. "Friendly competition," Warren said.

Noah chuckled. "When we were younger, it was the only way we could fight with each other without our parents getting upset."

"We'd just save it for the mat." Warren snapped Noah's leg with a towel. "I can still kick your ass."

Noah scowled at him, but there was no anger in it. "Yeah, right."

I watched them together, so at ease despite the beating they had obviously exchanged. My sisters and I would never do such a thing. Imagine, me and Ivy kicking the snot out of each other over Mom. It was almost laughable it was so absurd. But maybe I'd talk to her more often if we had a chance to work off the tension between us.

But it was never going to happen, so why even think about it? Really, did it matter that Ivy thought I was wrong—that I wasn't a good enough daughter? I knew that some great tragedy hadn't befallen Mom. I knew that she hadn't been "taken" from us, so instead of fighting with my sister I should just feel sorry for her and take my lumps as they came.

"You have enough energy left for me?" I asked Noah as I set down my bag. He was giving me another aikido lesson tonight. "I just might kick your butt."

A flirtatious grin curved his lips. "I always have energy for you."

I blushed. Noah chuckled, and Warren looked as though someone had just flicked him in the eye. He was obviously not used to hearing his half brother flirt.

"I'm going to leave before I'm scarred for life," Warren

announced as he headed toward the locker room. "Don't do anything lewd until I'm gone."

I went to the other locker room to change, but not before Noah gave me a "hello" kiss that had me tingling all over. "You smell," I told him when we parted, my nose wrinkling. "Bad."

"I smell manly," he corrected without so much as a grin, but there was laughter in his eyes.

When I came back, Warren was gone, and Noah was ready for our lesson. We sparred for almost an hour and by the end of it I was a little annoyed. Noah kept pulling his punches with me. He went out of his way not to hurt me, which was sweet, but at the same time didn't do me much good in the defense area. How was I going to mount a good defense when I had no idea what he was capable of?

"I need you to stop being so careful," I told him. "Karatos wouldn't hesitate to kick my ass."

"No." He reached for a towel and used it on his head and neck.

"Oh, come on." I wiped the sweat from my forehead with my arm. "I know you don't want him to pulverize me."

Noah peeked out from beneath the snowy white edge of the towel. "Of course not, but I'm not going to try to hurt you."

"Because I'm a woman?" I couldn't figure out if I was amused or annoyed.

The towel was around his neck now, his hair standing out on all sides. "Yeah."

I liked that he was honest, but I didn't like the honesty per se. I suppose it was nice that Noah didn't think boys should hit girls, but some girls needed to be hit—like those ones on TV trash shows that start hitting guys with their shoes. On the other hand, Noah was bound and determined not to hit a girl—so determined that it made me wonder why. But that was his secret, not mine. It was connected to his dream about his mother, so I had my suspicions.

For that reason I decided not to push it.

We showered upstairs at his place. Okay, we showered *together.* It started out purely as a practical thing—why use more hot water than we needed to? And there's something so good about having someone there to wash your back— Noah went so far as to throw in a little back rub while he was soaping my skin. It wasn't until after we were clean that his hands slid around to my front and did some interesting exploring in wet, slippery areas.

I was gasping and trembling by the time he turned me around, a tightness wound deep inside me.

No guy had ever gone down on me in a shower before, and once I got past the initial surprise of having Noah on his knees in front of me, I relaxed and gave in to it. And it was good. Two fingers inside me stroked while his tongue found exactly the right spot to lick. I grabbed the back of his head with one hand and the top of the stall door with the other and held on as the things he did made my knees go weak. The orgasm that followed hit me so hard I thought I was go- ing to take a header right through the glass doors, but Noah kept me on my feet. Feeling naughty, I returned the favor, and by the time we finally left the shower, the water was cold and we both had the muscular stability of wet noodles.

"You realize that every time we're together we have sex?" I said to him, as we dressed.

He shot me an amused glance before pulling a black T-shirt over his head. "So?"

"Don't you find that strange?" I fastened my bra. Maybe it

was just me. It had been a while since I had dated anyone, and I'd never felt as comfortable with anyone as I did Noah.

He sat down on the bed to put on his socks. "Are you complaining?"

"No, it's just . . . I don't know." I pulled on my sweater and went to stand in front of him. "You don't mind?"

"Mind?" His tone was incredulous, if I do say so myself. He rose to his feet and lifted my hair free of the neck of my sweater. He pressed his lips against my forehead—I loved that he was tall enough to do that—and placed his hands on my hips. "Don't speculate why I'm with you, Doc, and I won't ask why you're with me."

I pulled back and lifted my face to look up at him. "Why would you ask that?" I mean, that was just ridiculous. He was gorgeous and warm and funny and sweet . . .

He smiled—a little sadly I thought. "I've wondered if you just want to fix me."

That broke my heart. "You're not broken." Oh, he was dented and scuffed and probably needed patching in some areas, but didn't we all? Hell, I wasn't even totally human!

He gave me a hug, and we went downstairs to order dinner. His words stayed with me for a while, though, and they made me think. I had avoided talking to him about Morpheus's plan to lure in Karatos because I wanted to protect him. But Noah didn't want protection any more than I did.

He was right, I was something of a fixer. Even though I didn't think he was broken, I was driven by my own nature to try to help him.

I was chewing on a piece of General Tso's chicken—so fattening but so good!—when I decided to stop trying to protect him and let go of my own need for control.

"How do you feel about facing Karatos again?" I asked.

Noah had chopsticks in one hand, a carton of beef and broccoli in the other, and from the way he was sifting through the contents, I knew he was picking out all the beef.

"Face Karatos how?" he asked after he swallowed.

"My father—Morpheus—he thinks we'd catch Karatos faster if we lured him in."

Noah nodded slowly as he chewed, the two happening in unison. "The lure being me?"

There was no other way around it. "Yeah." And me, I guess.

"And if I don't do this, you go back to hunting for the Terror?"

I knew where this was going, but I answered anyway. "If my father lets me, yes."

He didn't even pause. Didn't even think about it. "Tell your father I'll do it."

I laughed out loud. Couldn't help it. "If I had said no, would you be so gung ho?"

Noah smiled at me. "Still think I'm not broken?"

I kicked him in the thigh—not hard, of course, but enough so he knew how frustrating he was. "I think you're exasperating and an overbearing jerk, that's what I think."

His expression sobered. "I want my life back."

I knew exactly how he felt. "So do I."

"So, we'll do this together?" As brave as Noah was, we both knew the risks involved.

I shifted on the couch, moving over so that we were side to side, thigh to thigh. "Together," I replied. Hopefully we'd survive it. "Now quit hogging the beef and broccoli."

Chapter Twenty-one

My hope was short-lived.

Friday ended up being not a bad day at work because my appointment load was light, giving me time to work on research, and because Dr. Canning avoided me like the plague. That pretty much allowed me to do my own thing, and after I was done with my obligation to the clinic and to my patients, I sat down at my desk with a Venti white mocha latte and went to work on research of my own.

It was amazing what you could find on Google if you looked.

There were rules in The Dreaming about things such as human-world and dream-world interaction. It was what had gotten Antwoine kicked out and me born. I was a living example of what could happen when the two worlds collided, and for that reason, I wanted to appear as normal as possible for both sides.

Growing up in the human world, I had a pretty good idea of what normal entailed here. I needed to read what was normal for a Nightmare.

According to the Internet—and hey, it wouldn't lie, would it?—Nightmares were gifted with quick reflexes, agility, telekinesis, and strength. Okay. That would explain how fast I moved that time with Verek and why I was able to hurt him. It also explained why I had been able to fight Karatos at all. Although, by rights, I should have been able to squash him like a bug.

If I hadn't freaked out as a kid and decided to shut myself off from the truth, I would have known what I was doing because my father would have trained me. The Nightmare Guild would have trained me. And I would have destroyed Karatos by now.

Crap. Running away had seemed like such a good idea at the time.

I left work having resolved that I would work on my abilities that night, even if only within the confines of the castle. Morpheus was bound and determined to keep me safe, it seemed, but was he also determined to keep me stunted? It wasn't as though he had taught me a whole helluva lot since my return to The Dreaming. Maybe he wanted to keep me ignorant.

Or maybe he knew that as soon as I learned what I wanted, I'd stop visiting so much. Maybe his reticence was nothing more sinister than a father's ploy to keep his daughter close.

Maybe. Or maybe he didn't want me to know just how bad the situation was.

I stopped by an Asian grocery on my way to Noah's. He had planned to spend the day in his studio painting, so I offered to make dinner. I suppose I could have invited him to my place, but it seemed so much easier to go to his. Besides, Lola was having a "sleepover" tonight with her latest, and four was definitely a crowd. It would feel weird, both of us having sex in our rooms—too much like an orgy or something.

Knowing that Lola had someone physically with her, as well as a Dreamkin watching over her in The Dreaming, made me feel a heckuva lot better about staying at Noah's. Noah was alone. Maybe that played too much to my Cancerian "gotta be needed" nature, but I felt wanted when I was with him. So long as he stayed out of The Dreaming, he was safe, but I didn't want to put all my faith in the pills he was taking. A dreamer like him just might slip past that barrier.

I bought all the fixings for a stir-fry, including fresh ginger, bamboo shoots, and bok choy. I bought stuff for hot-and-sour soup as well, but the stir-fry would be more than enough food for dinner tonight. It never seemed to matter how small an amount I tried to make, I always ended up with enough chicken, veggies, and noodles for six people.

Juggling the bags—why couldn't they use plastic?—I rang the buzzer at Noah's shortly after six. He answered barefoot, in baggy jeans and an old Nine Inch Nails T-shirt. He took the bags from my arms and kissed me. Maybe it was my imagination, but he seemed happier to see me than usual—no, not happy. He seemed relieved. Weird.

He helped me cook and asked about my day. He let me do most of the talking, which wasn't all that strange, but just off enough that it made me suspicious. Occupational hazard maybe, but I'm usually pretty good at knowing when someone has something on their mind. I gave him until we finished eating to tell me, and when he hadn't said a word, and we were sitting on the couch drinking coffee, I finally came out and asked.

"What's wrong?"

He looked up from his cup. Maybe it was the lighting, but I saw shadows beneath the slight arch of his brows, a slight bruising on the skin just beneath his eyes. There was a grayish cast to his skin that I had never noticed before. He looked sick.

"I can't paint," he announced, the words coming out precise and slow, as though he had chosen them carefully.

I frowned. "Are you blocked?" I've heard of writers hitting hard patches in their work, maybe the same happened to artists.

"No." He stared at me, his gaze boring into mine, trying to make me understand. "I *can't* paint. It's like that place inside me is dead. There's no inspiration."

It was strange, that was for certain, but Noah was acting like it was something more significant than that. "Maybe the stress of all you've been through—"

"Doc, I've never not been able to paint, even when my father put my mother in the hospital. I'm telling you it's gone."

The look on his face scared and confused me, even though my brain lurched toward a rational explanation. "It can't be gone. It's part of who you are. How can you simply not be able to paint anymore?"

"It's not the ability, it's the capability."

I was still confused.

"I can't dream either."

Oh, now I understood. I wasn't sure how it was possible, but if my mere existence taught me anything, it was that strange things sometimes happened. Noah's painting was closely tied to his dreams, so if he couldn't dream . . .

"It's the depressants," I told him. "Once you stop taking those, you'll be able to paint again."

Noah dropped his gaze, and with it went my stomach. He couldn't even look me in the eye?

"I haven't been taking any depressants," he confided softly.

"But . . ." For once in my life I was at a loss for words. "But you haven't been in The Dreaming. Karatos . . . you . . ."

Now his gaze met mine. "I think Karatos did something to me."

Sweet God. "You haven't taken any sleeping pills, no anti-anxiety meds, no booze?"

He shook his head. "Nothing."

Anger pierced my concern. "Not even when I asked you to?"

He didn't even have the decency to look sorry. "No."

"Asshole." I think I might have snarled at him. "You let me think you were safe when you were really risking your life? For what?"

"Obviously I wasn't risking anything if I can't dream."

"Don't argue semantics with me. You didn't know you couldn't dream at the time." I rubbed my forehead with the heel of my hand. "Maybe Morpheus banned you from The Dreaming, too." I was stretching, but it was possible.

Noah looked hopeful. "You think?"

I glared at him. "I can't believe you'd be so stupid to risk yourself like that."

His eyes narrowed as his nostrils flared. He was on the defensive now. Good, because I was feeling decidedly *offensive* at the moment. "I can take care of myself."

"Who the fuck are you trying to kid? I can't even take care of myself in The Dreaming, and I'm from there!" I jumped to my feet. "Jesus, Noah. What did you think you'd do if Karatos came after you again? I can't go anywhere but my father's castle. I wouldn't have been able to help you."

He stood as well, face tight and flushed with anger. "I swore I'd never hide from a bully again, and I don't mean to start now."

There was something for me to think about later. Right now I was too angry to think of anything else. I got in his face. "Karatos is a soulless being who lives off fear—not just a bully."

"I'm not afraid of him."

"There's a fine line between bravery and idiocy, Noah, and you've crossed it."

"Fuck you."

It didn't hurt—I was too scared and angry to feel anything else. "Oh, nice. Did you once stop to consider how I would feel if Karatos seriously hurt you? Or worse, if he killed you? What about Warren or your mother or your sisters?"

He paled a little, and I knew I was getting through his layers of self-defense.

"I'm sorry if I've offended you," I told him, my voice shaking with emotion. "But you've offended me. You don't trust me, and you obviously don't care about me at all to lie to me."

"Doc . . ."

I held up my hand. "Don't. Rationally, I understand you have reason to behave like this. But emotionally, I don't understand at all." I couldn't be much more honest than that.

He shoved his hands in his pockets. "So what do we do?"

Back to "we" now, huh? Oh, I could have slapped him silly at that moment, for all the good it would have done. He hadn't done this to hurt me, and I knew that, but it drove home that little fear I'd had ever since we got involved—that we wouldn't have a relationship at all if not for Karatos. When this was all over—and if we both lived through it— I expected that Noah and I would soon cease to be anything at all to one another.

And the thought broke my heart.

"We find out exactly what's been done to you. That's what we do now." I turned to the side and held out my hand. I probably didn't have to do that to open a portal, but for now it helped me focus. I didn't even try to relax, I just pushed hard with whatever power I had inside me.

Which was much more than I ever thought because one push was all it took for a portal big enough for me to walk through to zip open. I didn't have to tug or wiggle through.

"Jeez-us," Noah breathed behind me, and I knew he could see The Dreaming from over my shoulder.

I reached back and grabbed his hand. There was no time for preparing him or coddling, and I wouldn't have bothered even if there were, I was that pissed at him. His fingers tightened around mine, but he walked behind me, not even hesitating at the threshold between the worlds. Maybe he trusted me more than I thought.

We walked into Morpheus's study. He was there along with my mother, Verek, other members of his Royal Guard, and a few other Dreamkin I didn't recognize. They all turned and stared at us—at me—with open mouthed astonishment.

"Good gods!" someone exclaimed.

I looked at my father. "I'm sorry to interrupt, but I need to talk to you. Now. It's important."

He nodded, still staring at me as though he had never seen me before. "Leave us," he commanded.

It must be nice to have people obey your every whim. Some of his companions obviously didn't want to leave, and those same ones shot daggers at me with their eyes as they left. Verek, however, looked at me as though he felt sorry for me, and that bothered me more than anything else.

My mother didn't leave, but she looked equally shocked to see me. What the hell was the big deal? I had opened a portal to The Dreaming before.

But I had never brought company. I looked at Noah, who was gazing around the room with thinly veiled wonder. Was it against the laws to bring a human into the Realm? Personally, I wasn't all that worried about decorum at the moment. I was pretty sure Karatos had broken more laws than I ever had, so I was vindicated in breaking as many as I had to in order to stop him.

"What did you need to discuss with me?" Morpheus's voice was softer than usual, his expression caught somewhere between pride and alarm—a bizarre combination if you ask me.

"Noah hasn't been taking sleep aids." I felt like a third grader tattling to my teacher. "And he hasn't been able to dream."

My father turned his pale blue gaze to the man beside me. Noah stared back. "Do you feel strange at all, Mr. Clarke?"

Noah nodded. "Like something's missing."

Morpheus walked toward us. My father didn't look much older than I, and his uniform of jeans and a sweater didn't help. The way he looked never bothered me before, but right then I wished he looked more fatherly—like someone capable of protecting me from bad guys and monsters.

He stopped in front of Noah and looked him over. "Something is missing."

My heart jumped. "What?"

Both men turned their attention to me. Noah's face was relaxed as usual, but his fingers tightened around mine.

"He's like a zombie," my father explained. "Part of him is dead inside—the part of him that dreams."

"How is that possible?" I demanded.

Morpheus glanced at Noah. "I wouldn't have thought it possible, but I think Karatos took it."

No, that couldn't be right. But I had seen Karatos plunge his hand into Noah's chest. What if he had ripped out his dream-self? "But a person has to be able to dream. Without dreams they'll . . ." I stopped then, because my father was watching me, and so were Noah and my mother. We all knew what happened to persons without dreams.

They died.

Chapter Twenty-two

"How much time do we have?" I wanted to have this conversation with my father in private, but Noah wouldn't let me.

"A few days maybe," Morpheus replied. He handed Noah a glass of scotch. "Then the reservoir of dream energy stored inside Noah will be depleted."

This was ridiculous. This could not be happening. "Can I give him energy?" Technically, I could draw power from the stuff, so maybe I could share.

Morpheus shook his head. "No. Our only hope is finding Karatos."

I rubbed my eyes. "And he's eluded you again."

My father ignored my barb, as any good father would. That only made me angrier. "Karatos has worked very hard to come this far. I don't think he's going to let go so easily."

"So now what? We just dangle Noah out there like a carrot and hope Karatos takes a bite?"

The grim expression on his face told me it wasn't Noah we needed to dangle. It made sense. After all, having Noah was just gravy. This was really all about getting rid of me—the freak who scared them. The freak who was heir to the king they were rising against.

"No," Noah insisted, understanding Morpheus's expression as well. "No fucking way."

"We have to," I told him. I didn't like being Terror bait, but I'd rather me than him. "You are so not dying."

He smiled a little, his eyes warming as he looked at me. "You're so bossy."

I could have cried at that moment. Forget how angry I had been when he told me he hadn't listened to me earlier. I didn't care about any of that right now. All I cared about was keeping him alive so that I could be angry at him later.

I turned to my father, tears stinging my eyes. I would not let them fall. "How do we bring Karatos out?"

"He'll have felt Noah's presence here. He'll know that you've discovered the truth, and he'll feel cocky over it. I think he'll come to you, Dawn—without any further prompting on our part. All you have to do is show up."

I swallowed. The idea of facing Karatos terrified me, but at the same time I wanted it to happen. I wanted to beat that bastard. "You'll lift the barriers and give me access to The Dreaming again?"

Morpheus inclined his head. "Yes. Karatos isn't stupid. He'll feel safer closer to Icelus's domain. You'll have to go there."

Fabulous. Icelus was my uncle and had dominion over all

things disturbing and terrifying. If Morpheus was king of The Dreaming, Icelus was a prince. Karatos, though part of my father's world, had been created by Icelus, who would protect his creation simply because he didn't like Morpheus getting in his business. Maybe Icelus was behind this rebellion.

So why didn't Morpheus put the smack-down on his brother? It wasn't done that way. Icelus was necessary to the balance of things, just like everything else in the natural order of things. He could be punished, but only if he directly did something that was against the rules—and if Icelus was the mastermind, he was too clever for that.

"I'll go tonight." Pop into Icelus's Realm, hope Karatos showed up, then what? "What if he doesn't have Noah's dreams with him?"

"He'll want to bargain." Morpheus's gaze was intense as it settled on the man beside me. "The Terror's own desires are getting ahead of what he's been ordered to do. For him, the most important thing is getting Noah, and he won't want to risk losing that."

I didn't want to risk losing Noah either. That was why this whole plan made me want to puke. I was going to be playing with Noah's very life.

"It's too dangerous," Noah interjected. "I'm coming with you."

I turned my head toward him. "No."

His eyes lit with challenge. "It's my fight."

"No, it's not. Not anymore." There, I'd gone and done it. I'd taken any power he might have thought he had. I felt like crap for it. His jaw tightened, but he said nothing.

"You'd better go," Morpheus suggested. "The more time Noah spends resting, the more energy he'll conserve."

Meaning the longer his life span would be.

Noah and I rose to our feet. As we reached the portal, my father asked me to wait. "You can go ahead, Noah," Morpheus said. "It's quite safe."

It was painfully obvious that my father wanted to speak to me alone, and Noah didn't argue. He didn't even look at either of us; he simply disappeared through the portal. Morpheus beckoned me closer, and I went, just in case Noah was listening from the other side.

Warm, strong hands came down on my shoulders. I wanted to sag under them, fall against his chest and be a little girl for a minute or two, but I didn't. "Dawn, I know you're concerned about him."

"Damn straight."

"You can't bring him here again—not physically."

"Because of your rules?" I probably looked as snarly and mean as I sounded.

"Just don't." There was more to it than he was telling me. Even if the insistence in his tone hadn't told me that, the pleading in his gaze would have.

"Okay." I knew then that I had messed up royally on some scale—in front of witnesses—and that somehow Morpheus was going to have to make it right. If he could.

He kissed my forehead. "Be careful."

I nodded, acting braver than I felt. I wanted to ask him to come with me, but that would defeat the whole "keeping Karatos off his guard" plan. "I will."

"If you get in trouble, just call for me."

Sure. If Karatos didn't cut out my tongue.

It was the determination not to let that happen that kept me from crying as I slipped through the dimensional rift into Noah's apartment.

* * *

Noah and I didn't speak until I was about to walk out the door.

I had returned to the apartment to find him loading our coffee mugs in the dishwasher. He didn't look at me, and that was fine. He was angry at me, and I was angry at him and the world in general. In fact, I was angry at the fact that I was so angry. I gathered up my things, which took all of about five minutes, grabbed my coat, pulled on my shoes, and made for the door. I had no intentions of even saying good-bye at that point, I was feeling so wildly resentful and defiant. I'd show him. I'd save his ass or die trying. And then he'd be sorry he put me through this.

But Noah wasn't putting me through anything, and I knew it. Noah was just as much a victim in this as I was. Even more so.

"Hey." His voice stopped me as my hand closed around the doorknob.

I looked up as he bounded down the stairs to where I stood. I didn't speak. I just raised a brow and waited.

He sighed as his hands closed around my arms. "Don't go."

Both eyebrows went up. I hadn't expected that. "I really think I should." I didn't want to. What I wanted to do was crawl into his arms and do my best to make the world go away.

"Look, I know you're pissed at me," he said, "but I don't want you to do this alone."

I eased out of his hold. "I have to."

Noah frowned, but there wasn't any anger in it. "You're right." He ran a hand through his hair, mussing it further. The worry in his gaze warmed me a little. "I hate this."

"Me too."

"Call me after? Let me know you're all right."

How could I stay angry when he said things like that? "I will."

Then he kissed me. Long and soft, and so sweet I was tempted to stay, but I pulled away instead. Then, before he could tempt me further, I opened the door and walked out into the chilly darkness.

Lola was home when I got there. She was sitting on the couch, watching TV with Fudge on her lap. She looked up as I closed and locked the door. "Hey you."

"Hey, Lo." Fudge jumped off her lap and pranced across the assortment of rugs tossed over the hardwood floor to rub against my legs and meow in greeting.

I picked him up and buried my face in the soft thickness of his fur. Somehow, this cat gave me all the comfort I needed without doing anything at all.

"There's a pint of Coffee Heath Bar Crunch in the freezer for you," Lola said, as I kicked off my shoes and padded toward the kitchen with Fudge purring in my arms.

Screw the diet. Since it could very well be the last pint of heaven I ever ate, I was going to enjoy it. If I screwed this up, not only could I die, but Noah would for sure.

I wanted this over. I was tired of being afraid. Tired of wondering if Noah and I would have a relationship after all was said and done. I was just plain tired.

"I thought you had a sleepover tonight?" I remarked as I carried my frozen goodness into the living room.

My roommate shook her head. "He got called into work."

"You don't seem too disappointed."

She shrugged. "It happens. I'm trying to learn to just accept things as they come. Nothing I can do about it."

"You are very wise, grasshopper." I sat on the couch

beside Lola. Fudge lay between us, purring and wheezing as he sucked up the pets and scratches both of us gave him. I ate my ice cream—all of it—while we watched *Four Weddings and a Funeral*. Nothing like British comedy/drama to make the world go away for a little while. Plus, it had Hugh Grant. You had to love Hugh.

After the movie, I knew I couldn't wait any longer. Lola went to bed as well, and I waited a bit before opening the portal to make sure she was asleep. The last thing I wanted was for her to come knocking on my door only to find me gone.

Inside The Dreaming, I was once more confronted with the mists that swirled and snarled inside that world. Tendrils of fog reached for me, hissing softly. The mist didn't like me. The mist was there to keep humans from wandering the Dream Realm—subconsciously or in physical body—which I think had actually happened once many years ago.

I had a feeling the mist wasn't simply reacting to the human in me. The mist didn't like me, period. If it could kill me and get away with it, I think it would.

"Don't belong," I heard a thready voice whisper.

"Should have been destroyed at birth."

"Abomination."

"Monster."

It was the last one that got to me. I could have easily believed it. Maybe I would still, but the nerve of that mist—that sentient, swirling bank of fog—calling me a monster when it was no better really pissed me off.

"Fuck you," I muttered. And then I felt the stirrings of something inside me. It felt like embers in the ashes of a fire coming to life under the breath of an evening breeze. I drew in a deep breath, fanning the coals. They flickered. Another breath, and they sparked. One more, and the fire leaped to life within me. It surged through my veins and along my skin. My eyes grew warm, and I knew without seeing that my irises had lost color and were edged with jagged black.

"Let me pass." I spoke the words. I recognized my own voice, but not the power in it.

The mist wavered and thinned a little before becoming almost solid once more. It was an act of defiance, but instead of adding to my anger, it gave me an amazing sense of satisfaction.

I guess I had been looking for a fight.

I had brought my dagger with me and now it was in my hand, the moonstone in the hilt shimmering in the silver of The Dreaming night. I held it so that the guard rested against the outside of my hand. I felt a little bit like Norman Bates's "mother" when I lifted it so that the dagger was level to my eyes, pointing outward like a little spear. Holding it this way made it easier to slash into the wall of mist.

It actually cried out in pain as I tore through it with my Morae blade. Three sweeping arcs of my arm, and the mist began to shrink back, pulling apart to open a path for me. It was a path wide enough for two of me to walk through, shoulder to shoulder. The mist obviously wanted to stay the hell out of my way.

Good.

The duchy of Icelus lay at the end of the path. Was it there because that's where I wanted to be, or because I had actually entered The Dreaming at a point this close? I didn't know, but I had a feeling that if I had entertained the idea of having to drive to the duchy, there would have been a car waiting for me instead.

I didn't go looking for entry to my uncle's home. This wasn't a social call, and I didn't need to be in his house to call down Karatos. In fact, it was probably better that I stayed outside. First of all, I didn't know whose side Icelus was on, and if he was on Karatos's, then I didn't want to be alone with the two of them.

"Karatos." I whispered the name. Then, like that old game of "Bloody Mary," "Karatos, Karatos." Three times fast. That was supposed to call down the very devil, wasn't it?

Apparently so, because as I stood in a six-foot clearing of mist just outside the walls of Icelus's manor, I felt a stirring in the air. And then Karatos was there.

"Little Light," he said sweetly as he smiled at me like a shark at a seal pup. "I've been expecting you."

I ignored the clenching in my stomach as I met his gaze. "I bet you have."

"And here you are, strolling through the badlands as bold as brass." He glanced around me. "I see you've brought the mist to heel." He sounded a little surprised, and I allowed myself to take some pleasure from that.

"We need to talk," I told him.

His gaze locked with mine—and widened. He saw my eyes. He saw that they were no longer the eyes of a human. "Well, look at you." It came out breathy—full of wonder.

"You need to let Noah go."

He hesitated, still staring at my eyes. "No."

"He's dying."

"Yes, I know."

"So, what are you going to do about it?"

"It's not what I'm going to do about it, Dawnie. What are you going to do about it?"

"You can't have him."

"He'll die."

"You're going to kill him anyway when you take him over."

Another shrug. He didn't seem the least bit impressed that I knew what he had planned. "Probably. Or maybe he and I can learn to live together. We're very compatible, you know."

I snorted. "Yeah. Practically twins."

But instead of looking offended, the Terror seemed amused. "That's why I chose him, you know. Because of all the rage and violence in those delicious dreams of his. I've been watching our Noah for some time. He'll bring me into flesh, and the damage I do will be lasting."

I didn't like the way he said "our Noah." "He's nothing like you."

"He's my very own dream come true," Karatos rhapsodized. "Just think of all the fun he and I will have."

The thought made me sick.

"I know you're worried about losing him," the Terror went on, almost sympathetically. "But if it's any consolation, I'll fuck you whenever you need that particular itch scratched."

I sneered at him. "Not freaking likely."

"Oh, come on. Don't you remember what it was like with us? I get hard just thinking about it."

The roiling in my stomach had gotten worse, but I tamped it down. "Aren't you supposed to kill me, too?"

He moved closer, smiling that seductive and disturbing smile of his. "You could join me. Imagine what we could achieve together."

I tried to look haughty. "You'd just be a regular mortal. What would I want with you?"

"I know things. Things that your daddy would find very interesting—like who I work for."

Morpheus would want to know that. Would he give Noah's life for the information? I wouldn't. "Let me guess, and all I have to do is side with you, and you'll tell me who that is?"

"And bring Noah to me."

"I don't know how to do that."

He made a tsking noise. "Just like you took him to see your daddy," was the drawled reply. "Open a portal and bring him through."

"How do you know about that?"

He smiled. "I know a lot of things. I know that your mother was wearing a beautiful set of pearls two nights ago, and I know that Morpheus can't figure out why I always seem to be one step ahead."

"Christ," I whispered hoarsely. "You've got a spy."

Karatos's smile became a full on grin. "And I know that a lot of Dreamkin are scared of Morpheus's little girl and the things she can do—things even her father can't do—like bring a human into the Dreaming."

I swallowed. "Now you're lying." My head was reeling. A spy. Karatos had someone inside my father's house— someone who had Morpheus's confidence—feeding him information. No wonder we hadn't been able to find him unless he'd wanted to be found.

The Terror shot me a smug glance. "Don't you think that if he was physically able to bring your mama into this world, he would have done it by now? You're a special one, Little Light. People aren't sure whether to embrace you or destroy you."

Oh God. Somehow I managed to hold my ground, to keep my feet beneath me and my head high rather than collapsing to the ground like my trembling knees insisted I do. I didn't want to be destroyed.

I knew better than to take Karatos's words as absolute truth, but I heard the truth in them all the same. The villagers might not be readying their pitchforks and torches for me, but they were eyeing them. The Dreamkin, after so many centuries of human contact, weren't that different from mortals after all. And they didn't like what they didn't understand. Me.

"You and I could wreak so much havoc together," Karatos told me, taking a couple of steps closer. "I could help you hide from them, Dawn. Teach you how to use your powers."

I raised my gaze to his. It creeped me out knowing our eyes looked almost exactly the same. "You don't know my powers," I informed him. "No one does, because there's no one else like me."

Suddenly, Karatos swooped toward me, his face coming to within just a breath of my own. "That's right." He sliced my cheek with his fingernail. I hissed at the pain as blood trickled down my face. Then I felt searing cold just beneath my sternum. I looked down and saw the Terror's hand buried in my chest just past the wrist.

He shook his head, laughing. "Silly little Nightmare. I've been working toward this for years. Did you really think you and your daddy could trick me?"

I opened my mouth, but the smart comment died on my lips as a wave of pain washed over me. I could feel his fingers inside me, feel him claw into my very soul. He seized me—he was going to do to me what he'd done to Noah. I could feel my life draining. He pulled.

And then he got stuck.

As a strange energy buzzed in my veins, I realized what had happened. I smiled at the Terror—giddily, foolishly.

"Shit out of luck, Karatos. This world is part of me, and you can't take it away."

He was trying though. Sweat beaded on his brow as his beautiful face contorted with concentration. He was trying to take my power, and he was succeeding in small degrees. He might not be able to take my dreams, but he could weaken me.

I grabbed his arm, digging my own fingers into his flesh, the hard muscle just below the skin. The buzzing I felt in my veins intensified. I was taking something from him as well.

"What would happen if I stuck my hand in you?" I wondered out loud, and laughed when his eyes actually widened. "Wanna find out?"

Karatos wrenched his hand free.

"Aghh!" I doubled over from the force of the release and the heat flooding back into my body. Christ, it hurt. I gasped for breath as I struggled to stand upright. Tendrils of gray drifted in front of my eyes as my gaze jumped to the Terror.

The mist folded and thickened, closing around him, drawing him in until I wasn't sure if Karatos had actually vanished or if the fog had swallowed him.

It was closing in on me now as well. I hadn't done anything to Karatos that the Terror hadn't done to me, but I was the anomaly here, not he. The mist knew this, and its fear of me evaporated. I could hear it whispering—harsh and low. It would hurt me now if it could—payback for the damage I had done to it earlier.

I didn't waste any more time waiting to see just what that revenge might be. I was too weak to do anything but run.

I raced toward my portal and dove through, the mist nipping at my heels like a rabid spaniel.

One of my feet was actually bleeding when I tumbled into my bedroom. I had to walk on my tiptoes to the bathroom to avoid leaving bloody tracks on my carpet and the floor outside.

I wiped most of the blood from my face and foot with toilet paper, then cleaned both wounds with soap and water with just a touch of witch hazel. With antibiotic cream underneath the bandages on my cheek and my heel, I tottered back to my bedroom and climbed into bed.

I hummed a dee-dee-dee song to help myself go to sleep, to take some of my attention away from the pain in my face and foot. My body was humming like a cheap harmonica, and I felt strangely good. Like I had kicked some ass and taken names. I wasn't as easy to destroy as Karatos had originally thought, and that had to be a victory of some kind.

All in all, it was one hell of a way to pass a Friday night.

Chapter Twenty-three

Just before sunrise, I felt a familiar tug at my dream-self. I had intentionally kept myself from physically entering The Dreaming again, and instead made myself a sweet little paradise beach all of my own. I was lying on a blanket on the sand, soaking up the warm rays of a late-afternoon sun when my mother called.

She had obviously learned from my father how to project across one person's dreams into another's. I had been expecting one of them to contact me about my meeting with Karatos, and I was surprised that it was Mom. Did Morpheus suspect that there was a traitor in his own circle? Or had my mother chosen to do this, knowing it would be one time when I couldn't turn my back on her?

I sat up on the blanket, then rose to my feet. I was wearing a simple blue tankini, and I looked good in it. I always looked good in the dreams I controlled.

I followed the essence of my mother—her "signature" if you will. It was like following the scent of her perfume, catching the briefest of glances, or hearing the softest of whispers all at once. It was faint, but undeniable, and I walked across the beach toward it, the sand silky and warm beneath my feet.

I walked up the boardwalk and opened my mind to another's dream. The scenery changed as I walked. My oceanside paradise gave way to a park with wrought-iron benches and well-manicured lawns. It was like one of those old-fashioned botanical gardens, and I recognized it as one my family had visited in Nova Scotia when I was a child.

I changed my clothes so I wouldn't seem out of place to whoever was dreaming this. Jeans and a blouse were more fitting for the late-spring day that welcomed me with sun and the scent of roses and popcorn. Gulls cried overhead as I passed by a murky pond packed with ducks and a pair of snowy white swans. Gravel crunched beneath my shoes, driving home the contrast between my faux-rural setting and the traffic bustling outside the park's iron gates.

On a bench on the opposite side of the pond, facing the water, were my mother and my sister Ivy. They had a bag of bread between them and were tossing bits off the chunks in their hands to the ducks quacking greedily in the water before them.

I hadn't expected her to use Ivy's dream to draw me in. Was it merely for my benefit, or was she sincere?

She gestured to a path to my right. It led to a couple of

large weeping willows that would hide us from Ivy's view. No sense in letting my sister see me. She often dreamed of Mom, that I didn't doubt, but she might find it weird to see me and mention it later. It might stick with her.

I didn't wait long. I don't know what my mother said to my sister to excuse her sudden departure, but she said it quickly and joined me within a few minutes, there behind the weeping willows, bowed like grieving driads, their tangled locks of stringy green hair hanging toward the grass.

"I don't have long," my mother told me, as a young woman walked by with a child in a stroller. "I told her I was going to get ice cream, but she panics if I'm away too long."

I bit my tongue, fighting back the response that leaped there so eagerly. Surely my mother had to know *why* my sister was like that, even in her dreams? It didn't matter what age you were; you were never too old to have abandonment issues.

"Did you find him?" she asked me, her gaze darting over my face.

"Yeah," I replied, and I gave her the *Reader's Digest* version of what Karatos had said. I left a few things out—like me being able to do things Morpheus couldn't and the fact that Karatos had tried to do the same thing to me that he had to Noah. I didn't want to go there right now. Saving Noah—and yes, myself—was much, much higher on my list of priorities.

But most importantly, I told her that there was at least one spy feeding the Terror information. "That's how Karatos is staying ahead of us. Someone in Morpheus's inner circle is a traitor."

My mother's face took on a stricken expression. I could only imagine how awful this news was. God only knew how many secrets had been betrayed. "The Terror has to be stopped," she whispered.

"No shit," I replied snappily, surprising us both. "Finally figured that out, eh?" Okay, it was no secret that I had some bitterness toward my mother, but where the hell had that sudden outburst come from?

We blinked at each other.

"I'm sorry," I said, and I meant it. "I don't know why I said that."

"You're under a lot of stress." As big a brat as I'd been to her, she was still making excuses for her baby girl.

"Yeah," I agreed lamely. I guess it was as good an excuse as any. "I guess. Karatos got away, though. I'm going to have to try again."

She opened her mouth to protest, but Ivy called out to her. My mother glanced over her shoulder, then back to me. "I'll pass this on to your father. Don't do anything until you've talked to him."

I nodded. "Go spend some more time with Ivy." I didn't mean for it to come out all judgmental, but it sounded that way to my ears.

My mother, however, didn't seem to notice. "Be careful," she whispered, her dark eyes filling with tears. Then she hugged me. Not a loose hug shared between people parting for a brief time, but the desperate, hard embrace of a mother scared for her child. My throat tightened, and the back of my eyes burned, but I managed to keep it together.

It was strange, because underneath those burning eyes and the need to hug her back was a little voice telling me that now would be the perfect time to slap her across the face or yank out a handful of her hair. I didn't know for sure whose voice it was.

But it sounded a helluva lot like mine.

Noah looked like crap. A reminder I didn't need that time was running out. He arrived at my place at ten o'clock Saturday morning while I was eating toast and drinking my third coffee in an attempt to get out of this crap mood I was in.

"What happened to you?" he demanded as he crossed the threshold into my apartment, his gaze locked on the side of my face where Karatos had left another reminder—a taste of what would happen to me if I crossed him.

I was going to cross the bastard anyway.

"Karatos," I replied as I closed the door, irked. "Who the hell do you think?"

If Noah heard the snark in my tone, he totally ignored it. He stood close, invading my space as he always did, studying the damage the Terror had done to my face. His hair stood up, his beard was patchy, and his face was pale beneath the flush of rage that bloomed in his cheeks. I thought he was beautiful.

His gaze locked with mine, and it was so hard to hold it. There was no life in his eyes, just anger. It scared me—more than Karatos ever could. And it got rid of my bitchiness in a hurry. "I'm okay, Noah."

I don't think he believed me. Frig, I didn't believe me, but hearing the words seemed to take him down a notch anyway.

Cool fingers touched my cheek, careful to avoid the scabbed and torn flesh higher up. "Does it hurt?"

I closed my eyes, swamped by a rush of emotion I didn't want to feel—not now. His concern made me want to melt against him, made me want to hide away for a while. It was little more than a scratch in the grand scheme of things—nothing compared to the loss he faced. I wasn't going to run away. I was stronger than this.

I took his hand in mine and pulled it away from my face, but I kept my fingers tight around his. "I'll heal it later. There won't even be a scar."

His smile was a little smug. "He won't like that. They never do. Scars and bruises are trophies to fucks like him."

Goose bumps danced across my back at the darkness in his tone. And I wondered just how many scars Noah had. I hadn't seen many all the times I'd explored his body, but not all scars were outside. I didn't have to be a psychologist to know *that*.

"How are you doing?" I asked, wanting very badly to switch the focus of this conversation.

He shrugged. "I'm all right."

I arched a brow. "Why do I get the feeling you could be bleeding from the ears and still tell me that?"

He chuckled. "I'm okay, Doc. Not great, but okay."

Those words made me feel so good I can't describe it. It was like someone flipped a blind inside me and let a whole day's worth of sunshine pour in. Probably I shouldn't feel so hopeful, given what we were up against—given that I was all that stood between Noah and Terror-possession—but I did.

I was meeting Antwoine in a little while for coffee but didn't want to make Noah feel like I was tossing him aside. "Want to come with?"

He shook his head. "I've got something I have to do. Call me when you're done and let me know where to find you."

There was something oddly guarded about his expression—more than usual. "What are you up to?"

"Bossy and nosy," he muttered, then sighed. "I'm seeing my lawyer."

He had a lawyer. As in, a lawyer he used on a regular basis. Sometimes I forgot he had major money. "Oh?" A sense of dread settled over me, as though some part of me already knew why he was seeing a lawyer.

"I'm making out my will."

"Oh, Noah. No." And suddenly, I wanted to bawl.

He took me in his arms and held me tight against the solid wall of his chest. "Shh. It's not a big deal. If anyone can beat this thing, I know you can, but I just want to be prepared. Just in case."

I raised watery eyes to his. "You are not going to die. How many times do I have to tell you that?"

He smiled slightly. "If you have to keep telling me, that means I'm alive to hear it. Promise you'll call me later?"

I nodded, but I couldn't think of a damn thing to say. He kissed me at the door before leaving, and I watched him walk down the hall before shutting the door. His shoulders were back, his spine straight, so if his head was a little bowed, I wouldn't make too much of it. I thought the both of us were holding up better than most people would in the same circumstances.

Of course, I was still holding to some small hope that I would wake up, and this would have all been a bad dream.

Unfortunately for me, it really was a bad dream. A potentially deadly one.

Antwoine was already at a table when I arrived for our meeting. He was very dapper in a black leather blazer, black dress pants, and a cranberry red turtleneck. He smelled good, too.

"Did you have a date?" The question came out sounding a bit more dubious than it had in my head.

He raised graying brows at my rudeness and pushed a large Styrofoam cup across the table at me. I picked it up and sniffed. A chai latte. Yum.

"Not a date, no," he said in a low, cultured tone I didn't recognize. He sounded different. Looked different. He looked like an older man of means—confident and regal, not like the strange little man I first took him for.

I scowled. "Why do you sound different?"

A secret smile curved his lips. "This is how I sound."

"And your appearance?"

"This is how I appear."

The liar. I didn't know whether to hit him or laugh. "Why?"

"I thought it would be easier for you if I seemed a little . . . less in the beginning."

I watched him, tilting my head to study him from all angles. "And?"

His smile didn't so much grow as it deepened, became more intimate. "I didn't want to reveal my true self until I could be certain you trusted me."

Narrowing my eyes, I leaned forward. "Thought I'd be less likely to sic my daddy on a feeble old man?"

Now his eyes were sparkling, not the least bit sorry for the trick he had played. He looked like an impish Morgan Freeman. "Something like that. Morpheus might relish the chance to smack me around again. I, on the other hand, am in no hurry to be smacked."

I laughed. It was such a relief in some ways, realizing he was more than he had seemed. It gave me hope that he'd prove himself to be more still.

"So tell me," he said after taking a sip from his cup. "Why did you call?"

"Do you know a Terror's weaknesses?" I dared to ask. "Does he have any?"

Antwoine looked at me. "Some dreams linger. Most fade, even the bad ones."

"Karatos hates fading away. He wants to be significant."

He nodded. "You know it. And now you know his weakness. Exploit that, and you can bring the Terror to his knees."

I thought of Jackey Jenkins and how I had made her ugly and twisted in her dreams. Every fear she had I used against her. I had been in her head, and all her hopes and fears had swarmed me like chickadees after a handful of seed.

I didn't know if I could do the same thing to Karatos. It wasn't just his mind I was up against in The Dreaming; he was a true being there.

Antwoine must have seen the fear in my face because he leaned forward and put his hand over mine. "What does a Nightmare do, Dawn?"

I met his gaze and almost lost myself in the chocolaty depths of his wise eyes. "Protect dreamers."

He smiled. "That's right. You protect them from things like this Terror. You are stronger than him, you just remember that."

Hearing him refer to Karatos as a thing helped, it really did. Silently, I vowed to do that once more myself. "I'll remember."

A woman juggling a tray of coffee and sweets bumped into our table, sloshing latte over the sides of my paper cup onto the table.

It made me angry.

I grabbed her by the wrist, looked up into her apologetic brown eyes, and whispered, "Spiders."

Her tray dropped to the floor, spilling coffee and tea and food all over. She screamed and started stomping her feet, as though stepping on bugs.

Bugs that weren't there.

She swatted at her arms as well, clawed at her clothes and skin. And her face was contorted into the most beautiful mask of terror I had ever seen. I smiled.

"Girl, what have you done?"

I turned to Antwoine. "What?"

His dark eyes widened—then narrowed as he looked at me. Picking up a spoon, he shoved the curved side of the bowl at me. "Look at yourself."

My eyes were pale and black again. Bright and scary in my happy face. I was happy that I made a woman hallucinate about spiders. WTF? Why would I be happy about that? How could I even do that?

I thrust Antwoine's hand aside, fear souring my stomach. "What's happening to me?"

He wasn't impressed. "First you fix that poor woman."

I glanced at the woman, who was openly sobbing now—people stared at her. "How do I do that?"

"Same way you broke her."

I couldn't do it without people noticing, so I stood up. "I'm a psychologist," I told one concerned onlooker. "Maybe I can help."

I went to the woman, whose arms were covered in red marks from where she'd hit herself. Tears ran down her cheeks as she sobbed and begged for the spiders to stop. God, what had I done?

I put my hand on her shoulder, cupped my other hand around her chin to make her look at me. "They're all gone," I told her, willing her to believe. "The spiders are all gone. It was just a dream."

It worked. She struggled for maybe a couple of seconds, then went still. She blinked at me. "What happened?"

"You thought you had spiders on you," I told her.

She looked confused as she glanced at the mess on the floor. "Yes. I thought there were spiders on me." She chuckled self-consciously. "How foolish of me."

I helped her replace her order—and made her take the money for it. It was the least I could do. She thought I was just being nice.

Finally, I sat down with Antwoine, who was still looking at me like I was that kid from *The Omen*.

"Something happen to you?" he demanded. "Did Karatos try to do to you what he did to your friend?"

I literally felt the blood drain from my face. "How did you know?"

He shook his head, looking at me like I was a damned idiot. "We've got to stop this thing. Tonight. And *you*—you had better get control of yourself."

"What did it do to me?" I demanded, beginning to feel almost as hysterical as the woman with the spiders had been.

"He left some of himself behind, and it's calling to your darker nature. Power like yours is a dangerous thing in this world. Can't be brushed off here like it can be in The Dreaming."

My darker nature. Great. That explained the snarkiness, the snapping. I had liked freaking out that poor woman. My mouth tightened. This had to stop. Antwoine was right. Tonight, I faced Karatos and put an end to this. He might have taken a little of me, but like Antwoine said, I had taken some of him. I could find him now.

I could beat him. Tonight, I took back myself. Tonight, I was going to save Noah and destroy a Terror. It wasn't going to make me a favorite with my father's enemies, and at that moment, the darker side of me didn't care. Bring it on.

I met Antwoine's sharp gaze across the table. "Will you help me?"

My eagerness continued into the evening, lasting until Antwoine arrived at Noah's at exactly ten o'clock. Even then, knowing what was coming, I felt a positive vibe deep within myself.

I could do this. I wasn't alone with this task. I had Antwoine and my father—who had Verek—and I had Noah. Together, we would beat Karatos. That was the thought I kept in my mind whenever I looked at Noah and realized that he looked even more tired and pale than he had earlier in the day.

He was slipping away.

He and Antwoine sized each other up as men often did, and obviously did not find each other lacking. In fact, Antwoine actually nodded at Noah, as if giving him some kind of approval or blessing, a gesture I found strangely endearing as well as amusing.

"Take this," Antwoine said, as I slipped the sheath for the Marae dagger onto my left forearm. It was a jeweled cuff that he placed around my right wrist. It snapped shut, shaping itself to my arm as though made for it, the seam at the catch disappearing so that it was one continuous shackle.

"What is it?" I probably should have asked that before he'd put it on me.

"A succubi tether," he replied, snapping an identical cuff on his own wrist. "In the old days—and I do mean old—the succubi were sometimes kept in harems. Each wore one of these bracelets, the master of which was worn by their keeper. Whenever he wanted one of them, all he had to do was think of the succubus he wanted and pull. The same worked the other way as well, and if any of the ladies was ever in trouble, all they had to do was tug, and he'd come running."

I stared at the beautiful jewelry on my wrist, then at Antwoine. "How do you know this stuff?"

He didn't smile, but he didn't frown either. "I guess I've made it my business to know all I can about the Dream Realm."

I smiled at him and held up my arm. "How can these survive in this world if they're from The Dreaming? Nothing is supposed to last longer than a few hours outside of its home realm."

"That's true between The Dreaming and earth, but these cuffs weren't made in The Dreaming or on earth. Just like your dagger, these were made in the Underworld."

The immortal race that my father belonged to had many names. The Greeks had names and stories for them, as did the Romans and the Chinese, the Minoans and Aztecs. Every race has given these creatures its own names and identities, but at the core they are always the same. I don't even know my father's *real* name—or if he even has one. The Greek is the most familiar, so that is the one that often gets used the most. The Egyptians called him Serapis. In Hindu he is actually a woman—the goddess Maya. Try wrapping your head around the fact that your father is actually a cross-gender anthropomorphic being sometime and see how messed up you get.

Regardless, I was glad for whatever help Antwoine could

give. "So if I'm in trouble, I just tug?" I made a tugging motion with my arm. "But you can't come get me."

"No, but hopefully I can pull you out."

That would work. "Nice."

Antwoine shrugged. "We probably won't need them. I imagine your daddy will take care of things lickety-split if you start screaming, but it never hurts to be prepared."

And prepared we were. In fact, ten minutes later, I couldn't find a reason to delay the inevitable any longer. It was time to go.

I was nervous, and that worked against me, just as anger seemed to work in my favor. The fact that I had an audience didn't help, and it took me longer to open a portal that night than it had in the past. I managed to get a small rift started with my mind, but then I had to pull it open like I used to. It wasn't a huge setback, but a setback I didn't need all the same.

Finally, when the portal was large enough, and I had beads of sweat on my upper lip from the exertion, I turned to my left and offered Noah my hand. "Ready?" I asked.

His fingers were cold in mine. All the warmth was leaving him, and more rapidly than I wanted to admit. He was almost totally white now, the golden hue of his skin bleached by the loss of *anima*—if Jung was right in calling it the source of creative ability—or the true inner self.

His gaze met mine, flat and black. "I'm ready."

I turned my head to glance back at Antwoine. He nodded solemnly at me. This was it.

Noah and I walked through the portal together, into the mists of The Dreaming, and toward whatever was waiting for us there.

Chapter Twenty-four

"Jesus Christ."

Noah was looking around in awe—or maybe it was fear, I wasn't sure. Could have been both since it was the swirling eddies of the mist that had his attention.

And the mist saw him as well. Those angry tendrils smelled human and writhed together to form rippling snake-like bodies. There were talons in swirls, sharp and brutal. The talons were for me—the anomaly. All they would do to Noah was set him somewhere else—somewhere not off-limits to dreamers.

I needed him with me, so I had to keep him close and not be distracted by fighting off the mist.

I tore my dagger from the sheath and held it aloft. Too bad it wasn't bigger. This would go a lot faster with a sword.

The Marae blade hummed in my hand—hummed and shifted. I watched as it changed, felt the movement of the bone beneath my hand. The guard widened, as did the blade, lengthening as well. When it was done I held a sword in my hand rather than a dagger. The only thing unchanged was the moonstone in the hilt.

"Did you do that?" Noah asked, eyes wide.

My eyes were just as wide. "I think so."

Sword aloft, I led the way. Noah's hand was firmly clasped in mine as he walked slightly behind me. I don't know if it was my imagination or what, but the blade of my new weapon seemed to glow a little as we approached the mist.

"Out of my way," I commanded, in my lowest, fiercest "don't fuck with me" voice. Inside I was quivering. How could I defeat Karatos if I couldn't get past the mist? How could I save Noah?

To my surprise, the mist did as I asked. Pulling back, it formed a path as it had before. Maybe it remembered me slicing through them.

"Nightmare," it whispered. "Not a Nightmare."

"I *am* a Nightmare," I said, inching closer to the entrance of the path. It could be a trap—the walls could close around us once we were inside. The fog would rip Noah from me and send him away, and I had no idea what it'd do to me since it had already tasted my blood.

"I'm here on Nightmare business," I told it again. "For the Terror Karatos."

"Karatos," the single, yet many-voiced mist repeated. "Terror." The fog walls remained, and it was all I could do not to run the length of that path. As it was, I walked quickly, and Noah, obviously sensing that something wasn't right, kept pace.

We walked out of the mist into the waiting area of the sleep clinic.

"Morning, sunshine," said Bonnie from her usual post behind the counter. "You're first appointment is here. He's waiting in your office."

Karatos. I could feel him here, and no doubt he could feel me as well. He was playing with me. Bonnie hadn't been conjured. She wasn't some illusion Karatos had brought with him, she was actually dreaming this. Somehow Karatos had brought her into this scenario, or had manipulated her dream for his own purposes, but upon waking tomorrow, there was a good chance Bonnie would remember this.

I lowered the sword and flashed her a smile. "Thanks. Lunch later?"

She winked. "You know it."

We continued toward my office. Hopefully, Bonnie wouldn't give much thought to Noah being with me in her dream. I hoped she would chalk it up as speculation about our relationship. Other than that, I had nothing. At the very least I figured she would ask me what the sword meant next time she saw me. I'd have to make something up about penis size or something.

Karatos was in my office, waiting. The bastard was sitting behind my desk. He—It—looked up and smiled when we walked in. "I was beginning to wonder if you kids were going to show."

"Get out of my chair," I told him. "Now."

His smile continued, grating every nerve I had into raw awareness. "Dear me, what are you going to do with *that*?"

I followed its gaze to the sword in my hand. Slowly, I willed it back into original form. "Whatever I need to do."

Brave talk, but true. I'd slice him from what my grand-mother used to refer to as "asshole to appetite" if necessary.

"I like you, Dawn. I really do."

"Spare me. Why don't you give Noah back his ability to dream, and you and I can settle this the old-fashioned way." God, I sounded like something out of a Western!

Karatos rolled his eyes at me. "Well, of course I'm going to give it back! He's useless to me without that."

I didn't quite understand how that worked, but I figured that for some reason Noah had to be able to dream for Kara-tos to take him over—it was some kind of conduit, perhaps?

Karatos reached a hand inside himself—right into his own chest cavity—and pulled out what looked like a palm-sized crystal. It was brilliant in all its facets and colors—so bright it hurt my eyes. Swarovski had nothing on this.

"Beautiful, isn't it?" Karatos asked, voice heavy with pride. "I knew as soon as I saw it I had to have it." With that an-nouncement, his gaze lifted to Noah.

The crystal was Noah's inner self. His creative being. And yes, it was beautiful.

Karatos came around my desk to stand before us, still holding the crystal in his outstretched palm. "Take it."

I watched as Noah reached out a trembling hand to take the crystal. "Now, hold it against your chest," the Terror in-structed.

Noah did just that. I think both of us forgot to breathe at that moment. Would it work? Or was this a trap? Would I have time to intervene before Karatos took Noah? Should I call Morpheus now? No. I had to get Noah to safety first. I had to make sure Karatos was contained first.

The crystal pulsed and glowed as Noah held it against his

shirt. Slowly, the light waned as his body absorbed it back into itself. Color bloomed in Noah's cheeks and hands as his flesh returned to its normal hue. And his eyes brightened with the spark of life once more.

I could have cried, he looked that beautiful to me.

"Now," Karatos said, clapping his hands. "My turn."

That's when I acted. Dagger in hand, I turned myself inward. I can't begin to tell you how to do it, only that a split second later I was seizing hold of something deep inside me, a well of knowledge and power that I recognized as my Nightmare-self. I grabbed it and surged upward with it, bringing it out of myself, letting it wholly envelop me.

It took a second—maybe two.

Karatos reached for Noah just as I whipped open a portal. I grabbed Noah by the arm, then shoved hard, pushing him toward it.

"Go!" I cried. He hesitated, because Noah was the kind of guy who had a hard time leaving a woman alone in a dangerous situation, but in the end he did as I asked and lunged through the opening. If I survived this, I was going to kiss him so hard for listening to me.

Karatos roared behind me. It felt as though a Mack truck had struck me from behind, and I flew into the wall face-first. I felt my nose crumple under the impact, and my mouth split in two places.

"You bitch!" the Terror screamed.

I peeled myself off the wall. My blood left a bright crimson smear on the sage paint as I moved. I think a rib or two was broken as well. I was not off to a good start. But at least Noah was safe. Right?

I had to check. The portal was closed, I saw, much to my relief. Karatos couldn't open a new one—it wasn't one of his

abilities. It wasn't anyone's ability except for me and my
father.

I propped my back against the wall and smiled, despite
the blood streaming down my face. "He's gone."

Karatos turned on me. He was incredible in his rage. Pale
eyes blazed from within the dark of his beautiful face. His
high cheekbones were flushed with crimson, and his wide
lips were pulled back from the perfect white of his teeth.

"I'm going to skin you alive," he snarled.

He could probably do just that, I realized. I was immortal
in this realm—or at least I thought I was. There were probably ways to kill me that I didn't know about. Unfortunately,
I didn't know any ways to kill Karatos either.

"You didn't actually think I'd go along with your plans,
did you?" I asked, wiping my nose with the back of my hand.
I don't know why I bothered. It was bleeding really hard—
not fast, which was good because it wouldn't take long for
my head to start swimming—but it was a slow, heavy bleed
that would catch up with me eventually.

"I had hoped," Karatos replied as he flipped my desk on
its side with a casual touch of his hand. "But this will be so
much more fun."

I swallowed. Gross. "Then let's do this."

He—damn it, *IT*—chuckled. "I am going to miss our little scuffles, Dawn."

I cocked my head. "Don't go getting all emotional on me.
We're not done yet."

Pale, spidery eyes lightened. "Soon. I will get Noah, or
someone else. And when I do, I'm coming for you."

I reached up, pushed my nose back into place, and healed
the damage. It was mostly bravado that did it. I needed to
show off, and so the ability came readily. I think I was

finally starting to figure this stuff out. Karatos blinked as I fixed myself before his very eyes.

"I'll be ready," I assured him, and flashed my dagger. "Let's go, bitch." Oh, it felt so good to taunt him! To feel this new power surging through my veins. My vision altered, became more clear. My eyes had gone like his, I knew it. I could feel my muscles rippling beneath my skin, becoming stronger and more fluid. I felt like Wonder Woman.

Karatos sprung at me. I managed to slip to the side and avoid the attack. "That all you got?"

That remark got me a left hook to the jaw. Stars sparkled before my eyes, but I shook them off and stayed on my feet. I lashed out and was rewarded with the Terror's astounded cry of pain as I moved faster than he could and slashed him across the chest. His white shirt blossomed with crimson.

I bounced on the balls of my feet, adrenaline pumping.

"I'm so going to fuck you over," the Terror promised, circling like a hungry wolf. "And when I cross over, your father will be blamed for letting it happen."

My eyes narrowed. "Please. You've admitted to having help."

He smiled a little. "Only to you. People here have been waiting years for him to make a slip-up like this. First, he brought in his human lover, then he spawned a half-breed brat, and now he's let a Terror loose in the world. What kind of king is he?"

"Let's ask him," I suggested, but inside I was troubled. Was this really all about rebellion? Like Julius Caesar, it seemed my father needed to watch his back.

That was why he had told me not to bring Noah into the Realm anymore. He knew what trouble it would cause for both me and him—especially him. And yet, he had allowed me to bring Noah in tonight in order to save his life.

I brought things out of this Realm that I shouldn't, and brought things in, too. And my father never told me no—just that it wasn't a good idea. He didn't want me to think there was something wrong with me, but it was obvious that I wasn't normal, not even here.

"Are you going to cry?" Karatos taunted with a harsh bark of laughter. "Don't waste your tears, Little Light. Everything King Morpheus does is for himself. He'd toss you to the wolves in a minute to save himself."

"Sounds like you have issues with your own father," I replied lightly. "Ever thought about going into therapy for that?"

He lunged again, and this time I kicked him in the stomach, an effort for which he thanked me by grabbing me by the jaw and slamming my head into the wall until the plaster rained down on my shoulders.

Like my muscles, my bones seemed stronger, too. Lucky for me, or my skull might have gotten fractured.

I slid to the floor, blinking, trying to force the pain away, but I didn't know how. How could I concentrate when I hurt so freaking bad?

"Done already?" he asked, kicking me in the ribs as he spoke. I think I might have screamed. "We're just getting started. But then, you always were a quitter."

Ah yes. I had been waiting for this. Arm wrapped around my torso, I sat against the wall. I had blood and plaster all down the front of my black shirt and blood on my hands. My dagger was beside my thigh on the carpet, and I reached for it.

Karatos sat in my chair, rocking back and forth like a kid,

beside the overturned hulk of my desk. He'd changed and looked just like the puppet on a kid's show I used to watch back in Canada. Mr. Make Believe, the host of the show, had a "son" named J. T. who was played by a marionette with a bowl cut and rosy cheeks. Damn thing used to scare me.

Seeing a life-sized version didn't exactly assuage that old fear.

"This is really lame," Karatos informed me. "A puppet?"

I shrugged. "He was creepy."

The Terror shook his big, shiny wooden head. The yellow strands of his yarn hair waved slightly. "This isn't your real fear, is it, though, Dawnie?"

I stayed where I was, trying to look calm. The pain had subsided enough that I was trying to concentrate on patching up my ribs. The longer Karatos took listening to himself talk, the more time I had. "I guess not."

He straightened and started walking toward me, arms swinging at their jointed elbows, the skinny fingers brushing the thighs of his denim overalls. He was going to keep this form just for fun, I realized. Because even though it didn't fill me with terror anymore, it unsettled me, and he knew it.

"What you're really afraid of," he remarked casually as he squatted in front of me, "is being a freak."

Shit. "That lacks a little punch coming from a being dressed up like a puppet."

He laughed—J. T.'s laugh. I shivered. "You try so hard to protect yourself with sarcasm and that glib tongue of yours, but I can see inside you, Dawn. I know what Jackey Jenkins did to you. I know what you did to her."

It was the last sentence that chilled me. "I never meant to hurt her."

"No, but you kind of liked it, didn't you?" Big blank eyes stayed fixed on me as he tilted his shiny-cheeked head. "You're afraid of what you are. Afraid that you really are a big fat freak." Then his trapdoor mouth dropped open in a parody of a grin. "A monster."

For a moment I couldn't speak. I was too afraid of what he might do next. He didn't disappoint. J. T's face wilted, melted away to more human features. And wouldn't you know it? The features were mine.

Karatos turned into me. Bloody face and all. It was like looking into a mirror—an evil one at that. I saw my strange eyes and pale cheeks. Saw the blood all over my mouth and throat. It even had a mock version of my dagger.

"How rich," this other me said with a throaty laugh that made me shudder. "The thing you're most afraid of is yourself."

And then it started laughing, and it kept laughing. And the more it laughed, the madder I became. Maybe I was afraid of what I might be, but I also knew that I could control what kind of person I was. I made the decisions for myself—no one else did. Part of being a therapist was undergoing therapy—and no one was more self-aware than I was. It was a point of self-mockery sometimes, but I knew myself inside and out, and even if I didn't want to face the truth, I saw it with perfect clarity whenever I could.

And Karatos had made me see the answer with perfect clarity when he mentioned Jackey Jenkins had used Jackey's fears against her, just like Karatos was trying with me. There was just one difference.

I had done it better.

My dagger in one hand, I lashed out with the other and

grabbed the Terror by the front of the black shirt that matched my own. I smiled cruelly into my own face. "What are you afraid of, Karatos?"

My eyes blinked back at me, bewildered. My smile grew. "You think you have it all figured out? Think you can survive in the real world? Let's find out."

I shoved the Terror backward as a portal sliced open behind Its shoulder. Just to make sure it worked, I gave my arm wearing Antwoine's cuff a shake. An answering tug came from behind—a strong tug that I pushed into. Both of us rolled through like a big Dawn-donut into the familiar surroundings of Noah's living room.

We fell apart, both of us sprawling on the gleaming floor.

Both of us identical.

Noah and Antwoine were suddenly there, staring at both of us with horror.

"Which one is which?" Antwoine demanded of Noah. Karatos was wearing a bracelet just like my tether—there was no way to tell us apart.

I didn't look at either of them. I kept my hand on my knife and my gaze on Karatos. "Get back," I ordered. "Both of you!"

"The bossy one's Dawn," Noah stated, just before kicking Karatos in the head with such precision and certainty that my stomach almost fell to my toes. The Terror fell backward, his-her-Its head smashing the floor with a dull thunk.

"Get up, asshole," Noah commanded, standing over It with legs splayed and fists clenched.

"This is why I wanted you," the me on the floor rasped. "So much hate. So much rage."

Noah's only response was to kick It again. And again.

And again. And when Karatos tried to rise, Noah beat It down again. My stomach churned even as I cheered him on. I knew it was Karatos he was beating, but seeing Noah do so much damage to my doppelgänger gave me sickening chills. Thank God he knew the difference between me and the Terror. But didn't it bother him at all that It was wearing my face?

The Terror cried out as Noah kicked It again. Blood sprayed from Its nose as Its head snapped back. *Take that, you bastard.* How did Karatos like pain now that It was on the receiving end?

I tried to get to my feet, but it hurt just trying to sit up. I paused to catch my breath, and that's when Noah made the mistake of turning his attention to me.

It all happened so fast. Karatos, even though It didn't belong here, was still very strong and fast, and the second Noah let down his guard, the Terror leaped to Its feet. It grabbed Noah by the hair and yanked his head back. I yelled at it, bothered deeper than I could fathom at the sight of myself looking so battered and twisted and gleeful as Noah winced in pain.

"Time to go, sonny." Karatos flung Noah toward the still-open portal, and as Noah stumbled toward it, I found my own strength and lunged to my feet after him.

But it wasn't me who stopped Noah from going through the portal, back into The Dreaming, where Karatos certainly would have taken possession of him. It was Morpheus. He caught Noah by the shoulders.

"Steady there," he said, and gave Noah a gentle shove to the side—closer to me. I went to him and put my arms around him, so relieved that he was still here. That the goddamn calvary had finally arrived. Noah's arms were warm around me, and I didn't care that my ribs were still bruised and tender. I let him hug me as hard as he wanted, despite the blood on his hands from the beating he had given Karatos.

My father, dressed in a dark blue shirt and jeans, looked like a construction worker dressed up for a date as he fixed his pale gaze on Karatos. "You. Come with me."

The other me shook its head. "No."

Morpheus shrugged. "You have no choice."

"I will stay here." Karatos lifted Its head. "I will die here." And it would—within the next few minutes It would begin to lose form and dissolve into nothingness. I suppose that was better than facing the people who had sent It in the first place.

Okay, so was it wrong that at that moment I actually felt a sting of sympathy for the damn thing? True, my father would probably destroy It once they were back in The Dreaming, but there was something pathetic about choosing to end life in a world that wasn't yours.

Morpheus crossed the floor, work boots thudding softly with every step. He put his arm around the shoulders of the Terror, and for a moment I saw how the two of us must look together. I saw the resemblance between us. "Come home, little dream. We have much to discuss."

Like who Karatos was working with, for example.

The Terror looked up at him—a frightened little girl. "You're not going to unmake me?"

My father smiled the kindly smile of a father with a wayward child. "No."

I might have voiced my outrage at this had his voice not appeared in my head saying, *Unmake, no. Remake, yes.* "Remaking," if I was not mistaken, was the term for recycling Dreamkin. Weird, but true. Karatos would be made into something else—something not so twisted and awful. A second chance, I suppose.

I wasn't so certain the Terror deserved one, but that wasn't my decision. It belonged to the King. To the God of the Dreamkin.

"I'm going to make sure you don't try to run away." Morpheus said as he snapped some kind of collar around Karatos's neck. It looked like a big gold choker set with gems. Based on how it settled around the Terror's throat, I knew I would look really good in it—without the bloody face, of course. The collar was obviously some kind of low-jack device. I wouldn't mind having one of those in my own arsenal someday.

Karatos shifted to Its original form as It walked through the portal, into the custody of the Royal Guard waiting on the other side. My father didn't follow immediately after It. Instead, he turned to me and held out his arms.

"Are you hurt?"

I left Noah's embrace and went to Morpheus. He took me against him gently, and I felt a strange warmth tingling through me from head to toe. He was healing me. In this world, he could heal me.

Seemed I wasn't the only one who could do some things I shouldn't be able to do.

"You took a big risk doing what you did," he murmured. I merely nodded against his chest. "I'm proud of you."

Okay, now I was going to cry. I sniffed. I was just so damned relieved . . .

"All better," he murmured against my hair, and he was right. I was all better. I looked up at him.

"How did you know which one was me?"

My father's smile was lopsided and small, but it was

heartfelt and sweet. "You're my kid. I'd know you anywhere."

And as if that wasn't enough to bring tears to my eyes, he kissed my forehead. "And don't you worry about your mom and me. We'll find a way to make things right with her other family."

And then, after giving Antwoine a brief nod, he let me go and walked away, disappearing through the portal, which zipped shut behind him, leaving no trace of any of the night's events.

Noah and Antwoine crowded around me, but we were subdued in our celebration. I don't think any of us could quite believe what had just happened. Couldn't believe that it was all over.

"Are you all right?" I asked Noah.

He nodded. "I think so. You?"

I smiled, sagging against him. "I need a bath."

Chapter Twenty-five

Two weeks later

"Get your sorry butt out of bed. You're going to be late."

I opened my eyes, still bleary with sleep, and looked into Noah's smiling face. "My butt's not sorry for anything."

He laughed as he rolled off the bed. He was wearing a white T-shirt and the Spider-Man bottoms I liked. I may not like his little sister much, but I couldn't find fault with how much she adored her big brother. "You have eye snot. And you're going to be late for your first day at your new job."

I wiped at my eyes as I sat up. We were at my place, and Fudge was at the foot of the bed, licking his paws. I smelled bacon and eggs and coffee drifting in from the kitchen, and my stomach growled.

The clock by the bed said it was twenty before eight. I didn't have to be at work until nine. "I'm not going to be late," I called after him, as he walked out.

He stuck his head back through the doorway, a grin lingering on his lips. "You will be if you want to shower, have breakfast, *and* then have me before you go."

Well, when he put it that way . . . Laughing, I jumped out of bed. Life was good. Almost too good, but I wasn't about to start analyzing that. Noah was one hundred per cent okay after the whole Karatos thing, and so was I. The edginess he'd given me lingered, but I managed to subdue it, and now it had faded like a bad case of PMS. My mother and father had held true to their agreement not to ask me to interfere on their behalf with my family. Because of that, I didn't mind visiting The Dreaming so much. My relationship with Morpheus was better than with my mother, but there was hope for her and me, I thought.

My father—the human one—had made an appointment to see that big-shot specialist. He would be coming to Toronto in a few weeks, once he'd cleared his schedule. I didn't give it much thought, but I wasn't so blasé that I didn't think about it at all. I was more concerned about the effect his efforts would have on my family than whether or not he would actually succeed in waking my mother up. Morpheus and my mother acted like they weren't the least bit concerned, but I think my mother's conscience was giving her a hard time. I tried not to feel too sorry for her over that.

And I had a new job. The Monday after bagging Karatos, I had walked into the clinic and told Dr. Canning that I was done. Facing my fears—and the possible loss of Noah, as well as my own life—was a real eye-opener for me. Dr. Canning was a jerk, and I was done being bullied and used.

I was able to work wherever I wanted now, and I had been made an offer on Sunday afternoon to set up my own office in the prestigious clinic belonging to Drs. Edward and Warren Clarke.

It was Warren's idea, not Noah's, so that made it easier for me to accept. And there was an offer for Bonnie as well. We were both starting today. Yayee us. I would be able to do some real good there. I could continue my dream research, and treat patients that suffered not just from sleep-related issues, but a variety of others as well. I had this theory that I might actually be able to help people from *inside* their dreams. If I could go into the dreams of a person suffering from post-traumatic stress disorder and see the horror for myself, it would give a new depth to my counseling. Not only that, but if I could slowly start to change their dreams, bend them so that they weren't nearly so horrible, I could help my patients face their issues and begin the healing process all the faster. It was all very exciting—and for the first time in a long time I felt like I had something to contribute to the world.

So I showered quickly and went out to the kitchen, where Noah was setting plates on the table for the two of us and Lola, who was watching him with a big grin. My friend liked my guy, a fact that pleased me. And I wasn't the least bit insecure about Lola being hot and outgoing. Noah didn't look at Lola the way he looked at me. Noah didn't have a painting of Lola hanging on his bedroom wall. When I was with Noah, I felt smart and fun and sexy, and all my hangups disappeared for a while. I was a little scared that I might be falling in love with him, but I wasn't about to pull back. Not after all we'd been through.

We had plans to have dinner with Noah's family later in

the week, so we'd see if I could win them over as easily as he had won over my friends. It was his mother's idea to have dinner, so I didn't expect to have issues with her. I knew she liked Amanda, but she loved her son, and what she wanted most was for him to be happy and well treated. At least, that's what I hoped she wanted. As for his sister . . . well, I wasn't going to let a teenager intimidate me.

Besides, if the kid was too much of a bitch, I could always give her a few nightmares. I'm joking, of course, but I wouldn't be above making her dream of Wayne Newton concerts for a few nights in a row. Maybe I'd put her up front for Céline Dion as well. If that didn't scar a kid like her for life, nothing would.

After breakfast, Lola left to go to the gym, and Noah and I went back to bed—even though I should have used the time to get ready. We made love fast and without finesse, laughing about it almost the entire time. I didn't know what was going to happen between Noah and me, or how long we were going to last, but we had made it this far, and that was something to be thankful for. Afterward, he helped me get dressed, and I let him apply my lip gloss. He seemed to like painting my lips, and I liked that he found me so bloody fascinating when I was, in reality, just me.

No, I didn't know if Noah was going to end up being the man of my dreams, but I had a strong suspicion that he was. I knew one thing for certain, however.

I'm the woman of his.

*Next month, don't miss these exciting new
love stories only from
Avon Books*

The Devil Wears Tartan by Karen Ranney

Marshall Ross, Earl of Lorne, is certain he's going mad. Not the best time to get married, but he has no choice if he wants to continue his line. What began as a marriage of convenience becomes a battle of wills . . . and against time, as Marshall's past continues to haunt him and threaten the woman he's come to love.

Killer Charms by Marianne Stillings

An Avon Contemporary Romance

Andie Darling is a cop out to get her man. Logan Sinclair is a con man who's just looking to have some fun. The game is on, and surrender may turn out to be the most pleasurable outcome of all.

Passion and Pleasure in London by Melody Thomas

An Avon Romance

Winter Ashburn, bored with society, takes a page from Robin Hood's book. When her path crosses with the bitter Rory Jameson, Earl of Huntington, things become much more serious. Can two people who've had their dreams destroyed rediscover their passion for life in the love they have for each other?

Secrets of the Knight by Julia Latham

An Avon Romance

Diana Winslow will do anything to keep her position as a Bladeswoman . . . even if it means kidnapping a peer of the realm. Duty and desire are put to the test in this latest medieval romance from Julia Latham.

Unforgettable, enthralling love stories,
sparkling with passion and adventure
from Romance's bestselling authors

At Avon Books, we know your passion for romance—once you finish one of our novels, you find yourself wanting more.

May we tempt you with . . .

- **Excerpts** from our upcoming releases.

- Entertaining **extras**, including authors' personal photo albums and book lists.

- Behind-the-scenes **scoop** on your favorite characters and series.

- **Sweepstakes** for the chance to win free books, romantic getaways, and other fun prizes.

- Writing **tips** from our authors and editors.

- **Blog** with our authors and find out why they love to write romance.

- **Exclusive content** that's not contained within the pages of our novels.

Join us at
www.avonbooks.com